YOU
HAVE
GONE
TOO
FAR

Books by Carlene O'Connor

Irish Village Mysteries
MURDER IN AN IRISH VILLAGE
MURDER AT AN IRISH WEDDING
MURDER IN AN IRISH CHURCHYARD
MURDER IN AN IRISH PUB
MURDER IN AN IRISH COTTAGE
MURDER AT AN IRISH CHRISTMAS
MURDER IN AN IRISH BOOKSHOP
MURDER ON AN IRISH FARM
MURDER AT AN IRISH BAKERY
MURDER AT AN IRISH CHIPPER
CHRISTMAS COCOA MURDER
(with Maddie Day and Alex Erickson)
CHRISTMAS SCARF MURDER
(with Maddie Day and Peggy Ehrhart)

A Home to Ireland Mystery
MURDER IN GALWAY
MURDER IN CONNEMARA
HALLOWEEN CUPCAKE MURDER
(with Liz Ireland and Carol J. Perry)
IRISH MILKSHAKE MURDER
(with Peggy Ehrhart and Liz Ireland)

A County Kerry Mystery
NO STRANGERS HERE
SOME OF US ARE LOOKING
YOU HAVE GONE TOO FAR

Published by Kensington Publishing Corp.

YOU HAVE GONE TOO FAR

CARLENE O'CONNOR

KENSINGTON
PUBLISHING CORP.

www.kensingtonbooks.com

KENSINGTON BOOKS are published by

Kensington Publishing Corp.
900 Third Avenue
New York, NY 10022

Copyright © 2024 by Mary Carter

All Kensington titles, imprints, and distributed lines are available at special quantity discounts for bulk purchases for sales promotion, premiums, fund-raising, educational, or institutional use. Special book excerpts or customized printings can also be created to fit specific needs. For details, write or phone the office of the Kensington Special Sales Manager: Attn. Special Sales Department, Kensington Publishing Corp., 900 Third Avenue, New York, NY 10022. Phone: 1-800-221-2647.

The K with book logo Reg. U.S. Pat. & TM Off.

Library of Congress Control number: 2024939435

ISBN: 978-1-4967-3758-8
First Kensington Hardcover Edition: November 2024

ISBN: 978-1-4967-3760-1 (e-book)

10 9 8 7 6 5 4 3 2 1

Printed in the United States of America

To Jill Carter, Susan Collins, and Bethany Carter-Giles,
three strong, bad-ass women

*May you have the hindsight to know where you've been, the fore-
sight to know where you're going, and the insight to know when
you have gone too far.*
—Irish proverb

ACKNOWLEDGMENTS

Thank you to my editor, John Scognamiglio, my agent, Evan Marshall, and my publicist, Larissa Ackerman, as well as the many additional folks at Kensington Publishing who help bring a book into the world—Lauren Jernigan, Robin Cook, cover designers, copy editors, et al. Thank you, booksellers, for your passion for reading and kindness to authors. Thank you, Irish friends, for always answering questions and offering support, and, of course, as always, thank you, reviewers and readers!

AUTHOR'S NOTE

Although the wonderful town of Dingle exists, like many other locations in the book, this is a work of fiction, and sometimes I take liberty with the landscape, creating bogs and structures where there are none.

CHAPTER 1

*D*EAR *B*UTTERFLIES,

My darlings. The time has come for you to flap your wings. Secrets never stay buried, and in due time, I will provide the shovels. I won't lie, I made a deal with a pair of devils: a wolf and a hound. (We were the sheep and their clothing.) And these communications may very well cost a life. But it will be well worth it in the end. I have spent the rest of my life watching, fearful of this very moment. As much as I'd like to deny it, it is happening. I will not sit around and watch history repeat itself. You now have the ability to contact each other. There is safety in numbers. After this letter, you will see a link to a private messaging page. USE IT. I assure you it is secure and cannot be traced. That said, do erase it from your history <u>each and every time</u>. This is essential. I am trying to help, but they are watching me too. I am sorry to tell you this, but you <u>MUST</u> listen: Do not trust strangers. Do not fall for sweet talk or promises—and STAY AWAY from anyone who preaches dogma of any kind. Do not go anywhere alone. You are safe as long as you are carrying your babies. Once you deliver, you are in extreme danger. They won't hesitate to kill. #Run. #Hide. #Fight. I will try to help, but they are watching me.

Never, ever forget: You are your mothers' savage daughters.

Butterflies are free!

Love and kisses,

One Who Has Not Forgotten

PS. This email box does not accept replies.

FiFoFum@gmail.com: **WTF?**

DeafGirlsRule@gmail.com: **You took the letters right out of my fingers. Seriously, WTF?**

FiFoFum@gmail.com: *I am my mother's savage daughter . . .* **Is this, like, an advert for Sarah Hester Ross? Love the song but hate being spammed!**

DeafGirlsRule@gmail.com: **I don't know the song. #Clueless. But it read***: You are your mothers' savage daughters . . .*

FiFoFum@gmail.com: **I got that, but whoever wrote the email is obviously referring to the song.**

DeafGirlsRule@gmail.com: **You sound snippy. Never heard the song. I'm deaf. I was only pointing out the differences. #Facts.**

FiFoFum@gmail.com: **I was being kind of snippy. Sorry, sorry, sorry! Hormones!!!**

DeafGirlsRule@gmail.com: **Is this you, Baby Daddy? If so—this isn't funny . . .**

FiFoFum@gmail.com: **Definitely not your Baby Daddy. This is getting weird . . .**

DeafGirlsRule@gmail.com: **Getting weird? It started weird. I'm not falling for this. HOWEVER—I eagerly await my shovel!**

FiFoFum@gmail.com: **Are you pregnant? I'm 7 and a half months.**

DeafGirlsRule@gmail.com: **7 months. But still not falling for this. I am not DUMB! Deaf people can do everything but hear.**

FiFoFum@gmail.com: **I NEVER said you were dumb. Either you are messing with me, or someone else is messing with US. Should we show the letter to someone?**

DeafGirlsRule@gmail.com: **Like who? We probably both shopped for baby stuff online. #BOTS**

FiFoFum@gmail.com: **I'm from County Kerry—what about you?**

DeafGirlsRule@gmail.com: **I am not giving you any more information. #PeaceOut.**

FiFoFum@gmail.com: **Could we meet? In a public place? (In case one of us is a serial killer?)**

DeafGirlsRule@gmail.com: **Like where? (And I'm <u>totally</u> a serial killer!)**

FiFoFum@gmail.com: **Spring Festival in Dingle is next month. Murphy's Ice Cream Shop? Noon—first day of the festival? That way, if you stand me up, I still get ice cream.**

DeafGirlsRule@gmail.com: **Still think you're taking the piss. But whatever. I'll be there. #You'reBuying #NotScaredOfYou.**

FiFoFum@gmail.com: **Perfect. Let's have a code word.**
DeafGirlsRule@gmail.com: **Lol whatever Jane Bond!! Like what?**
FiFoFum@gmail.com: **Butterfly.**
DeafGirlsRule@gmail.com: **Okey-doke. Guess we're flapping our wings. Wonder if we'll set off a tornado.**

FiFoFum@gmail.com: **I think you mean hurricane . . .**

DeafGirlsRule@gmail.com: **Chill out, Tiger Mom.**
FiFoFum@gmail.com: **It's hard to convey humor through an online chat. See you there. Don't forget: Butterfly. Just in case . . . I am deleting this chat.**

DeafGirlsRule@gmail.com: **Fine. Whatever. #MeToo.**

CHAPTER 2

JOHN MALONE FACED A DILEMMA. MR. AND MRS. SHEEHAN WERE ON holiday, and they hadn't been home in a fortnight. On a cruise, no less, some fancy thing destined for Italy. But John only knew this because he heard the missus on the phone the day before they'd left. Breanna Sheehan liked to take her mobile phone into the front garden and chat with her friends—and, boy, did she have a set of lungs on her. They hadn't been the friendly sort, so it was the only reason he knew anything about them at all. Age discrimination—what else could it be? He was an old man, and she probably assumed he was nearly deaf, but the joke was on them; he'd always had excellent hearing. This was also how he knew that they'd been calling him "the nosy old goat next door." After that, he never bothered to say hello or even make eye contact. Nosy old goat his arse! He was the one who'd lived here over sixty years. They were the blow-ins; he could count the years they'd been here on one wrinkled hand, and even then, he'd gone out of his way to be neighborly.

Still. His dear late wife would want him to stand on higher ground, and if there wasn't any, she'd tell him to pull up his wellies like a big lad. And he certainly wasn't earwigging. But if your one was going to pace outside and holler, he couldn't *not* hear it.

Apparently, it was the Sheehans' twenty-fifth wedding anniversary, and they needed a break from "the whole mess with Fiona." Breanna said it wasn't how they imagined becoming grandparents.

He had no clue what she was on about, and he'd been disappointed that their lovely grown daughter hadn't been around in six months. Unlike her parents, she was the friendly sort, and they'd stood by the wall and had a nice long chat the first time she had visited. The lovely angel and the parents had obviously had a falling out, and he was firmly on Team Fiona. What a colleen. Man oh man, if he was forty years younger. Dark hair, light eyes, and that smile! She could bring ships to shore with that smile. Once he heard Fiona was with child, he'd bought a teddy at the shops and had been eagerly waiting her next visit so he could present it to her. But months rolled on, and there'd been no sign of Fiona. He finally put it together that she was an unmarried woman and the Sheehans did not approve. John didn't approve either, but that was the world now, wasn't it? And it was still their job to love and support their daughter, regardless of her sins.

And even after the "old goat" comment, John would have been delighted to gather their mail had they only asked. It was no skin off his back. He was long retired, and aside from his weekly shopping and whatnot, and his twice-weekly forages to his local pub, he was a homebody. But his neighbors didn't ask. And now their mail was falling out of the postbox at the end of their drive, and he had no idea when they would return. He missed the days when neighbors were friendly, because you never knew when you might need a helping hand.

He'd been watching the mail bulge out of the postbox for days, and then he could not take it anymore. The weather was grand at the moment, but rain and nothing but rain was coming in. For days on end they'd been issuing flood warnings.

John retrieved an old tin box from his shed and walked to the end of the road, where their postbox yawned open, envelopes spilling out. He grabbed a handful. They had a load of bills alright. Electric, water, internet, and telly. John was a man still content with the newspaper and the radio. Suitable, perhaps, for an old goat. Their *Irish Times* subscription needed to be renewed, and it seemed Gary Sheehan received a lot of solicitation from various financial corporations. That explained why he suited up for work every morning and was out before the sun, although John had no idea what line of business he was in. Perhaps he was in banking or an investor. They shouldn't have any problems paying these bills; if they were past due, it was down to pure laziness. There were no personal cards or notes; he wondered where Fiona lived and if she ever wrote to them.

He opened his tin box, set it underneath the post, and pulled until nearly all their mail tumbled out. He felt a certain satisfaction as the postbox started to empty. Anyone driving by would have seen the over-stuffed postbox and realized they weren't home. That was a safety concern. For all John knew, he was preventing a robbery. They didn't have to bake him a cake, but dollars to donuts, they wouldn't even thank him. *Typical.* The mail was nearly out now, but there were some odd bits still shoved in the back. John had to strain to reach all the way in.

The top item he pulled out was a flyer—an advert for Super-Value, and given that the coupons would expire in a few days, he tucked that into the pocket of his trousers. No sense letting good coupons go to waste. The next item was a flyer for the Spring Festival he was just on about. The first of its kind, the festival would be held on Strand Street, and apparently it was happening rain or shine. It boasted of arts and crafts and produce—farmers selling eggs and whatnot, he supposed. There was also going to be a petting zoo, of all things. You couldn't pay him to endure those crowds. He liked it when people talked to him over his fence. Like sweet Fiona. The last bit, shoved way in the back, was the oddest of them all. A mobile phone taped to a sheet of paper. The phone was the old-fashioned flip type. The paper blared a message in bold type. He read it once, and then again, and then a third time, wondering if someone was taking the piss:

WE HAVE FIONA
AND YOUR GRANDCHILD TO-BE
THEIR RETURN WILL COST YOU
ONE HUNDRED THOUSAND EURO
OR SHE DIES
KEEP THIS BURNER PHONE
GET THE MONEY TOGETHER

**CASH ONLY
OR SHE DIES
WE WILL ONLY CALL ONCE
AFTER INSTRUCTIONS
YOU WILL HAVE 6 HOURS TO DELIVER
WE ARE WATCHING
NO GUARDS
OR SHE DIES**

A ransom note? Did someone really have poor, dear Fiona? That wasn't possible. Was it? There was no proof attached. No photo of Fiona holding a newspaper or tied up, and although he was grateful for that, he didn't know whether or not someone was just messing. His heart thumped louder with each read. It had to be a joke. Some young ones acting the maggot. He hadn't seen anyone suspicious hanging around the postal box, and he usually had his eye out. The only way someone slipped this past him was if he was at the shops, or the pub, or watching telly, or eating, or sleeping. Who in the world would think this was remotely funny? He wished he had a phone number for Fiona, or even the Sheehans, so he could put his mind at ease straightaway. What kind of neighbors didn't exchange phone numbers for emergency situations?

His stomach twisted with worry as he flipped open the phone. One missed call. Jesus, Mary, and Joseph. What if this was real, like? They'd not only missed the call, but the letter and phone were in the very back of the box, which meant it had been delivered *first*. Most likely right after they left. That was nearly two weeks gone by. Was Fiona alright? For the first time in John Malone's life, he wished he had a neighbor on the other side. His panic was so great he probably would have flagged down the nearest vehicle, but this was a quiet road. He was going to have to go to the guards, wasn't he? The note clearly stated "no guards," but it was also too late now, wasn't it? Clutching the ransom note—maybe he should have worn gloves; also too late now—he ran for his truck. God help her, please let this be nothing more than pitiful shenanigans. Minutes later, he was screeching down the road in his truck, headed for the Dingle Garda Station.

CHAPTER 3

SHE LAY IN THE DEGRADED BOG, LIT BY THE MOONLIGHT. THERE WAS beauty in her stillness; there was grace in her death. A white silk scarf was wrapped around her neck, thick enough to disguise the jagged slash beneath it. She was dressed in a short, flowing, white robe that strained against her swollen belly. Her secrets were now their secrets, and they would take them to the grave. Night after night, they carefully returned to the area, expecting any day now to see a flood of guards. Why hadn't anyone found her? Each day, they checked the paper, only to find the usual headlines—politics, sports, petty crime, and the frivolous coverage of the upcoming Spring Festival.

This remote spot had once seemed poetic; now they were thinking it was foolish. Storms were predicted, warnings of severe flooding. They needed her to be found.

Local reporters would soon be slapping themselves. The story of their lifetime lay a mere thirty-minute drive (less, if they had lead feet) from the bustling Dingle Peninsula. Where were all the spring hikers? The wandering tourists? The lads acting the maggot? The bog was a bit remote; it was a bog, after all, but it was degraded, so she was clearly visible, even from a distance, and although a good pair of wellies was a given, the field was completely accessible. The tree that many called the Cross Tree, due to the branches on either side spreading open like arms, hovered in the distance and often drew lookie-loos. And yet here she lay. They hoped folks felt like utter fools when she was finally discovered. Her beauty was decaying with every rise of the moon. They did not like what she was becoming. They had to do something. The clock was ticking. Ever so loudly.

CHAPTER 4

SHAUNA MILLS STOOD IN FRONT OF MURPHY'S THIRTY MINUTES PAST the time she was supposed to meet FiFoFum. It was becoming apparent that she had been played. She wasn't entirely surprised that it had been a trick, but she couldn't deny the twinge of anger. She'd been a fool. At least she was in front of a delectable ice cream shop. Handmade with milk from Kerry cows, it never failed to satisfy the cravings of her onboard passenger. Now she really needed her dose of mint chocolate chip. She wondered if FiFoFum was a fat lad with thick glasses hiding behind his laptop. *Arsehole.* At least the day wasn't an entire waste; she'd get a fat cone and have a wander around the festival. According to weather reports, this was the last day before heavy rains and floods were predicted. The wind was whipping a bit, and the smell of rain was in the air, but for now it was dry. She took a moment to see if there was anyone gleefully watching her get stood up, but it was crowded, and no one seemed to be paying any particular attention to her.

The line for ice cream was long, and so was the line for the jax, and she really had to pee. It seemed all she did now was pee, and it was a struggle to get everything off, and then it was another struggle to get it all back on, even though she was practically wearing nothing but stretchy leggings and maternity tops these days. By the time she finally used the restroom and bought her cone, she was knackered. She was so ready for her onboard passenger to be born, although she was still petrified at the prospect of giving birth. So many things could go wrong. So many things had gone wrong for so many women throughout history. *Died in childbirth.* Shauna couldn't help the awful images that assaulted her daily. It wasn't right, something so large trying to force its way out of such a small opening. What was God thinking? She needed to "redirect" her thoughts, as her doctor had told her many times, but now all she wanted to do was go home and curl up into a ball. Into a fetal position. Ironic. But she had to stick it out; she was due at the Griffins' in a few hours.

The Griffins. Thinking about them made her take a huge bite of her ice cream, and then she was struck with brain freeze. Jane Griffin was to blame. Lately, she'd been onto Shauna about a natural childbirth, a home birth no less. She'd even researched local doulas without discussing it with Shauna first. No way. Shauna was going to hospital, and they were giving her drugs. All the drugs. She wanted to lie down, then wake up when it was all over. If she could somehow take it all back, she would. Liam insisted to this day that he had not messed with her birth control, but Shauna knew that a few of the pills had been replaced. They had tasted sweet. Like candy.

She was having second thoughts. About everything. Was that why they had invited her over tonight? At first, they bribed her with an offer of supper. *Home-cooked meal.* But Shauna had learned her lesson that last time. Nothing but soggy green vegetables and plain chicken and a small amount of rice—because she didn't want to risk gestational diabetes, did she?

Jane had never shown this side of her before. How many times had she spoken with them? How many applications had she poured through? Not that Shauna wanted to keep him. (She just knew she was having a boy; she could feel it.) But she couldn't provide for a baby. And no matter what he said, neither could Liam. He stayed out drinking too many nights, and he didn't wash his cereal bowl, and sometimes he didn't even wash himself. Yes, he was kind, and he worked hard at his handyman job, not to mention overseeing all those rentals, but he was immature, and it wouldn't be long before the poor baby was taking care of *him.* And the Griffins had money. Babies needed things all the time. Nappies, prams, outfits, high chairs, bibs, pacifiers, changing tables, toys. Most of Shauna's possessions could be contained within a few luggage bags, and it had been that way her entire life. The thought of providing everything a baby needed was overwhelming.

It was settled; Jane and David would be much better parents. They were schoolteachers even. He would be smart. But she didn't want to live near them after the baby was born; she worried it would hurt her heart to see him. She nearly had Liam convinced that they should move to the States. There was a university for the deaf there, and even though they used American Sign Language, and Shauna barely knew a bit of Irish Sign Language, maybe they could teach her. She'd never been around a group of deaf people before, and she wanted to know what that was like. Liam was still resisting, but no matter where they went, it would be somewhere that they didn't have to see the baby—and he didn't have to see them. She'd refused the Griffins' offer of supper, but she said she'd turn up and listen to Jane wax on about a doula. But she already knew what her answer was going to be. No, no, no. Jane had better watch her step.

Shauna pushed past a fat man in a flat cap and sunglasses, lurking on the corner. Eejit. The sun wasn't even out. She watched his head dip as if he was gazing at her big belly. "Take a photo, fatty," she said, startling him. "It lasts longer." She had no idea whether or not he understood her voice, as per usual. But she liked that she'd startled him. He turned his back on her. Laughing, she continued on her way, strolling by the tents, stopping only at ones that weren't too jammed with folks. How did people have all this money and all this time on their hands? So many people. They were swarming all over the booths, picking up candles and sticking their noses into them, winding colorful scarves around their necks, and molesting handmade soaps. Normally, Shauna kept her head down because, more often than not, when she looked up, there would be a pair of lips flapping at her. Then she would have to either shake her head and point to her ear, or vocalize, "I'm deaf." This either produced embarrassment on the hearing person's face or induced them to exaggerate their mouth movements, or suddenly they would expect her to read their lips, despite the fact that she hadn't understood them in the first place. She wasn't in the mood for it today.

She'd wasted too many years of her life in speech therapists' offices, striving to be understood. The speech therapist would clap her hands and grin whenever Shauna spoke, forcing air up, up, up *from the diaphragm*, hands squeezing the spot. Shauna would try and do what she was asked. Then came the clapping, as if Shauna was a trained seal who had just learned her first trick. And the worst bit was that Shauna would actually feel something like love wash over her from the rare praise. Then she'd try the very same words out in the real world, and instead of claps, she would get eyebrows furled in confusion and blank faces staring at her. Having someone turn his back on her, like the fat pervert had just done, was something new.

And yet they still forced her to practice: *Try, try, try.* The problem with swallowing other people's expectations your whole life was that eventually you choked on them. *Not today, thank you.* It wasn't deafness that was her disability; it was hearing people. They'd been doing it to her her whole life. She'd grown up in a group home, but instead of placing her in a school for the deaf, they'd put her in a school with handicapped children.

Her entire life had been hearing people sticking labels on her and lying to her face. And now she was supposed to trust these people when it came to pushing a human being out of her fanny? She also didn't want to watch it happening, and she certainly didn't want other people to watch it happening. Jane and David Griffin had actually said they wanted to be by her side when the baby was being born! No. Fucking. Way. She wished she could take it all back. And when she said all, she meant all.

She was about to find a bench to perch on when she came across a booth selling baby clothes. Holding her ice cream cone in one hand, she scrounged around in her pocket to see if she had any euros, but the only thing there was the last email correspondence she'd had with FiFoFum. They hadn't spoken since this first exchange. The least the woman could have done was message her to cancel. Shauna always checked her messages, so she knew she hadn't overlooked a cancellation. She had even printed out the message before deleting it. She took it out now and read it one more time. It was rubbish. There was a bin near one of the last tents at the end of the street. The banner read WILDE'S VETERINARIAN CLINIC. Next to it was an enclosure with lambs, and their banner read DOOLEY'S FARM, and just beyond it a parade of Irish wolfhounds. Shauna had always wanted a pet. Any pet. A dog or cat, of course, but she would have settled for a budgie or a goldfish.

The Griffins had an ugly dog, but she wasn't supposed to say that. Hearing people got so uptight when she called things like she saw them. Somehow it wasn't nice to call things ugly, or fat, even if they were ugly or fat. That was just lying! And the Griffins' dog *was* ugly. He was a hairy little thing that always looked as if he'd stuck his paw in an electric socket. He had bad breath and pointy teeth, and one eye was bigger than the other. He constantly yapped at her, only she couldn't hear it, so she didn't care. It was funny, though, watching him flap his gums at her. Maybe once she moved to the States and finished college at Gallaudet University—that's where she intended on going, even though she hadn't applied yet—but after she graduated, she would get a good job, and an apartment, and a load of pets. Only hers would be cute.

She was headed for the rubbish bin to throw away FiFoFum when someone bumped into her, sending the paper flying out of her hand and her ice cream cone smashing into her breasts. *Fantastic.* Someone's hands were moving toward her, and before she knew what was happening, a tiny woman with white-blond hair and green eyes the exact same color of her mint ice cream was blotting her chest with napkins. Her mouth was moving too, and Shauna caught: "Sorry, sorry, sorry."

"It's okay," Shauna said. "I was finished." She looked at the paper that now rested at the woman's feet. There was no way Shauna was bending over. The woman took the dripping, mangled cone out of her hand and pointed in the direction of the ice cream shop. "No, I'm full," she said, patting her belly and laughing. The woman joined her in laughter, and even though she was clumsy and hadn't been watching where she was going, Shauna liked her. She started to move on when the woman bent over and plucked the paper off the ground, then held it out to her. Shauna shook her head and continued on her way. It had all been a prank anyway; there was nothing to fear from the letter. All that secret shite about deleting the email and being in danger. It was laughable. Shauna could not believe she fell for it. The tiny woman could throw it away; it seemed a fair exchange for dumping ice cream on her and then pawing at her. Shauna tilted her head back and calmed herself in the skies. Whereas most people would see splotches of gray and the obvious signs of an approaching storm, Shauna saw so much more.

Stripes of hopeful blue peeked out from beneath those gray clouds, interspersed with fluffy white ones. She spotted the shape of an owl, about to take flight. She spotted the face of a beautiful woman. She spotted a newborn baby. Shauna had spent her lifetime watching the skies, learning every trick of light and shapes they had to offer. Endless faces and shifting patterns. The skies talked, and Shauna listened. She considered herself an expert and could accurately forecast storms, if anyone cared to listen. How the hues shifted, light blue sliding into grays and blacks, how the breeze ticked up, how she could smell the rain long before it came. Snow had yet another smell, deeper and earthier than rain, and if the hairs on her arms prickled, there was sure to be thunder and lightning. Some people claimed they could feel the weather in their bones, but Shauna could feel it in her soul. Floods were coming alright. Shauna had told Liam to buy extra food and batteries for the torch, and she was going to be browned off if he didn't listen. They'd be spending the next few days indoors; hopefully they wouldn't kill each other. But otherwise she was looking forward to the storm. Shauna relished her relationship with Mother Nature, the only mother she had ever known.

You are your mothers' savage daughters . . .

What shite! She'd had enough of the festival; hopefully the Griffins wouldn't mind if she turned up a bit early to use the jax. She turned and continued toward the end of Strand Street; from there it was a left up the hill and then a right to the Griffins. She imagined them all walking to Mass on Sundays, then to a harbor restaurant for fish and chips. Hopefully, they would let him have more than soggy green veggies. The Irish wind picked up as she plodded uphill, and it was not at her back. Her onboard passenger kicked his disapproval, or maybe he was cheering her on. Her lad. Whom she would never get to know. Who would never miss her.

But what if he did?

You could miss something you never had. Shauna missed a lot of things she never had, especially parents. Which meant she couldn't give her baby fabulous grandparents either. She couldn't give him a real home, with a garden and a big kitchen filled with yummy smells, and a grand school down the road. She wanted him to have it all. Loving parents, loads of friends, and a house full of love.

The only person who had tried to talk her out of giving him up for adoption (besides Liam) was the homeless woman who sat on the wall near the group home. She was dirty, her blond hair greasy and always shoved under a red bandana, and she smelled, but she was friendly, and Shauna couldn't help but like her. She wasn't like the others. She didn't frown when she couldn't understand Shauna's speech. When she told the woman that her baby was going to have fabulous parents, the woman held up a finger and then jotted something down on the pad they used to communicate and turned it around: *You would be a good mother.*

Shauna hadn't expected that. And, for some reason, it made her feel a little stab of pain in her heart. But the woman on the wall was only trying to be nice, and Shauna knew her baby needed a bigger life than she could give him.

By the time she arrived at the Griffins' semi-attached brick house, her "light" backpack was heavy, and her bladder was about to burst. She passed their lovely front garden and mounted the steps to the front door. But when she went to knock on the door, she could see that it was already open a few inches. She stepped in. "I'm coming in." She wouldn't be able to hear their answer, so there was no use stalling. She really, really had to pee, and they had already told her she was welcome anytime, and so she made her way down the small hallway and into the kitchen. A shocking sight greeted her. At first, she couldn't make sense of what was right in front of her eyes.

Mr. and Mrs. Griffin were sitting in their dining chairs, facing her, eyes wide and terrified. Their mouths were covered with silver tape, rope covered their torsos, and their ankles were zip-tied to the bottom rungs of the chairs. But that wasn't what had Shauna rooted to the spot, heart thumping, piss coating her thighs. Standing behind the Griffins was a man. He was dressed in a bulky black coat and wore a dark mask. Given that it was made from black and gray feathers, at first she thought he was a bird. But as she continued to stare, she realized the sides of the mask had a very distinct shape. A dark butterfly—or a moth. It covered nearly his entire face, and it was one of the most terrifying things she had ever seen. She thought of the letter. *Butterflies are free!* Code word: Butterfly. That's when she knew. He had been waiting for her.

He held up large sheets of white paper and began to shuffle through them in slow motion. Large words in black marker screamed at her:

**YOU CAN COME QUIETLY
AND LIVE
OR YOU CAN STRUGGLE
AND DIE**

CHAPTER 5

*D*IMPNA WILDE STOOD IN FRONT OF INK-LING, DINGLE'S NEWEST—
and only, for that matter—tattoo parlor. She was still in shock over
the news that her brother Donnecha was not only a budding tattoo
artist, but the owner of this little shop. He'd been keeping his new
vocation secret for a few years now, and it was only because her son,
Ben, had taken his shirt off while helping her clean out the kennels
that Dimpna had learned of it. She spotted what she had thought
was a smudge on his left triceps. She licked her thumb and tried to
wipe it off, which elicited a rare belly laugh from her grown son. It
turned out to be a miniature Tree of Life, all in black. She had
been about to lecture him when he preempted that with the news
that he'd received the tattoo from Donnecha, and that he'd
opened his own shop, and that Ben was working there part-time.
That little avalanche of information had knocked every other
thought out of her poor head. *Well played, Benjamin.*

A bell dinged as she entered. The shop was so small it was claustrophobic, and it didn't take long to spot Donnecha. He was
hunched over a woman who was lying prone in a chair next to him.
The walls were painted a dark orange and covered with images of
tattoos. There was a single station, the one now occupied by Donnecha and his client, and a counter with a cash register. The place
smelled of ink and stale cigarettes, and overhead a bank of fluores-
cent lights buzzed and popped. Dimpna felt a pang akin to home-
sickness. He'd left her out of all of it.

"Busy now, leave your name and digits in the guest book on the counter, and I'll give you a bell," Donnecha said, without turning around.

"Lovely," Dimpna said. "I'm thinking of getting the name of me business tattooed on me arse." She laughed, imagining their official name: Wilde's Large and Small Animal Veterinarian Clinic. She was a tiny thing; she doubted he could even fit "Wilde's" on both cheeks.

The buzzing stopped. Donnecha apologized to the poor girl in his chair, then swiveled around and grinned. "Turn around," he said. "Let me see if I have enough to work with."

"Sod off." Seconds in her brother's presence, and they were both acting like children. She'd missed this.

"What do you think?" he said, gesturing around the shop with his needle.

"I'm gobsmacked."

"Let me guess," he said. "Ben spilled the beans."

"Through no fault of his own," Dimpna said. "I thought he had a smudge on his arm."

"Smudge!" he said. "That tree was a work of art."

"Tree," the girl said, a tinge of panic in her voice. "Maybe I should have gotten a tree."

"You're grand," he said. "Who doesn't love a panda?"

"But maybe he could be, like . . . eating a tree," the girl said. "Don't they eat trees?"

"Bamboo," Donnecha said.

"That's sorted," the girl said. "I want him eating bamboo, like."

Donnecha sighed and rolled his eyes at Dimpna. "Brilliant," he said to the girl.

"Why didn't you tell me?" Dimpna asked as she looked around once more. She recognized the self-pitying tone in her voice, but she couldn't help it. Did he think she wouldn't have been supportive? She would have been supportive. *Mostly*.

"Can we chat later? I'm in the middle of something here."

The girl raised her free hand. "Me," she said. "He's in the middle of me."

Lovely. "You're a piece of work," she said. "Sorry—me brother, not you. But congrats. Again. Me brother, not you. But . . . congrats to you too."

"I'm covering me ex-boyfriend's name," the girl said.

"Excellent." Dimpna tried to drum up some enthusiasm. "Congrats are in order after all."

"Thanks." The girl stared at Donnecha as he worked. "Do you think I should, like, add the panda's name or something?"

"Why don't we save that for another day," Donnecha said.

"Right," the girl said. "No. I want it now. Padraig. Padraig the Panda."

Dimpna turned and covered her laugh with her hand. When she'd sorted herself out, she addressed her brother. "You'd better have me over later when you're free. I want to hear all about this venture."

"Only if you get a tattoo," he said. "I'm a busy man."

"Nice try."

"Jokes aside, it's a busy week," he said. "I have a primo tattoo artist coming to train me."

"Lucky you."

"Train you?" the girl said. "*Train* you?"

"Advanced stuff, like," he said. "Don't worry; you're grand, like." He turned to Dimpna. "This lad is *talented*. He gave up a high-tech job in security systems to pursue being an artist."

"Living the dream," Dimpna dead-panned.

"What kind of advanced stuff?" the girl asked. "Do you think I need something advanced?"

"I think you need a psychiatrist," Donnecha said.

Dimpna's phone buzzed, and she looked down to see a message from Niamh, her clinic manager. **Emergency. Dooley's Farm! (Your Father!!!)**

Dimpna groaned.

"I don't want to hear it," Donnecha said.

"It's not about you, it's about Da," Dimpna said. Donnecha repeated her groan. Eamon Wilde was suffering from dementia, and lately he'd been a handful. They needed to get him into a proper home with care, but so far her mother had been resisting it. "Later," Dimpna said as she headed for the door. "And congrats again. I didn't have an inkling." She laughed. "Get it?"

"Har har."

"Congrats. I mean it."

"Ink it," he said. "If you mean it, ink it."

The lambing shed was filled with a pungent mix of sweat, fluids, and hay. Lambing season was well underway, and a casual observer might not see anything wrong with the tall veterinarian who had climbed into the nearby pen, his white coat hanging off his thin frame. He was ordering everyone around—anyone, that is, who would listen—but, at the moment, his only audience consisted of a chubby lad who looked to be nine or ten years of age and, of course, the sheep themselves. The owner of the sheep farm, Peg Dooley, had stepped away to report an emergency.

He was the emergency. Dr. Eamon Wilde, a once-renowned veterinarian in the Dingle Peninsula, who had been retired for years now, had bouts of time where he thought he was still practicing. Normally, he barged into the clinic, and Dimpna would have to gently redirect him. This was the first time he'd shown up off-site. His visit came much to Peg's surprise, and although so far he hadn't done any damage that she could see, Dimpna learned that Peg had not been able to coax him out of the lambing shed.

By the time Dimpna and her vet tech, Patrick, arrived, with Peg Dooley chattering on their heels, Dr. Eamon Wilde had actually helped deliver five healthy lambkins. Their bleats made for a joyous chorus. Dimpna hurried over to her father.

"He just showed up out of nowhere and climbed into the pen, like," Peg said. She'd already said as much on the phone, but now that Dimpna saw her father was doing no harm (so far), she had to wrestle with herself not to lash out at Peg.

"Luckily, everything is in order, and we're here now," Dimpna said. The hard part would be getting her father to leave.

"In order?" Peg said. "He doesn't even have a wash bucket—he's not wearing gloves."

"He let me help too!" The chubby lad grinned and flashed palms filled with unknown fluids. Maybe he was doing a little bit of harm.

"Dylan Walsh!" Peg let out a shriek and grabbed the lad by the collar. "Wash those hand now!" She gave him a little shove; presumably, he knew where to go. "Me grandson," she said to Dimpna as he ran out of the shed. "He's going to be the death of me."

He was back so soon that there was no way his hands were sanitized. "Why do we need *three* vets, like?" Dylan said. "Me and the old man were already doing it."

"Young man, I am not old," Eamon said, turning to Dylan. "I am forty-two years young."

"Oh my God," Dylan said. "That old?"

Eamon Wilde was in his late seventies. Dimpna felt as if she was watching a Vaudeville act, and she didn't know whether to clap or throw tomatoes.

"Dylan Walsh, how many times do I have to tell ya?" Peg Dooley said. "Do not take the Lord's name in vain." Peg clutched her hair with both hands. "He's on spring break, yet he's nearly breaking me."

Dimpna couldn't help it; she laughed. "Da," she said, "why don't you step out and use the wash bucket?" She turned to Dylan. "You can use it too. You need to get those hands sparkling clean." Dylan stared at his hands in wonder as Patrick took the hint and set off to fetch the bucket from Dimpna's VW bus. Her son, Ben, was supposed to be watching her father. His third caregiver in less than a fortnight had quit. Eamon's behavior was growing more and more erratic. It was heartbreaking. And exhausting. But at the heart of it all was a man who deserved respect. He had spent his lifetime earning it. Dimpna texted Ben to come to Peg's farm right away to collect him, and then she tried once more to get her father to climb out of the pen. She took in the surroundings—as usual, Peg Dooley was ready for her busiest season of the year. And this week the Spring festival was taking place; both she and Peg had been there earlier today, and Dimpna was running on fumes. Peg must have read her mind, for she brought out a thermos of coffee with some Styrofoam cups, along with a tin of biscuits. It was enough to distract her father, and minutes later, Dimpna was holding a nice hot cup of java. She loved how the smell of the coffee mingled with the hay. The wind was picking up, storms were coming in, but the lambing shed was well-protected.

The sheds were separated from the main barn, with everything one needed for successful birthing—a series of pens that were designed to house several lambs, outdoor green curtains that would be pulled up or brought down, depending on the weather, and a bay they could lift up so that when the forage truck went by with the feed, the ewes could stick their heads out to feed. There were also plenty of viewing spots for the visitors. Every year, people flocked to the Dooleys' to witness the miracle of birth. The visiting hours were in the morning and early afternoon; it was nearly half-three now, and Dimpna was grateful not to have spectators for her father's episode.

Dylan was swinging around one of the beams. He was adorable, with his full cheeks and little belly hanging over his T-shirt, and although she also feared his weight would make him a target of his schoolmates, Dimpna was a strong proponent of acceptance when it came to body sizes. Animals came in all shapes, and so did people. But as someone who had always been tiny and thin, she was also aware that those who carried extra weight faced struggles she had never imagined. And she got the distinct feeling he was bereft of a close friend group, which was why he seemed to be thrilled hanging around sheep and a seventy-something-year-old man with dementia.

"Da," Dimpna said, as Patrick returned with the bucket and began filling it at Peg's water source, "take my hand."

Eamon Wilde squinted at her, and then, to Dimpna's surprise, he stepped forward to take her hand. But instead of allowing her to help him over the barricade, he yanked her forward, and then, before she knew what was happening, his teeth had dug into her bicep, and he clamped down hard.

Dimpna screamed and jostled the rest of her scalding coffee over her arm. "Let go, let go."

Patrick came rushing over. "Mr. Wilde," he said. "Mr. Wilde."

Her father released his bite, but still gripped Dimpna's arm. He lifted his head to Patrick. "It's Doctor Wilde." His tone was suddenly professional, as if he hadn't just bitten his grown daughter's bicep.

Patrick held up both hands. "Of course, of course, my deepest apologies. Doctor Wilde, please let go of Doctor Wilde."

Eamon released her arm and grinned. "Don't bite the hand that feeds ya," he said.

"Oh my God," Patrick said. He looked at Dimpna. "Are you alright?"

"I'll be grand," she said. It really hurt.

"Shall I get you some disinfectant?"

"The skin isn't broken," Dimpna said.

"He said, 'Oh my God,' he said, 'Oh my God,' he said it," Dylan sang, finger pointed at Patrick. "Me grandma said you're not supposed to take the Lord's name in vain. And you said it. You said, 'Oh my God.'"

Eamon looked stricken, as if he was the one being blamed. "You'd better not tell her," he said.

"Once again, I apologize," Patrick said. "I apologize to everyone for everything." Patrick, in addition to being young and handsome, was a stand-up lad, and Dimpna could tell he was getting frazzled.

"Everyone, settle," Dimpna said. "Da, we need to get you home."

Eamon tilted his head. "What did I tell you, Dew? If you're going to come with me to a job, you have to sit and watch. Sit. And. Watch."

Dylan opened his mouth wide, then slid his gaze to Dimpna and Patrick.

Patrick gently took Dimpna's arm to examine the bite. Although it hadn't drawn blood, she could see the indents in her arm, and it hurt something fierce. "Out of the pen right now, Da," she ordered, raising her voice. "Ben is on his way; why don't you watch for his car?"

He'd better be on his way. He had yet to text back.

"Ben?" Her father eagerly jumped over the barricade. "I haven't seen Ben in ages. How old is he now?" He went over and ruffled Dylan's head. Patrick handed Dimpna some disinfectant and cotton balls.

"Thanks."

Peg, who had stepped out of the barn, returned, this time with two plates, each with a large slice of apple pie. "Listen lads. If you wash up real good, you can have my apple pie. Hot out of the oven."

"Yes!" Eamon said, making a run for the wash bucket. Dylan

trailed after him. Minutes later, they were seated on hay bales lost in their pie.

Ben texted his apologies; he had fallen asleep and hadn't realized Eamon had snuck out of the house. Fallen asleep? This late in the day? Dimpna had been awake since half-four. She loved her son but was, she had to admit to herself, disappointed. He appeared to have no career ambitions whatsoever. Working at a tattoo parlor, of all things. At his age, she was running a practice, keeping up a home, and raising him. She never thought she'd be one of those mothers who nagged, and for the most part, she kept out of his business. To an extent. She was still a mammy. The urge to lecture him was itching at her.

He was so smart. So capable. He could do anything he put his mind to. Look at Patrick. Even younger than Ben and well set up for a fantastic career. Not that she expected Ben to follow in her veterinarian paw-steps, although it had always been a fantasy of hers to go on jobs with her son. It wasn't the life for him, and she understood that. But wasn't it time he figured out what was? Didn't Ben want to seize the day? These were supposed to be the good years. He was young and healthy. He was at an age where he should be well into a line of work and looking to settle down. Her brother, Donnecha, and his carefree lifestyle must have been rubbing off on him. Then again, Donnecha was a business owner now; maybe it was only a matter of time before Ben found his passion. Understandably, Ben's life had been shaken up when the man who raised him as his own was caught in a financial scheme and then took his own life. Prior to that, Ben had planned on working in finance himself. Niall's tragedy had become their tragedy, and to some extent, they were still dealing with the fallout. Ben didn't even have his own flat; he was living at the house with her father now, and although she appreciated the help, it just wasn't a long-term solution. But that conversation would have to wait for another day. She was here, and given the crooning sounds around her, several of the ewes were in labor. Dimpna washed and suited up, then climbed into the pen to help. Soon Patrick joined her, and they got to work. Half an hour later and they had three newborn lambs, all wobbly and adorable.

"It really is a miracle," Patrick said, as the sounds of newborn lambs echoed around them.

"So it is, lad, so it is," Peg said. "It never gets old."

Dylan set his empty pie plate on the haystack next to a now-sleeping Eamon Wilde and ran to Dimpna. He looked up at her (barely, since Dimpna was under five feet herself) with wide and terrified eyes as he pointed to the ewe giving birth. "She's in pain," he said. "Why don't you just put them to sleep, and they won't know they're in pain, and then they wake up and they're, like, oh, here's me baby. I didn't even know I was having him." He talked in a rush as if he was used to being interrupted and had learned to shove as much as he could into a single breath. His level of empathy at his age touched her.

"It is very nice to care about someone else's pain," Dimpna said. "And there are things we can do to ease their suffering, but we need the mother to push, and there are some experiences that are worth it in the end."

Dylan scrunched his face and shook his head. "How can that be worth it?"

"Giving birth is one of the greatest miracles in this world. There's an unbreakable bond between mothers and babies." She wasn't really talking about ewes anymore; frankly, she'd never had a single one of them tell her they were happy for the experience, but here was this lad in front of her with questions, and she wanted to plant a little seed of hope in him, so he would know that it wasn't all doom and gloom.

"It's worth it when it's all over," Patrick agreed, sticking his fist out to bump Dylan's. Dylan frowned, then shrugged and resumed twirling himself around the pole. Dimpna hurried in front of Patrick and gave him a fist bump.

"Thanks," he said with a laugh.

Dimpna grinned. "Not a bother."

"I'm glad I never have to give birth," Dylan said, as he continued to swirl. "If I were a girl, I'd say let's just adopt." He was making Dimpna dizzy.

"Dylan. What did I tell ya about hanging around here when it upsets you so much?" Peg said. "Why don't you ring one of your friends, and we can arrange a play date?"

"Lads don't have play dates," he said. "They just see each other, and one might be, like, do you want to hang out, and the others, like, shrug or something, but they do want to hang out, so they just start doing stuff. Like ride their bicycles. They don't have to ring each other about it." He stopped. "Do I have me bicycle here?"

"You do indeed," Peg said. "Your mammy brought it along; it's in the garage."

"Can I ride it?"

Peg put her hands on her hips and stared her grandson down. "Well, where can we take you that you might see these friends of yours?"

Dylan shrugged. "Dunno."

Peg glanced at Dimpna. "He struggles a bit to fit in." She leaned in and patted his back. "Where's your inhaler, lad? I can hear ya wheezing."

"In me room."

"I think you need to take a rest from the barn and calm your lungs down."

"What about later?" he asked.

"What about later?" she responded.

"I could go bicycle riding," he said. "Michael and James ride their bicycles every night."

"In the dark?"

"Just around the harbor." He clasped his hands together. "*Please?* We're going to have a storm, and then I'll be stuck in your barn with nothing but little lambs."

Peg laughed. "Let's see if we can get your breathing back to normal first."

"If I do, can I go?"

"If your lungs are clear, I don't see why not." She glanced at the sky. "The weather's expected to take a bad turn late in the evening. I suppose you might as well get some exercise while it's still behaving. But you must stick around the town square, do you hear?"

"Yes, granny."

"And not for long. Thirty minutes, and I'll pick you back up."

"One of their mammies can take me home. They take turns picking them up with a truck for their bicycles and everything."

"I already said yes, and I don't mind picking you up. Tell their mammies I can take the other lads home as well."

"Yes!" He whooped.

"Until then, why don't you rest up?"

"I don't need rest," Dylan said, as he continued around the pole.

Just then, a pained sound came from one of the ewes. Patrick hurried over.

"Another one," he said. "It's a breach." Two legs with tiny hooves appeared at the vaginal opening.

"Maybe the lad needs a glass of milk," Dimpna said to Peg before joining Patrick.

"I want to watch! I want to watch!" Dylan's voice was thick with excitement; his previous hesitations seemingly had vanished.

"This might not end well," Dimpna warned Peg. The mother was already exhausted, straining, her heart no doubt racing too fast. This little runt was not expected, which was another bad sign.

"He might as well learn," Peg said. "Death is a part of life on a farm. Just a part of life."

Dimpna wanted to argue, but she didn't have time. The lad was already sensitive, and he didn't need to learn life's harsh lessons right now. But Dimpna had to focus, and she'd learned long ago that arguing with fools made her one too. Patrick, sensing Dimpna's ire, stood behind her. Whereas Dimpna was so small she was often mistaken for a child, Patrick was tall enough to block Dylan's view. "Good man," Dimpna said, as she positioned herself near the little hooves.

"I want to see! I want to see!" Dylan continued to shout. "Are they going to die?"

Like a lamb to the slaughter, Dimpna thought. *Like a lamb to the slaughter.*

It took considerable effort, but Dimpna was finally able to turn the lambkin around, and once that was sorted, they were able to pull him out. The mother let out a groan, then set her head down, exhausted, as they cleaned the baby. This one wasn't breathing. "Come on, luv," Dimpna said, clearing its little mouth, pressing gently on its chest. She continued the palpations, fearing the worst, but seconds later, the wee thing gasped for breath and kicked its little legs. The mother lifted her head and then sat all the way up to lick her last born.

"Well done, you!" Peg exclaimed.

"What's she done now?" a familiar voice said. Dimpna turned to see Ben standing in the doorway of the barn.

"Ben," she said. "I'd hug ya, but I'm covered in slime."

"Story of me life," Ben said with a laugh. He glanced at Eamon, who was still sleeping. "Sorry," he said. He then turned to the newborn lambs and took out his phone as he began to record. "Do you mind?" he asked Peg. "It's for my YouTube channel."

"YouTube channel?" Dimpna said.

"Yes, Mam. I'll send ya the link."

"Why do you need a YouTube channel?"

"It's a form of artistic expression. And you can get sponsors. Sponsors that pay."

"You're telling me you have sponsors that pay you?"

Ben's neck flushed. "Not yet. I'm building me audience. American girls go bonkers for life in rural Ireland."

Dimpna had to talk herself into not responding in a negative way. "Send me the link," she said.

"I said I would, but you know, you could open your own account and give me a follow."

When pigs fly. "Is there a theme?" She paused. "Other than making American girls go bonkers?"

"Just the days of me life, Mam," he said as he filmed.

Fantastic.

"Film me! Film me!" Dylan said, going faster around the pole.

"Do you need anything else, Peg?" Dimpna asked, hoping the answer was no; she needed to get back to the clinic.

"That's it, Doc," Peg said. "I can't thank ye enough."

"You have a nice batch here," Dimpna said. "It will keep you busy."

"So it will, Doc. So it will."

Dylan followed her as she began to scrub up in a bucket.

"What are you doing?"

"It's my turn to clean up. This is how I do it."

"You don't take showers?" He sounded horrified. Then he leaned down, his breath syrupy. "You're lucky. I don't like taking them either."

From the ripe smell of him, he was telling the truth.

"You'll have a bath tonight, lad," Peg said.

"After my bicycle ride," Dylan chimed in.

"We had a nice crowd in this morning, watching the lambing," Peg said.

"Lovely," Dimpna replied.

"Sheila Maguire brought in a few, alright," Peg added.

Sheila Maguire. Even now Dimpna felt a sad tug at the mention of the woman who had once been her best friend. She was a local tour guide, and it didn't surprise Dimpna that she'd brought folks here.

"I saw a baby lamb come out dead yesterday," Dylan said, back in her face. "It was sad."

Dimpna ruffled him on the head. "That is sad," she said. "And it's okay to be sad for a bit. But then we can turn our focus to the happier results, can't we?"

"What do you mean?"

"We focus on all the ones who have been born." She took his hand and led him to the pen with all the babies. Adorable, stumbling, little fluffy white babies nuzzling at their mothers.

"They're sooo cute," Dylan said.

"They are indeed," Patrick said.

"Where there's life, there's hope." Dimpna resisted the urge to pat him on the head again. "Where there's life, there's hope."

Ben groaned. "I wish I had a euro for every time you've said that."

"How many euros would you have?" Dylan asked. "Does she owe you two euros right now?"

Ben laughed and rumpled his head.

"I have a dog at home," Dylan said. "She's cute too."

"I bet," Patrick said. "What breed is she?"

Dylan shrugged. "Dunno. Just a regular one, I guess."

Dimpna's mobile phone rang. Dimpna fished it out of her bag and glanced at the screen. It was her clinic manager, Niamh. She would only be calling if it was important.

"How ya," Dimpna said.

"Sorry to bother ye," Niamh said, sounding out of breath. "Are ye almost finished?"

"You have excellent timing," Dimpna said. "We're just about to pack up." She waited through a few seconds of silence. "What's the story?"

"First, Liam McCarthy is here and wanted to speak with ya. I don't know what it's about; he'll only speak with you, but he's pacing in the courtyard."

"Got it." Liam was a local handyman whom she hadn't seen since his dog had passed away last year. "What else?"

"The Griffins never came to pick up Milly." Milly was a Kerry blue terrier that they loved more than life. They'd never once been late picking her up; in fact, they were normally there an hour early because they said they didn't want Milly to come to the reception area, not see them, and think they'd abandoned her. If they were a no-show, that was unusual. Then again, they were adopting a newborn in a few months, and it was such a dramatic and exciting event that she could see them dropping the ball.

"Did you ring them?"

"I rang both of them. Neither of them picked up."

"If we don't hear back in a few hours, I'll take Milly over myself and make sure they're alright," Dimpna said. "I'm sure they just got tied up."

CHAPTER 6

*L*IAM McCARTHY WAS STILL IN THE FRONT COURTYARD WHEN DIMPNA and Patrick arrived. Niamh was correct; he seemed agitated. Dimpna flashed a smile, and Patrick gave a nod.

"Hey, Doc." He then nodded at Patrick.

"What brings you here?"

Liam ran a hand through his dark hair and studied her with gorgeous blue eyes. He was a handsome lad, although he didn't seem to know it. He was nearing thirty. Dimpna wondered if he had a girlfriend. He was one of Niamh's many crushes. No doubt she was devastated he was pacing out here instead of inside with her.

He glanced at Patrick, then his shoes. "Just had a couple questions."

Something private, from the way he was acting. Dimpna turned to Patrick. "I'll be in shortly." Patrick nodded and headed into the clinic. "What's the story?" She thought of his former dog, a sweet golden retriever named Pancake. Liam cried in her office when they had to put her down. Pancake was fifteen, and Liam had had her since *he* was fifteen. Was he thinking of getting another? Dimpna always hoped he would. But the look on his face made her wonder if something was wrong.

"My neighbors' dog is pregnant," he said.

"Nice," Dimpna said. "Are you thinking of getting a pup?"

"The thing is, she's a very nervous dog."

"Is she?"

Liam nodded. "Like *very*. Like the most nervous you could ever imagine."

"Okay. That might be wise to pay attention to, although that doesn't necessarily mean her pups will be nervous too."

"I'm just wondering—if the dog is afraid to give birth, how do I help her?"

Dimpna's heart melted a tad. "When the time comes, she'll know what to do."

He shook his head. "But what if she rejects her pups?"

"I don't think you need to worry. What breed is she?"

"Let's just assume that she is freaking out at the thought of giving birth and I want to help. Is there, like, a book or something?"

"If you're that worried, why don't you have the owners give me a bell? I can have a look at her."

Liam kicked a rock and slowly nodded. "Okay."

"Really. Most dogs do just fine. Even the nervous sorts." She paused. Liam remained silent. "When is she due?"

"Soon," he said. Then without another word, he took off. *Strange,* Dimpna thought. Then again, plenty of people thought the same of her.

Once inside, Dimpna was swept up with the needs of her furry clients. Milly, who wasn't used to being without the Griffins, and perhaps sensing the oncoming storm, followed Dimpna around everywhere she went. The sour cherry on top—Dimpna had three missed calls from Sheila Maguire, and when Dimpna didn't respond, she received a disturbing text:

Why are you ignoring me? My father is dying. He wants to see you. Call me!!!

It was the last thing she'd expected to hear. Dimpna's stomach twisted at the thought of Sheila losing her father, Danny Maguire— or Mr. Maguire, as she had always called him. He and Sheila's mom had been pillars of the community back in the day. A nurse and a chemist. They'd been members of nearly every organization, the first ones at church every Sunday, and the ones most likely to sign up as volunteers for the charity of the moment. But Dimpna had never really liked Mr. Maguire. He'd been the intimidating sort, always trying to control his wild horse of a daughter. And when Dimpna left for Dublin at the tender age of eighteen, Danny Maguire had a scandalous affair and moved away with his mistress for several years before crawling back home and begging for forgiveness. Sheila's mam gave him another chance, but in the end, the betrayal proved too much. They divorced years ago, but despite his faults, Sheila had remained a daddy's girl. There was no reason on earth why Danny Maguire would want to see her. This had to be Sheila, trying to manipulate her. Sheila often had a hidden agenda. Dimpna sent a text back, writing and deleting until she settled on a polite version:

I'm so sorry. Please send my regards.

It's lambing season, as you know, and I'm truly swamped.

I'll say a prayer.

Sheila was not going to like that, and Dimpna knew she hadn't heard the end of it. But it was closing time, she was exhausted, and her pack needed a stroll. Dimpna owned three dogs and a cat. "Any word from the Griffins?" she asked Niamh.

"Nada." Niamh frowned. "I hope they're alright; it's so not like them."

Dimpna agreed. "I'm taking my pack for a walk. I'll take Milly along and then pop by their house on the way home." They didn't live far from Strand Street, where Dimpna was headed. Just as she announced her plans, the Universe laughed.

The doors opened, and Sheila Maguire entered, accompanied by yet another young and very pregnant woman. She had strawberry-blond hair and a bright smile. Next to her, a handsome young man clutched her hand. Young love. Dimpna had become a mother all alone, and it was hard not to look at them and imagine what it would have been like to be in love and expecting.

"I'm glad we caught you," Sheila said.

Caught. Definitely the correct word choice. "I'm sorry I was late responding to your text, and I'm truly sorry about your father. But I was just on me way upstairs to grab the pack, and I have to get this one back home." She gave a nod to Milly, who, sensing an oncoming walk, was dancing around her feet.

"This is my cousin and her husband," Sheila said, as if Dimpna hadn't spoken. "This is Orla and Kevin, and the one-on-the-way makes three."

"Lovely to meet you," Dimpna said. "Congrats on the little one. Is it your first?"

Orla and Kevin grinned. "It is," Orla said. "We're over the moon." She believed them. They had that glow. Dimpna's thoughts flitted to the deaf pregnant woman from yesterday. Hopefully, she had a fella supporting her as well. Then again, Dimpna had done a damn fine job as a single mum, if she did say so herself. And for a time, her husband, Niall, had been a good father figure to Ben.

Dimpna had never met Orla or even heard a thing about her. She was half Sheila's age, in her early twenties at the most, but the family resemblance was obvious. "Is there something I can do for you?"

"Orla and Kevin have just moved to town. They had to move in with Kevin's mam, because the flat they rented is an absolute wreck," Sheila said. "And I hear it smells." She smiled at Orla, who nodded. "Liam McCarthy manages it," Sheila said. "He tried to accuse them of causing the odor."

Liam had just paid her a visit after a year, and now Sheila was mentioning him. Synchronicity. *Fascinating.* Dimpna wasn't going to mention it; he'd come to her privately. With a very odd question— but still, he was a client and deserved respect.

"Disgusting," Orla said, wrinkling her nose. "It smelled like that from day one."

"I don't even want to know what caused it," Kevin said. "Personally, I think an animal crawled in there to die. Whatever it was—not good for Orla."

It was possible. Animals gave no thoughts to the humans when they were seeking someplace to die. "Not good for anyone," Dimpna said.

"My mam rents a town house, also managed by Liam," Kevin said. "But not many wives want to live with their mother-in-law, I've learned." He slid a glance to his wife. Her expression made it clear that she did not want to live with her mother-in-law.

"They'd be welcome to stay with us," Sheila said. "But with Da being sick, it's not exactly a cheerful environment."

"This one is coming soon." Orla patted her belly. "It's more that we don't want Mr. Maguire to have to listen to a screaming baby." She glanced at her husband. "We don't want your mam listening to it either."

"Mam wants us to stay," Kevin said. "She wouldn't mind."

Orla gave Sheila and Dimpna a pointed look. "I'm sure she wouldn't mind you and the baby," Orla said. "Not sure I can say the same for me."

"Now, now," Kevin said. "Mam loves you."

"She's obsessed with her son," Orla said.

Kevin flushed red. "Just a normal mammy."

"I saw her take the fork you were using and tape it in her scrapbook," Orla said. She looked at the women in the room. "Did I mention she's an avid scrapbooker?" She rubbed her belly. "She's already documenting this little one—wanting to know every second I feel movement and then writing it down." She shook her head. "She's a bit much."

"What can I say?" Kevin said with a grin. "I'm the Golden Boy." He winked.

Orla rolled her eyes. "I know she's looking forward to becoming a granny, but you'd swear she was the one having the baby." Kevin laughed and ambled over to a nearby bulletin board that featured photographs of all their furry clients. *She's awful*, Orla mouthed and mimed someone smoking, then mimed shooting herself in the head.

"In front of you?" Sheila couldn't help but ask as she repeated the smoking gesture.

"She smokes in her room," Orla whispered. "But we can still smell it." She shook her head as she rubbed her belly.

"I wish you the best in your search for a rental," Dimpna said, hoping to distract Orla from her family problems. "Is that the reason you stopped by?" Sheila always had an ulterior motive.

"It's actually Niamh we came to speak with," Sheila said. "If there's anyone who has her pulse on Dingle, it's her."

Niamh, who had just put on her jacket and grabbed her handbag to make her exit, laughed. "I do hear all of the gossip, alright. I don't know of any place for let at the moment, but now that I know you're looking, I'm going to keep me eyes and ears open. Why don't you write down what you're looking for—how many bedrooms, location, and whatnot—and your mobile number."

"Thanks a million," Orla said as she stepped forward to write everything down.

The clinic door opened again, and a tall man with dark hair hidden under a pea cap and large sunglasses entered. He seemed to command attention, and everyone fell silent. Dimpna couldn't put her finger on the exact reason, but something about the man set her on edge. Over the years, she had learned to trust her instincts, that little voice inside her warning of danger. But this time it wasn't whispering. It was loud and insistent. She'd very rarely taken such an instant dislike to a person, but there was something about him that set off all her alarm bells. Maybe it was his intense eyes, and the way he seemed zeroed in on Orla's swollen belly. Dimpna wanted to shove the stranger out the door, then slam and lock it tight behind him.

"How ya," Niamh said to the stranger. "Welcome to Wilde's Veterinarian Clinic."

"I'm sorry," Dimpna said. "We're closed." The man turned his head to Orla and dropped his chin slightly. "How can we help ya?" she asked the stranger. Her tone, even to her own ear, was not friendly. Sheila looked at her and raised an eyebrow before glancing at the man.

Because her small stature contrasted with her booming personality, Dimpna was often called a miniature Viking. She'd learned early on that she had to assert herself or else she'd be treated like a child. That said, sometimes she wore her hair in pigtails and donned flowery dresses with wellies just because wearing them made her happy. She derived a great deal of satisfaction from smashing norms. It was fun to let her hair down and dress how she liked on her days off; it was a nice contrast to her drab, fur-covered work attire. She had no qualms about her size. But this man instinctively made her want to make herself bigger, like an animal in the wild confronting a predator.

"I'm on the hunt," the man said. His voice was low and gravely.

"Excuse me?" Dimpna said. "The hunt?"

His lips slowly stretched into a smile. It was the creepiest thing Dimpna had ever seen. "For a wolfhound."

"We don't have animals up for adoption," Dimpna said. "We're strictly a veterinarian clinic and boarding facility." Last year, she had transformed the mechanic's garage across the street into a lovely boarding space. "We're having a bit of a staff meeting here; I'm afraid I need you to leave." Patrick, the strongest of them, had already gone home. At her feet, Milly started to growl, a low sound that made the hairs on Dimpna's arm stand up.

"I was hoping you could recommend a reputable breeder," the man said. He continued to gawk in Orla's direction. That had to be the reason for the sunglasses. To behave like a letch and get away with it.

"You'll want to contact the Irish Wolfhound Club," Dimpna said. "They can point you in the right direction." She headed for her counter, where she grabbed a calling card, and on the back, she jotted down the name of the organization. When she handed the card to the man, he took it and slipped it into his pocket without looking at it.

"Small world," Orla said, turning to the man. "I just met a wolfhound breeder." She turned to Kevin. "Isn't that what Cara does?"

Don't talk to him, Dimpna wanted to shout. *Don't even look at him.* She was confused at why her body was pushing panic buttons. It was her mother who claimed to be psychic. But there were times when a person's energy field was so strong that Dimpna felt as if she knew exactly who they were. And this man was trouble.

"Something like that," Kevin said. He too seemed disturbed by the man. *Good.* "But it's not like she has any pups at the moment."

"Sorry we couldn't help." Ignoring her pounding heart, Dimpna headed for the door, then held it open and stared at the man so that there was no doubt she wanted him to leave.

The man stared back at her for a moment, but instead of exiting, his head swiveled back to Orla. He reached into the pocket of his jacket and brought out three calling cards. He handed one to Orla and the other to Niamh. He then held one out to Dimpna. She couldn't help but look at it. Instead of his name, it seemed to be a business card. It read: NEW AWAKENINGS.

"No thank you," Dimpna said.

He simply shrugged and returned the card to his pocket. "To each his own."

"New awakenings," Orla said. "What is it?"

The man smiled. "What *isn't* it?" he said. "It is everything."

"Is it a spa?" Niamh said. Niamh loved a good mani-pedi. Today her nails were bright orange.

"No," the man said. "It's a way of life." He didn't offer anything more.

"Intriguing," Orla said.

"Isn't it?" Kevin replied, giving the man a hard stare.

"Have you owned wolfhounds before?" Orla asked.

Dimpna bit her lip. Orla seemed unable to pick up on his dark energy. She was the trusting sort, which could be sweet but also dangerous. Given that the wind was now whipping into the clinic and the man was making no move for the door, Dimpna reluctantly closed it. She stood by it, ready to start the routine over again in a few minutes if he didn't leave. If need be, she'd get her pack down here, as Milly wasn't exactly intimidating; she was small with a lop-sided eye and a "just rolled around a field and drank a few pints" look about her. Still, she continued to growl.

"I can tell ye anything ye want to know about Irish wolfhounds," the man said. "Throughout history, *cú* were used only by royalty." His spine straightened as if he was including himself in that lot.

"*Cú?*" Niamh repeated.

"Wolfhounds," he said.

"Really?" Orla said. "That's mad."

No. *He* was mad. All of this was mad.

The stranger nodded. "Chiefs and kings trained them to fight and hunt. They were not for the common man."

"We'd better be off," Kevin said, placing his hand protectively around Orla's waist.

"Right," Sheila said. "I need to get back to my father before he steals me car again."

"He stole your car?" Dimpna asked.

"Figure of speech," Sheila said. "He should be resting; instead, he took my new car for a spin and was gone all afternoon."

Sheila wanted Dimpna to know she'd bought a new car. Good for her, but Dimpna wasn't going to ask about it. If she wanted to brag about her car, she could do it without all the game playing. Sheila stared at Dimpna, then shrugged. "Call me later if you're not too busy."

"It's lambing season," Dimpna said weakly.

"Good luck finding your wolfhound," Orla said to the man. "If Cara knows when any of hers will be having pups, I'll give you a bell."

"Do that," the man said. "Any time." And then he was gone. The wind slammed the door shut behind him.

Kevin stared at the door, then looked at Dimpna. "Is it just me, or was he a bit . . ."

"Off?" Niamh said. Kevin pointed at Niamh and nodded. "He was a bit off alright."

"He seemed alright to me," Orla said. "He was very tall."

Dimpna turned to Sheila. "Have you ever seen him before?"

Sheila shook her head. "Never." Sheila knew everyone in town. If she didn't know him, then he was an outsider.

"Do you think he was blind?" Kevin asked.

"Blind?" Orla said with a laugh. "He was getting around without any cane or other such help."

Kevin stared through the windows as the rain beat down. "Nobody wears sunglasses inside when the skies are this dark."

"I was thinking the same thing," Dimpna said. She turned to Orla. "If I were you, I wouldn't ever call him. You should throw that card away."

Orla tilted her head. "I don't know what you lot are on about. He seemed fine to me."

They headed for the door with Sheila in tow. "Give me a ring next week, and I'll let you know if I've heard of any place to let," Niamh called out.

"Preferably next week," Orla said forlornly, as she rubbed her belly.

"Tell ya what," Niamh said. "Give me a few days."

"We can't thank you enough," Kevin said.

"But we'll try," Orla added.

"Call me," Sheila said.

And then they all did the thing they did when saying goodbye; they said it over and over and over until they were finally out the door. Minutes later, as Dimpna exited the clinic with Milly and her pack, her thoughts once again turned to the stranger. Whoever he was and whatever he was up to, she hoped he would do it far, far from here.

CHAPTER 7

WHEN MILLY STOPPED TO DO HER BUSINESS, DIMPNA STUCK HER hand in her jacket pocket for a poop bag, but instead she pulled out a piece of paper. She glanced at what looked like texts between friends. Then she remembered—the young pregnant woman whom she had bumped into at the festival. Poor thing, Dimpna had squashed the girl's ice cream all over her chest. She had been rambling a long apology and insisting she would buy her more ice cream, not to mention pay for her dry cleaning, when the girl told her she was deaf and moved on before Dimpna could make amends.

Dimpna cleaned up after Milly and was about to throw the messages into the bin, along with the plastic baggy, when she hesitated. If Dimpna did see her again, the paper was the perfect excuse to start a conversation. Dimpna tossed the baggy and tucked the paper back into the pocket of her jacket. The wind was getting worse. "Come on, lads, let's do this." She and the dogs started up again. Walking her pack was often the best part of her day.

There was E.T., her sheepdog, Pickles, her border collie, and Guinness, her English bulldog. E.T. and Pickles vied to be in the lead, whereas Guinness was always holding up the rear. Milly was getting the leashes tangled by running between them. Her black cat, Spike, had remained indoors; he was not a fan of storms. None of them were, to be fair, including Dimpna, and maybe she could get David Griffin to give them all a ride home. He had a pickup truck, and she didn't even mind sitting in the back with the doggos.

Strand Street was closed to cars and dotted with white tents that had been shuttered for the evening. The food trucks had gone home, but the smell of donuts, popcorn, and chicken curry still filled the air. The streets had been jammers a few hours ago, but now there wasn't a soul about. Docked boats rocked on the water. It was getting choppy.

Dimpna broke into a jog and was relieved when they finally reached the Griffins' semi-attached house. Their car and truck were parked on the road in front of the house. That was odd. A prickle of worry came upon her, and as she approached the front door, the dogs all started to bark at once. When Dimpna hesitated, Milly emitted a shrill bark. It startled Dimpna; she'd never heard the old girl bark. Not even once. And when she saw the door was half-open, her heart was thumping, and her hand was already reaching for her mobile phone. She thought she heard the sound of something from within the house, some kind of banging noise.

"Hello? It's Doctor Wilde here. I brought Milly home. I have three big dogs with me." Guinness wasn't really big, but just in case someone had broken into the house, she wanted the person to know she was well protected. She let Milly go, mostly because the dog was about to pull her arm off. She entered the foyer and watched as Milly dashed down the hall to the kitchen. Damn, she'd wanted a more cautious entrance—again, just in case.

But so far, nothing looked amiss. The entrance was tidy. It consisted of a side table with a vase and a bowl for keys, and an area rug that wasn't askew; the windows weren't broken. Had they forgotten to lock the front door and the wind had simply blown it open? She released her dogs and followed Milly into the kitchen. And what she saw there was unbelievable.

Mr. and Mrs. Griffin were tied to their dining chairs, tape around their mouths, rope around their chests securing them to the chairs, and zip ties at their ankles. Tears streamed down both of their faces. Mrs. Griffin's face was smeared with makeup. Milly had already put her front paws on Mrs. Griffin's thighs and was sniffing at the ropes. Dimpna hurried over while calling 999. She was quick in giving them the address, and when she hung up, she called Cormac, a detective inspector she had a friendship with. She stayed on the phone as she hurried over to Mrs. Griffin.

"Dimpna?" Cormac said. "How are ya?"

Dimpna got straight to it. "I've already called 999, but I'm at the home of some clients, Mr. and Mrs. Griffin, and they're tied to their kitchen chairs with tape around their mouths. There's so much of it—and it's so tight—I don't think I can get it off." It was the same with the ropes. It was thick, and she would need something sharp to release them; she was terrified of cutting them in the process. "Same with the rope around their torsos, and their ankles are zip-tied."

"Jesus," Cormac said. "Don't try—wait for the paramedics. I'll be right there." Cormac clicked off. She felt horrid, not being able to help them. She returned to the front of them and before she could apologize, they nodded their understanding.

"You're alright, loves, you're alright. Help is on the way, not much longer now." A stench rose from the pair. They had both soiled themselves, striking a chord of deep empathy in Dimpna. Tears continued to run down Mrs. Griffin's face. "I'm so sorry we didn't cop on earlier; you're always right on time to fetch Milly. I swear to ye this will never happen again." Dimpna fetched a kitchen towel and gently dabbed Mrs. Griffin's face. Then she let the dogs out in their small backyard, realizing all of them, as well as herself, had already trampled over a crime scene. Thank God they were alive and, it appeared, had no serious injuries. She was so confused; she still had not seen anything to suggest a break-in. The Griffins were salt of the earth, both of them primary schoolteachers, and everyone in town unanimously said the baby they were adopting had won the lotto getting them as parents.

"As soon as the paramedics arrive, we'll put on the kettle for tea, will we?" She felt like the young lad Dylan as she rambled on, and an eternity passed before she finally heard sirens. "I'm going to wave them in." In reality, she wanted to get away from them; it was the worst feeling leaving them tied and taped. By the time she stood outside, tears of relief were coming down her face as well. She'd never been so happy to see emergency services in her life.

CHAPTER 8

Seven Star—My Journal
Lessons from the Womb—1994

Yesterday was the worst day of my life. I still don't know how to process it. And so I am writing it down. Purging my demons. No one knows I have started this journal, and it's the first secret I've kept from the Shepherd or the Flock. But if I do not write about last night, it will eat away at me, and that will distract me from my duties. Writing was always something I took to, something that eased my troubled soul. This is all to explain my thievery. I saw this empty journal in the storage room—no doubt put there by Eternal Mist to keep logs of our food—and something wicked came over me. I had to take it. She had a total of three piled one on top of the other, and a fourth into which she had begun logging our inventory. The Shepherd ventures out daily, and he often returns with supplies. It will be a while before we can fully live off the land and the fish in the pond. I know that taking the journal is stealing. I will have to silently ask forgiveness for my sin. The Shepherd preaches that we must act as one. I am striving toward that goal, but I struggle. Keeping a journal is like medicine to keep me balanced. Eternal is often scattered, and I do not think she will even notice that a journal is missing. The Shepherd must have brought them from town, and it stings a little how willing he is to give Eternal Mist anything she wants. She is a child, if you ask me, and I am glad she is not yet with child, for I do not feel she has the skills yet that are needed for motherhood. Then again, that's what the rest of us are for.

I'd forgotten the hit of pleasure I receive from starting a new journal. The blank page, the poise of my biro, the bubbles in my tummy. Just writing my name and the date and the name of our compound was thrilling. I see those blank pages, and I cannot wait to document our adventures. Every society needs a historian, and I will gladly take on the mantle. How many people get to be in this position? Creating a new world. A fair and just world. A world that runs how the Grand Ruler always intended it to run. Why everyone isn't doing this is lost on me. Together we are powerful. Intentions lead to creation. And creation is life. And although I believe the Shepherd when he says that for doing this work we will be rewarded beyond our wildest dreams, it is actually the act of creating this utopia that excites me the most. I am part of something that matters. I am not wasting my life. Life is short, and life is precious, and so many people just throw it away, take it for granted. I know I might sound preachy, and of course I am not as eloquent as the Shepherd, but his passion ignites me.

Living like this, with a true community, is my wildest dream. I only wish the people in the outside world could understand. I would happily bring a few into the fold, but right now their hearts are closed to eternal wisdom. For once in my life, I feel as if I belong. I am a vital part of this community, and they are a vital part of me. I've always been a bit out of step with everyone around me, and finally I am marching in rhythm. I wish they could see me now.

I know there are people who would call us a cult, or too new age, or even crazy, but we are simply living in the moment and paying attention to what is truly holy. The sun. The moon. The earth. The stars. Animals. Nature. Fire. (And that's both literal fire and the fire within each of us.) And each other. We are one. If that's a cult, sign me up! I am present, and I am fulfilled. But I digress. *I know I must write about what happened yesterday.* I am rambling because it is very difficult to talk about, and I am terrified of losing my faith. I find myself wanting to change what happened, yearning for a different outcome. *The truth shall set you free.* I cannot let yesterday destroy everything we are working to build. Every major achievement in history has its tragedies. And yesterday was one of ours.

It began around four in the afternoon. I was in the Sustenance Field, bent over pulling potatoes out of the ground, when I heard Golden One scream. I knew immediately her baby was coming. A sense of dread struck me as I calculated the distance I had to cover to reach her room. First, I had to cross the field, and then I had to maneuver around the lake.

Most days, I love the man-made lake that surrounds the Womb. I can spend an hour staring into its depths, getting lost in the ripples, watching the life that it now holds. And life is a miracle. (Sorry, doing it again!) But even now, six months since I moved in, I am enthralled with our blessed compound. Where once there was nothing but a raggedy field (so I was told, and it's easy to imagine), there now stands a glorious structure made of concrete and embellished with limestone and tiles, and steel. If nothing else, it is solid.

It is shaped like a giant womb (the female goddess;

we are the makers of life); there are fireplaces, and
built-in furniture, and separate corridors that wind
around and lead to thirteen smaller wombs spaced
evenly around the structure for privacy. The Shepherd
bought this place off an old man who started building
it in the 1970s. For what purpose, nobody knows, but
the Shepherd believes that this old man had been
building it for us, even if he didn't know it.

There is so much power in that thought; our purpose
is so strong that someone saw it coming over five
decades ago. The Shepherd says we are aligning with
our true purpose, and it's a glorious feeling, a natural
high. I have never been happier. And I am the first to
be chosen, and it is an honor. But as I hear Golden
One scream, as I do my best to run, first I must maneuver all the way around the water.

The lake teems with life—fish, and ducks, and frogs,
and turtles. The surface ripples, and shines, and calms.
But yesterday it was an obstacle, a barrier forcing me
to run all the way around to the back, where a single
wooden bridge is hidden from view, cocooned by
thick trees and unwieldy hedges. I had the strangest
feeling that morning that today was the day Golden
would deliver, and I begged the Shepherd to allow me
to stay by her bedside today. Why did he not listen?
And where were the others?

"Eternal Mist," I yelled. "Morning Sun? Red Rose?
Shepherd?" I will probably be the third to give birth,
and at seven months, this baby is big so I'm not very
fast. I hoped my panic was not seeping into my baby. I
am still learning to override my emotional states, but at
that moment, I was losing the battle. As I drew closer to
the back, I could see the round patio that juts from
Golden's room, and to say I was surprised to see the
Staff planted there is putting it mildly. He was holding
that hideous gun. The sun lit up the barrel, making it

gleam. I do not know much about guns, but this one is terrifying. I want to say it's a machine gun, but why on earth would he need a machine gun? Dread flooded my body. Something was happening. Something bad.

Although there are thirteen wombs (our rooms), there are presently only five of us in the Flock. This has nothing to do with why I was dubbed Seven Star. The number 7 marks Athena, Goddess of War, Protector of the City. It is a symbol of faith and awareness, and its Angel number signifies the bridge between heaven and earth. And, of course, the stars. The stars are what we are all made of; the stars hold the secret to the Universe. I'm sure you can see why I must live up to my given name. It is both an honor and a burden. The Shepherd chose us carefully, and he will continue to do so. But I do not know how he chose his Staff. He seems more monster than man. His height, his bulging arms, his slicked-back hair, his everlasting sneer. His menace is amplified by the gun. Why was he on guard? There were no signs that the perimeter had been breached, and the only sound I heard was the wind, and the birds, and poor Golden One. I wished she wasn't the first, as she was the most afraid. I suppose she was the most fertile as well; after all, it took no time at all for her to get pregnant. And the order is not up to me.

In the distance, I could see the Shepherd hurrying toward his vehicle. He parks it near the enormous iron gates. He was dressed in his formal white robe edged in emerald green, and in his arms, he held a pile of satin blankets. I've only seen him wear that robe for ceremonies—and then it dawned on me that, of course, our very first birth should be a ceremony, but why were we not all involved? "Shepherd," I yelled again. I was breaking another rule—yelling is not permitted—and I wondered, with a flash of terror, how he would respond, but he did not even turn his head.

It was then that I realized what I did not hear. I still did not hear any of the others. Red Rose should have been playing the harp. She is the most timid of us; she much prefers music and animals to humans. Eternal Mist should have been in the kitchen, and Morning Sun should have been fishing at the lake. Were the others at Golden One's bedside? Everything felt so wrong, and an overwhelming sense of panic made me feel too much like my former self. My original-sin name was on the tip of my tongue, and I could feel my undeserving core rising to the surface. *You are not her, she is gone, you have been saved, you are so, so grateful. Look at this beautiful, magical, miraculous place. It is here that matters. It is here that I belong.*

By the time I was crossing the bridge, ducking under branches, ignoring the scrapes against my face and arms, I could hear the Shepherd's car taking off, the iron gates creaking, and the sound of Golden's screams. They all echoed across the lake. As I entered the Womb and reached Golden's room, the Staff was now guarding her doorway. His stance was wide, a snarl played across his face, and for a moment, I feared he intended to stop me.

"What's the story?" I was not supposed to speak first; this is twice now, and my words crackled like an electric shock. The Staff turned his predatory gaze on me, sending chills up my spine. When will the Shepherd see that his Staff is irrevocably broken? I am twenty-four, but the way the Staff gazes at me, I feel more like a frightened child. Why was he holding that gun? "Is the baby alright?" His sinister mouth did not give an answer. Golden wailed again, a sound so pitiful it made every hair on my body stand up. I hurried past the Staff and rushed inside. Golden was on the bed,

and it took me an eternity to make sense of what I
saw. Her wrists were chained to the bedposts. She was
crying and drenched in sweat. Her dress was gathered
at her waist; she was naked and bloody below. I knew
I was looking at the placenta; we've been studying
the book, but how could I be looking at the placenta
when I didn't see a baby? Golden's eyes were fever-
ish, and she turned them on me. "He took my baby,"
she cried, as she pulled against the chains. "Did you
see him?"

"Him?" Those of us who are pregnant do not know
the sex of our baby. The Grand Ruler is in charge, and
we will each find out the sex at birth. I could not help
but feel excited. Our first was a boy. I remember thinking that the Shepherd must be over the moon. But
there was no time to celebrate. Something went
wrong. It all made sense now. The bundle in the
Shepherd's arms, the truck speeding away, the
absence of a baby's cry. Something went terribly
wrong.

"He's gone," Golden cried. "He's taken him."

"To hospital," I said. "He's taken the baby to hospital." I did not know if this was true, but it was the only
thing that made sense. "It's going to be alright, Golden
One." I neared the bed, then immediately looked
away; the sight of the chains filled me with confusion
and horror. Why was she lying in her mess? Where were
the others? Why was she chained?

"Look what he did!" Golden shouted. "Look!" And I
couldn't help it, I *looked*. The chains wound around
the bedposts, and a lock was secured to each wrist,
assuring they stayed in place. No doubt delirious from
the pain, Golden must have tried to claw at the
Shepherd. It must be for her own good, her own safety.
Why does he have locks and chains in the first place?
The thought wound its way through me, constricting

my breath. There had to be a reasonable explanation; we are goddesses, not prisoners. But horrible thoughts continued to barrage me: *She's chained up. Her baby is gone; she gave birth all alone. The Staff is standing guard with a machine gun. The Shepherd fled with a pile of blankets . . . No, not a pile of blankets . . . Golden's baby.* He must have been rushing to the hospital. I glanced at the bedside table, praying there was a key for those locks. There was no key.

"Where is he?" Golden cried. "Where is he?"

"Have faith in the Grand Ruler and the Shepherd," I said. "He's going to save him." I loathed how there was a part of me that didn't believe it, a part of me that was being contaminated by her hysteria.

Golden's eyes flashed with a rage I had never seen in anyone, let alone her. "How can you speak of God and that man right now?"

"How can I not?" I said, and it was impossible not to hear that I was pleading. Even now I wondered: Was I trying to convince Golden or myself? "Now is when we need our faith the most." We were being tested, and I was not prepared. I should have been more prepared. How weak my faith! How ashamed of myself I was in this moment. I knelt and begin to pray.

"Help me. Help me!" Golden was jerking her hands, making the chains rattle. "Get me out of these."

"I don't have the key. The Shepherd will be back soon." *Won't he?* We could not lose our first baby. "Where are the others?"

She scoffed and looked at me as if she pitied me. "He locked them in their rooms too. He would have come for you, but you were too far out in the fields." Golden's gaze landed on my rounded belly. She dropped her chin, jerked her head, beckoning me to come closer. I edged in. She stopped thrashing. "Run," she said. "You need to run."

A shadow fell across the wall—broad shoulders and that horrible, horrible gun. He was listening.

"You need to rest," I said loudly. "Everything is going to be alright."

"Don't you see?" Golden moaned. "He's not going to bring him back." She thrashed some more. "I want my baby boy. I want my baby boy." Her eyes fixed on the Staff. "He's *your* baby too. Don't you even care?"

The statement startled me. I assumed her child was conceived by the Shepherd. Perhaps I was special to him. What about the others? Was I the only one carrying the Shepherd's baby? I tried not to feel the warm glow of attention, but for a moment, it rippled through me.

"We are merely vessels; we do not make the rules," the Staff said. And then he turned his back to her.

"You bastard. I'm going to kill you. Do you hear me? I'm going to kill you!"

"You're delirious," I said. "Listen to me. The Shepherd is saving the baby. He's taking him to hospital." I was practically yelling now, angry at Golden for making me doubt, making me panic. *Should I run?* If I didn't, would I end up in chains, watching my baby be taken away? Where would I even go? I hadn't spoken to my friends or family in over six months. I had no money, no mobile phone. I don't even know exactly where the hell we are. For our own safety, we arrived blindfolded. Otherwise, the Shepherd explained, we might be tempted to give our location away if, by chance, one of us reconnected with our past. It's part of the process, exorcising who we used to be, and it is not always a smooth transition. The Shepherd is helping us through it. We are still in County Kerry; I am pretty sure we are still in County Kerry.

"He's *taking* my baby," Golden continued to wail. "He's *kidnapped* him."

"That's not true." But . . . *It felt true.* Nothing else made any sense.

"A baby boy. It's a wee baby boy," Golden wailed. "My son. My son. Not his."

"Please," I begged her. "Calm down."

"He's stealing him. I'm never going to see my baby again."

"Stop saying that," I said. "Don't say it again." She was making me doubt. She was making me angry.

"He's a liar and a kidnapper," Golden said. "Look at me! It's all been a damned lie."

"Golden One!" My hand raised, and before I even realized what I was doing, my palm made contact with Golden's cheek. *I hit her.* Dear heavens, I hit her.

I write this with shame coursing through my body. I had never slapped anyone in my life. And I have never felt worse. Golden stopped crying, and her mouth opened in shock. I will never forget the stunned look on her face, her wet eyes grief-stricken and blinking. I was filled to the brim with my old self, my old anger, my old shame. I want to make it right, I want to erase what I've done, I want to give Golden her baby back. I knelt next to the bed and tried to grab her hand, but it was too awkward; her hands were chained up next to her head. I placed my hands in prayer position, and I begged the Grand Ruler for forgiveness. "He's coming back with the baby," I told her over and over again. "Let us pray. Oh Golden Ruler, look upon us with your radiant love—"

"Shut up!" Golden yelled. "Shut the fuck up, you stupid cunt." I felt as if she had struck me back, only ten times harder. None of us have ever cursed at all at the compound, let alone uttered such a horrible word. I feared then that the real reason he had chained her up was that she had been possessed by the Devil. She jerked the chains again and let out a primal scream.

Golden One was not acting like herself. *Fool's Gold.* *She's not in her right mind, she's not in her right mind, she's not in her right mind.* I needed to be a calming influence. We cannot lose our first baby, we cannot. We have come too far. I handled this so poorly. I failed. I have given up everything, and I still failed.

"Where did the Shepherd go?" We turned to see Eternal Mist in the doorway. Her long, brunette hair was flowing wild, as per usual, her energy too buoyant for the situation at hand. She seemed nonplussed about Golden's hysteria.

I looked at Golden, but she refused to meet my eyes. "I thought you said they were locked in their rooms."

"Why would we be locked in our rooms?" Eternal Mist said.

I must say, this brought a bit of relief. If Golden was lying about that, what else was she lying about?

"Go to the others; you'll see," Golden said. "She is not pregnant, so there's no need to lock her up."

"Where is he?" Eternal Mist asked again.

"He's trying to save the baby," I said. "They've gone to hospital."

"Liar," Golden said. "He's taken him. He's taken him, just like he's going to take yours. We've been played. We're so fucking stupid." Golden's face crumbled as sobs overtook her. "I want to go home. I want to go home. I want to go home."

"You are home," I said. My heart bled at her words, and the tiniest thought of my home crept in. My mam and my da and my brother and sisters. Do they still love me? Do they miss me at all? Are they sorry for how they reacted when I told them I was pregnant? Do they still think I'm nothing but a whore?

"Hormones," Eternal Mist said, staring at Golden. (She's as cool and opaque as her given name.)

"What is wrong with you two?" Golden One struggled to sit up. "We need to go," she said. "We need to find him." She looked from me to Eternal and back again. "Please," she crooned. "I'm begging you. I'm begging you. Help me find my son."

"Get back." The Staff entered, his chest puffed out. The gun was strapped diagonally across his chest. He held a syringe.

"What are you doing?" I demanded.

"She's hysterical," the Staff said. "She needs her rest."

"My baby," Golden moaned. "I want my baby."

"Our baby," the Staff corrected. "Our baby."

"Staff," I say. I tried to block him, tried to stop the needle from going into her. He glared at me, and for a moment, I thought he was going to hit me. "Tell her he's bringing the baby back," I begged him. "Tell Golden One it's going to be okay."

"That's not my name," Golden One said. "That's not my fucking name." She was delirious, but that didn't mean the Shepherd wouldn't punish her for blasphemy.

"You're doing God's work," the Staff said, hovering over a terrified Golden. "We're so proud." He sounded insincere. Golden One was out cold seconds after the syringe pierced her arm.

"Do you have the key?" I asked, pointing to the locks. "She shouldn't be chained."

"Mind your own business," the Staff said.

I felt my fists curl, and I wished I could punch him in the mouth. I imagined snatching the gun, I imagined shooting him and dumping his body in the lake. My old self was back, and I was too weak to fight her. "Take me to hospital," I said, placing my hand over my belly. "I don't feel well." I had to find Golden One's baby. I needed to prove to her and to me that the Shepherd had taken that precious baby boy to hospital. The

Staff's vehicle was also parked by the iron gate. What if I found the keys and drove away? What if Golden is right? What if we are prisoners? What if we've been prisoners all along?

"Clean her up," the Staff said. "You're not going anywhere."

CHAPTER 9

*T*EN EUROS. TEN WHOLE EUROS TO GO TO THE BOG. FOR JAMES AND Michael, it was as if the stranger had handed them a pile of gold, but Dylan had a bad feeling. Not that it would do any good; even if he tried to talk them out of it, James and Michael wouldn't listen. They would have done it for a single euro. They would have done it on a dare. It would be enough money for crisps and chocolate bars and cokes, maybe even ice cream. And this evening might be their last chance before the storm comes in. "Lads," Dylan yelled, as James and Michael ran for their bicycles. "Lads, wait up." Dylan nearly tripped trying to keep up with them. The clouds were swollen, gearing up for the next unleashing, and his runners were brand-new. When his mammy dropped him off with Granny Dooley, she'd warned him not to dirty them, and the ground all around the bog was mushy. They'd only be able to take their bicycles so far; the rest would have to be on foot.

Dylan had heard that one step into the bog and you could sink and disappear forever. The bog was the enemy, and it was rumored that some portions were still deep enough to swallow you whole and spit out your bones. James and Michael weren't scared. They liked to play sink hole. Whoever sunk down the deepest was the loser. Dylan was always the loser.

"Why does he want us to go to the bog?" Dylan whined, as they reached the alley and mounted their bicycles. He didn't like the man in the pea cap. He didn't like him at all.

"He gave us ten euros, eejit," Michael said. "Mind your business." Michael and James took off, leaving Dylan to scramble after them. Dylan knew he was more than a little chubby, but he thought he did a pretty good job of keeping up. Michael was the biggest and the meanest. If Dylan stopped doing what they wanted, they would be his worst enemies. Normally, he kept his gob shut. But his new runners gave him pause. If his granny picked him up and his runners were dirty, would she tell on him? His mammy's anger could be worse than James and Michael's. And she could ground him. She *would* ground him. But only if Granny told on him. Maybe he could wash them and they'd look new again by the time his stay in Kerry was over. Then again, he liked his shiny white runners. He wanted them to stay that way a little bit longer.

"You said it yourself. He *already* gave us the ten euros," Dylan said. "We don't have to go." It bothered him, that. What was the point of a dare if you already had the money? Why couldn't Michael and James see that was messed up? There was something wrong. *Listen to your inner voice, Dylan,* his mammy once said to him. "It will never steer you wrong."

But Michael and James weren't the kind of lads who wanted to hear about inner voices. They were constantly hungry for trouble, and they were after it today. "We could buy sweets right now—I don't think he's here—he'll never know," Dylan pleaded as he pedaled like mad to keep up with them. They were tearing through the streets like they were on fire. Dylan wished the stupid man would have given the ten euros to him. They'd already be eating sweets by now.

"If we don't go, he might come after us," James said.

"We can tell an adult," Dylan said. "Then he'll stay away."

Michael braked abruptly, and Dylan had to swerve to keep from slamming into him. "Be a pussy if you want," Michael yelled as he resumed pedaling. "More sweets for us."

"Spot on," James said. "More sweets for us, like."

"But I can't get my runners wet. They're new, like." Michael and James had better bicycles than Dylan, and all it took was a little effort and they were way ahead again. Dylan just knew he was going to spend his entire life behind everyone else. It wasn't fair. "He just said go *to* the bog. He didn't say we have to go *near* the bog," Dylan yammered on. His mammy only let him have sweets at holidays and his birthday. If he wanted them at any other time he had to sneak them, and he wasn't very good at that. Technically, the entire surrounding field could be considered the bog. If he went *to* the bog but not *near* it, would they still share? Probably a few bites. He could live with that. "Do I get my share if I just go to the bog but stand back far so I don't get me runners dirty?"

"No," Michael shouted back.

"But he didn't say we have to go near the bog. Just *to* the bog."

"Go home, you big baby," James yelled. "Right, Michael?"

"I have something you lads will want to see," Dylan yelled. "A secret." When the man pulled out the ten euros, something fell out of his pocket. The good thing about being the youngest of the lads was that people hardly ever paid attention to him. Dylan knelt and pretended to tie his shoe so he could have a look. It was a silver bracelet with a swath of rectangular silver. It read: MÍORÚILT—1994.

Dylan didn't know what the word meant. Was it real silver? Was the man in the flat cap a pirate? The back read: LOVE FOREVER AND EVER AND EVER. Dylan stuck it in his pocket right quick. But now he was wondering if he'd made a mistake.

What would the man do when he realized it was gone? Was it valuable? Would he remember Dylan kneeling next to him and realize he had nicked it? Michael and James were nearly to the hill that led down to the bog. The lads ditched their bicycles at the top and tore off. Dylan hesitated.

"We can't leave them here," Dylan said. "Someone will nick our bicycles." Not only would he return home with dirty trainers, if his bicycle was stolen, his granny would never let him borrow another one.

"There's nobody around, you eejit," James said. "Right, Michael?"

"We'll be quick," Michael said.

"He won't even know we were here," Dylan said. Unless the man in the cap had followed them. That hadn't occurred to Dylan until just now. The bad feeling was back, and it was making his stomach twist something awful. *Go home, go home, go home.* But before he could decide whether or not to share his new fear with the lads, they were already tearing across the field, whooping with joy.

Dylan felt tears coming on, and he bit his lip hard. He should have told them about the yoke in his pocket; that would have distracted them. He always waited too late to act. He was a baby. A coward. He felt himself filling up with shame. He gave it a few more seconds, then, before he knew it, he had ditched his bicycle next to theirs and was flying down the hill after them. Michael and James were way past the tree shaped like a cross. Dylan ran faster. By the time he was a few meters away from the bog, his trainers were covered in muck, and he was wheezing. He reached into his pockets and began to search for his inhaler. It was gone. He must have dropped it somewhere between where he left his bicycle and here. He was allergic to everything, and the field around the bog was thick with weeds and bramble. He didn't want to go back to look for it. He knew he had to calm down. It was when he got too worked up that he couldn't breathe. He tried to think calming thoughts. *Do not think about your runners. They were ruined. His mammy would be so mad.* Dylan started to wheeze.

Dylan cupped his hands on either side of his mouth and shouted into the wind. "We did it, lads," he yelled. "We did it. Cop on, it's going to lash something fierce."

But the lads weren't copping on; in fact, they were nearly at the bog.

"What's that?" he heard Michael yell. "There's something in the water." Were they taking the piss? Trying to scare him? It was working. He was scared.

Dylan watched as they scrambled around the bog, moving closer. "It's a floating monster!" James said.

"Stop messing," Dylan yelled, picking up the pace.

"Monster," Michael yelled. "Monster in the water!"

"Fuck," James said. "Holy fuck."

James dropped the F-bomb. Dylan had never done that. He knew that was really, really bad. They had to be messing, right? But what if there *was* something in the water? Dylan didn't believe there was a monster, but there had to be *something*. Dylan did not want to get any closer. But then *he* would forever be the one who missed it. And if he missed it, then on some future date, when

Michael and James told the story—the one about finding the monster in the bog—they'd say Pussy Dylan missed it all because he didn't want to get his runners wet. That he was afraid of his mammy. Anger coursed through him, fueling him into an all-out sprint. *Cop on!* There was no such thing as monsters.

Just as he was finally within spitting distance, James and Michael came sprinting toward him. As they drew near, he clocked an expression on Michael's face he had never seen before. *Fear.* He didn't realize until that moment that fear had a presence. He could feel it coming off them in waves.

"I want to see it," Dylan said as they pushed past him.

"Run," Michael screamed, grabbing his wrist and pulling him. "Run!" But Dylan was almost there. He yanked his wrist free and soldiered on toward the bog as the lads' screams echoed behind him. The skies opened up, and the rain bucketed down, drenching him instantly. Dylan stood paralyzed by indecision. He was so close, he wanted to see what it took to strike fear into the hearts of lads like Michael and James. He wouldn't be left out of the story. Dylan continued toward the edge of the bog where they'd stood, the wind at his back, encouraging him, shoving him along.

Michael and James had disappeared into the thick of the rain; they weren't even sticking around to see if Dylan would do it. Maybe he was braver than them. Maybe he was braver than *anyone.* It was his story now, and when they told it, they would be the little crybabies. And he didn't ruin his trainers for nothing. He wasn't even afraid of his mammy anymore.

He reached the edge of the bog where they'd been standing and made sure to keep his heels far back as he tried to peer into its dark center. He had to concentrate, and it took what felt like forever until he saw it. A blob was lying in the middle of the muck, something big and round. Dylan stepped closer, his trainers squelching as they sank into the muck. His shoes were already ruined. Now he could see there were *two* blobs, and something that looked like hair snaking out from the one blob. He clomped forward, trying to keep his balance on the slick field. He moved closer. That's when he saw it. It wasn't a blob at all. It was a head. A human head.

A woman. Or used to be. She did look like a monster; her face was swollen and ghastly white, rimmed in shades of blue and purple, like something out of a horror film. The second blob was her belly. It was so big it was sticking up. *Pregnant.* He was looking at a dead pregnant corpse lying in the bog. With real hair. Her hair. He'd only seen one dead body before, his nana, lying in a coffin, looking like she always did when she napped, dressed in her Sunday best. They even did her hair and put makeup on her. But this body was different. He knew he would never get her image out of his mind. He was going to vomit. He turned, his stomach heaving, as he began navigating the sticky muck, making his way back to dryer land.

The man in the flat cap. He knew she was here. That's why he wanted them to go to the bog. He wanted them to see her. Why hadn't the man called the guards? *Because he's the one who killed her.* This thought assaulted Dylan and brought a new wave of terror crashing down on him. *Was* he the man, the one who did this to her? Had they taken ten euros from a murderer? Did that make them murderers? Now his fear had a thick, rusty taste and he could feel his teeth chattering. He was a very bad lad. He'd gotten his trainers muddy, he'd said the F-word in his head, he'd gawked at a dead body. He was probably already going to hell, and now there was nothing he could do to stop it. He was sorry. He was so, so sorry. And look at him feeling sorry for himself. What about the woman and her baby?

Was her baby still alive in her tummy? Would they be able to cut it out? Should he cut it out? He didn't have a knife. He wasn't even allowed a mobile phone. "Help," he screamed, although he knew it was of no use. Help did not come for her, and it wasn't coming for him. He stood slightly back, staring once more at the dead woman, his stomach heaving. *Run,* his little voice said. Run like Michael and James. Just then, a hand clamped down on his shoulder. Rancid breath assaulted him as a mouth came near his ear.

"Don't turn around," a man's voice said. "Do you understand?" And now Dylan knew his mammy was right. He should have listened to that inner voice. He should have listened to his mammy and granny. None of this would be happening if he had just listened to them. Bad, bad, bad. He was bad, bad, bad. He was so sorry. So, so sorry. This was all his fault. He was being punished for being such a naughty lad. For stealing that silver bracelet. For getting his trainers muddy. And probably other things too. Maybe he was hallucinating. Maybe it was a dream. Maybe if he prayed hard enough, God would let him wake up in his own bed, his new trainers lined up shiny and white by the press. He'd never disobey again. He wouldn't even care what Michael or James said about him. He would listen to his elders. He would listen! He wanted to scream, but his mouth wouldn't move. Why wouldn't it move? The hand squeezed his shoulder. *Hard.* "Do you understand?"

Dylan bobbed his head as hard as he could. In addition to the chattering, he was shivering now, trembling from head to toe. He could feel himself wheezing, and his heart thudded in his chest. Was it just going to burst out of him and kill him instantly? His bladder released, filling him with even more shame. At least no one would know, due to the sheets of rain.

The man pulled Dylan's hands tight behind him, and soon he felt rope winding around his wrists. Dylan didn't scream. Next, he heard something rip, and soon tape was over his mouth. Last, a dark cloth was laid over his eyes and tied so tight in the back that Dylan winced. The feel of the tape stretched across his mouth made him panic. Could he breathe? Could he breathe? *Nose. Breathe through your nose.* He thought of his mammy. *I'm sorry,* he thought. *I'm really really, really sorry about me shoes.* Was the man going to kill him and throw him in the bog next to the dead woman? Would he sink to the bottom or float alongside her? Would they think *she* was his mammy? His mammy wouldn't like that. He wondered if they'd call him the Bog Boy. The man hoisted him and began dragging him backward. Dylan had been dead wrong about one thing. He had been all wrong about monsters. Monsters did exist.

CHAPTER 10

*J*ANE AND DAVID GRIFFIN REFUSED TO BE TAKEN TO HOSPITAL. ONCE the guards had gathered all the evidence they needed and bagged their clothing, they were allowed to shower and change. Despite sore wrists and ankles, they insisted they had not been physically harmed. And they wanted to give their account to Cormac while all the details were fresh in their minds. Cormac and Garda Barry Lennon were seated across from them in a meeting room at the Dingle Garda Station, the cheeriest room on the premises, which wasn't saying much. It was going on half-seven in the evening, and the storm was due any minute now. Everyone was wrecked, but Cormac needed to know everything they could possibly tell them. Time was not on their side. "You've experienced a trauma," he said. "I'd like you both to see your doctors as soon as possible, and don't hesitate to ask for mental help."

The couple stared at him as he spoke. They looked so young, and objectively they were—in their early thirties, both schoolteachers, attractive, and distraught.

"We'll look after ourselves," Jane said. She was trying to hold back tears but failing. Cormac gently shoved a box of tissues her way and gestured to the tea in front of them.

"Get that into you; it will do you good." She nodded but didn't touch it. "Let's start at the beginning. How did Shauna come to be at your house this evening?"

"We invited her for supper," Jane said.

"How long have you known her?"

"I know this is part of your job," David said, before his wife could answer. "But I feel this clock ticking in my head. Every second we do nothing, that evil man—that *thing*—is getting away. We have to find Shauna."

Cormac understood where he was coming from. Hell, he wanted to rush out and find this costumed psychopath, but investigations didn't work that way. He had to remind himself that the quickest way to succeed was through a methodical process. Slow was fast. He needed every scrap of information he could get. "Let me tell you what's happening right now as we sit here. We have guards going house to house, looking for witnesses. If we get an identification on an unknown vehicle in the area, we'll be able to put out an alert. This could be someone Shauna knows, which is why I need to know everything about Shauna that you know. We're pulling CCTV footage from the festival—specifically, to see if there was a booth selling the type of mask you describe him as wearing. Some kind of bird, was it?" They had found a few feathers on the floor of the kitchen.

"Butterfly," Jane said. "A dark butterfly."

"Or moth," David added. She gave him a look, and he shrugged.

"Right," Cormac said. "Got it. Dark butterfly or moth. See? Every little bit helps, and whether you feel it or not, you are helping us find Shauna. Your house is now cordoned off and being combed for clues. I know it feels as if we are wasting time, but I assure you we are not."

David took this in and nodded. "Thank you," Jane whispered. They clasped each other's hand.

"Back to an earlier question," Cormac said. "How long have you known Shauna Mills?"

"We met her through the adoption agency," Jane said. "We've been on the list for two years." She hesitated, chewing on her lip. "We know that older children need homes too, and we're open to that in the future, but for our first, we wanted a newborn."

"We'd been trying for years before that," David said.

Cormac nodded. "And Shauna chose you?"

"She did," Jane said, the tears flowing once again. "We were over the moon."

"And you had a close relationship with Shauna?"

"We wouldn't have wanted it any other way," David said. "We liked Shauna." He stopped, his eyes widened. "Oh my God. I mean like her. We *like* Shauna."

"It's alright," Cormac said. "And you saw her regularly?"

Jane nodded. "Shauna has some fears to work through. She's terrified of giving birth. We've even attended doctor's appointments with her."

No doubt she was even more terrified now. "Do you know who the father of Shauna's baby is?" The Griffins glanced at each other. "We're not accusing him of anything, but I need to know," Cormac said. That was partially a lie. In his head, he would accuse everyone until he proved them innocent.

"Liam McCarthy," Jane finally said. "We like him a lot."

"In fact, he's our handyman now," David said.

"I take it he wasn't there when all this went down?" They shook their heads. "And was he on board with Shauna giving the baby up for adoption?" Jane opened her mouth and then shut it again. David tensed. "I need the facts," Cormac prodded. "Just give me the facts."

"Initially, he was against it," David said.

"I think he wanted to raise the baby with Shauna," Jane added. "But he was also trying to respect her decision."

"Do you know if the pair argued about it?"

"Not in front of us," David said. "But we can't say for sure." He hesitated. "But Shauna did mention they had quite a row when she found out she was pregnant."

"Oh?" Now this Cormac wanted to hear.

"Apparently, she accused him of messing with her birth control." David grimaced, and Jane sighed.

"I don't think that's true," Jane said. "But she was convinced that a few of the pills had a sweeter taste. As if he'd substituted some candy or something. But I think she was just scared and lashing out."

"Scared?" Cormac asked.

"Her phobia," Jane said.

"Right," Cormac said.

"We keep trying to tell her it's going to be okay," Jane continued. "We keep going over her birth plan—she has a fantastic doctor—but she's still terrified." She swallowed hard. "I even suggested a doula. They can be very helpful in situations like these."

"I see," Cormac said. "Is there any chance Shauna is afraid of Liam in general?"

Jane shook her head. "He wouldn't hurt a fly."

"Jane," David said. "The facts, remember? We can't say that for sure." Jane clamped her lips together. David turned to Cormac. "We never witnessed anything violent between them—nothing that would raise an alarm."

"What did he say to this accusation?" Cormac said. "When Shauna accused him of messing with her birth control?"

The couple exchanged a glance. "It was so long ago," Jane said. "They're way past that by now."

"I need to know," Cormac said.

"He blamed it on a break-in," David said.

Cormac lifted an eyebrow. "Say more."

"A few weeks before the birth-control fiasco, he said he could have sworn someone had been in the flat while they were gone. At the time, he couldn't find anything missing; he just said things were moved around."

Interesting.

"But Liam couldn't be the man in the mask," Jane said.

Cormac leaned in. "Why? Different height? Different build?"

Jane bit her lip. "I mean, I guess technically I can't rule him out. I think the height is the same; the man was wearing bulky clothes and a mask"—she stopped and her mouth dropped open. "Do you think that's why he was wearing the disguise? Do you think it's someone we know?" Cormac could see the entire scenario playing out as he watched her face. Then she shook her head as if to rid herself of the thoughts. "But why would Liam do this? They're already a couple."

"Maybe he does want the baby," David said. "Maybe he intends to hold her hostage until she caves to his demands."

David Griffin was getting worked up now, but Cormac had no interest in maybes. "We didn't see any signs of a break-in. Do you have any idea how this man got into your house?"

"We left it unlocked," Jane said. "For Shauna."

"Never again," David said. "Never again."

"Maybe it is someone you know," Cormac said. "Someone who knew Shauna was due to arrive."

Jane squirmed in her chair.

"The man also held up those signs," David said. "Presumably because Shauna is deaf. Another indicator that this is someone who knows her."

"Maybe," Jane said. "But they do that on social media. Usually for happy things, like asking someone to marry you."

Cormac didn't reply. If they were telling the truth about these signs, the perp took them with him. He only had their word for it. If the Griffins were innocent, they needed to get their heads around the fact that this was probably someone close to them. It was usually the case. "At this moment, Liam McCarthy has no idea Shauna was taken?" *Unless he was the one who took her.*

"We haven't told a soul yet," Jane said. "He will be beside himself."

"I kind of hope it is him," David said.

Jane gave her husband a look. "How can you say that?"

"I just mean—if it's him, he's not going to hurt her or the baby," David explained. "Right?" He looked to Cormac for confirmation. "Right?"

Jane shook her head. "If he dressed up just to tie us up and kidnap her—we can't be sure of that, now can we?"

"I'm going to need Liam's number and address," Cormac said. He slid a pad of paper over to the couple, and the husband jotted it down. "Now. When did you arrange for Shauna to come over to your house?"

"This morning," Jane said. "I checked in with her by text, as per usual. Just to see how she was doing. Shauna told us she was going to the Spring Festival, and that's when I said she should stop by for supper." She bit her lip. "I worried about Shauna's nutrition. She wasn't used to preparing healthy meals."

Despite their good intentions, Cormac was starting to see that this couple had quite a bit of control over Shauna. Her everyday movements, her boyfriend, her doctor's appointments, her meals. Did she resent this? What if this was all an elaborate plan to get out of their grasp? Or what if Shauna had told them she'd changed her mind? Things could have gone terribly wrong; an argument could have ensued—an accident. Emotions would have been riding high. Cormac could not lose sight of the possibility that this couple knew exactly what had happened to Shauna and where she was. They could not have both tied themselves up, but that didn't mean they weren't involved. It was a stark reminder about one simple adage when it came to investigations: *Trust no one.* Cynical? Absolutely. Necessary? Absolutely.

Cormac nodded to the pad of paper. "I'm going to need you to write down the names of all the agencies, as well as her doctor, friends, boyfriends, employers, anyone Shauna had contact with."

"She was very private," Jane said. "We can write down the agencies and her doctor, but she never talked to us about friends or family."

"Not even to give you a medical history?"

"The adoption agency covered that as best they could; however, Shauna was an orphan. She grew up in a group home, and she never knew her biological parents."

"I'm going to have you each fill out an incident report," Cormac said. "We need the story written down in your own words. Once you're finished, I'll have guards escort you to your house, where you can pack an overnight bag. I'd like at least two days to process the scene."

"What do you expect to find?" David asked, sounding none too happy about this. "He wore gloves."

Cormac didn't hesitate. "We could find a hair, we could find skin particles, shoe prints—I agree it probably won't yield much, but it has to be done."

"Of course," Jane said. "Whatever you need."

Cormac stood. "One more thing," he said. "Do you know a

woman named Fiona Sheehan or her parents—Gary and Breanna Sheehan?" He hesitated. "Or did Shauna?" When Cormac was told an old man brought in a supposed ransom note from his neighbor's postbox, he had thought someone was taking the piss. He knew better now. These incidents were related; he could feel it in his bones.

Frowns came over their faces. "No," Jane said. "Should we?"

"Not at all," Cormac said. "Do you know if Shauna was in a childbirth class? Anything of the sort?" There had to be a connection between the two women.

"We had asked her about that," Jane said. "But . . . she told us to mind our own business." She dropped her head. "We didn't mean to treat her like a child. It's just . . . it's our first baby."

"Who are these people?" David asked. "What do they have to do with Shauna?"

"It may be nothing, so I'll have to leave it at that for now," Cormac said. "And I'm going to ask you not to contact Liam McCarthy, and if he phones you, do not answer. Let us handle him."

Garda Lennon poked his head back in the door. Cormac knew right away something was wrong; the lad didn't have a poker face.

"Can I speak with you?" he asked, chewing on his bottom lip.

"I'll send in a family liaison," Cormac said to the couple. "They'll take care of you from here." He started to the door, then stopped and turned back to them. "What were you having for supper?"

"Pardon?" David said.

"You mentioned you had asked Shauna over for supper. I just wonder what you were planning on serving."

The pair looked at each other.

"Chicken curry," Jane said.

"Takeaway," David said at the same time.

He watched as they both took on the expression of someone who had been caught in a lie.

They looked at each other. "We were waiting for Shauna to choose," Jane said.

"Right," David said, sounding relieved. "We were waiting for Shauna to choose."

Cormac stared at them. He couldn't help it; he liked the Griffins.

But he liked them a little bit less now that they seemed to be lying straight to his face.

Out in the hall, Cormac didn't waste any time filling Lennon in on the next steps. "I need you to call one of the guards at the Griffins' house. Have them check the fridge and the cupboards; see if they have the ingredients to make chicken curry."

Garda Lennon looked stricken. "And those are?"

"I dunno. Chicken and curry. Let's start there, shall we?" Lennon jotted it down. "Send another team straight to Liam McCarthy's house, and bring him into the station." He handed Lennon the paper with the address. "Straightaway," Lennon said. Cormac could feel worry coming off him in waves. "What's the story?"

"We received two panicked calls. The first was from Peg Dooley, saying her grandson Dylan, aged ten, wasn't at the harbor when she went to pick him up from a bicycle ride, and the second was from a pub in Tralee. They had two panicked lads rush in saying they saw a monster in a nearby peat bog."

"A monster, is it?" Cormac groaned. Cormac wasn't so old that he couldn't remember being a lad in short trousers. It didn't take much to get them wound up, especially in groups. Little terrorists, the lot of them. "Was one of these lads Dylan?" The last thing they needed was a distraction like this.

"He had been with them, but they left him at the bog."

"Are you joking me?" He could hear the wind howling around them and the rain drumming on the roof. He wouldn't want a mouse out in this. If there was a lad stuck at a bog in this storm, that was plenty of cause for alarm.

"Peg Dooley is losing her mind. We haven't told her about the call from the pub yet; the calls came in back-to-back."

Cormac mulled it over. "Are we sure these lads aren't messing?"

Lennon swallowed hard. "Guards found Dylan's bicycle at the top of the hill, just where the other two lads said they'd find it."

"Who are these lads? How old are they?"

"Michael and James. Twelve years of age."

"You're telling me they left the one aged ten alone in a bog in the dark by himself?" Cormac found himself clenching his fists. He didn't have children of his own, and he'd already decided he wasn't having them. Given that he literally wanted to shake some sense into these lads, it was probably for the best.

"They said they told him run, but he wanted to see the monster."

"Monster. Jaysus." He started down the hall. "Let's get our rain gear on," he said as Lennon followed him. "Looks like we're headed to the bog."

CHAPTER 11

*B*OGS WERE AN ECOSYSTEM ALL THEIR OWN, AND CORMAC HAD A healthy dose of respect for them. Most of them were classified as degraded, having dried up over the years, and to the average eye looked unimpressive—soggy brown fields. In County Kerry, they had both raised bogs and upland blanket bogs. Both were formed by a combination of peat, water, and plants growing together, and he vaguely remembered that raised bogs contained a deeper layer of peat. The one in question was the latter, thin soggy layers spreading across the field without much depth, but still too mucky and slippery to have a walkabout, and the rain would fill it up right quick.

The storm was in high gear when he and his men arrived, making the ground even slicker, and their sight line abysmal. In addition to the heavy rain, the absence of city lights rendered the area as dark and unforgiving as a black hole, but they were prepared with high-powered torches. In the police vans, they had portable lights at the ready. He had been praying this was just lads acting the maggot, but once Cormac saw Dylan's bicycle at the top of the hill, he could no longer hold onto positivity. Next to one of the tires, they found an inhaler. His grandmother confirmed that Dylan had asthma. Cormac had brought a team of three guards; the rest were occupied with the investigations revolving around missing persons Fiona Sheehan and Shauna Mills, and so he called out the paramedics to be on the safe side.

"Let's walk the perimeter," Cormac said, looking down at his wellies. They were all wearing them, no choice but to respect the bog. Cormac took the right-hand side, making long strides, his torch sweeping the grounds in front of him. His raincoat flapped, and his hood continuously flew off as the wind howled around them. He couldn't remember the last time he'd been out in a storm of this nature. The caw of a crow broke through the sound of the rain, and it sounded like someone crying for help.

He was halfway around the bog when a beam of light caught something in the middle of the field, where water was starting to rise, snaking in all directions. He could make out a couple of lumps and some kind of material—something that was once white. Was it clothing? *Please don't let it be the lad.* Cormac called out, then picked up the pace, and soon the guards in the vicinity followed.

Cormac reached the object and shined his torch. A second later, he nearly dropped it. A bloated corpse confronted him, wrapped in a white satin robe. The now-hideous face that stared upward had a ghastly white complexion, tinged with purple. It was a woman. And she was pregnant, nearly to term from the looks of it. "Jesus." A pregnant mother lying dead in a field of muck. He then did something his mam would have done; he crossed himself. For a moment, he wondered if they had just found Shauna, but this corpse was too decayed. Could this be Fiona Sheehan? The neighbor who'd brought in the ransom note guessed it had been in the postbox for at least two weeks.

"Jaysus," a guard behind him echoed. "Holy Mother of God. Is she pregnant?" The guard began to dry-wretch.

"Stand back," Cormac said. He needed the area cordoned off before too many wellies stomped any closer. "We're going to need a coroner, the Technical Bureau, and every single guard you can reach both here and in Tralee. Take them off the Sheehan and Mills cases for now. We may be looking at the same perpetrator."

"Yes, Inspector."

Cormac had yet to voice one of his worst fears. That their young lad may have been kidnapped, just like Shauna Mills and possibly Fiona Sheehan. What kind of monster were they dealing with here? Guards hurried toward their squad cars, voices raised, wellies making sucking sounds as they tried to cover ground quickly. Cormac turned to another as he pulled booties and gloves out of his pockets. "Garda, I need portable lights pronto and crime-scene tape."

"Do you think they'll stand in this wind?" a nearby guard asked, his voice nearly drowned out by the rain.

"We'll make them stand," Cormac shouted back.

"Yes, sir."

He turned his attention back to his surroundings. He had a feeling they were looking at the secondary location and she'd been killed elsewhere. Otherwise, what would a woman near term be doing at the bog? He turned to the remaining guards. "Everyone have their booties and gloves?" Heads around him nodded. "Suit up."

"Inspector," a nearby guard called. "I see a child's shoe. A runner."

Cormac hurried over. There on the ground was a single white runner, and indeed it was child's size.

Cormac whistled for all the guards. "We need to expand our search." Torches lit up the ground surrounding the shoe. "I need everyone looking for shoe prints," he said. "Both child- and man-sized." He knew it was a ridiculous request. The rain had turned everything to mush, and their boot prints were already marred by the lashing rain. This was biblical.

"Maybe he was so scared he left his shoe behind and kept running," a guard yelled.

"All possibilities are on the table," Cormac said. "Including an abduction. Look for prints. Look for objects. But, most of all, look for the lad. His name is Dylan Walsh. Maybe he found shelter. Keep yelling his name." What they were really looking for was a miracle. Cormac wished he believed in them. As guards fanned out, scouring the area and yelling for Dylan, Cormac shone his torch across the field. "Hello?" he shouted into the darkness. "It's the guards, lad. Dylan? Dylan Walsh, are you out there?" He gestured to another guard. "Stay near this shoe until we have the crime-scene tape and evidence bags." They'd be lucky if the crime-scene tape stayed in place. There could not be a worse night for a lad to get lost in a bog. And maybe that was exactly what someone had been counting on. If he had been taken, Cormac prayed the lad was alright. But anyone who murdered a pregnant woman close to term and left her body in a degraded bog was probably not the type who gave a shite about a kid. If they wanted to find Dylan Walsh alive, the clock was ticking.

"Inspector," Garda Lennon yelled.

Cormac hurried in the direction of Lennon's voice. He was standing over a patch of dirt, his torch shining down. "Footprints?" Cormac asked.

"No. But it's some kind of mark—like a bicycle wheel."

Cormac reached the spot and shone his own torch. He saw the mark, then swept the ground until he saw another mark running parallel only a bit of distance between them. "A cart," he said. "Or a wheelbarrow."

"You think?"

"It's how someone transported the body to the bog." He looked off in the distance toward a tree line. "Nearest road is that way," he said. "Let's get guards searching from these marks to the road. Let's see what else we can find." Lennon whistled, a piercing sound that brought other guards running. They set up a formation and began sweeping the area in the manner Cormac had instructed. Closer to the woods, they clocked more cart or wheelbarrow indentations, but most of the tracks had been washed away by the rain. Once in the woods, they tried to maintain the same line as the wheelbarrow marks, and when they finally reached the single road, they fanned out. "Here," a guard farthest to the right yelled. Cormac and Lennon hurried over. There they found tire marks and deep ruts in the mud. "He was stuck," Cormac said. They continued the search and found loose branches discarded as if someone had used them to hide the vehicle and then what appeared to be a partial boot print. "We need this cordoned off. Mark all around the boot print as well as the other wheelbarrow marks, and let's get a few guards on this road. Look for skid marks, and then find the nearest house or business. Maybe we'll get lucky and be able to pull CCTV."

"I know this road," Lennon said. "You won't find a camera for quite a stretch."

That's why the killer had chosen it. "Let's canvas the road anyway, including on either side. Maybe he tossed something out the window."

"Of course, Inspector."

Cormac knew he was grasping at straws, but straws were all he had. Cormac pulled out his mobile phone and brought up Detective Sergeant Barbara Neely's number. He hated disturbing her this late, not to mention ending her holiday early, but time was not something he could afford to waste.

Cormac and Lennon stood by and watched as the coroner began his work. An entire team was still canvassing the area for the lad, a search grid had been set up, and they were once more fanning out from where they'd found his shoe. A command tent was being set up nearby. The Dooleys had arrived, which Cormac had mixed feelings about, but he knew if his kid or grandkid was missing, he'd do the same. Peg Dooley stood in the corner of the tent, clutching coffee and crying. Cormac approached and introduced himself. Her eyes were swollen and red. "He was happy-out staying home. I thought he should be with lads his own age and get some exercise before the storm. I only left him for thirty minutes! He's usually an obedient lad." She bit her lip as tears rolled down her cheeks.

"We're going to do everything we can," Cormac said. "What you're feeling is normal, but let's concentrate on finding Dylan."

"I'll never forgive meself if something horrible has happened to him."

Something terrible *had* happened to him, but that was best left unsaid. "Do you know of anyone who had any kind of quarrel with Dylan?"

"Are you joking me? He's a chubby lad who talks too much. No one pays him any mind at all."

"The other lads said something about a man in a pea cap giving them ten euros to go to the bog," Cormac said.

"Who was it?" Peg asked. "Why would he do such a thing?"

Because he wanted them to find the body. Just like the man in the dark butterfly mask left the Griffins alive. He *wanted* them to report Shauna missing. Just like he expected the Sheehans to report the ransom note. Only whoever this bastard was, he hadn't realized the Sheehans were on holiday. Someone wanted to overwhelm the guards. Spread them too thin. And it was fucking working. Cormac was livid and panicked, neither of which would help him at all. He had to keep his emotions in check.

"Inspector," a familiar voice said. He turned just as Detective Sergeant Barbara Neely entered the tent, and judging from her facial expression, she had been told at least a portion of the grim news. She peeled off her hood and shook out her honey-colored bob. In her mid-sixties, she was an attractive woman with a lean, strong body, a giant heart, and the kind of mind Cormac would always want on his cases.

"I'm sorry about cutting your holiday short," Cormac said.

"There are more important things." Neely walked up to Peg Dooley and embraced her. Peg sobbed on her shoulder. Neely pulled away, grabbed a napkin from the nearby table, and handed it to her. "We're going to do everything we can, Peg. Try not to project or let your mind run wild. We're going to do everything we can."

"I shouldn't have let him go," Peg said. "He would have been happy-out at my house."

"Inspector, Detective," Lennon said, hurrying into the tent. "Dan O'Neill wants to speak with you." The coroner. Neely and Cormac exchanged eye contact, pulled their hoods over their heads, and plodded over, fighting the wind with every step. By the time they reached the spot, they were both out of breath. Dan O'Neill was a bit pale in the face, bald, and sporting a round belly. It was a stressful job; Cormac couldn't blame him if he was compensating with food. Cormac had seen him before, but they'd never been chatty. But he was competent, and that was all that mattered. Everyone had to yell to be heard over the wind.

"I've spoken with the assistant state pathologist. She's given her permission for us to transport the body to the Kerry Hospital morgue," he said. "If you look here, you'll see that her throat is slit." Cormac stared at the jagged red slash, repulsed by such a violent and intimate act. "It's a reasonable assumption that's the cause of death," O'Neill continued, "and she's definitely close to term. *Was* close to term." He looked up at them. "This next bit is even more gruesome," he said. "Fair warning."

"Go on, so," Cormac said.

The coroner shone the light several meters away from the deceased woman. Cormac had seen a lot of things in this line of work, but never this. He couldn't call it a fetus. She'd been so close to term. He was looking at the remains of a dead baby. He instinctively covered his mouth with his hands. "Dear God."

Neely cried out, once, then twice, then cursed.

"I don't understand," Cormac said. "She . . . gave birth, and then he killed her?"

"No," O'Neill said. "It's called coffin birth, or postmortem fetal extrusion. It's the expulsion of a fetus—nonviable at this stage, mind you—caused by increasing pressure from intro-abdominal gases."

"If we had found her earlier, could we have saved the baby?" Neely asked, her voice thick with emotion.

"No," O'Neill said. "The baby would have died within minutes of its mother."

Cormac tried to keep his emotions at a distance. He did not want to imagine her last horrific moments. *Their* last horrific moments. "How long would you say she's been out here?"

"At least ten days or more," the coroner said. "That's my guess." Beside him, he saw Neely shiver. "I'm sorry," he said. "This is the worst of the worst." Neely did not answer. That was not like her. "Mostly likely she was killed from behind," the coroner continued. "I'd like to think she never saw it coming."

"Why do you think she's dressed like that?" Cormac asked.

The coroner shrugged. "Dunno. Maybe they wanted us to see *this.*" With gloved hands, Dan lifted the left edge of her robe, then adjusted so he could shine the torch. There, on her thigh, was a tattoo of a blue butterfly rimmed in black. Neely and Cormac both kneeled to have a closer look at it. It looked new, but the strange thing was there was another tattoo underneath it. White and black in little swirls. "What is it covering up?" It didn't appear to be the name of an ex-lover, which would have been extremely helpful, and it would have explained why she got another tattoo to cover it up. But instead of a name, it looked like some kind of animal.

"Looks like she covered up a sheep," O'Neill said.

"Mother of God," Neely said. "Tell me it's not a sheep."

"I believe it is," O'Neill said. He traced the head and then the tail on the other side. "That's definitely what it is."

"No," Neely said. "No, no, no."

"What's the story?" Cormac asked.

Neely held up a finger, then turned and walked away. She began to pace. Cormac was feeling impatient and wanted to know what in the world was going on, but he was trying to give her a bit of space. When she returned, her face had drained of all color. "The baby wasn't cut out of her?" Neely asked O'Neill. "Are you sure the baby wasn't cut out of her?"

"I'm sure," O'Neill said. "This is a straightforward case of post-mortem expulsion."

"Then it's not him. It can't be him. The baby wasn't cut out of her; it's not him."

The baby wasn't cut out of her? Cormac had always known Neely to be level-headed, but that comment was downright bizarre. "Not who? Who are you on about?"

"I'm sure the state pathologist will be able to tell you more," O'Neill said, throwing a worried glance to Neely. "Do you want me to use two body bags or . . ."

"Place the fetus with the mother," Cormac said. At least they could be together in death. The coroner nodded. "Thank you," Cormac said.

"This is the worst I've seen," O'Neill said, before turning back to his work. "This is the absolute worst." Cormac walked over to where Neely paced, took her gently by the elbow, and steered her back to the tent.

"Cup of tea?" he asked, once they were under cover. "Coffee?" Hell, he'd give her whiskey if he had it.

Neely crossed herself, then to his surprise removed rosary beads from her pocket. "It can't be them. They're in jail. They're in jail."

"Detective Sergeant," Cormac said as he laid his hand on her arm. She jumped. He removed his hand. "What's the story? Who's in jail?"

She shook her head violently. "Keep searching this field," she said. "Every inch." She began to back away. "I can't stay. There's something I have to do."

"Now?" She started off. "Care to tell me what that is?" He had to yell across the field; she was hauling arse.

Neely stopped, then shook her head, her hands in prayer position near her mouth. "I need to think."

"Can you tell me anything?"

Her face was a portrait in terror, half in shadow from the portable lights shining on her. "It's probably nothing. It has to be nothing. But if it is." She swallowed.

"If it is?" Cormac prompted.

"If it is"—Neely stopped as if trying to work out her words. "If you ever believed in God, or a Higher Power, now's the time to call on him. Now is the time to pray."

CHAPTER 12

*T*HE LONGER CORMAC LIVED, AND THE MORE HE'D SEEN OF WHAT men did to each other, the less he believed in any kind of heaven above. But it had been nearly a year since the death of his beloved mam, and her absence made him long for a belief in some kind of afterlife. He spent a considerable amount of time chatting with her in his head, imagining how she would answer, what topic of conversation they might be tackling, given the news on any given day. But now, with this grizzly scene, he was relieved his mam would not have to share in the horror. And he had to turn his attention to the ones he could save. The kid. Hopefully Shauna. Everyone knew the window to find a missing person alive was at best forty-eight hours, but more likely twenty-four, and a clock was ticking like a bomb in his head. He had to focus. He prayed Neely would get her act together; he was going to need every pair of capable hands he could get.

The entire bog was illuminated by the portable lights. At the command tent, they were trying to get a bead on search dogs. Peg Dooley had been driven home so they could collect a few items of the lad's clothing. Besides the wheelbarrow and tire tracks, the only hard evidence they'd found so far were a discarded cigarette butt, Dylan's single runner, the wheelbarrow or cart prints, the tire print, and the partial boot print. It wasn't much, but it was something. Dylan's parents, who lived in Dublin, had been notified and were on their way to Kerry. He could only imagine that it was going to be the longest drive of their life. He had to find Dylan and Shauna. Were they being kept together? There was no way the two—make that three, including the Jane Doe in the bog (most likely Fiona Sheehan)—there was no way these three incidents were not connected. Were they looking for a single individual or a group? It was a lot for one person to coordinate, and kidnappers often worked in teams. Cormac had the sense that he was facing a group. And whoever these people were, his opinion thus far was that this had been in the planning for quite some time.

The man in the flat cap sent three lads to the bog to find the body. Cormac was confident in that assumption. Was kidnapping Dylan part of the plan? Or had Dylan gotten a good look at him? Did Dylan *know* this man? Michael and James had said he was a complete stranger, but whoever took him was either worried he could be identified, or he saw this as an opportunity for another ransom. Cormac had to leave room for all possibilities. His best hope was that they would hear from the kidnappers. He'd already put Peg Dooley and Dylan's parents on alert, and headquarters was working on setting up a trace on all their mobile phones.

The smell of coffee brought by some genius at the station lured Cormac into the tent. He poured his into one of the large Styrofoam cups and turned to Garda Lennon, who was warming his hands on his cup. Once his coffee was sorted, Cormac joined him. "Neely was going on about someone—I don't know what—but—"

He didn't need to continue; Lennon was already nodding. "I don't know much," he said. "But I've heard tales."

Gossip wasn't Cormac's preferred mode of investigation, but he was desperate. "Go on, so."

"It's something to do with her first case nearly thirty years ago, when she first became a garda. A murdered pregnant woman." Lennon's lips stretched into a thin line. "The victim was young too. Barely thirty, and her baby had been cut out of her."

Neely had inferred as much, but hearing it from Garda Lennon made Cormac's stomach heave. He tossed his coffee in a nearby bin. "Was her throat cut?"

He pressed his lips tight as he nodded. "It was indeed."

"Jesus." He understood Neely's reaction now. You didn't get much more horrifying than that.

"Where was she found?"

"At the base of Mount Brandon."

Mount Brandon was a popular area for hikers and tourists alike. Although there were horrifying similarities—pregnant, near-term, throat slit, left out in the elements—these murders were nearly three decades apart. He was inclined to mark them down as coincidence. "Did they ever catch the bastard?"

Lennon crushed his Styrofoam cup and made a basket in the nearby rubbish bin. "I think I'd better let Neely tell you the rest of the story." He shook his head. "You wouldn't believe it coming from me."

That wasn't true; Garda Lennon was a straight shooter. But if it was Neely's story to tell, then it was Neely's story to tell. She had been on the force a long time and had seen enough to develop a thick skin. But there were some cases that pierced even the toughest armor. Darkness and light were parallel roads. At any given moment, someone was living their best life alongside someone living their worst.

But there were degrees of "bad," and a murdered pregnant woman and kidnapped victims were as low as you could get. Let's face it—it was pure evil. Evil disguised as normal human beings walking among the rest of them. There were times he was amazed any of them could function at all. His mam had always reminded him to look for the good, look for the helpers, and to understand that godly light was brighter than any man-made darkness. Cormac wasn't religious, but there were times he wanted the comfort. This was one of those times. "Flowers grow in the cracks," she liked to say. "The sun will shine again, Mac." Now that she was gone, he was going to have to remind himself. And he was going to have to remind Neely. Just as he took out his mobile phone to do just that, it was ringing, and as if he had just summoned her with his thoughts, her name lit up his screen. He hadn't spoken to her since she'd left the scene; at least six hours had passed. "Speak of the Devil," he said. "Are you at the station?"

"No," she said. "I'm at a pub. And I'm three jars in."

"You're drinking? Now?" That wasn't good.

"I am, so. And you'd better get here while I'm still sober enough to tell this story."

CHAPTER 13

*T*HERE WERE PLENTY OF CHEERFUL PUBS IN DINGLE, BUT NEELY HAD chosen an old pub situated far enough away from town that tourists couldn't find it. The kind of dark cave catering to the graveyard shift that welcomed established as well as burgeoning alcoholics. At the moment, there were only two old men at the bar and a publican glued to a small television. "Can't believe we still have power," the publican said to no one in particular. "'Tis miserable, isn't it?"

Cormac peeled off his raincoat and held it by the hood. When the publican didn't offer a solution, he hung it over the spoke of a nearby chair. His coat was soaked, but at least he was relatively dry.

Neely was huddled in a booth in the corner. Cormac slid across from her, already appalled by the wet marks on the table. One of his many little quirks was that he could not stand wetness on a table. He wasn't going to touch it. Neely was indeed staring into the bottom of a pint glass. "This isn't like you," he said.

She tossed a file across the table, and Cormac visibly cringed. "Sorry," she said. She produced a napkin and wiped the table. "Sometimes I forget about your little dislikes."

He rose, went to the bar, and asked for a clean cloth. The publican frowned, but then shrugged and tossed him one. Cormac returned her empty pint glasses to the bar, asked for water, then wiped the table properly before setting the water in front of her, placing it on a coaster like a human being. Then he picked up the file. It was half-wet and soggy. "Why don't you tell me the story in your own words?"

Neely nodded; she'd already planned on this. "Twenty-nine years ago, the area was terrorized by a man who called himself the Shepherd. His real name was Cahal Mackey."

"Cahal Mackey," Cormac repeated. The name sounded vaguely familiar, but he couldn't quite put the pieces together.

"He lured young, pregnant girls into his web. They went of their own accord. We believe he had a commune somewhere in County Kerry, but we never found it."

Cormac frowned. "A commune?"

"I'd call it a cult," Neely said. "He started a cult."

If Cormac didn't know Neely better, he'd have thought she was taking the piss. "A cult. In Ireland?"

Neely nodded. "It's not common, but it wasn't the first. Did you ever hear of the Atlantis Primal Therapy Commune?"

Cormac shook his head.

"You weren't even born. They were established in 1974 in Donegal. Better known as the Screamers. And, yes, you can take that literally. But I don't think Cahal Mackey ran a true commune, after all. I think he convinced the women it was a commune. One of those 'we all raise each other's babies' kind of shite. I suspected a baby-smuggling ring, but could never prove it." She shook her head. "And that's only because the entire thing imploded before it even got off the ground."

"That's dark." He wanted to say that kind of depravity didn't exist here. But he knew better. When it came to money, for some men there was no bottom.

Neely ran her finger along the pint glass. "I was new on the force then. Greener than Garda Lennon. From missing persons reports and family statements, we believe that, at one point, a total of five women were living with Cahal, aka the Shepherd, and another man, Flynn Barry; he was the second in charge. All good communes need prison guards, I suppose. They called him the Staff."

Nicknames. A way of asserting control. "I take it the women were called by something other than their names as well?" Cormac asked.

"They were indeed. And I apologize because I know you're busy, and I know you have a lot of questions, but I'm only going to tell this story once, so if you don't mind, I'm going to take it step-by-step."

"Not a problem." It was; he had a million things to do, including interview Liam McCarthy, who was at this very moment waiting at the garda station, but he had too much respect for Neely to rush her.

"The entire situation didn't come to our attention until a hiker found a body at the base of the mountains. Young woman. Her throat was slit—and her baby . . ." Neely swallowed. "Her baby had been cut out of her." She grimaced. "One of the most disturbing things I've ever seen. No fingerprints. But she had a recent tattoo. And get this—it was a sheep." She shook her head. "But no butterfly. The butterfly is new."

"Butterfly," Cormac said. "My God, I nearly forgot about Shauna's kidnapper."

"What?" Neely sounded panicked.

"You wouldn't believe the day we've had. I haven't even had time to tell you about our other incident—a ransom note for a pregnant woman named Fiona Sheehan, left in a mailbox for two weeks, along with a burner phone and a missed call. The note threatened they would kill her if they didn't receive a hundred thousand euros within six hours."

"You think that's the woman at the bog?"

"Highly likely." He held her gaze. "That's not all. Another young pregnant woman by the name of Shauna Mills was taken in front of the parents-to-be."

"Parents-to-be?"

"She was putting her baby up for adoption. To Jane and David Griffin. Do you know them?" Neely shook head. "They said the kidnapper was a man dressed in a black coat, bulked up as if he had layers of clothing underneath. And get this—he had on a black butterfly mask." These cases were related. Now he knew for sure they were looking for the same perpetrators.

"I knew it," Neely said, her voice nearly a growl. "I knew it was them. I knew it."

"Why a butterfly?"

"I have no idea," Neely said. "But the sheep . . ."

Cormac frowned until the lightbulb went on. "The Shepherd."

"Indeed," Neely said. "Cahal Mackey essentially branded her. He probably branded all of them. Sick bastard." She swallowed hard.

"And our Jane Doe had a butterfly imposed over a sheep," Cormac repeated. Repetition helped him think. Cormac was beginning to see why Neely was so weighed down by this case. "The murder victim from thirty years ago. Any other evidence at the scene?"

Neely tilted her head, as if trying to remember. "Nothing concrete. She had no abrasions, vaginal scarring, or bruises. Nothing that suggested rape. We did find some hairs on her that were later identified as a female, and they did not belong to her. Interpol did an exhaustive search for us, but we never got a hit on the DNA."

"You think she was killed by a woman?"

Neely half-shook her head. "I don't know. There have been cases of women so desperate for a baby that they resort to such evil things. But the hair could have been from one of the other women in the commune, or it could have even been from someone who found the body but didn't want to get involved. But I know it was orchestrated by—if not done by—Cahal Mackey and Flynn Barry. Mark my words, this isn't going to be a case of whodunnit. This is going to be a case of how do we nail the bastards?"

Some days Cormac loathed his job. This was one of them. "Did you ever get any leads on what happened to the baby?" Neely shook her head. "We have no idea if the baby lived or died." She pursed her lips. "It took ages to identify the woman. Alana Graves. What little we could find out about her life was one of those sad stories. A 'troubled' girl. Bounced from home to home. When we finally located her parents, they told us that she had run away and joined some kind of a cult."

"What all did they know about this cult?"

"After she left, she only spoke to her parents once. She called them from a pay phone. Said she had a new name, but she didn't tell them what it was. She said their 'protector' was called the Shepherd and they worshipped the Grand Ruler, and they lived somewhere they called the Womb."

Cormac shook his head. He was having trouble processing this. He had very little experience with cults, and by little, he meant none. "I don't even know what to say."

"Neither did I. Alana told her mother she had found a home

where she lived with other pregnant goddesses, and they were going to live off the land and raise each other's babies. The mother said she'd never heard her daughter so excited. She begged her to let them come see her—tell her where exactly she was—but she hung up. That's the last time they ever spoke with her."

"How did you connect Cahal Mackey and Flynn Barry to the cult?"

"That would be our sole witness, Erin Tanner. Believe me, I'm getting to her. But before she came forward, we received an anonymous letter. The writer said that previous to Alana, whom the writer of the letter called Morning Sun, another woman from the cult had been murdered. The letter stated that she had given birth, but her baby had been immediately taken, and the next day she disappeared as well."

This was insane. Cormac could hardly process it. "What do you make of this letter?"

"I believed it. But I've never been able to prove it."

"Did this anonymous letter writer give you a name of this second victim?"

Neely nodded. "Moira Baird, or Golden One. And before you ask—yes, we did find mention of a Moira Baird in old records from a Dublin orphanage. There was a single photo of her. Erin Tanner later confirmed that was her. We were never able to find anyone who'd heard from her after she joined the cult."

"Which puts it at two unsolved murders from the past and two missing babies."

"According to Erin, there were three. The third was called Seven Star. She insisted she never knew her birth name."

"Who is this woman? Erin?"

Neely sighed. "Right, sorry. She was a former member of the cult, and once we arrested Cahal Mackey and Flynn Barry, she finally came forward." Neely shook her head at the memory. "There was something very cold about her. Matter-of-fact. But I give her credit for coming forward."

Cormac nodded. "Five women in the commune. Erin makes four. Did she have a baby taken?"

"She said she never conceived."

Cormac replayed what he'd learned of these women so far. Erin Tanner, witness, former cult member, never conceived. Seven Star, reported murdered and baby taken. Alana Graves, body found at the base of Mount Brandon, baby cut out of her. And Moira Baird, also known as Golden One, baby reported taken, and the next day, she too is gone. His head was going to be done in for quite some time. "And the fifth woman?"

"Erin Tanner refused to name her. I always wondered why."

"She wouldn't even tell you her 'given name'?"

"She would not."

"Garda Lennon mentioned that these men have been in jail the past few decades?"

Neely swallowed. "That is true."

"On what charge?"

"About a week after we found Alana Graves's body, we received another anonymous tip. This time via a phone call with voice distortion. The caller told us they had information on the cult leaders, and said, and I quote, 'Where there's smoke, there's fire. That's where you'll find them.' And sure enough, we saw the smoke. Thick black stuff that you could see for miles. In addition to volunteer firemen, we sent every garda on duty. It was an old farmhouse, large enough for a group of women, but we never found any evidence that they had been there. What we did find at the scene were Cahal Mackey and Flynn Barry. They each wore a white robe edged in emerald green. It was the strangest thing. They didn't even try to run when we pulled up. They were just standing there, watching the place burn. Cahal was still holding the gas can. We found evidence of drugs and guns in the charred remains. Cocaine and marijuana, and unregistered rifles, which added time for possessing firearms. And finally, they resisted arrest something fierce; that gave us yet another charge. They've been in prison the past twenty-nine years."

"Did this Cahal Mackey or Flynn Barry own the farmhouse?"

"No. It had been abandoned since the owners died. The Meehans. Lovely couple, well liked in town, although Noel Meehan had been in poor health most of his life. They didn't have any children. Noel passed away first, and Margaret lived about a year after his death.

And when she died, there was no will, and the property just sat there, forgotten by time. We believe Cahal and Flynn were squatting."

"Their starter commune," Cormac said, without any real humor. "You said you never found proof of the women living there. Do you think you had the right property?"

Neely nodded. "Erin Tanner verified that the farmhouse was indeed their commune, and that it did not have electricity or running water. The things she told us about the way they lived still makes the hair on the back of my neck stand up. What started as kumbaya ended in the total dismantling of the woman as human beings. Tattoos, dress code, chains. Flynn Barry stood guard nearly twenty-four/seven with a loaded rifle. They were nothing to these men but wombs."

"Jesus. How did they sell that as utopia?"

"Your guess is as good as mine. But even with her testimony, the men wouldn't cop to it, and we couldn't prove it."

"Did Ms. Tanner have anything to back up her story?" Witnesses, as they both well knew, could be unreliable. Memories weren't always accurate, and sometimes they outright lied. Neely seemed to have full faith in this woman's account, but Cormac knew he needed to keep an open mind. "Did you find anything to corroborate her story?"

"The Devil was in the details. She described exactly where the property was located and what it looked like before it was burned to the ground. She described Alana Graves in great detail. Brown hair, hazel eyes, slim build. She confirmed that Alana's nickname—or 'given name,' as she phrased it—had been Morning Sun. And Erin also had a tattoo of a sheep on her left thigh, identical to Alana's."

"Do you think Erin also wrote the anonymous letter and made the anonymous call?"

"She said she didn't, and she seemed genuinely intrigued that someone had. We obtained samples of her handwriting. They were not a match to the letter."

Cormac steadied his breath. "Dirty Old Town," by the Pogues, began to play. "How does this relate to the woman in the bog? Do you think we're dealing with a copycat?"

"Aren't you going to ask me where I went after I left the bog?"

"Where did you go?"

"The station. To phone the prison. They've been released. The bastard and his cohort were released three weeks ago."

"And you didn't get any heads-up?"

Neely grimaced. "They blamed a technical error. Said something about thirty years being a long time. They have no idea who these men are. None. Someone dropped the fucking ball."

And then some. Cormac gave it a beat. "You think it's them? The minute they're released after twenty-nine years in prison, they immediately start targeting pregnant women again?"

"That's exactly what I think."

He wouldn't dare accuse her of being emotional, but there was no denying her feelings were raw and strong. "Walk me through that."

"It's who they are."

"Maybe so. But that's not evidence."

"They've had time to plan. And I don't think that man could stop if he wanted to."

"Let's have a chat with these men. Are they in the area?"

She nodded. "It's part of their parole. They're at a halfway house in Dingle and working at the harbor." She chewed her lip. "The thing is, the guards have had eyes on them since they've been released. They both signed up for a monitored transition program. It consisted of rooms at a boardinghouse and the jobs at the harbor. In exchange, they knew they were going to be watched like hawks. And supposedly they have been. I was told they rarely venture from their routine: home, work, and a few local restaurants, pubs, and shops. Believe me, I'd love to go and haul them in right now, but as you've stated, we don't have any hard evidence. This is like twenty-nine years ago all over again."

"We could still rattle their cages."

"You need to catch up to speed before we do that," Neely said. She leaned forward, radiating intensity. "Trust me when I tell you that if we don't nail these bastards, this case is going to eat away your very soul. I will not fail twice. This time, *we* need to be the ones three steps ahead."

Cormac gave it a beat. "What about this property that was burned down? We should check it out."

"I already did. As soon as I learned that Cahal and Flynn had been released from prison."

"And?"

"There's a new family there now. A new build. Modest home. Lovely people. They haven't seen or heard anything out of the norm in the five years they've been there. They let me look around. I have no reason not to believe them."

"You left the bog, went to the station, called the prison, grabbed the file, then checked out this property? All before coming here to drown your sorrows?"

"What can I say. I've been on holiday. I was rested."

Obsessed. That was the word he was looking for. Cormac lifted the file. "I'll get on this today." He stood, then nodded at her water. "Drink that and more of it. Then get some more rest. I need you raring to go for the press briefing bright and early tomorrow morning."

"How long are guards going to search this evening?"

"We had to call it off. Its dark; it's lashing. They'll start again at the first sign of daylight."

Neely sighed, but she took a sip of water. "We had another version of Garda Lennon back then. Paul Bryne."

Cormac wondered if he was ever going to stop hearing about Paul Byrne, Dimpna Wilde's unrequited love from long ago. He had nothing against the man, but he had nothing for him either. The man used to be a detective sergeant, and for that, Cormac respected him. That didn't mean he had to like him. "Alright. Is there a reason you mention it?"

"I know you've had your issues with Paul, but back then, he threw himself into this case. You should definitely speak with him."

"I have no problems with Paul Byrne." If anything, it was Paul who had a problem with him. No doubt he was still in love with Dimpna. It occurred to him that Dimpna had been pregnant when she left Dingle, and it was around the same time Cahal Mackey was actively "hunting." The thought of anyone manipulating a young pregnant woman, the thought of Dimpna sharing the fate of those poor young women—if he let his mind go down that dark alley, he'd be ordering pints along with Neely.

"If it's starting again . . ." Neely closed her eyes. "I don't think I can do this."

"I'm sorry," Cormac said. "But you have no choice." He placed his hand on her shoulder and gave it a squeeze. "See you in the morning."

"Not if I see you first," Neely said, lifting her pint of water. "Not if I see you first."

CHAPTER 14

The Womb—1994

Golden One is gone. All traces of her have been removed from The Womb. The Shepherd sat the remaining four of us down and informed us that Golden had
asked to leave the Flock, and he had driven her to
town. He explained that her baby had been born frail,
and he'd rushed him to hospital, but there was nothing
they could do.

We huddled inside the main portion of the
compound by the fireplace. Moonlight streamed in
through the round windows, and the flames from the
fire cast dancing shadows on the walls.

I didn't understand what he meant by "born frail." I
could tell the others didn't either, but I didn't want to
be the one to ask for clarification.

"If anyone would like to say anything, you can speak
now," the Shepherd said.

For a moment, none of us spoke. Not Eternal Mist, or
Red Rose, or Morning Sun. It was up to me. The Staff
stood near the lake, the black gun still strapped to his
chest.

"Why is the Staff carrying a gun?" I asked.

"We've had some threats from the outside world,"
the Shepherd said. "It's only for precaution."

"The chains?" I continued, my voice wobbling. "Why was Golden One in chains?"

"She was trying to prevent me from taking the baby to hospital. Had I known the poor thing wouldn't survive, I would have let her hold him. But time was of the essence." The Shepherd was a man who felt deeply. His voice was low; his eyes were wet. He had been looking forward to their first baby as much as any of us.

I had to step carefully. What I really wanted to know was why he didn't listen to me when I told him she was close to giving birth? Why didn't he allow all of us to be at her bedside? I didn't even know if it was a difficult birth or what her condition was when her son was born. We'd been preparing for this for so long. "I feel bad," I said, putting it on me. "I should have been by her side."

"The baby was early. You couldn't have known."

I nodded, but I was wrestling with my inner doubts. *That wasn't what I meant.* Why was I nodding when that wasn't what I meant? And why was I sitting there thinking that he knew exactly what I meant and was trying to twist my words? Because the Shepherd was mistaken. The baby *wasn't* early. And would Golden really have left without saying goodbye? She had been in an absolute rage when I saw her last. She'd also been terrified, not just for herself, but for us. We were now to believe that she'd simply been taken to town and what? Walked away? *Not possible.*

And if what the Shepherd said was true, and she had been chained to the bed so that he could take the baby to hospital, why was she still in chains the last time I saw her? The Staff could have actually done something useful for once and unchained her. I had not even been allowed to stay with Golden after I had cleaned her up and administered pain meds. And what about the fact that Golden said the others had been locked in their rooms? Eternal Mist said it wasn't true. But I wanted to hear from the others. None of them would talk about that.

I glanced at Eternal Mist. She was smiling at the Shepherd. *There is something wrong with that woman.* If I was going to take a risk and talk to any of the others about my fears, it was not going to be her.

"We'll find another goddess," Eternal Mist said. "Those who lose faith do not belong here."

"Indeed," the Shepherd says. "But in light of this, we have decided that we need to ensure that each and every one of you know that you are part of a family. My family. You are a Flock, I am the Shepherd, he is the Staff, and we obey the Grand Ruler. To honor that, we are all going to get a tattoo."

"A tattoo?" Red Rose spoke for the first time today, her voice laced with fear. She was arguably the prettiest one of us all, with dark hair that spilled down her back and pale blue eyes. One might think only a redhead would be given her moniker, but the Shepherd named her so because she is sweet with a thorny side. I have a thorny side too, but perhaps I have hidden it well.

"Don't worry," the Shepherd said. "The pain won't last, but what will last is our everlasting bond."

Branded, I couldn't help but think. *We will be forever branded.* I wanted to get up and walk out. Would they chase me? Would I see the barrel of the gun? I did not want a tattoo. Was Golden onto something? Were we prisoners?

"Where will we go to get these tattoos?" I asked. If we were going out into civilization, I would have a chance to escape.

"The Staff and I will do them," he said. "There's nothing to it." He stared into my eyes as if daring me to resist.

I felt a shiver up my back.

In that moment, my mind was made up. This was not

going to be the utopia I had been promised. And they had never intended it to be. Fear and rage twisted inside me like the flames from the fire. I wanted to run then and there. But that was not a smart move. I needed a plan. I needed to figure this out before the next baby was born. Before *my* baby was born.

"It's settled then," the Shepherd said. He rose and stood over us. He wasn't a handsome man, but he had an energy field around him that was irresistible. When I'd first encountered him, he'd filled me with so much hope. Even now, I wavered. Was this simply grief getting the better of me? "I am so proud of my Flock and so humbled that I get to watch over you. Protect you. We eagerly await our first baby." His gaze fell to my belly. I thought of my last conversation with Golden. I think I knew then that she was no longer alive. But her spirit was still here, and she was talking to me. *Run*, she said. *Run*.

CHAPTER 15

THE COLD WAS GETTING TO SHAUNA. THE ROOM WAS ALL CONCRETE, and the walls were rounded like a cave. The one window (also round) was boarded up, and the door was made of steel. Mounted next to it was a keypad blinking red. *Locked.* What was this place? It was damp and moldy. There was a single cot on one side, and on the other, he'd placed big jug of water, a loaf of bread, an apple, a bucket, and adult wipes. How nice of her kidnapper to attend to her hygiene. Arsehole.

She felt the cold in her toes, and her fingertips, and the tip of her nose. Like ice. She didn't want to get sick. She was already "compromised," according to her doctor; he'd warned her over and over not to let her stress level get too high, not to let her "phobia of birth" run away with her. The fear was building now; she was afraid of having a panic attack so big it would kill her baby.

She tried to concentrate on her breathing. For the past hour, she'd been trying to memorize every detail of the incident, up to the moment he wrapped a blindfold around her eyes; he'd also put a gag in her mouth and held something metal against her throat. *A knife.* Then he made her climb into the boot of his car. She thought about kicking him in the balls and hoping he would be in too much pain to reach for the knife, but it wasn't just herself she had to consider; it was also her onboard passenger. He was the only reason she had climbed into the boot. The drive felt like it was less than an hour, and toward the last bit of it, the road was bumpy. And then he'd opened the boot and marched her quite a distance to this room. She felt grass under her feet and then wood, and then this concrete. She'd peed her pants again in the boot of the car, and now he'd given her this long gray dress; not only was it drab, it covered nearly every inch of her, like something from hundreds of years ago—and plain white panties and a maternity bra. Hideous. She wanted to strangle him with it. But at least she was out of her soiled clothes. He'd taken them away and had brought in three more dresses, nearly identical to the one she was wearing, only slightly different shades: brown, off-white, and another gray one. Three more sets of white panties and maternity bras. Whoever he was—he'd never taken off that mask, and his figure was hard to discern; she got the distinct feeling he was wearing multiple layers of clothing to bulk up—but whoever he was, he had been planning this for quite some time.

She had been thinking about that letter and email exchange. Fi-FoFum. Did she even exist? Had Moth Man, as she'd taken to calling him, written that strange letter? Pretended to be FiFoFum? Had she told FiFoFum about her meeting with the Griffins? She couldn't quite remember; on the other hand, it wouldn't surprise her if she'd mentioned it. What she did not do was give away the Griffins' address, and she was damn sure she hadn't mentioned their names. But local people knew all about the adoption. The Griffins were primary schoolteachers. Well-known and well-liked. They had been congratulated on Shauna's pregnancy more than she had. One couldn't keep secrets in Dingle; they were carried along by the ocean wind. This person could be a friend of the Griffins. Or, she should say, an enemy. However, if FiFoFum did exist, where was she? Had she been taken too? Was she in this very building?

And what about Liam? He had to be worried about her. Had he been talking about her with his workmates? Someone nasty who then decided to kidnap her? Was Moth Man going to send a ransom note to the Griffins? That didn't make any sense. They made a decent living; they were rich compared to Shauna, but they weren't rich compared to, well, rich people.

The reason she'd been taken wasn't hard to suss out. It was the baby he wanted; and once he got him, what would happen to her? He hadn't harmed the Griffins. Did that mean he wouldn't hurt her? Had anyone found the Griffins? How long had they sat there, tied to their chairs? Did they blame her? Did they think she was involved in this?

She'd said some things she'd regretted to the Griffins. They'd had an argument, and she'd told them maybe they weren't the right parents for her baby, after all. That's why they'd asked her to come over. And now look at what had happened to them. Unless . . . were *they* setting *her* up somehow? Was the kidnapper someone who was working for them? Were they afraid she wasn't going to let them have the baby and they were taking control? No. This couldn't be them. They were teachers. They'd had background checks.

None of it made sense.

She rubbed her belly and made cooing noises, trying to push away the fury. Mostly at herself. Her baby had an eejit for a mammy. He was almost in this world; all she had to do was follow the doctor's orders and stay home. Would God even listen to her if she begged him now? Maybe God hated her. She wore a gold cross. Didn't He see she wore a gold cross?

She felt for it and was shocked that it was no longer around her neck. Was it in the boot of his car? She didn't go to church every Sunday, but mostly it was because they didn't always have interpreters. And the one they did have was too old; her hands shook when she signed, which was totally distracting, and she was always winking at her. Shauna disliked her intently. Maybe Shauna was too mean, and that's why she was being punished. She might deserve everything that had happened and was happening to her, but her baby did not. Her baby was innocent. Pure. He was the only good thing about her. Tears came and, with them, congestion. Her nose always ran like a waterfall when she cried. She wiped the tears with her stupid, long, ugly, ruffled sleeve—seriously, what kind of costume was she wearing?—then with one of the sheets. *Cry later.* She had to do something, she had to focus. She had to figure out how to get out of this mess. But she was tired, so, so tired. It was tempting to just lie down and go to sleep and pray that, when she woke up, it would all be a horrible nightmare.

She stared at the door. Was there anyone on the other side? What would happen if she pounded on it and screamed? Unlike a hearing person, she could not listen for him to come and go. Had he counted on this? She would have to be patient and watch. She could stare at the door until he came. He was coming, wasn't he? Otherwise, why give her food, and bed, and water, and a bucket? How long did he plan on keeping her here? He didn't expect her to give birth in this strange room, did he? *Never.* Rage bubbled up in her again.

Settle. Down. Think. There was a tiny space underneath the door; she'd felt it with her pinky finger. Would she see a shadow when someone stood on the other side? She would find out. Just having a goal, even if it wasn't yet a plan, gave her a boost of adrenaline. There was only one thought keeping her blood pumping and her determination to escape sky-high. And that was imagining the moment when he realized something. When he realized that he had messed with the wrong fucking girl.

She felt a gush of air, and just like that, the door opened. Moth Man was back. He was tall and wearing a long dark robe. He still looked bulky, but she still felt as if that was part of his disguise, for all she saw was robe; there was no making out his arms, his chest, his legs—just layers and layers of robe. The moth mask covered so much of his face she couldn't even guess his age. It took another few seconds to realize he wasn't alone. At his side was a chubby young lad. Was it his son? If he had a child, maybe he was here to help her. But just as her hopes raised, they were cut down. Moth Man shoved the boy into the room. He landed on his knees on the concrete floor.

"Hey!" Shauna said, instinctively moving toward the boy. "Shame on you." She pointed at Moth Man, just in case he had any doubt she was referring to him. It was eerie, not being able to rely on his facial expression for information. Shauna was very, very good at that. Much better than hearing people. He'd taken away one of her key strengths. *He knew her. He knew she was deaf.* The lad was shaking.

"Don't cry, don't cry," she said to the boy. He did not respond; he remained hunched over, curled in on himself. She scooted close, but stopped short of touching him. It wasn't nice to touch people who didn't want to be touched. Once more, she turned to the man. He did not move a muscle. She wanted to flip him off, but she had not learned enough about him yet. She had no idea what he would do to her. She turned back to the boy. "I'm Shauna," she said. "I'm sorry this happened to you too." The boy looked up at her, his eyes wide with terror. He darted over to the blankets and curled into a tiny ball.

Shauna waited for the man to leave, but he was just standing there. She pointed to the boy. "Why?" Once more his lips did not move. "Let him go." He straightened his arm, and in his gloved hand, he held a bag from SuperValue. He tossed it onto the pile of cushions. It yawned open. She could see a vitamin bottle on top, some bottles of water, toilet paper, and sandwiches. Why was the creep just standing there? That's when she realized he was holding something else in his hand. Some kind of syringe—a tube—and poking out of it was a long needle. She hated needles. Had been terrified of them ever since childhood. When hearing kids could be calmed down by whatever the doctor was saying when he flapped his lips, she had always been traumatized. What was that? What was he doing? In two shakes, the man was in front of her.

"No!" Shauna screamed. "No." Her throat burned from the effort. The gloved hand grabbed the back of her hair tight and pulled her head back. His lips were moving through the hole in his mask. His breath smelled of cigarettes. Pain thumped through her head. His eyes were dark, nearly black. Evil eyes. She wished she had something with which to poke those eyes out. She vowed to find something. Next time, she would do it. She would poke his eyes out, grab the boy, and run. He held up the strange syringe. Was he going to drug her again? Was this it? Would she ever wake up? He wasn't going to try and take the baby *now*, was he? He lifted the mask higher, and now she could see his entire mouth. He moved his lips slowly as he brought the needle closer to her. She understood him now, but she wished she didn't.

This is going to hurt.

CHAPTER 16

*B*RIGHT AND EARLY THE NEXT MORNING, LIAM McCARTHY SAT straight in his chair in the interview room at the Dingle Garda Station. He looked as if he hadn't slept, and to be fair, he probably hadn't. He also hadn't touched the bottle of water or cup of coffee that had been set in front of him. Cormac let him sweat it out a bit longer before he and Neely entered and took the seats across from him.

"Do you know why you're here?" Cormac asked.

He bit his lip and nodded. His eyes were red. "Shauna was kidnapped," he said. "And instead of letting me get out there and look for her, you've had me waiting here for hours since last night. Like some kind of criminal." His entire body radiated anger.

Cormac didn't react to it. "Can you take me through your day yesterday?"

He nodded. "I helped set up tents for the Spring Festival in the morning. Ate me lunch from one of the food stalls. Went home. Showered. Took a nap. Got up. Got dressed. Went and saw a veterinarian. Then I was home, waiting for my girlfriend to call, when a guard knocked on me door and asked me to come here."

"What is the name of the veterinarian?" Cormac asked.

"Doctor Dimpna Wilde." He crossed his arms. "I believe you know her, Inspector." Cormac could feel Neely smirking beside him. Dingle was too small of a town. "And why were you at Doctor Wilde's clinic?"

He looked away. "I just had a question for her is all."

"What question?"

"Are you joking me?"

"No, Mr. McCarthy, we are dead serious."

"I just asked her about my neighbors' dog. She's going to have pups, and I'm thinking about adopting one."

"You went all the way to a veterinarian to ask her if you should adopt a dog?" Cormac asked.

Liam frowned. He leaned forward. "Yeah," he said, maintaining eye contact with Cormac. "I did."

"And if we ask her what you talked about, that's exactly what she'll say?" Cormac kept his voice steady.

"I suppose."

"It's either a yes or a no."

"I can't remember every single word we exchanged, but yeah, that's the gist of it, alright."

"And when is the last time you talked to Shauna?"

"I've never talked to Shauna," Liam said.

Cormac stared at him. "Excuse me?"

"She's deaf," Liam said. "We don't *talk*. We *communicate*."

"How do you communicate?"

He sighed. "We text. We write. Sometimes she talks. Sometimes she reads my lips."

"When is the last time you *communicated* with Shauna."

Liam removed his mobile phone from his pocket and thumbed through it. "Half-eight yesterday morning. Told her I was setting up tents. Sent her a picture. She sent me a tongue-out emoji. I asked what she was doing. She said she had a doctor's appointment, then was meeting up with someone from her group, then she was going to the Griffins', then she was coming to see me." He placed his phone on the table. "Read it," he said. "I know you have to investigate me. Do your thing. And then please move on, because I can't stand sitting in here knowing she's out there somewhere with God knows who."

"And that text is the last time you communicated with her?"

He sighed and picked up the phone again. "No. She texted me

again at half-two. She said her friend had stood her up. She was going to wander the festival before going to the Griffins'."

"Who is this friend she was meeting?"

He shrugged. "Friend is the wrong word. She said she and another pregnant woman had received some kind of mysterious email, and they were going to meet up to discuss it."

Cormac was paying attention. "Did you read this email? What was mysterious about it?"

"I have no idea." Liam shook his head. "She was a bit secretive about it. Shauna liked her secrets. I just thought she'd tell me about it later."

"Yesterday, between four and six in the evening, where were you?" Cormac asked.

"Home."

"Is there anyone who can verify that?"

"What do you mean?"

"Between four and six, did anyone see you at home?"

"No."

"How did you find out what happened to Shauna?"

He scoffed. "I should have found out when I was sitting here for hours. But no one would say a word. When they finally realized you weren't coming in to see me and I was allowed to leave, I tried texting Shauna. When I couldn't reach her, I called the Griffins." He bit his lips and curled his fists. "Tell me you know where she is. Tell me you know who did this."

"Do you have any idea who might have done this?" Cormac asked.

"No," Liam said. "But you had better figure it out before I do."

"Should we take that as a threat?" Neely interjected.

"No," Liam said. "You should take that as a promise."

Cormac let it go; hell, most people in Liam's position would feel the same way. "Were you angry that Shauna wanted to give the baby up for adoption?"

He screeched his chair back and stood. "Are you accusing me of doing this?"

"Sit down," Cormac said, "or you'll be thrown into a jail cell."

He remained standing. "You have no idea what I'm going through right now. I love Shauna. I want her back. I want to kill whoever took her."

"Sit. Down."

He glanced at Neely, then finally sat. He crossed his arms and bounced his leg. "I've been thinking about this all night. I hate saying this, but do you think the Griffins are involved? Do you think they set this whole thing up?"

Cormac continued to portray a non-emotional façade. "Why do you ask that?"

"Jane Griffin was starting to get on Shauna's nerves. She was—is—a bit controlling. Was I angry that Shauna wanted to give our baby up?" He shook his head. "No, Inspector. If I was angry at anyone, it was myself."

"Why is that?"

"Because Shauna was right. I've been immature. I don't make much money, and what I do make, I waste at the pubs. Even after I knew she was pregnant, I stayed out all night with the lads. I didn't try hard enough to prove I could be a good dad. I didn't try at all. To be honest, it kind of freaked me out, and by the time I came around to the idea, she had already made up her mind. We didn't plan on having a baby. And if she was the mom and she didn't want to raise a baby, what right did I have to talk her into it?"

"Did Shauna ever accuse you of messing with her birth control?" Cormac could feel Neely lean in. He hadn't had time to tell her everything he'd learned from the Griffins.

"The Griffins told you about that, did they? Are they accusing me? Because I want it on the record that I'm suspicious of them."

"Did Shauna ever accuse you of messing with her birth control?" Cormac asked again.

"Yes, Inspector. She said I switched a couple of pills with candy. That it tasted sweet."

"And did you?"

"No."

"Why do you think she thought that?"

"Someone broke into my town house. *Our* town house. I mean, I own it, but Shauna lived with me, and I love her, so I consider it hers."

"When was this break-in?"

Liam shrugged. "About a month before she found out she was pregnant. I came home, and the door was ajar. Nothing was missing, but I swear things had been moved around."

"What things?"

"Stupid things. The remote for the telly. I always leave it on the stand. It was on me chair. My whiskey had the cap off, and there was less in it than before. And yes, Shauna's birth control was on the bathroom sink, and she usually keeps it in the cabinet above the sink. I just assumed it was her. She swore it wasn't. It definitely wasn't me."

"Why would someone break in just to mess with Shauna's birth control?"

"I have no idea."

"Why don't you take a guess?" Cormac prodded.

"Because it doesn't make sense, alright? I honestly have no idea. Up until now, I still thought it was Shauna. I thought she didn't want to admit that she forgot to shut and lock the door. That she drank my good whiskey—which I don't give a fuck, but she could have put the cap back on. That she forgot to put the remote back on the stand. Like, who cares, right? I see that now. But I was immature. I was a jerk. So I accused her, and she accused me right back." He leaned in. "I'm never going to be like that again. We have to find her. I have to show her that I'm never going to be like that again." He leaned in. "Please," he said, his voice thick with emotion. "I'll do anything. Anything. Please. Bring her back. Bring her back right now."

"What boot size do you wear?" Cormac asked.

"Why?" He narrowed his eyes. "Is there a clue? Did he leave his boot print?"

"Answer the question," Neely said.

"Forty-six," Liam answered.

They didn't have any information back on the boot print, but Cormac jotted it down and treated Liam to a grim expression. He wanted to rattle him. "And what vehicle do you drive?"

Liam crossed his arms. "Should I have a solicitor present?"

"You are within your rights," Cormac said. "Say the word, and we'll stop the interview."

"Fine," Liam said. "I want to stop."

"Not a bother," Cormac said. "It just means more time wasted, more resources going to checking into you, less resources dedicated to finding Shauna."

"I drive a Fiat."

"We'd like to get your prints and a DNA swab," Cormac said. "For elimination purposes." Right now, they had nothing to compare either to, but if something turned up and they had them on hand, it would speed up the process.

"I'll get back to you," Liam said. "After I speak with a solicitor."

"Smart," Cormac said, standing up. "I would do exactly the same thing if I were in your boots."

CHAPTER 17

THE DEMAND TO ATTEND THE PRESS BRIEFING WAS OFF THE CHARTS. IT was not only the media that was hungry for answers, but the panicked public as well. RTE was on-site, and the briefing would be broadcast live to local stations all over Ireland. They were also dealing with the logistics of the storm. The heavy rains and wind had abated for now, but damage had been done. Branches were down, debris littered the streets, and everywhere one looked, there was standing water. They were stretched beyond capacity. Although Cormac knew this press briefing was a high priority, he hoped he could end it sooner rather than later. He needed to focus on finding their missing persons. They chose the largest meeting room in the station, and Cormac had never seen it so jammed. It made him claustrophobic; one wrong shove and they could have a stampede. And so much was riding on how they presented these cases. This was their only chance to try to control the narrative and hopefully contain the public's fears.

And on this point, on what exactly to say and what not to say, Cormac and Neely disagreed slightly. She thought the public should know everything they knew. Pregnant women especially. Cormac thought it was wise to keep pertinent details, ones only the perpetrators would know, to themselves. They also disagreed on whether or not to discuss Cahal Mackey and Flynn Barry. Cormac did not want to supercharge angry residents and turn them loose onto these men. Whether or not Neely liked it, there was no evidence at this stage that pointed to either of them, yet they had plenty of evidence that they had been under such strict surveillance that it couldn't possibly be them.

A podium and microphone were set up on the grounds, as well as tables to distribute missing-persons posters for Dylan and Shauna, and volunteers could sign up to join search parties. Well before they were slated to begin, people began to arrive. The grapevine had been swift and fierce. Everyone wanted to do something about the missing lad and pregnant woman. As long as no one crossed any lines into vigilante territory, Cormac welcomed the help. Guards were currently conducting house-to-house inquiries, and both Dylan's parents and the Griffins were in the station, being prepped on what to say at the briefing. Cormac never thought that pleas directly to kidnappers ever yielded any positive results, but maybe it would help the victims themselves feel less helpless. Helplessness in the face of evil was debilitating. Being a "helper" in times of crisis was a way of taking one's power back.

After the briefing, they'd immediately utilize volunteers to help with the search for their missing persons. They had already issued a Child Rescue Ireland Alert, and tip lines were open. Cormac prayed they would have an identification on the deceased woman from the bog sooner rather than later. They had yet to get ahold of Fiona Sheehan's parents, and they had no evidence yet for a judge to allow the guards into her flat. Guards had gone to her place of work, a touristy pub in town, but Fiona Sheehan had not been in contact with anyone there since she'd taken maternity leave. They were still reaching out to the names they were given as possible close contacts. Somewhere loved ones had to be missing her. Cormac stood at the podium over a sea of faces, people who were understandably on edge. Cormac couldn't help wondering if the perpetrator was standing in this crowd, blending in with everyone else. The very thought sent a charge of electricity through him. Cameras flashed as he began. The press was both a blessing and a curse.

"Good afternoon. I'm Detective Inspector Cormac O'Brien, and we're here today on a somber and urgent mission. We've had a series of disturbing and violent acts, and I'm going to address them in sequential order. Yesterday morning, a witness brought forth a ransom letter that had been sitting in his neighbor's postbox for at least a fortnight. He discovered it when he was retrieving the mail, which was spilling out of the box. The letter named a particular victim and claimed that this person was being held against his or her will. The letter contained a demand for money and gave a time line for when the money needed to be delivered. When this letter was finally retrieved, that time line was well in the past. To date, we have not located the victim mentioned in the letter, nor have we located the victim's family, so we are obliged not to release any names until we know whether or not this person has even been taken."

Murmurs rose, along with the tension in the room. This incident had not yet reached the grapevine. Cormac had debated whether or not to bring it up, but given that he believed all these incidents were related, he felt it was important to be as transparent as possible. "Then, later that same afternoon, a young woman by the name of Shauna Mills was kidnapped by a man in a mask in front of two witnesses. Shauna is eight and a half months pregnant, and she is deaf. Guards will be distributing her photo. She's approximately nineteen years of age, and the witnesses, Jane and David Griffin, are in the process of adopting her baby."

He paused as the crowd absorbed the information. "As we were investigating her disappearance, hours later the guards were alerted to reports that a young lad, Dylan Walsh, ten years of age, had been left alone by the two lads he was with at a nearby peat bog. The two lads who reported their friend missing had also reported seeing something in the bog. They described it as a monster."

Murmurs went through the crowd. They already knew what the boys had seen; gossip in Dingle was swift.

Cormac took a breath. "Upon arriving at the bog, we found Dylan Walsh's bicycle, his inhaler, and a single runner. There we also discovered the remains of an unidentified woman." He paused again and tried to dispel the image of her swollen belly and the jagged knife wound across her neck. The less information they gave out, the better. He didn't even want to mention that she was pregnant, but they had already let that cat out of the bag with

Shauna, and Neely insisted that pregnant women in the area needed to be vigilant. On that point, he firmly agreed. "The deceased woman was also pregnant, and although we do not yet know how many months, she appeared to be close to term." The crowd began to chatter, voices rising in concern. "At this time, we are not revealing any more details about our Jane Doe, and I would ask the press to respect our intentions in regards to what we feel we are able to reveal. The body is currently at the state pathologist's office, and we will release more information when we are able to do so. For now, we are asking for all of your help. Not only do we want parents to keep their children close; we strongly urge any pregnant women and their families and friends to be on alert until we know exactly what or who we are dealing with."

A reporter, a young woman in her early twenties, shot her hand up. Cormac gave her a nod to speak. "Amanda Bailey with the *Dingle Daily News*. I'd like to go back to the first item you mentioned, a ransom note and a demand for money. Is there any chance that the person mentioned in this ransom note is the deceased pregnant woman in the bog?"

Cormac feared that this question would arise. "At this time, I cannot release any information about the person named in the ransom note," he said. "And we do not yet have an identification on the woman found in the bog. But, rest assured, we are working as quickly as possible to identify her and to locate the person named in the ransom letter."

"Do you have reason to believe that the person or persons who kidnapped Dylan Walsh are the ones who kidnapped Shauna Mills?" This came from a male in the front with a goatee and thick glasses.

"We're going to investigate all possibilities," Cormac said. Given that kidnappings were so rare, it was more likely than not that all of these cases were related, but Cormac was not about to present his hunches as fact.

Amanda Bailey piped up again. "Do you have reason to believe there is a threat to pregnant women in general?"

Cormac was prepared for this question. "As of yet, there is no overt threat to anyone else in the community. But we would rather take all precautions now than be sorry later." Agreement rippled through the crowd.

The man in the goatee spoke up again. "What exactly are you asking pregnant women to do? Hide away in their homes?"

"And you are?" Cormac finally asked.

"Aidan Kehoe with the *Dublin Times*." Cormac gave the question a beat; he didn't like the way the man had phrased the question.

Neely, picking up on this, moved over to the podium. "I'm Detective Sergeant Barbara Neely, and we all stand behind this advice—not only for pregnant women but for the parents of children. Do not go out alone. Take a buddy. Keep your eyes open. If you hear or see anything suspicious, call our anonymous tip line. We're going to have our hands full with all of these inquiries. We are enlisting the help of the Tralee Garda Station, and headquarters will be closely involved as well. But even with all hands on deck, we will be busy. Please do your part as citizens. Do not give us anything more to investigate. Watch each other's backs. If you do that and let us do our jobs, we'll do what needs to be done. I promise ye that."

Cormac held his breath, wondering if Neely would go rogue and mention the case from three decades ago. It was another element that eventually the media would pick up on, but he wanted to bide them time. He could only imagine the panic that was going to result from resurrecting the memory of a cult that had terrorized pregnant women in the area twenty-nine years ago. The downside of this tactic, as Neely had reminded him over and over, was that when the correlations to the past came out, it might erode trust in the Gardaí. It was a tightrope, and he was walking it the best he could. The crowd was growing restless, and Cormac already felt as if he was losing them.

Cormac stepped back up to the podium. "Let me tell you exactly how you can be of help. I know the people of this community care, and we want you involved, but let me stress: We want your involvement to be on the periphery. If you see or hear anything that you think could be related to any of these cases, call the tip line. If and when we confirm that the ransom note is legitimate, we will immediately release the name and photo of that victim and ask anyone who has any pertinent information to come forward. For now, if you have had any contact with either Dylan Walsh or Shauna Mills in the days leading up to their kidnappings, we want to know. Even if you passed by them and said 'Hello,' we want to know." He turned to Jane Griffin, who was standing behind him. David had not wanted to speak in front of a crowd. "I'd like to introduce Jane Griffin, one of the witnesses to Shauna Mills's kidnapping. Please quiet down and allow her to speak. Then we will hear from Dylan Walsh's parents, Ava and Joe Walsh."

Cormac and Neely stood by while Jane Griffin pleaded for the kidnapper to release Shauna. She spoke of Shauna's kindness, her rough upbringing, her selfless act of finding the best home she could for her unborn baby. As requested, she did not mention that the mask worn by the perpetrator was a butterfly. A dark, demented one, but a butterfly, nonetheless. Next, Ava Walsh took the podium, but halfway through begging for them to be kind to Dylan, to let them have their sweet lad back, she went off the rails. "Dylan," she said. "If you're listening, Mammy isn't upset about your runners. It's okay if you got them dirty. Daddy and I love you very much. Do whatever the people say, and you're going to be home soon, pet." She was then too choked with tears to continue. Her husband pulled her back, then, to Cormac's surprise, stepped up to the podium. Joe Walsh was a big man, but his tough exterior was crumbling. He trembled in front of the room, then raised a finger.

"I'm speaking directly to the son of a bitch who took me son. You have one chance to bring Dylan back unharmed. One chance. Drop him off wherever you'd like. Somewhere he can run for help. If you touch a single hair on his head, if you harm him in any way, mark me words, you're going to wish you had listened to me. Are you listening? You have one chance. If I do not have me son back *today*, I promise you this. I am going to find you, and I'm going to kill you with me bare hands. And it's not going to be quick, I can promise ye that."

The crowd erupted in cheers. "You won't be alone," a man in the back yelled out. "Release the woman too. Let them both go, or you'll be dealing with the whole lot of us."

"And we won't go easy on ye," another man yelled out. Others confirmed the statement.

Cormac and Neely exchanged a look, and then Neely quickly stepped forward and guided Joe Walsh away from the podium. The meeting had gone pear-shaped fast. Cormac stepped up to the podium. "Although I understand the sentiments expressed, and I know emotions are high, that kind of rhetoric is not helpful." The crowd immediately booed.

"Do your job, then," a man yelled. "Or we'll do it for ye."

"We are doing absolutely everything we can to solve these cases and bring our victims home as quickly and safely as possible." There was no use trying to convince them; the testosterone in the room was palpable. With a pregnant woman and a young lad missing, he had expected no less. "That's all we have for you at this moment, but there are tables set up in the lobby where you can sign up for search parties, and take flyers to post and hand out, as well cards with our tip line number. We will be conducting house-to-house inquiries; expect the guards at your door. You never know when one tiny observation might lead to a big break in a case. We will schedule another briefing as soon as we have any clarification in any of these cases."

Reporters shouted more questions to their backs as Neely and Cormac started to push their way out of the room.

"Are there any similarities in this case to the murder of a pregnant woman in 1994?" Aidan Kehoe shouted, just as they had nearly made their escape. His voice was loud and carried through the crowd. Silence fell as everyone awaited an answer. Pure terror shot through Cormac as he and Neely were forced to return to the podium. He had completely lost control over this briefing. He had completely fucked it up. "Do you remember the case?" the reporter continued. "The woman's name was Alana Graves. She was found with her throat slit, and her baby was cut out of her. Are you familiar with this case? Her mother said she had been in some kind of a cult?"

How was it possible that someone was already making a connection to that case? It seemed highly unlikely unless . . . unless Aidan Kehoe had been tipped off. By whom? One of the guards? It wasn't out of question to imagine one of them going home after their all-night search and repeating all their suspicions to a wife. And then the wife talks to a friend. His eyes slid to Neely standing next to him. It could not be her. Could it? She would never undermine him like this. Would she? Either way, he was not letting her take the podium. He needed to salvage whatever he could of this colossal fuckup of a briefing.

"We will pursue all avenues of inquiry," Cormac said. "But, as of yet, we have no solid evidence on either the murder or the abductions. And I do not wish to see anyone report otherwise," he added.

But Aidan Kehoe wasn't finished. "Is it true that the men suspected of the murders twenty-nine years ago, Cahal Mackey and Flynn Barry, were recently released from prison?"

Rumblings ascended from the crowd, the loudest yet. There was no way Cormac could hold in his suspicions. Later, he was going to have to confront Neely and pray that, if he was wrong, his question didn't destroy their friendship. Because he did consider her not just a colleague but a friend.

"We are aware of this past case from three decades ago," Cormac simply said. There was no stuffing this genie back in the bottle. "But let me repeat. We have no firm leads. No current suspects. And to report otherwise would be negligent."

"Is it also true that the men are here and working at the—"

"Enough," Neely said, shoving Cormac aside, despite his conviction that he would keep her out of it. "Shut your mouth."

"Excuse me?" Aidan said, clearly enraged. "I'm doing my job, and I will not shut me mouth."

Hell. Neely knew better. Cormac should have insisted she go home. He had to physically move her aside. "I understand you're doing your job," Cormac said. "And we'll have our media rep keep you in the loop with developments as it's safe to do so. I'm sure you don't intend to start trouble and redirect our resources away from finding a young pregnant woman and a lad ten years of age, do you, Mr. Kehoe?"

He stared at the reporter, hoping to drive his warning home. The reporter stared back. "If I don't report it, someone else will."

One thing was apparent. These men could no longer work at the harbor. Now they would have to use resources to protect them. Protect men who could be their kidnappers and murderers. Cormac could not imagine a worse scenario. He could feel his own temper coming to a boiling point.

"Let me assure everyone that we are following every single lead and suspect. And I repeat: Stand back, and let us do our jobs." He was nearly pleading. It wouldn't be long before others knew where these men were living and where they were working. And there was nothing stopping Kehoe from reporting it. The last thing they needed was vigilantes. And once they removed Cahal Mackey and Flynn Barry from their work-release program, they were going to have two unemployed criminals—a much more dangerous situation than keeping them busy at the harbor, keeping them where they could watch every move they made. Kehoe had already endangered his cases. "That's all the questions for today," Cormac said.

"Don't you think these cases are related?" Aidan persisted. "Or is it a coincidence that weeks after an alleged cult leader was released, we have a dead pregnant woman?"

Against his better judgement, Cormac returned to the podium. "We don't act on coincidences or speculations, Mr. Kehoe. I've just finished telling you that we're following every lead, and we need you not to be rash." Neely elbowed him out of the way. Her face reflected the anger he felt.

"I promise ye we're going to find Dylan Walsh and Shauna Mills, and I promise ye we are going to catch the person or persons responsible." *Jesus.* Cormac gently took her arm and pulled her away, as the crowd began to buzz. As they ducked back into the hall, a feeling of foreboding seized Cormac. He knew in his bones that if he was alive twenty years from now, he'd still be traumatized by this case. As Neely was now. But she was out of control, and he was going to have to rein her in.

"You *promise* them?" Cormac said the minute they stepped into his office and he closed the door. "You can't make promises."

Neely's face portrayed no shame. "These are going to be the last two cases I ever work," she said. "After this, I'm retiring. But I do promise: We're going to stop this. We're going to stop the next pregnant woman from losing her baby and her life. Before I go, I'm getting this bastard, and the only happy ending I will accept is him six feet under."

"Tell me you didn't tip Aiden Kehoe off about the case from thirty years ago."

"Twenty-nine years and sixteen days ago," she said.

"That's not an answer."

"I don't think you really want the answer. Do you?"

Neely's face was uncharacteristically red. Cormac gave it a beat. She was right. He didn't want the answer. He'd probably have to drop her from the investigation. And he could only imagine what she'd do if she was no longer required to conduct herself lawfully. He could already feel these cases spinning way out of his control, and it terrified him. "We're going to do everything we can," he said. "And I mean everything. But do me a favor. No more public promises."

Neely stared at him for a long time. "I can't promise that," she said. "And I *won't*."

CHAPTER 18

*D*IMPNA STOOD IN THE RECEPTION AREA OF HER CLINIC, GLUED TO the telly in the corner, along with Patrick and Niamh and two folks in the waiting room, one with an obese cat, the other with a hyperactive Jack Russell terrier. Neither case was an emergency, and everyone understood the need to watch the briefing. It had disturbed Dimpna to her core. Was Shauna Mills the deaf woman she had literally run into at the Spring Festival? The briefing was now coming to an end, and finally the screen flashed a pair of photos: one of poor Dylan Walsh, looking a bit tidier than when she had seen him—no doubt this was a school photo that he'd been forced to dress up for—and on the right-hand side was a close-up of Shauna Mills. It was them. That sweet, sweet grandson of Peg Dooley and the woman she had bumped into at the festival. Dimpna cried out.

"What's the matter?" Niamh asked, sounding just as panicked in advance.

"Dylan was at Peg Dooley's helping us with the lambing—a wee dote he was—and Shauna is the woman I crashed into at the Spring Festival." How could this be happening? Dimpna fervently wished this was nothing but a nightmare. That she'd wake up and none of it would be true.

"The one whose ice cream you spilled all over her, like?" Niamh asked.

Dimpna nodded; her throat felt as if it was closing. A moment in time frozen. Before she was taken. And Shauna's bad luck had started with Dimpna.

"Hey, hey," Patrick said, putting his arm around her. For a second, Dimpna wondered why, and then she realized that tears were rolling down her cheeks.

"The piece of paper," she said, gently pulling away from Patrick. "Oh my God." Where had she put it? Where was the jacket she'd worn to the festival? Dimpna was looking at her coat hanger in the hall near the reception area, and it was not there. She had not moved it. "Do either of you know what happened to my jacket?" She pointed at the hanger. "My black jacket? I wore it to the festival?"

Niamh frowned as she stared at it. "I remember seeing it after you came back," she said. "But I don't know what happened to it."

The last time she'd seen the email exchange had been when she took Milly back to the Griffins. She'd considered throwing it away and then changed her mind. Had she dropped it? Discovering the Griffins tied to their chairs had knocked everything else out of her head. She'd either dropped it, or someone had taken it from this very clinic. "Patrick?" Dimpna asked. "Have you seen a black jacket?"

"I'm sorry, I don't remember seeing it at all," he said. "What's wrong?"

"I just . . . need something from the pocket."

"Someone might have accidentally taken your jacket home by mistake," Niamh said. "An honest mistake."

"Of course," Dimpna said. "Would you mind calling the clients I've had since it was hanging there? There was a piece of paper with an email exchange in the pocket."

"Of course," Niamh said.

"Is this it?" the woman with the obese cat piped up. She pointed to the far corner of the clinic, where indeed something black was balled up, and lying on top of it was the cat. Dimpna hurried over. It was her jacket. When she reached for it, the cat hissed.

"Mable!" the owner chastised. "Be nice."

Mable hissed again. "Do you mind?" Dimpna said.

The owner glanced at Mable as if she too were afraid to touch her. She reached down, and Mable hissed again.

Dimpna sighed, wondering whether or not she should fetch heavy gloves, when she smelled tuna. She turned to find Niamh with a freshly opened can that she soon set down on the floor. Mable immediately bounded off the jacket and stuck her face in the can without a single hint of table manners.

The owner pointed. "I thought she was supposed to be on a diet."

"Desperate times," Niamh said with a grin. "I guess it's her lucky day."

"Thank you," Dimpna said.

Niamh grinned. "Not a bother."

Dimpna grabbed the jacket and stuck her hand in one of the pockets. *Empty.* She searched the other one. It too was empty. "It can't be," she said. "It was here." Unless Mable ate it, which she doubted, although anything was possible. She stared at the corner, then began looking under all the seats in the waiting room. The Jack Russell hopped off his owner's lap and followed her around, sniffing. "Patrick, can you help me search the rubbish bins?" They'd stuck their hands in worse.

"Not a bother," Patrick said.

"I'll help too," Niamh said. The three of them searched every bin in the clinic, and then Dimpna searched her flat upstairs, this time followed around by her three dogs and a cat. Nothing. It was gone. Had someone taken it? *Impossible.* No one knew what she had. How could they? She hadn't even known. Dimpna was going to have to tell Cormac about this, and then break the news that it was missing. She was just about to ask Patrick if he could handle the remaining clients when he beat her to it.

"Go on, so," he said. "I've got this."

"Thank you. I'll only be an hour or so. I'm going to talk to Cormac and then sign up for a search party."

"Can you sign me up as well?" Patrick asked.

"And me?" Niamh said. "I'll text you our schedules. You can book me for any time slot I'm not working."

"Ditto for me," Patrick said.

"Of course." Dimpna loved her staff fiercely, and their unwavering kindness made her want to cry even more. She exited the clinic into the front courtyard and was just about to head for her VW bus when she saw a familiar figure striding into the courtyard. Her father. Even from a distance, Dimpna could tell that he was having a better day. His walk had purpose. It gave her heart a squeeze. He was holding a newspaper, and as he entered the courtyard, he made eye contact with her. He wasn't supposed to walk about by himself; they had hired a day nurse, but he must have given her the slip.

"Da," she said. "I'm on me way out. What's the story?" His timing couldn't have been worse, and she had no idea if he even recognized her.

He held up this morning's newspaper: PREGNANT WOMAN FOUND DEAD IN BOG.

On it was a photo of the bog. Although thankfully there was no photo of any person in the image, it still gave Dimpna the chills. After that circus of a press conference, she could only imagine tomorrow's headlines. "This could have been you," her father shouted, shaking the newspaper. "We have to get you out of Dingle."

He was back in the past again. What a frustrating disease. Before she could figure out what to do with her father so she could continue to the station, another familiar figure was approaching the courtyard, and she lit up when she saw it was Ben.

"Pappy," he said. "There you are." Eamon did not turn around or even show any signs that he knew Ben was there. Ben entered the courtyard, shaking his head. "Sorry, Mam. I stopped by to see if he wanted to go for a walk-about. He wanted to buy a newspaper. I was paying for it, and when I turned around, he was gone." He studied Eamon. "You're fast, old man."

Eamon held up the newspaper. "It's not safe," he said. "Not for you or the baby."

"He's been pretty worked up about the woman they found in the bog," Ben said. "Awful business altogether."

Dimpna looked at her grown son, and a slideshow of him as a little boy played in her mind. She couldn't imagine her life if he had never been born, and she couldn't imagine her sorrow and rage if someone had done to her what had been done to those women. She started crying again, then grabbed Ben's arm and pulled him in for a hug.

"Sorry, Mam," he said as he rubbed her back. "Sometimes I forget how attuned to the world you are."

Dimpna got ahold of herself and dried her eyes. She made eye contact with her handsome son. "You're the best thing that ever happened to me. And I love you to the moon and back."

"Wait. Could you say that again for TikTok?" Ben took out his phone. "Do you think you can bring the tears back?"

Before she could think of how to politely decline, when what she really wanted to was throw his phone over the stone wall that surrounded their courtyard, her father came between them. "Do you see now?" Eamon said, towering over Dimpna. "Did you see why you had to go?" Memories assaulted Dimpna. Leaving Dingle pregnant at eighteen years of age, a baby conceived from an assault. She glanced at Ben. Empathy shone in his eyes, as if he knew where her thoughts were going. She'd always made every effort not to let him know how he was conceived; she'd wanted to save him from that. It all blew up a few years ago, and now he knew. Everyone knew. Small towns soaked in secrets until they became part of the scenery.

She'd wanted to leave Dingle back then; there had been no argument from her. But suddenly she remembered how dead-set her father had been that she leave straightaway. At the time, she thought he was embarrassed by her, by the ugly truth of it all. She hadn't learned about pregnant women going missing until she was in Dublin, and she had so much on her mind, a baby on the way, a new life to figure out, that quite frankly she hadn't paid much attention to the larger world around her. But now she wondered. Were rumors of this cult luring pregnant women into their web part of the reason why her father had been so frantic for her to leave? It had felt a little like rejection back then, for even if she wanted to go, she kept waiting for him to ask her to stay.

She reached out to touch her father, but he flinched and backed away. She tried not to take it personally, but the pain bubbled up. It was surreal to miss the man who was right in front of her. "Thank you," she said. "You kept me safe."

"Can you say that again, but a little louder?" Ben asked with his phone aimed at them.

"No," Dimpna said.

Eamon frowned, and he glanced at the paper, which was now in Dimpna's hands. "Whatever you're selling, I'm not buying," he said. Then he headed for the clinic.

"Da," she said, throwing a desperate look at Ben. "There's no need to go inside." The last time he'd barged into the clinic, Dimpna had been in the middle of surgery. He'd burst through the door with a haggard Niamh running after him shouting, "I'm so sorry, I couldn't stop him."

"Eamon Wilde," a female voice said. Dimpna turned to see her mother, Maeve. It was as if the Universe had summoned her entire little family to the courtyard; all they were missing was Donnecha. Given that her mother mainly lived in a caravan in the field adjacent to the clinic, her presence wasn't much of a stretch. Her father stopped, turned, and looked at his wife. Today she was dressed in a rose-colored pantsuit with a crisp white blouse and white heels. Her black hair (meticulously updated by a colorist) was piled on top of her head. Her makeup looked recently applied. She was the epitome of an aging actress, and even though the town of Dingle was her only stage, she never failed to find her mark. "You're looking well today, luv," she said. Then she turned her gaze on Dimpna and squinted as if Dimpna had been up to no good and Maeve Wilde was on to her. *What now?*

"We only treat animals," Eamon said, giving his somewhat estranged wife the once-over. "You'll need to find a human doctor."

Dimpna couldn't help but laugh. "Are you not human, Da?" she couldn't help but say. The newspaper in her hand was snatched away, and she turned to find her Mam ripping it up.

"Evil is all around us," she said. "And it doesn't intend on leaving anytime soon."

"I take it you watched the press briefing," Dimpna said.

"What press briefing?" Maeve asked.

"And this, my dear followers, is my psychic grandmother." Ben turned his phone to Maeve. She looked startled for a moment, but quickly recovered.

She struck a pose, right foot out, hand on her hip, head tossed back. "I wouldn't say I'm psychic," she said. "But I am tuned into higher vibrations."

"Perfect," Ben said. "Perfect on one take."

"If that had been me planning to make a living off TikTok, the two of you would have been frothing at the mouth," Dimpna said.

"And yet they're fully supportive," Ben replied. "Unlike some people."

"You can do anything you set your mind to," Dimpna said. "You could be a filmmaker."

"I already am," Ben said. "I'm just doing it my way."

Now that the camera was off her, Maeve narrowed her eyes and focused on Dimpna. "Why does this recent trouble involve you? For once, could this not involve you?"

Dimpna felt the hot shame of someone who had been caught doing something wrong, only she had done nothing wrong. "What are you on about, Mam?" Dimpna shook her head. "It doesn't involve me." *For once.*

Maeve put her hands on her hips. "Who have you been around who's pregnant?"

Shauna Mills. Orla. At times, her mother's abilities freaked Dimpna out. This was one of those times. She didn't need this now. "Why are you asking?"

"She's not safe." Maeve shivered as she wrapped her arms around herself. "I feel trapped. And cold. Is the baby cold?"

"Mam?" Dimpna pleaded. Maeve Wilde was deeply in touch with her supernatural side. Appropriate for a tarot card reader. Dimpna wasn't exactly a believer, but she had to admit there were times her mother knew things that she couldn't possibly know. Sometimes Dimpna was in absolute awe of her. She did readings in her caravan, and because she had a stellar (if not spooky) reputation, she made quite a good living at it. But there were other times, like now, that Dimpna wished she wouldn't do this. Couldn't she see they had their hands full with Eamon, not to mention everything else that was going on?

"I asked you a question," Maeve said. "Who have you been around who's pregnant?"

Dimpna pointed to the newspaper shreds that were now littering her courtyard. Her parents were like tornadoes, sweeping in and destroying the status quo. "I ran into the missing pregnant woman at the Spring Festival. I didn't realize she was the kidnapped woman until they showed her photo at the press briefing." She hesitated. "And Sheila Maguire's cousin Orla is in town. She's pregnant as well." There was no use hiding things from her mother.

"Orla," Maeve said. "Is she married?"

"Yes." Dimpna gritted her teeth. Her mother could just be guessing.

"I need to meet with Orla," Maeve said. "Tell her to come see me."

Dimpna shook her head. "I'm not going to do that."

"You will do it. Whether she wants to come see me or not will be up to her. But you will tell her. Do you know how to get in touch with her?" Dimpna bit her lip and looked away. "I thought so," Maeve said. "Now. That's settled."

There was no point in arguing. "I'm on me way to sign up for the search for Dylan Walsh," Dimpna said. She couldn't stop thinking of him. They had to find him.

"I'll be signing up as well. As soon as I get this one home safe," Ben said, nodding toward Eamon.

"He can stay with me," Maeve said. She took his arm and headed out of the courtyard. "Not safe," she called behind her. "They're running out of time."

"Who is they?" Dimpna shouted after her. She was starting to think her mother *had* watched the press briefing. "And what am I to do about it?" Her phone rang. *Sheila. Again.* When she wanted something, she was relentless.

"I want to go home," her father shouted as he headed across the field with her mother. "I want to go home! I just don't know where that is."

"Hey, Sheila," Dimpna answered. "Ben and I are on our way to sign up for the search parties. Can we chat later?" Dimpna also needed to call Cormac about the email exchange, then tell him she hadn't read it, then tell him it was missing. Maybe they could search Shauna's computer; she had to have printed it and carried it with her for a reason.

But she hadn't seemed interested in it when Dimpna tried to give it back to her . . . had something happened between printing it out and arriving at the festival that changed her mind?

"My father is asking for you." Sheila had that tone. The tone that said, you are not going to ignore me. "He specifically wants to see you."

Dimpna took a breath. "Do you know why?" She couldn't think of a single reason why Danny Maguire would want to talk to her.

"He has some kind of envelope he says is for you. He won't let me look at it."

"Why don't you tell him you'll make sure I get it?"

"Dimpna Wilde. Me father is on his death bed, and he's insisting on seeing you. Now. When can I expect you?"

CHAPTER 19

SHAUNA'S LEFT THIGH WAS BURNING FROM THE HOT NEEDLE THAT had pierced her skin. Tattoos. Ironic. She had always wanted a tattoo, but she never imagined she'd have not just one but two forced on her. She didn't know it would hurt so much. She prayed the baby couldn't sense or feel her pain. When he was finished, Moth Man had placed a thin film over it, patted her on the head, and left the room. A butterfly on top of a sheep. The butterfly was blue, edged in black, with flecks of green and gold. Had she chosen it herself, she would have thought it was pretty. The face and tail of a woolly sheep peeked out from underneath. Bizarre. It filled her with a rage she'd never known before. She'd been called a lot of things in her life: *Dummy. Slow. Retarded. Mute. Deaf and dumb . . .* the list probably went on; she just hadn't been able to lip-read all the insults. A lifetime of oppression had formed a volcanic-like rage inside her, one she'd spent her life trying to tame. But now she needed her rage. Her baby and that kid were getting out of here alive, no matter what it took. That was her new purpose.

She envisioned the volcano inside her erupting and coating everything in sight with lava. *He marked her.* Like she was his property. Patted her on the head like she was a household pet. *Property.* A sheep. A butterfly. Why? Did this mean he was going to let her live? She didn't think so. In fact, she knew with every fiber of her being that, after the baby was born, he planned on killing her. He had also brought into the room a short, white silk robe. There was a single hook in the wall that she hadn't noticed before. He hung the robe on the hook. "For later," he said. "Don't touch."

Like she wanted to touch anything he'd had his hands on. Like she wanted to wear that stupid robe. But it rattled her. She was wearing long dresses that covered nearly every part of her. They were maternity dresses too; someone had specifically made these for pregnant women who apparently wanted to pretend it was two hundred years ago. The robe was so short she wouldn't have worn anything like it either. Extremes. Everything was to the extreme. It didn't make sense. He didn't make sense. Maybe he was just crazy. A mad man. That was the most frightening possibility. How did one reason with a mad man?

She needed to see him without the mask. She wanted to rip it off, and whenever he came in the room, it took everything she had not to attack him. She would lose, she knew it, but maybe it would be worth it to get this over with. But there was her onboard passenger to think about. He was innocent, just along for the ride. She would not let this man intimidate her into hurting the baby. He had wonderful parents and a wonderful life waiting for him. It was painful to think about the Griffins, and even more painful to think about Liam. What were they going through? Did they know that she had nothing to do with this?

And what about the kid? His chest was moving fast, as if he was struggling to breathe. He still wouldn't let her come near him, although while she was enduring the pain of the tattoo, she looked up to find him staring at her. He waved. She waved back. He pointed at her tattoo. *Sorry.* She pointed at him. "I'm sorry." She pointed at the door. "Bad man."

She tossed him a bottle of water and half a sandwich, then pointed to the bucket. His mouth dropped open in horror. She mimed shutting her eyes, letting him know she would give him privacy. "I'm deaf," she said. "Shauna." She pointed at the door. "Bad man." *Moth Man.*

He pointed to his chest. His mouth moved. She had to move closer. What was he saying? *I hate her?* It looked like *I hate her.* He pointed to chest again. *I hate her. I hate her.*

"I hate her," she said. He shook his head no. Then mimicked

putting something over his nose and mouth. It took a minute before she understood him, and then her rage turned to fear. "Inhaler?" He nodded, his head bobbing up and down, his face red.

Shauna was at the door in a flash, pounding on it. "Help! Help! Help!" This time she wanted him to be on the other side. "Help. Inhaler. Inhaler. Inhaler." She had no idea if he could understand her, if anyone out there could. "Help!"

She felt the door jerk, and she stepped back. It opened, and the man stuck his head in, his mask askew. His mouth moved, and it was obvious he was yelling at her.

She pointed to the boy. "Inhaler." He frowned and glanced at the boy. "Breathe. Can't breathe." She was so angry, yelling back now. It was bad enough that he'd taken her, but to take this poor lad. It made her want to kill the man. She would have lunged for him if she hadn't been carrying her son.

He uttered another word, and this one she could lip-read: *Fuck.* He didn't know the kid needed an inhaler. Like her, the lad was a stranger to him. He said something to the boy, moved closer to him, stood over him, talking. Then he left. Shauna scuttled over to the lad. "Hey," she said. "Hey."

He lifted his head. Panic covered his face as he struggled to breathe. The man was getting him an inhaler, wasn't he? Shauna had learned breathing techniques from her childbirth classes. The lad was slouched over. She mimed sitting up straight until he finally copied her. His lips were quivering, his eyes large and wet. The poor thing was terrified. She needed to make him feel better. It gave her a purpose. She pointed at Dylan, then herself, as she started going through the breathing exercises. She didn't know if she was doing the right thing, but maybe if she could get him to calm down a little, his breathing would steady. Given that she did not know where they were, she had no idea how long it would take for the man to return. At least he was looking at her, his eyes large with fright, dried tear stains down his cheeks. "Count," she said, taking a deep breath, using her hands like a conductor. "One . . ."

It took him until the count of five to join in. By the count of ten, they stopped. He seemed a little better.

"What's your name?" she asked, enunciating carefully.

"Dylan," he said. It took her five tries to get it.

Shauna began spelling his name in Irish Sign Language. He perked up, and it didn't take long before he was imitating her.

"Good job," she said. "Smart lad."

He smiled, then pointed at the door. This time she could lip-read him easily. "Why?" he asked. "Why?"

The magic question. One she intended to figure out. His eyes started to well again.

"Sky," she said, pointing up. "Do you like the sky?"

He looked at the dark ceiling and frowned. He said something about not being able to see it.

"Imagine," she said. "Is it blue? Gray? Clouds?"

"Dark clouds," he said making an angry face. "Mad."

"Mad sky," she said. "Do you see faces?"

He grabbed her hands. "Sky?" He wanted to know the sign. It was working; she was distracting him, and his breathing had slowed down. In that moment, she had nothing in her mind other than to keep him as calm as possible. They had all the time in the world. "I teach you ISL," she said. "Irish Sign Language. And you tell me what you see in the sky."

Cormac met with Paul Byrne under the command tent by the bog. He wanted any background he could get on Paul's experience with the case, but there was no time to stop what he was doing. He was grateful Paul had agreed to come to him.

"How can I help?" Paul's tone was brisk, all business. That suited Cormac just fine.

"To be honest, I don't know if you can. But I need everything you remember about that case nearly twenty-nine years ago. Cahal Mackey."

"I was new on the force, and it was an all-hands-on-deck situation. I was tasked with getting to know as much about Cahal's personal life as I could find."

"And?"

"Orphaned. Grew up in a boys' home, one focused on troubled lads." No surprise there. "He's wicked smart, but didn't present that way."

"How do you mean?"

"He looks like he's been living in the woods. Wild thing. At first, I didn't even know if he spoke English." Cormac nodded and jotted down a few notes. "From what our witness said back then, he purported to be religious. Witnesses said he'd go on tangents about the need to create new ways of living, a pure society or some shite."

"Neely thinks he's at it again," Cormac said. "What do you think?"

"He's just out of prison, and we have a murdered pregnant woman," Paul said. "I think it's a safe assumption."

"Yet her baby was not taken," Cormac said. "And she's dressed in a mini satin robe."

"But her throat is slit, just like Alana Graves."

Alana Graves. The woman found at the base of Mount Brandon with her baby cut out of her. Since hearing the story, he'd been able to pull up the cold-case file. She'd been a beautiful young woman about to become a mother. Her entire life ahead of her. If these cases were connected, Cormac wanted justice for all of them. "I see the similarities," Cormac said. "But there are major deviations in the pattern." And the heart of this case, he believed, centered around those deviations. He now believed he was dealing with a copycat. One who was trying to send a very clear message. He just did not know what that message was. "Our Jane Doe had a butterfly tattoo on her left thigh. Underneath it was a tattoo of a sheep."

Paul frowned. "Our cult survivor has a tattoo of a sheep on her left thigh."

"Exactly. Someone is referencing the past, then imposing a different future on it." Cormac knew he was making some leaps, but he wanted to see what Paul thought.

Paul stroked his chin. "He's been in jail a long time now. He's had time to think about how he would alter the pattern."

"Why?" Patterns were a detective's best friend. Patterns revealed the people underneath. The habits they could not, or would not, change.

"He's wicked smart," Paul said. "I think he's playing a game. Throwing a grenade into this case so that you can't see what he's really up to." Paul glanced away. "I'd say it's working."

Inwardly, Cormac bristled. But that was just ego. He needed to put that aside. Was it possible? Was he doing just what this Cahal Mackey wanted him to do? Cormac gazed out at the bog. "He chose this place. Why did he choose this place?"

"He's a showman," Paul said. "He likes the desolate atmosphere."

"One more hitch to the theory that it's him," Cormac said. "I've learned that Cahal Mackey and his cohort Flynn Barry have had eyes on them ever since they were released from prison. They signed onto a transition program. They're in government-run flats with arranged working assignments at the harbor. They voluntarily agreed to this program *knowing* that their movements were being watched." He shook his head. "They've been out for less than a month. Why would they finally get out, agree to a supervision program, then somehow manage to murder another pregnant woman and kidnap two others?" Neely was convinced this was them, but Cormac was not. "I think someone else is doing this and using their release as the grenade. I think the perpetrator wants us chasing these two men."

"Cahal Mackey is a master manipulator," Paul said. "Like most cult leaders. He may have someone else doing the dirty work. But make no mistake—he's behind this."

Cormac took in the opinion, but did not reply. There was no use arguing. He was already going to have his hands full convincing Neely to look elsewhere. "If they were selling babies, why didn't you find a money trail?" He'd seen the men's financial records from twenty-nine years ago. There was no large influx of cash.

"We only have Erin Tanner's word that more than one baby had been successfully taken," Paul said. "According to her, four babies in total. I don't know how they funneled the money. But you're right to try and trace it."

"I'm not convinced it's them," Cormac said. "But I'll be paying both men a visit sooner rather than later." Erin Tanner was also high on his list to visit. Who else but a former cult member could give him insight into what might be going on. "Any advice for me?" He didn't really want it, but Neely had asked him to talk to Paul, and he was giving it his best shot.

"Play to Cahal Mackey's ego, and don't let him get under your skin."

Cormac groaned. That wasn't in his nature.

Paul slapped him on the back. "I don't envy you," he said. "Get him talking about society and the modern world. Stoke the fire. Let him preach from the pulpit. Because when you see his real personality emerge? You won't have any doubt that it's him."

Paul Byrne was definitely convinced. Just like Neely. "And then?"

"And then?" Paul raised his eyebrow, then shook his head. "Then do what I couldn't twenty-nine years ago."

Paul started to walk away. "And what's that?" Cormac shouted after him.

Paul answered without turning around. "Get the narcissistic, evil son of a bitch to confess."

CHAPTER 20

Although the town house Shauna shared with Liam McCarthy was small, she seemed to keep most of her possessions in a guest bedroom. Liam said they had shared a bed until recently, when she'd wanted her own space due to restless sleep. He also admitted that she didn't like when he came home late from the pubs. Even if he'd only had a few pints, the very smell of ale on him could make her ill. Nearly everything at this stage of her pregnancy bothered her. Cormac and Neely stood inside the room, trying to get a feel for the young woman. The room was sparse, nothing more than a bed, two night tables, and a desk, but on the desk sat her laptop. It was open and plugged in, the screensaver flashing a spiral of colors against a black background. "It's here," he said. "Let's hope tech can get into it and figure out why she was carrying around a printout of an email." Liam had insisted he did not know her password.

"Or maybe Dimpna Wilde will figure out what she did with it."

It felt a little bit like Neely was dangling bait. She was on edge, which was understandable, but Cormac hated the wedge this case was already driving between them. "If you picked a piece of paper off the ground, you wouldn't consider it important either, and you know it." It wasn't fair to blame Dimpna for what happened after.

"It's too bad she didn't inherit her mother's 'psychic abilities.'"

"If you believe in Maeve Wilde's abilities, we can have her in for a reading," Cormac shot back. Neely grunted, and Cormac turned his attention back on the room before the tension heated up any further and they got in a row. Littered around the laptop were personal items. Chapstick. Bracelets. Magazines. Scissors. Tape. The wall behind the desk was covered with photos of clouds and the sky cut from magazines. He took a minute to study it. There was something beautiful about it.

"Creative," Neely said.

"She apparently liked clouds," Cormac said. "*Likes* clouds," he corrected.

Clothes were draped over chairs, in drawers, in the closet. Neely put on gloves and handed Cormac a pair. He followed suit. "Let's get this laptop to the team sooner rather than later, shall we?"

Cormac nodded, as he touched the mousepad on the laptop, hoping it wasn't password protected. But, of course, it was. They quickly gathered everything they could, including a few articles of clothing for the sniffer dogs. The motive for kidnapping Shauna was clear. Someone wanted her baby. But why the hell did they take Dylan? If it was for a ransom, the kidnapper would have been in touch by now. Given the position of the remaining footprints at the bog, the captor had come up from behind. The perpetrator's car had been hidden inside the woods by the closest road. Were they dealing with a pedophile? That was one of his worst-case scenarios, but it didn't fit with the reason for kidnapping Shauna. He couldn't help thinking . . . find the motive, find the man.

"What's this?" Neely pointed to a sliver of paper underneath Shauna's desk chair. She picked it up. "FiFoFum," she said. "That's odd."

"What?" Cormac looked over her shoulder, convinced she was messing with him. "That is odd. Fee Fi Fo Fum," he said. "I smell the blood of an Englishman."

"'Be he alive, or be he dead,'" Neely said.

"'I'll grind his bones to make me bread,'" Cormac finished.

"It's missing the 'Fee,'" Neely pointed out.

"Unless she knew something was wrong when she wrote this and is trying to tell us it's an Englishman who's behind this, I have no clue what that's about."

Neely sighed and stuck it in an evidence bag. "Story of me life."

When they were finished with the room, Cormac stopped to once again study her magazine cutouts. Spliced together, different photos of mismatched clouds, conflicting shades of blues and grays. She was artistic. He prayed she was alive. And he hoped that, wherever she was, she could see the sky.

"Wherever she went, she wasn't planning on being gone long," Neely said as she stared at her closet.

"She chose the Griffins as parents," Cormac said. "Maybe we need to see who else was in the running."

"You think prospective adoptive parents would do this?" Neely shook her head. "I'm not buying what you're selling."

"You know as well as I do that we have to investigate all possibilities, even if it's simply for the purpose of elimination." He tried not to sound snippy, but he knew he had only half-succeeded.

"I'm sure they all underwent extensive background checks. I hardly see them jeopardizing future chances of adopting." She turned her back to them. "Besides. We know who's behind this."

"Neely," he said. "We have to stay open to all possibilities."

"You're open enough for the both of us."

"Right," he said. "So this is how it's going to be?"

She stared at him. "I'm telling you. It's them. We just have to find proof."

He had worked several cases with Neely since his move to the peninsula. This was the first time he felt he was working one all alone. They had bagged everything they needed. "Whoever took her will need supplies," he said. "Baby things."

"True," Neely said. "How does that help us?"

"We could pull CCTV near any shops that sell such items, ask if anyone's recently stocked up on baby items."

"I think that's a waste of our time."

Everything felt like a waste of their time. "It might be less of a waste of time if Shauna and Dylan are being held together." He began to pace.

"How so?"

"We look for anyone who's bought an inhaler, maybe something for a young lad, along with anything related to pregnancy or having a baby."

"You think the kidnappers are waiting for the baby to be born?"

Cormac nodded. "Don't you? There's been no phone call, no ransom demand."

"That would explain why they kidnapped Shauna. But why kill the pregnant woman in the bog? And why take Dylan?"

"I've been wondering the same thing but can't come up with an answer. As far as our Jane Doe in the bog, I'm hoping the state pathologist will be able to shed some light on it."

"What are you thinking?"

"Maybe she found out something about the baby's health. Maybe there was a reason these vile men felt they could not get money for her baby."

Neely was listening intently. "Cahal Mackey and Flynn Barry," she said. "I wish I could beat the answers out of them."

He sighed. Here they were again, full circle. He just didn't think they should focus all of their attention on them. Guards had been watching them, and they had not varied their comings and goings whatsoever. Cormac walked over and stared at Shauna's collage of the sky. "If we are dealing with this same so-called cult, their first goal was to create some kind of utopia, was it not?"

Neely nodded. "We came to believe that's just the sales pitch they gave the women."

"I need to meet this Erin Tanner. Let's see if we can get her to open up before it's too late." Cormac took a deep breath. "I can't help thinking we're racing against the clock. If we don't find Shauna Mills before she gives birth . . ."

"Whatever that clock is, shorten it," Neely said.

"I don't follow."

"She has to be under a great deal of stress. It could bring on an earlier labor."

Fantastic.

"And Dylan?" Neely asked. "Why do you think they've taken him?" They had discussed this a number of times, but until they knew for sure, they would keep bringing it up, bouncing ideas off one another.

"At first, I thought maybe he was in the wrong place, but he was in the very place the man in the pea cap told him to go. So that means that either we'll get a ransom soon or they have other plans for him. What those plans are? I have no idea."

"No hits yet on the man in the flat cap?"

Cormac shook his head. "We've talked to all shopkeepers and festival organizers. No one remembers him. We're still sorting through CCTV and photos we've requested from the public." They'd sent out a plea for anyone who had photographs, especially of the man in the pea cap or of Shauna, to send them in.

Neely headed out of the room. Cormac stayed for a moment staring at the collage of the sky. "We're coming," he said to the wall. "Hang tight. We're coming." He understood now why Neely had been so adamant that they were going to solve this case. Because if they didn't, it was going to haunt him, steal a piece of his soul. He was going to pay a visit to Cahal Mackey and Flynn Barry very soon. They were expecting it, and Cormac wanted to let them stew. The only finding the state pathologist had confirmed thus far was that the tattoos on Fiona were postmortem. Some sick bastard tattooed her corpse. Guards had canvassed the property that was believed to be the location of their former commune, but there were no signs that anyone had been there in years. Fiona's parents, Breanna and Gary Sheehan, had finally been located and would be flying home from Spain. He found himself wanting to do it all at once, like some kind of superhero. Shauna and Dylan were constantly on his mind, staring at him, pleading with him to save them. He felt their lives in his hands. And even though he knew he was doing the best he could, everyone was doing the best they could, he also knew it wasn't anywhere near good enough.

CHAPTER 21

*E*RIN TANNER'S PROPERTY WAS IN DIRE NEED OF CARE. WEEDS choked the front garden, and the windows of her cottage were obscured by a thick layer of dirt. She was off the grid, at least a thirty-minute drive into town, and Cormac did not see any car other than his. How did she get around? Do her shopping? Had the Shepherd recruited folks who wanted to live off the grid, or had her commune experience molded the desire into her? He understood introverts and was one himself; were it not the job forcing him out of his comfort zone, who knew where he'd be? Playing the squeezebox on the Blasket Islands for donkeys or some such. Right now, that sounded like heaven. But this was beyond introverted; this was isolated, and he could already feel his mood plummeting. He wouldn't last a day out here by himself without tipping a bottle. They were having a break in the rain, but water pooled in the yard.

Suddenly a blur of pink streaked by, throwing up mud and the aforementioned water. It startled him, and he yelped. Neely chuckled, a deep sound that took him by surprise. He scanned the overgrown grass and weeds, but he had no idea what he was looking for until something grunted to his left. He whipped his head around, and it took nearly a minute of staring to believe his eyes. An enormous pig stood in the yard. It must have weighed nearly forty-three stone. Cormac felt as if he was going to hyperventilate "Jaysus," Neely said. "That nearly put hairs on your chest, did it?"

"Hilarious," Cormac said. There was no barn on the property, so where did this yoke come from? He could barely see the neighboring farm; had it wandered all this way? His heart pounded.

Neely whistled. "Somebody's been feeding Wilbur."

"Really?" he said. "Don't make him sound cute. Do they bite?"

"Wouldn't you, if you could?" Neely said. "Look at those sharp teeth."

"I think the word you're looking for is *fangs*." Cormac was trying to convince himself he wasn't afraid to move; only the thing was, he hadn't moved since the beast had grunted at him. Its hairy nostrils flared. Jesus, Mary, and Joseph. "Why is he just staring at me, like?"

"Maybe he thinks you're a long-lost relative, Inspector. Or he's fascinated by the terror in your eyes."

"Allergies," Cormac said. "I have allergies."

"To pigs? Pigs don't have fur."

"Are you joking me?" Cormac gestured to the beast. "That thing is hairy."

"Right, so. Allergies." A movement at the house drew their attention away from the pig, and Cormac saw one of the curtains twitch. "You're allergic to fur babies, and I'm allergic to liars," Neely said, staring at the curtain. "But now we know she's home." Neely had given Erin a bell earlier, and the woman had emphatically said she was not the Erin Tanner accused of being a member of the Womb, and then she'd cut the call.

The thing is, Neely hadn't called it the Womb at all. What she'd said was, "Were you a member of the Shepherd's commune?" The fact that it was referred to as "the Womb" was insider knowledge. They had the right Erin Tanner.

"Does she drive?" Cormac asked.

"The pig?" Neely asked.

"Hilarious," Cormac said again. In truth, he was happy to see Neely lighten up a bit. This job required it. "I don't see a car."

"It's a good observation," Neely said. "She lives here by herself, so if she doesn't have a car, I wonder how she manages her shopping."

"You can take the girl out of the commune . . ."

"To be fair, I think she has survived quite a bit of trauma in her life."

"She came forth as a witness back then," Cormac said. "Maybe there's hope she'll cooperate now."

"Unless our cult leader has already been in contact with her." Neely squinted. "She did just lie to me on the phone."

"Do you really think she's still under his influence?" Cormac asked. "All these years later? After what he did to the others?"

"I'd like to think not, but that's what's so perplexing about the cult dynamic. The things people will do."

"It's been nearly three decades."

"Look at where she lives. She hasn't spent the past thirty years reintegrating into society, that's for darn sure."

Cormac glanced at the massive pig, which hadn't taken his squinty eyes off him for a second. "Do you think there are more like him inside?"

"I'd say that is an excellent assumption," Neely said. "I'll ask Erin to step outside, will I?"

"Sure, lookit. It's a grand, fresh day," Cormac said, as a gust of wind blew him back a step. The pig toddled closer. "Barb. Can ya take this thing with ya?"

"Sorry. I left me pig leash at home. Besides. He likes you."

"Shoo," Cormac said. "Shoo." The pig did not move. Cormac took a step to the right. The pig moved closer. "Damn it."

Neely headed for the house. Soon she was banging on the front door with her baton. Cormac took out his inhaler. Big mistake. The thing must have thought it was a treat and sprinted for him. Cormac yelled and scrambled onto the hood of his Toyota. The pig toddled over to the entrance to the yard, as if blocking him, and Cormac could have sworn he saw a glint of victory in the beast's eyes. Cormac's breathing remained labored, and he began humming to himself, starting with "Black Velvet Band."

Her eyes they shone like diamonds . . .

Neely had stopped banging on the door and was now trying to peer into windows. "Erin. I know you're in there. We saw your curtains twitching." She waited. "I'll call backup and bang down your door. Is that what you want?

Cormac slid off the hood of his car, opened the door, and laid on the horn. The pig was not fazed.

"Hold your horses," a woman's voice finally rang out.

"Our horses?" Cormac said. "She can't even hold her pig."

"He just wants a cuddle," Neely said. Cormac took back his earlier thoughts. Neely was enjoying this way too much. The front door finally swung open, and there stood a tall, thin woman with long, wild hair down to her waist. She looked like a broomstick wearing a wig.

"Get this animal away from me," Cormac said straightaway.

Erin glanced at the pig. "Billy does what he wants."

Billy. Cormac thought that was for goats . . .

"This is Detective Inspector Cormac O'Brien, and do you remember me, Erin?" Neely said.

"No." Her voice was raspy, as if she hadn't used it in quite some time.

"I'm Detective Sergeant Barbara Neely, and I sure remember you. Now get your pig under control before I'm forced to call animal control."

The woman stomped and whistled. "Billy. Inside." The pig turned, trotted to the house, and disappeared inside the open door. *A pig. In the house.* Cormac didn't even allow shoes in the house. "What do you want?" Erin asked. "I'm not bothering nobody."

Cormac, buoyed by the absence of the pig, strode over and stood next to Neely. He could see a bit into the house, and the stench was overwhelming. From his vantage point, he could see at least six cats on her sofa. "How many animals are in the house?" It took everything he had not to itch his nose.

"I lost count," she said with a shrug. "Fifteen?"

"Fifteen?" Cormac felt his throat constricting. Sweat trickled down his brow. It could not be healthy to live with fifteen creatures in a tiny cottage. Was that legal? He wished Dimpna Wilde was here.

"I'm sure you're aware a pregnant woman's body was found in the bog?" Neely asked.

Erin's eyes were slightly cloudy. She gazed past them. "I mind me own business."

"I'm sure you're also aware that your pals Cahal Mackey and Flynn Barry were released from prison," Cormac said.

Her left nostril twitched. "Like I said, I mind me own business."

Cormac took a step forward. "Even if more young women are now in danger?"

"It's the way of the world. Women are always in danger, Inspector. But ye know that, don't ye?"

"You helped us back then," Neely said. "You tried your best."

"I've kept to meself. There's no help I can give ye now."

Neely refused to back down. "Has either Cahal or Flynn tried to contact you?"

Erin scoffed. "I don't even have a phone."

"You do so," Neely said. "We just spoke."

Erin shrugged. "It barely rings."

"Has anyone come a-knocking?" Cormac asked.

"Ye have." She crossed her arms.

Cormac was on Team Neely. Every instinct he had told him Erin Tanner was hiding something. "We have a missing kid and young pregnant girl. I want you to tell me every possible location where we might find them."

"Anywhere you can think of that Cahal or Flynn might take them," Neely prodded.

She shook her head. "I haven't seen the Shepherd in nearly three decades. I told you it's nothing to do with me."

They needed a different tack. Cormac relaxed his stance. "I'd like to hear about your time in the cult."

She crossed her arms. "It wasn't a cult."

"What do you prefer?" Cormac asked. "Commune?"

"We were a village. A flock." For a moment, her eyes lit up before hardening again. After all these years, part of the utopian dream was still alive within her.

"A flock," Neely repeated. Erin's eyes narrowed. "Do you still have the tattoo?"

Fury flashed across her face, and he watched her wrestle it

away. She was definitely putting on an act. To what end? Had Cahal threatened her? "You think you're so much better than me, is that it?"

"No," Neely said. "I think I'm different. Equal. Just different."

"You live in this world. You see the horrors. A few of us decide to take it off the grid, start over, do it right. Live by the land, follow the Grand Ruler's laws."

"That was the promise, wasn't it? A utopia?" Cormac was genuinely interested.

Erin blinked. "It would have worked. Only there was a Devil among us. Hiding in plain sight."

"You're speaking of Cahal Mackey?"

She grinned, showing teeth that looked as if they'd never met a dentist. "He was just a vessel for the Devil to corrupt."

"And are we talking the literal Devil here or . . . ?" Cormac asked. She refused to answer. "How did you first learn about the Shepherd? Who approached you? How and where were you approached?"

She stared at him for a moment, and then her gaze wandered to the fields. "I don't remember."

Another lie. He was losing patience. She obviously didn't like carrots; it was time for the stick. "I think there are ordinances around here when it comes to animal hoarding," Cormac said to Neely. "Am I right?" Dimpna would probably hate him for using her animals against her, but he would do anything he could to find their missing lad and young woman, not to mention justice for their unidentified woman in the bog. *Fiona.* He couldn't shake the feeling that their Jane Doe was Fiona Sheehan.

"Absolutely," Neely said. "It only takes a single call."

"Hopefully that won't be necessary." He stared at Erin. "Will it?"

"The past is the past," Erin said. "Now. I've already missed the first ten minutes of *Judge Judy;* are we done here?" And before they could answer, she went back in and slammed the door in their faces.

"*Judge Judy?*" Cormac's mouth dropped open, and he turned to Neely.

"And here I thought she wasn't a friend of the law," Neely said. "What now?"

"We call animal control," he replied, hurrying back to his car. "It's our only leverage."

"You mean you're going to threaten to take them if she doesn't talk?" Neely sounded as if she didn't approve.

"You're damn right I am. Starting with your pal Wilbur."

CHAPTER 22

*I*T SEEMED EVERY MAN, WOMAN, AND CHILD IN DINGLE HAD VOLUN-
teered to help in some way. MISSING posters plastered the streets,
shop windows, utility poles, the post office, and the garda station,
and, of course, their photos and details were all over the internet.
Flowers and Mass cards had accumulated just outside the search
area for Shauna, Dylan, and their Jane Doe and her baby. People
cared. Most people were not evil. And when trouble hit, people
banded together. There was comfort in that, there was strength. As
Cormac drove through town, he hoped that, wherever Dylan and
Shauna were, they knew people were looking for them. That people cared.

Cahal Mackey and Flynn Barry had been warned to stay in their
flats and not report to work, but apparently they'd refused. Cormac and Neely would be paying them each a visit in about an hour.
He could feel his adrenaline rise, just thinking about finally meeting them. Was Cahal still a smart, charismatic man, or had prison
changed him? Would Flynn, the supposed number two, be willing
to flip on the Shepherd? He needed something. If nothing else, he
wanted to get a bead on whether or not he thought they were involved. He also wanted Neely to open her mind to a copycat.

Cormac had just returned to the station when his desk phone
rang. He jogged back and picked it up. It was Joan, the front-desk
clerk. She was in her sixties, and she treated nearly everyone in her
station like they were one of her ten grandchildren. During stressful times, she was always a comfort.

"I've got a woman here to see you," Joan said. Her tone was subdued, which already had Cormac on alert. "She says she was an acquaintance of Shauna Mills."

"Name?"

There was a pause. "She doesn't want to give her name."

Interesting. "Send her back to my office straightaway."

The woman was appeared to be in her fifties, older than he had anticipated. She looked as if the time she'd spent on this earth had been hard. Her clothing was stained, she reeked of smoke, her blonde hair was in need of a wash, and she was so thin he immediately wanted to feed her.

"I'd like to get your name," Cormac said, as one of his guards brought her a mineral and biscuits, as he requested. She stared at the offerings without moving. "Help yourself." She looked up at him, then slid the can of Sprite closer, staring at it like it was something wondrous. Cormac edged the tin closer, and soon she was removing three. She placed them next to the can of Sprite and glanced at the tin. "Maybe you could do me a favor," he said, leaning forward. "I'm not supposed to eat too much sugar. Would you like to take that tin home?"

Her eyes reflected her surprise. She smiled to herself, and then immediately wiped it off her face and shrugged. "Whatever, if it will help ya."

"Brilliant." This way, she wouldn't stuff herself with biscuits in fear that the tin was going to be snatched away. He was going to have to find out her identity. One step at a time. "I'm Detective Inspector Cormac O'Brien, and I understand you know Shauna Mills." She nodded. "Let's start with your name."

"You don't need me name."

He'd have to circle back. "How is it you're acquainted with Shauna?"

"I like to sit on a wall near her house. She used to walk by every day."

"And where is it that you live?"

She narrowed her eyes. "I didn't come here to talk about me. I came here to talk about Shauna."

Tough audience. He wondered if she was homeless. She smelled as if she hadn't bathed in quite a while, and that scent mingled with the smell of stale cigarettes. Her nails were bitten to the quick. "When did you last see her?"

"Last week."

"Can you be more specific?"

"What do you mean?"

"What day last week?"

"I don't know."

"And what is it you came to tell me?"

"She told me she had a secret meeting, and it was going to take place at the Spring Festival."

A secret meeting. Now this he wanted to hear. "Do you know the nature of this meeting?"

"She was meeting with another pregnant woman. They both received some kind of email."

This matched the account Liam McCarthy had given. Cormac leaned forward. "Do you know what the email said?"

"I only know what I just told you."

"Anything else? Anything at all?"

The woman shook her head, then stared at her fingernails. "I think they were meeting for ice cream."

Murphy's. Dimpna had mentioned spilling ice cream on Shauna, but he'd been so overwhelmed, he hadn't even thought to follow up with the ice cream shop in town. Cormac would send guards there immediately. Maybe they could get something on CCTV. Maybe they'd be able to see Shauna and, more importantly, whether or not she met up with another pregnant woman. "How did you communicate with Shauna?"

"She carried a notepad. She would speak, and I would write."

He thought back to the name they'd found on a piece of paper near Shauna's laptop. FiFoFum . . . was that Fiona Sheehan? But if Shauna did meet Fiona at the festival, then she couldn't be the woman they'd found in the bog. Then again, Dimpna said that, when she bumped into Shauna, Shauna was alone, and she didn't want the paper with the email back when Dimpna tried to hand it to her. Was Fiona a no-show? Was Fiona a no-show because she was lying dead in the bog? Now that he was putting a few pieces together, he wanted more. "I'd really like to know your name."

"You don't need my name."

"I see. Well, thank you very much for coming in." He pushed away from the table.

"She was having second thoughts about that couple."

"What couple?"

"The ones adopting her baby."

"She said that?"

The woman nodded. "She said the woman wanted to control her. She didn't like that. She was worried she had chosen the wrong parents." The woman leaned in. "I told her. I told her she would be a good mother." She leaned back and shook her head. "Babies need their mothers."

Jane Griffin. Earlier suspicions rose before him. Had Shauna gone to her house that day to tell her she had changed her mind about the adoption? Had Jane and David Griffin hired someone to play the role of an abductor? Someone like Liam McCarthy? He was, after all, their handyman. But why would he turn on Shauna? Especially if he had been willing to raise the baby. Had things gone pear-shaped at that meeting, and they'd accidentally killed her? Or maybe they had hired someone to kidnap Shauna, scare her, and keep her under their control until the baby was born. But what about Dylan? And Fiona? Where did they fit in? *Patterns.* He could not ignore the pattern. These cases had to be related. "Are you from the area?" Cormac asked. He wanted to make sure this woman didn't have a personal vendetta against the Griffins.

She stood abruptly. "I hope you find Shauna. I liked her. She was funny." With that, the woman took the tin of biscuits and left. As he watched her go, Cormac felt a sadness he couldn't touch. Whoever that woman was, she deserved a home, indoor plumbing, friends. It was so easy to take a wrong turn in life. But that topic would have to get shoved away. There was no use confronting the Griffins just yet; the woman had simply floated a theory. He'd forgotten to ask Garda Lennon whether or not the guards who canvassed the Griffins' house had found any evidence that they had planned on making chicken curry that evening. Not that he could do much if the answer was no, but he could at least confront them with the lie. And why would they lie about something like that? He sent Garda Lennon a reminder text. Now he needed to send a guard to Murphy's ice cream shop to question the employees and pull CCTV. And while they were doing that, he had his very first meet and greet with a cult leader.

Cahal Mackey's flat was situated at the top of a long set of stairs in a semi-attached gray building a few streets behind John Street. It was known as transitory housing, often used by men just out of prison, as well as those just released from drug and alcohol treatment centers. "Do you think he'll be evasive?" Cormac asked as he and Neely stared at the door.

"Not if he's the same overconfident snake charmer from twenty-nine years ago."

"No snakes in Ireland," Cormac said.

Neely grimaced. "He's the exception."

Cormac knocked on the door. There was no buzzer, but he banged hard enough. "Would he keep a kid up in his flat?"

"Lennon has been watching him; he hasn't seen any evidence of that." They'd put Garda Lennon on surveillance duty; he'd been watching both Cahal Mackey and Flynn Barry.

"Hopefully he'll invite us and give us the tour," Cormac said. "We need eyes on the inside."

Footsteps could be heard tromping down the steps, and soon the door swung open. The man standing in front of them was tall, with dark hair in need of a comb, a scraggly beard, and sunglasses. He leaned his arm against the doorframe, filling the space. He reeked of cigarette smoke. "I knew you'd come a knockin'." He grinned like this was some sort of a game. He had a single gold tooth in his uppers. It glinted as if mocking them.

Smug bastard. Cormac, on the shorter side himself, spread his legs a bit wider, having no clue whether or not that would be perceived as a dominating stance, but he was giving it a go. He lowered his voice. "I'm Detective Inspector O'Brien; this is Detective Sergeant Neely."

"An inspector and a sergeant," he said. "I'm honored."

"What do you say we go upstairs and have a little chat?" Cormac said.

"I can chat right here," Cahal replied with a slow grin. "Unless the pair of ye are knackered and you need to sit down."

"I am knackered, and a seat and cup of tea would be lovely,"

Neely said. And then she pushed past Cahal and headed up the stairs. Cormac wanted to cheer, but he was also a little irked that she didn't let him keep ahold of the reins. He'd never felt competitive with Barbara before; she was an excellent detective sergeant, and the only reason she wasn't an inspector was she had decided she didn't want all the paperwork. Smart woman.

Cahal looked perturbed for half a second before gesturing up the stairs to Cormac. "By all means, Inspector. Are you going to stand out there like a vampire awaiting an invitation, or are your balls as big as the ban garda's?"

Ban garda. The old-fashioned term for a female guard. He'd done it to disparage her. "You'll address her as Detective Sergeant and myself as Detective Inspector," Cormac said, as he pushed past him. He had an urge to stomp up the stairs, but he held back. Seconds in the man's presence and he was already pushing Cormac's buttons. But at least they could look for any signs of Dylan Walsh inside the flat, which was no doubt what Neely was already doing. If she was truly retiring after this case, she was going to be sorely missed.

The interior of the flat was a mirror of the outside—basic, cheap, transitory. A small kitchen, a brown sofa and coffee table, a round dining table with two chairs. Depressing. Cormac was already itching to leave, and he was going to make damn sure Cahal was sitting down and he was standing up.

Neely had the kettle heating up and was rifling through his cabinets for cups.

"Help yourself, *Detective Sergeant*," Cahal said, emphasizing the title and treating Cormac to a cheeky grin.

"I will, so," Neely said. Cormac wondered if the tea was cheap and generic, but then spotted the box of Barry's. He could really do with a cup of coffee, but the tea was merely a bit of distraction, designed to put Cahal at ease while keeping him on his toes. Next to the sofa was a door leading to a single bedroom. Cormac wandered over and glanced in.

"Looking for that lad who went missing?" Cahal asked. "I've never met him in me life, nor did I kill that pregnant woman in the bog." He nearly sounded giddy. "Terrible pity, isn't it?"

There was nothing significant to see in the bedroom—a bed, a dresser, a suitcase. No sign of a kid or woman anywhere. That didn't mean he wasn't keeping them somewhere; it just wasn't here. Which meant Cormac was going to keep up the surveillance on him. It was risky. If Cahal knew he was being watched and he was the kidnapper, then he might leave their victims alone too long. And if he happened to drop dead, and no one else knew where he was keeping them, it could be the end of their lives too. Cormac returned to the table where Cahal had sat as instructed, but his legs were splayed as far open as he could plant them. Cormac removed an inhaler from his pocket and set it on the table. Then a pad and a biro.

Cahal glanced at them. "Funny housewarming gifts, that, but I'm sorted, thanks."

"Dylan Walsh has asthma. We found his inhaler by his bicycle. You should bring him that."

"I told you, I didn't take the kid, or the deaf woman, and I didn't kill the bog lady." He grinned again.

"Have you kidnapped *anyone* lately?" Neely asked as she returned with two mugs of tea. She handed one to Cormac and kept the other for herself. Cahal took out a pack of cigarettes. Benson and Hedges 100s Luxury. Another power play. Cormac could ask him not to smoke, but Cahal would then get the satisfaction of ignoring the request.

Cormac was trying to suss out whether Cahal would pick up on the significance of the notepad—that it was to communicate with Shauna Mills. He figured the man was too slick for that, but this was a throw-everything-at-the-wall situation.

"Let me see, have I kidnapped anyone lately?" Cahal said. "Would I be living here and working at the harbor if I had that kind of drama in me life?"

"How was prison?" Neely asked. "Apart from not fecking long enough?" Cormac nearly choked on his tea. Maybe bringing her wasn't the best idea.

Cahal glanced at the pad and biro, then reached for it. The hair went up on the back of Cormac's neck as Cahal Mackey jotted something down. When he finished, he slid it to the middle of the table. He'd written a single word:

Blessed

Neely's jaw tightened as she read it, and Cahal grinned. He spread his arms out. "These are the end of times, and blessed be those who recognize it." He dropped his arms and leaned forward toward Neely. She didn't back up. "You could never prove that I did anything wrong with me Flock, now could you, Sergeant?" He grinned. "You didn't sleep much those days, did ya?"

"A flock," Neely said. "Isn't that handy? You liked giving them all nicknames, including yourself, didn't ya? The Shepherd. The Staff. What were the women's names again?" She waited, but he did not answer. "Need to label and control others in order to feel like a big man?"

Jaysus, Barbara, easy now. Cormac had been unwillingly delegated to good cop.

Cahal flashed another nauseating grin. "If you're asking me to drop trou, all you have to do is ask, darling."

"Wipe that smirk off your face, and if you don't speak to her with respect, I'll make sure you regret it," Cormac said.

Cahal's grin did not fade. He threw open his arms. "I have no property. A criminal record. I'm working. You're watching me twenty-four-seven. Pray tell how you think I've managed to murder and kidnap in me free time."

"I see you smoke Bensen and Hedges," Cormac said. They'd found a butt in the field, and he was still waiting for the brand to be identified.

"Is that a crime?" He took out a cigarette and put it in his mouth, his lips curling up at the sides. He took his time lighting it, then tilted his head back and blew smoke up to the ceiling. He lowered his head after a minute. "Let's get right to it. You think I took the kid and deaf woman and killed the bog lady. I did not. Which makes this a fucking waste of your precious time, but, hey, do your thing. And when you're done wasting my time and yours, and you realize that the one thing you need to catch our little friend, maybe find the lad alive, is to curry favor with the one man who might be able to understand a mind like that." His gaze shifted to Cormac, and he kept eye contact. "What can I say?" he said. "I'm a people person." He blew rings of smoke in their direction.

"You're offering to be our Hannibal Lecter, is that right?" Cormac asked.

"I'm not much of a Chianti man," Cahal said. "A pint of ale will do."

"Why did you give the women you kidnapped new names?" Neely asked. "Was it to turn them into your property?"

Cahal stubbed out the cigarette. "My Flock followed me willingly, Detective Sergeant, but you already know that. I am but a vessel for our Lord above to use however he likes."

Neely leaned forward. "And you're saying God in heaven used you to slit a pregnant woman's throat and cut her baby out of her?"

Cahal crossed his arms. "I was never charged for such a thing," he said. "Not that you didn't try your best, ban garda."

Cormac slammed the table. "Detective Sergeant, or I'll haul you back to prison meself."

Neely crossed her arms. "It's alright, Inspector. Every word out of his mouth expresses his hatred of women." She stared him down. "I would expect no less."

Cahal kept speaking as if they had never interjected. "I spent many a night thinking about how hard you tried to prove it was me." He chuckled—a low, disgusting sound. "You have no idea how far off the mark you were. Still are." He shook his head. "Wonders never cease."

Despite her tough exterior, Neely was now literally shaking across the table, no doubt in a herculean effort not to lunge across the table with the biro and stick it in the softest part of his throat.

There was one thing Cormac knew about cult leaders; as Paul Byrne had suggested, they were hard-core narcissists, souls so depleted and starved of attention, they elevated themselves to godlike stature. Adoration was as essential as breathing. "Who do you think did this?" Cormac asked. "They're obviously trying to copy your previous work." He could feel Neely stiffen beside him, but she did not vocalize her displeasure.

Cahal flashed his gold tooth. "I've been in prison. I haven't a clue."

Cormac was not going to let up. "Take a guess then. A smart man like you."

Cahal squinted as if trying to figure out whether or not to answer. He swiveled his head toward Neely. "The blind leading the blind." Neely crossed her arms and glared at him. "Clueless," Cahal said, with a shake of his head.

"I hear your ex-wife and daughter did quite well for themselves," Neely said.

Cormac felt as if she'd just slapped him across the face. Ex-wife and daughter? She hadn't said a word to him about this.

"What can I say?" Cahal said. "I'm a provider. And regardless of what you think, I don't need the spotlight to shine."

Ex-wife and daughter. Why wasn't that in the file he'd read? What else was he in the dark about?

"You know what I find fascinating?" Neely said. "We haven't had the murder of a pregnant woman or a kid kidnapped in Dingle in the past twenty-nine years. But days after you're released, it happens again. I'd say that's one hell of a coincidence. Wouldn't you?"

"I've been thinking about that myself," Cahal said tipping his chair back. "I don't believe it is a coincidence. But I'm not the only man that was just set free now, am I?"

CHAPTER 23

*T*HE PUB WHERE FLYNN BARRY WAS HOLED UP PLAYING SNOOKER RE-
quired a drive outside of town. Garda Lennon had texted confirmation that the Griffins did indeed have ingredients to make
chicken curry; however, there had been no evidence that preparations had been underway to make it. Had Shauna's abductor interrupted it, or had Jane Griffin simply answered chicken curry
because she knew she *could* have made it? He still had to keep all
possibilities on the table. The rain was back, lighter than the previous days, but steady, and as they ventured farther into County
Kerry, the roads curved and the fields and hills outside became
nothing more than a background blur. Between the heat on in the
car and the swish of the wipers, not to mention his lack of sleep,
Cormac needed to talk to stay alert. He used the ride to quiz Neely
about the ex-wife and daughter.

"I'm sorry I didn't mention them," Neely said. "I hadn't planned
on it; it just came out."

"Do they fit into this picture at all?"

"I think they do," Neely said. "But it's open to interpretation."

"Try me."

"Right before Cahal Mackey and Flynn Barry went to prison, rel-
atives of both came into money. Mackey's ex-wife and daughter,
and Flynn Barry's sister. Both families claimed a wealthy relative
died, and get this: When we could find no evidence of any close rel-
atives dying, each claimed it was a distant relative. We tried leaning

on their solicitors, but they put up walls. They insisted there was nothing illegal about either of these inheritances. I have no doubt wheels were greased."

"You think that's how each of the men funneled their money." And if they had sudden money, had it come from selling babies? How many babies?

"I do think it's how they hid the money." She sighed. "But we could never prove it."

"Are they still living here in Ireland?"

"Mackey's ex-wife and daughter moved to Australia. Flynn Barry's sister is still in County Kerry. She leads a quiet life, still works as a hairdresser."

"We can arrange a video call. See if she's willing to open up, given the recent goings-on."

Neely shrugged. "You can try. But if he did pay her off, she's not likely to admit to it now." They stepped out of the vehicle. "Here goes nothing," Neely said as Cormac held the door open.

As they stepped into the smell of yesterday's ale, Cormac suddenly wished he were here to play his squeeze-box, wished Dimpna was here with her fiddle, wished none of this horror had ever taken place. It was like a cave inside, and it took Cormac's eyes a minute to adjust. When they did, there wasn't much to see. There was only one man at the pool table, a short but incredibly muscular man with a shaved head and small dark eyes. Flynn Barry. Number two, the Staff. Cormac had seen recent photos, and there was no doubt it was him. He was playing solo, and from the looks of it, he was winning.

The publican, a young skinny lad, was asking what they'd like until Neely stepped out from behind Cormac and flashed her badge. Without a word, he whistled, and Flynn jerked his head in their direction.

"What can I do for ye," Flynn said as he ambled over, the pool stick by his side.

"How's life since you broke free?" Cormac asked. He wasn't going to let Neely start the party this time.

"I didn't break free, mister. I served me time."

"Not for murder," Neely said under her breath. But Flynn had excellent hearing.

"I didn't kill no one," Flynn said. "Not that I'm proud of the man I was back then. Twenty-something years of age, rambling along, not knowing where he was going." He twirled the pool stick. He then pulled a gold cross out from under his shirt and pointed to it. "Since I've been in prison, I've found God. Not the blasphemous one the Shepherd waxed on about, but the God of the Bible and the Catholic Church, and now that the true Lord has seen fit to set me free, I'm going to dedicate the rest of me life to doing his work." He kissed the cross before tucking it back into his shirt.

"You want another double?" the publican said to him, holding up a whiskey bottle.

Flynn glared at the publican. "I'm sorted, thanks."

"What I see is a man playing snooker and day-drinking," Cormac said.

Flynn shrugged. "Idle hands," he said. "And I only drink *one* drink."

"It's a double, so you've had two, like," the publican said. Flynn pressed his eyes closed, as if trying to stop himself from erupting before opening them again.

Cormac removed a calling card from his pocket and held it out. "I'm Detective Inspector Cormac O'Brien, and this is Detective Sergeant Neely."

Flynn scratched his head, still not touching the card. "I don't have a phone yet," he said. "Only a burner for work, like."

Cormac kept the card held out until Flynn took it. Without looking at it, he shoved it in his pocket with a look that said it was going in the rubbish bin the minute he had the chance.

"Have you been watching or reading any news?" Cormac asked.

Flynn's eyes darted to the telly mounted in the corner of the room. Currently, there was a football match, muted, with captions on. He'd been hanging out here; he would have seen or heard the news. "I heard a bit alright," Flynn said. "I've been saying prayers for them."

Cormac didn't take the bait. "The woman is pregnant and deaf, and the lad is ten years of age. Her name is Shauna Mills. His name is Dylan Walsh. She has her entire life ahead of her, and the lad—who has asthma, by the way—has two loving parents who need him home." Cormac was just trying to see how Flynn would react to the information. He wasn't claiming to be a human lie detector, but there was value in watching a person's reactions. Everyone had a tell.

Flynn avoided eye contact. "I would have volunteered for the search, but they have me working long hours at the harbor."

Cormac took Dylan and Shauna's flyers out of his pocket, and held them up. "Have you seen either of them?"

"Your buddy Cahal thinks maybe you have," Neely said.

Flynn's nostrils flared. "Me?" He whirled around and put the pool stick back on the wall-rack with aggression. "I knew this was gonna happen. I said as much. I'm not out a few weeks, and I'm a suspect in another crime that I had nothing to do with." He looked to the ceiling. "You're testing me, God. But the joke is on them. I welcome your test." He squared off with Cormac and Neely. "I've never seen that kid, or those women, and I've only gone three places since I've been here. "Harbor." He flicked out a finger. "Home." Second finger. "Right here." Thumb.

"What about your pal, Cahal?"

"I don't know that man anymore; I barely knew him to begin with. And if it's up to me, I'll never speak to him again." He swallowed with the look of a terrified lad who had just stood up to a bully. "All I've ever done is me best to provide for me family. And, even then, I had to be away from them. But a man has to do what a man has to do." He was doing his best to put on a good act, but Cormac wasn't buying it.

"If you know anything, you're going to want to talk before he does," Neely said.

"If he says anything—anything that involves me? It's a damn lie, and you'll be wasting your time looking into it." He shook his head. "Don't say I didn't warn ye."

"Do you think it's possible that Cahal Mackey is involved with

YOU HAVE GONE TOO FAR

our missing lad or the women?" Unlike Cahal, Flynn showed some fear. Maybe good cop was the way to go with him.

"Anything's possible," Flynn said. "Some people can never cut ties with their past." He chewed on his lip. "I can tell you one thing. Are ye listening? I hope you are. The Shepherd never gets his hands dirty. Never. He always has someone else doing the deed."

"Someone like you?" Cormac asked.

Flynn stared at them, his face serene. "I am no longer a willing participant."

"Are you an unwilling participant?" Cormac asked. "Are you participating in any way?"

Flynn crossed his arms. "You tell me. You think I haven't noticed that young, tow-headed guard following me wherever I go?"

Garda Lennon. Cormac had hoped he'd be more subtle. He hadn't had time to have a proper sit-down with him yet or give him any guidance. These cases were stretching all of them.

"Have you seen anything suspicious about Cahal Mackey's behavior, anyone he might be hanging around?" Neely asked. She leaned in. "We're talking to him too. Whoever speaks first is going to be in our good graces."

"Whatever he said, it's a damn lie!" Flynn's eyes started darting again, and he licked his lips. "I only saw one thing you might be interested in, but unless you want me to be the next dead body in the morgue, you won't tell him it came from me."

"Go on, so," Neely said.

"Do you promise?" He looked genuinely frightened.

"I promise," Cormac said.

Neely slid him a look. "You really shouldn't make promises." Cheeky.

Flynn's gaze shifted between them, glued to their back-and-forth. "I'm going to make an exception to my really fine rule of not making promises," Cormac said. "What is it?"

Flynn swallowed again. "Those lads? On the bicycles? Three of them, right?"

Cormac stiffened. That had never been mentioned in the press briefing. "Yes?"

"The one trailing behind the other two was a little chunky."

"You saw them?" Cormac asked. "The night they went to the bog?" He was on high alert and had to remind himself that every single thing out of this man's mouth might be a lie.

"Aye. I saw them talking to someone on the footpath. I thought it was one of their fathers, and his head was down; he was wearing a flat cap."

"What exactly did you see?" Cormac asked.

Flynn shrugged. "Just saw him talking to the lads, and next thing you know, they veer off the footpath racing like hooligans and one of them almost runs me down as I'm crossing the street. That's when I looked to see if the father approved of their shenanigans, but he was gone." Flynn snapped his fingers. "Poof. Just like that."

"Did you hear the man?"

Flynn shook his head. "Barely saw him, didn't hear him, didn't talk to the lads; they were pedaling like mad." He paused. "But I was walking in the direction I saw the man, like."

He was leading up to something, but taking way too long. "And?" Cormac demanded.

Flynn reached into his pocket and pulled out a dark feather. "This was in the exact spot I saw the man in the flat cap standing when he was talking to the lads." He held the feather up. "It was as if he turned into a bird and just flew away."

Or a dark butterfly. Cormac removed an evidence bag. There was no sense using gloves; it had already been handled. Perhaps even by the perpetrator himself. "I'm going to be taking that." He plucked the feather out of his hand.

"You're joking me." He leaned in. "Does that have something to do with the case?"

"Did you see anything else but this one feather?" Cormac asked. Flynn shook his head.

"And you have no idea who the man was? No idea at all?"

Flynn seemed to be waiting for it. "I cannot tell you who the man was, but I can tell ye who he wasn't. He wasn't me, and he wasn't Cahal Mackey."

"How can you be so sure it wasn't Cahal Mackey?" Cormac asked.

"Because when I got back to the flat after seeing the man in the flat cap with me own two eyes, Cahal was coming out the front door." He shook his head. "And the look on his face? I don't know what terrible news he'd just received, but he ran outta that house like he was late for his mammy's funeral."

CHAPTER 24

DIMPNA STOOD OUTSIDE OF MR. MAGUIRE'S BEDROOM DOOR, PRAYing that, whatever it was he wanted to say to her, he would make it quick. He had been the local chemist in town, and Dimpna couldn't live down the moment, years ago, when she had to ask him for a pregnancy test. They were kept behind the counter back then, forcing young women to stand in line, then make eye contact with the chemist and state the request. Absolutely mortifying. To make matters worse, Dimpna had told no one at that stage what Sean O'Reilly had done to her. Not even Sheila. It took weeks after missing her period to finally get up the nerve to go into the chemist. She'd thought about going to one out of town, but on this particular morning, she could not take it one more second; she had to know now. She had been watching the shop to try to figure out when it was least crowded. On that particular day, there were only a few others in the shop, and they weren't in line for prescriptions. "Dimpna Wilde," Mr. Maguire had said. "What brings you here?" His voice carried throughout the small shop. She thought she was going to die, but there was no way around it; she had to ask for the test.

She tried to think of who else it might be for, but no one came to mind. She considered saying it was "for a friend," which would have caused Mr. Maguire to think it was his own daughter, so that was out. Standing there as he blinked at her and waited was one of the worst moments of her life. She nearly ran out of the shop then and there. It wasn't that he said anything; in fact, there was empathy in his eyes. Nonetheless, Dimpna had been mortified. To her, Mr. Maguire would forever represent two specific moments in time, and that was one of them. Even all these years later, standing outside his bedroom door, she could remember the hot shame she'd felt coursing through her tiny body. She was surprised it didn't swallow her whole. Standing here now, it was as if no time had passed at all. Sheila was in the living room. What on earth did he want from her?

Dimpna took a deep breath and opened the door. Mr. Maguire was sitting up in bed, oxygen mask over his face, the machine churning away. He raised his hand, and she waved. Stomach roiling, she approached the bed. "I'm sorry to hear you're feeling poorly," she said. *Feeling poorly.* He was dying. As a vet, she had to be blunt with her clients. But human to human, she pretended, like the rest of them.

He waved the sentiment away, then pointed to his bedside table. The surface was littered with pill bottles, a glass of water, reading glasses. She walked over to the table, and he gestured to the drawer. She opened it to find an envelope inside. She tried to hand it to him, and he motioned for her to open it as a deep cough shook his body. She opened it to find a single photo. It was from ages ago, and moments after studying it, she suddenly remembered the exact day it was taken. How could she not; the darkest time in her life was seared in her memory. This was the day after she'd taken the pregnancy test, the day after Mr. Maguire said what he had said to her (she still hadn't told a soul about the horrific thing he had uttered to her), the day after the pregnancy test had confirmed her worst fear. Now, of course, she wouldn't change a single thing, for it had given her Ben. And Ben was her world. But at the time, it felt like the dark night of her soul. And at this point, she still had not told anyone, besides Mr. Maguire, about her predicament. The photo was taken at their veterinarian clinic.

In the image, Dimpna and her father were in the foreground, standing in the reception area. Her father was standing next to her, his nose buried in a file. A red marker had been used to draw a circle around a man sitting behind them in one of the waiting-room chairs. He was handsome, with dark hair and a strong jawline. And if she wasn't mistaken, he was staring intently at her. There was something familiar about him, but she just couldn't figure out why. Looking at him gave her the shivers, and she had to remind herself this was from ages ago.

"What is this?" she said. She pointed to the man circled in red. "I don't think I know him, but I feel like I've seen him." She studied it again and then made eye contact with Mr. Maguire. "Did you take this photo?"

He reached over to the other bedside table, the one to the left of him, grabbed a newspaper that was sitting on top and handed it to her. She didn't realize until she was holding it that it wasn't just one newspaper, it was two. The one on top was recent, the same one her father had wielded the other day as he screamed that she needed to leave town, the headline one she was all too familiar with:

DEAD PREGNANT WOMAN FOUND IN BOG

She switched to the second paper and noticed the date. Nearly three decades ago.

PREGNANT WOMAN'S THROAT SLIT, BABY CUT FROM HER STOMACH

She studied the photo that accompanied the headline. To the left was a blurry image of the woods where they'd found the poor woman's body. But it was the photo on the right that caught her attention. A smaller headline read:

IS CULT LEADER CAHAL MACKEY, AKA THE SHEPHERD, A COLD-BLOODED KILLER?

He was young, with messy dark hair, standing in front of a field with three young pregnant women standing behind him. They were in long dresses that looked old-fashioned. Mr. Maguire coughed again as he pointed to the original photograph. She brought it up to the newspaper article and examined them side by side. There was no doubt. The man circled in red at their veterinarian clinic was the same man in the newspaper. The Shepherd. Watching her. That's when the lightbulb clicked. This was the same man who had recently come into the clinic just after Sheila, Orla, and Kevin. The one with sunglasses, asking about a wolfhound. The one who made the hairs on her arms stand up, the one staring at Orla's belly like a letch.

He was nearly three decades older, yet she had no doubt it was the same man. That could not be a coincidence. He must have followed Orla into the clinic. That's why he was wearing sunglasses. She looked at the photo again. Was he stalking Dimpna back then? After all, even though she wasn't showing, she was pregnant in this photo. And if so, how the hell did Cahal Mackey know?

Mr. Maguire coughed again. He gestured with his finger for her to come closer. "I'm sorry," he said. "It's my fault."

"What?" she asked. "What's your fault?"

It was difficult for Mr. Maguire to talk. In between words, he would pause to cough. "He was lurking in the chemist shop that day. He was there when you bought that test." Dimpna felt every hair on her body tingle. "I didn't realize until I read the article." Dimpna did not rush him; she felt a strange buzzing sensation as she listened to him. "I came to the clinic when I read that article. I knew immediately it was him. I came to warn you. But when I arrived, there he was, sitting in the waiting room, watching you. I didn't know how to protect you." A coughing fit seized him, and when he finally got control of himself, he gestured for a glass of water. Dimpna handed him a glass from the table and, after he drank, set it back down. He waited a moment, then continued. "I told your father. And I told him you had to leave Dingle immediately." His eyes were wet when he looked at her. "I should have told you everything."

Dimpna felt a sinking feeling in her body as memories assaulted her. Her father had started insisting she leave town. "This is not the place for you any longer," he'd said. And although she'd agreed and wanted nothing more than to leave this place, the place where Sean O'Reilly lived, at the time, she'd felt as if her father was rejecting her, rejecting everything about her. "Why didn't he just tell me?" she said aloud.

"We all made mistakes," Mr. Maguire said. "But we did the best we could."

"Why are you telling me this now?"

"Because he's free," Mr. Maguire said. "And I'm worried about my niece."

"Orla?"

He nodded. "I'm too weak," he said. "I can't watch over her."

"I'll tell the inspector everything you just told me," Dimpna said. "We'll watch her."

He reached for her hand and squeezed it. "You promise?"

"On me life," Dimpna said. "On me life."

Sheila was waiting for her downstairs. "What did he want?" She glanced at the envelope and newspaper articles in Dimpna's hand. "What's that?"

Dimpna wanted to just run out of the house, but there would be no getting away from the redheaded pit bull. "It's a photo of me from a long time ago," she said. "I guess he just wanted me to have it."

"What photo?" Sheila said. "Let me see."

Without the article, the photo wouldn't mean a thing to her, so Dimpna handed it over. "I don't understand," Sheila said. "My father took this?"

"He had his oxygen on; all he did was point at the photo. But I certainly didn't take it." It came out harsher than she meant.

"Who is this?" She pointed to Cahal Mackey.

"I asked him the same thing. He wasn't able to answer." *Liar, liar, liar.* There was a time she'd told Sheila Maguire every secret she'd ever had. Even now, the lessons she'd learned from doing so were seared into her bones. Dimpna might have let go of her past grudges, which she supposed was some form of forgiveness, but she'd never trust Sheila Maguire again.

Sheila studied her, distrust stamped on her pretty face. "What is going on?"

"I don't know."

"The man is circled in red. Who is he?"

"We've already been through this."

Sheila stared at Dimpna. "You think I don't know when you're lying?" She glanced at the newspaper articles. "What are those?"

Dimpna really did not want to get into this. If Mr. Maguire had wanted her to know, he would have shared it with her. But Sheila was a stubborn woman. If not now, she'd be answering her later. She handed her the articles.

Sheila scanned them, her frown deepening. When she reached the one with the photo of Cahal, she looked at Dimpna. "This is that cult leader. The one they think killed that pregnant woman from twenty-nine years ago."

"I'm aware."

"What does that have to do with you?"

"Until just now, I would have said nothing. Look at the clinic photo again."

Sheila did. "That's him?"

"It looks like it. And your father seems to think so."

"I don't understand. He's saying—he was after you?"

"I was newly pregnant then. Either somehow that man knew, and he was stalking me, or it's just an incredible coincidence."

Sheila tilted her head and stared at the photo. "I guess it's a good thing you left." They stared at each other. Just before she'd left Dingle, Sheila had slept with Paul Byrne. Dimpna's first love. She'd done it knowing how Dimpna felt. It had ruined their friendship, ruined everything. "Maybe everything that happened was meant to be," Sheila said.

"Maybe," Dimpna said, as a familiar anger swirled through her. She was not going to be goaded into discussing the past with Sheila. She handed the photo and article back to Dimpna.

"Wait a minute," Sheila said. She suddenly snatched the photo back. "Is this the man who was in the clinic the other day? Asking about wolfhounds?"

Dimpna swallowed. "I can't be sure, but that's what I think."

"Oh my God. It is him. He was staring at Orla."

"I know. I'm going to tell Cormac all about it." She paused. She might as well tell her. "Your father is worried about Orla. He wants to make sure we keep an eye on her."

"Oh my God." Sheila glanced toward the upstairs. "Why didn't he tell me?"

"I don't know. Maybe because he knows I have a . . . friendship . . . with Cormac. I'm going to tell him everything. But in the meantime, will you make sure she never goes anywhere alone?"

Sheila scoffed. "Like anyone ever listens to me."

"Then tell her husband. Please. If Cahal Mackey is following her, she needs to be careful."

"Stay for a drink," Sheila said, her tone softening. "Please."

"I really should be getting back."

"One drink. Please." Sheila Maguire nearly looked desperate. It wasn't her usual look. "I've been keeping a really big secret. And whether you like it or not, Dimpna Wilde, you're the only one I can trust."

CHAPTER 25

"ONE DRINK," DIMPNA SAID. "BUT THEN I REALLY MUST GET BACK." Dimpna had no idea whether or not Sheila had a secret, let alone intended to divulge it. Sheila was an excellent manipulator, and Dimpna was already regretting this.

"Grand." Sheila grinned and headed for the sitting room. She gestured for Dimpna to sit on the sofa and headed to the corner liquor cabinet.

"My father was never much a of drinker," Sheila said. "But he couldn't resist having one of everything." She poured two glasses of whiskey, then fetched ice cubes from the kitchen before returning. "I don't have much to offer in the way of food."

"I'm sorted," Dimpna said.

Sheila sat next to her and lifted her glass. "I suppose it's wrong to say cheers."

"May the end be peaceful," Dimpna said.

Sheila nodded, her eyes filling with tears. She turned her head for a moment, and when she returned her gaze to Dimpna, the tears were gone. It was as if Sheila had the power to will them away. When she wanted to, she'd always been good at controlling her emotions. They clinked glasses, and Dimpna took a sip. Sheila downed the entire thing in one go, then set the glass on the coffee table and stared at it. "I don't understand," she said. "He was fine last month. How did he go downhill so fast?"

"It happens that way sometimes," Dimpna said.

"Do you feel like you've lost your father?" Sheila asked.

Dimpna winced. Sheila had always been blunt. "Yes," she said. "In many ways. But I'm still glad to have him." There were even parts of her father that were much softer now. And sometimes he broke into childlike glee, something the healthy Dr. Eamon Wilde had never done. At least not in front of her. Those moments were like seeing a glimpse of who her father could have been.

"My father left us for a long time," Sheila said. "Not long after you left."

"I'm sorry to hear that."

Sheila snorted. "Don't act like you didn't know."

Sheila wasn't wrong. Dimpna had heard the gossip. Sheila's parents divorced, and Danny Maguire took up with another woman, another family. "Where are Orla and Kevin staying now?" Dimpna asked. "Still with Kevin's mother?" Was Orla a part of this other family? Was that the secret?

"My place," Sheila said. "I let them take my place while I've been staying here." She glanced upstairs in the direction of her father's room. "Just in case."

"I never even knew you had a cousin named Orla," Dimpna said. "Is she on your mother's side?" Dimpna intended to hurry this along. Sheila wasn't the only one who could play coy.

Sheila's mouth set in a hard line. "Father's."

As far as Dimpna knew, Mr. Maguire didn't have brothers or sisters. From the look on Sheila's face, she wanted to close the door on that subject. But there was more to the story; Dimpna could feel it. She wondered if Orla came because she'd heard that Mr. Maguire was dying. Not that she was accusing her of being after an inheritance. She and Thomas seemed genuine. If Orla was a product of Danny's second family, that had to sting. Sheila had welcomed them into her life. Was that a sign of maturity? Danny Maguire's career had taken off after he'd left Sheila and her mother, but unfortunately for Sheila, her father hadn't hung onto his money for long. It was rumored that he had gambled it all away. No doubt, now that he was dying, this was all rising to the surface.

"I feel like I should forgive him," Sheila said. "But every time I go into his room to say something, he barks at me about something else, and then I get angry all over again, and I can't bring myself to do it."

"Say what you need to say for you," Dimpna said. "But nothing more."

Sheila rose and fetched the whiskey bottle. Dimpna made sure not to set her glass down as Sheila refilled her own. "You never liked him, did you?"

Here it was, Sheila was going in for the kill. "I don't think teenagers pay much attention to their own fathers, let alone anyone else's," Dimpna said. She wasn't going to tell Sheila the real reason she didn't like him, the other memory of Mr. Maguire that had been lodged in her poor head the rest of her life.

Sheila snorted. "Always the diplomat."

"You said you had a secret you needed to share?" Dimpna wasn't going to wait for it all day.

"I spoke too soon," Sheila said. "Is that the only reason you stayed?" Dimpna set her whiskey on the table and stood. Not only did Dimpna want to avoid getting into a row, she had to get back to work. Sheila shook her head and then stood as well. "When are you going to stop acting like this?"

"Like what?" *Don't take the bait . . .*

"Like I'm rubbish. Like one mistake when I'm seventeen and you're never going to forgive me."

Mistake. Sheila deliberately slept with Paul; she'd done it to hurt Dimpna, to prove she could do it, and they both knew it. "I don't harbor any grudges," Dimpna said. "But we're not the same people anymore."

"That's shite. You're the same old Dimpna."

"I stayed because you said you wanted to confide in me." Sometimes it was impossible not to take the bait. "You manipulated me."

Sheila bit her lip and stared at a distant wall. "Everything is not about you, Doctor Wilde."

Dimpna counted to five in her head. It wasn't terribly helpful, but she managed to keep her next statement polite. "Keep an eye on Orla. I'm glad you have family during this difficult time." Did she have Paul Byrne as well? Dimpna couldn't keep track of Paul and Sheila's on-again-off-again love life. It was freeing that she no longer cared.

"She's getting paranoid about all the horrible news around here," Sheila said. "They're thinking of leaving Dingle and going back to Waterford."

"I wouldn't blame them," Dimpna said. "It might be the smart thing to do."

"They win then, is that it? We just let the bad guys win?"

"I didn't say that."

"Orla's not a coward. She's like me."

"Why are you so defensive? She's pregnant, and there is someone targeting pregnant women. She wouldn't be a coward if she left; she'd be looking out for her baby."

"So if she stays, she's a terrible mother?"

Sheila was certainly in a mood. "You're twisting my words." Dimpna grabbed the photo and newspaper article off the coffee table, where Sheila had set them. "I have to go."

"I'm sorry," Sheila said, following her to the door. "I'm just all itchy lately. Everything feels wrong. I can't focus. I don't want to lose my da, alright? I don't want to lose him."

"He's still there," Dimpna said. "It's not too late to say the things you want to say."

"But it is too late. I can't tell him how much he hurt me. How much he hurt Mam. He's dying." Sheila's mother lived in Tralee. She'd kept to herself ever since the public found out about Danny Maguire's second family. Despite her wild nature, Sheila had always placed an extremely high value on family. Dimpna knew she was telling the truth—and that she would have a difficult time letting go of her father, letting go of the life she'd always wanted but never really had. "Lean on Paul," Dimpna said. "I'm sure he wants to be there for you." Dimpna wasn't sure at all.

Sheila scoffed. "You must be so happy."

"Why is that?"

"That Paul and I never had a real love story. And we never will."

"That makes me neither happy nor unhappy," Dimpna said.

"You're Switzerland, is that it?"

"I'm detached," Dimpna said. "Happily detached."

"Is that so?" Sheila sounded smug.

"Yes."

"Ben asked me out. I'm thinking of saying yes." Sheila maintained eye contact. "And yes, your Ben." She shrugged. "I guess younger men these days love older women. And why shouldn't they?"

Dimpna froze. That was bullshit. Wasn't it? Sheila was way too old for Ben. A cougar. What was Ben doing around Sheila at all? He was probably just filming his TikToks, and Sheila was just trying to get under her skin. It was working. The smug look on Sheila's face was infuriating. Dimpna knew she was going to regret what she was about to say, but her mouth moved anyway. "You want to know why I stopped spending the night at your house?" Sheila stilled and waited. "It's because the last time I spent the night at your house—in this very room, as a matter of fact—I woke up to find your father hovering over me in the dark."

"What?" Sheila shook her head. "That's crazy."

"You're telling me. He was standing right over me. Watching me."

"You must have been dreaming."

"I wasn't."

"What are you trying to say?"

"He gave me the creeps. That's what I'm trying to say."

"You're spitting on the name of a dying man," Sheila said. "What's wrong with you?"

"Why am I not surprised?" Dimpna said. "You always have the wrong end of the stick." This was why. This was another reason why she had never told Sheila what happened.

Sheila crossed her arms and glared. "What's that supposed to mean?"

"It means you shouldn't be asking what's wrong with me. You should be asking what's wrong with him." Dimpna could go further; she could tell Sheila the vile word he'd called her that day in the chemist shop. *Whore*, he'd said, just as she was turning away with her pregnancy test. *Whore*.

* * *

Dimpna slammed the door to her VW bus, and the tears started immediately. She'd known she was going to regret accepting Sheila's invitation. She'd known it. Why was it that, no matter how far she'd run, it took nothing to bring her back to this same place? The place where she felt small and mean. The place where she was the worst possible version of herself.

And now she'd gone and told her about the darkness in her own father. As he lay dying. But that didn't make the incident less true. They had spent the night in the Maguires' sitting room. Sheila was all limbs and hair, and it was impossible to share her bed, so they'd take their pillows and blankets and sleep on the floor downstairs. Dimpna didn't know what time it was when she woke to find Mr. Maguire standing over her in the dark. She knew immediately it was him; there were no other men in the house, and through a faint light in the hall, she could make out his tall figure, his dark beard, the pudge in his belly. He stood there staring at her for what felt like a lifetime, while once again she felt hot shame run through her. What if he saw her wake up? What would he do? What would she say? Why was he hovering silently over her in the dark? She didn't know how long he stood there; it was probably only seconds, but it felt like forever. Relief flooded her body when she heard footsteps retreating, when the floorboards announced his exit with their telltale creaks. She'd never told Sheila. Even though she still had no idea what that was about, she did know that it was not the kind of thing daughters wanted to hear about their fathers. She'd just spilled a secret she'd kept for over three decades. Sheila was still capable of bringing out the worst in Dimpna.

Ben was not going to date Sheila. Dimpna needed to make that very clear. He knew the history between them. He wouldn't do that to her. Sheila was just trying to bait her. And she had more important things to worry about at the moment. Dimpna dug her mobile phone out of her handbag and called Cormac. Not surprisingly, she got his voicemail. "Something strange just happened," she said. "I know you're swamped, so I'm just going to text you a photo and a snapshot of two articles. They're from Sheila's father, Danny Maguire. I'll fill you in in person. It may be nothing, but I'll let you decide."

CHAPTER 26

The Womb—1994

He's branded us all with a tattoo of a sheep. The shame and rage I feel is consuming me. The physical pain is nearly gone, but the shame is deep and embedded. I feel like a piece of property, worth no more to the Shepherd than a farm animal. Why did these names seem so innocent before? And these ridiculous long dresses, most of them white. White like a flock of sheep. It was one thing to conceptually think of ourselves as a Flock, it was another to see the proof on my skin. It was also proof that I no longer had a say about my body. I had told both the Shepherd and the Staff that I did not want the tattoo. My wishes were ignored. Now, with only weeks before my baby is born, I can't concentrate on anything but the last time I saw Golden One. Correction. The last time I saw Moira. Her name was Moira. And I do not believe the Shepherd simply dropped her into town. The same woman whose baby he took. The same woman he had kept in chains. I had failed her. Her blood was on my hands. But I would have to make amends later. Right now, it is my life that is in danger. My baby's life. *Run,* Moira had said. *Run.* But where? And how?

There is another reason I believe Moira is dead. I

found her luggage bin in the storeroom. If he had really set her free, as she'd requested, why was her luggage still here? It made my blood run cold. And if I was caught rifling through it, I could only imagine what they'd do to me.

Inside the luggage, underneath her clothes, I'd found letters from a woman written to Moira. There was an address in Dingle. I assumed only a mother would keep writing to someone who did not answer. Had Moira even seen these letters? They were all still sealed.

I needed to go to this address. I needed to find her mother. She needed to know what had happened to her daughter. Those would be my amends. Was her baby alive? Where was he? If I ever escaped this place, I owed it to her to find him. I would escape. I would find him.

I have to find a way to escape. The Staff is the biggest problem; he's always watching. But there is another problem. Eternal Mist. I do not trust her at all. She is nearly as bad as the Staff. Worse maybe, for she is betraying all of us. I think back to how calm she had been when Moira was chained up, screaming that he'd taken her baby. How awful I had been, insisting that the baby was in good hands. Moira had been telling the truth, and we all made her out to be a lunatic. I slapped her across the face. And for that I will be forever ashamed. I will never forgive myself, but I will do everything in my power to make it right, even if it's not enough. I can't help but replay everything about our last conversation over and over.

Golden One . . .

That's not my fucking name . . .

She was right. And Seven Star is not my name. Have I been brainwashed? Or was I enamored because I thought Seven Star was a brilliant name? Much better than my real name. Somehow just being called Seven Star had erased the old me, the ordinary me, and the name I never really identified with. I actually thought it made me someone special. And her father. I thought that made our baby special too. But now I know that he has no regard for the baby whatsoever. The baby was a product with a price tag. And so is mine.

"My name is Tallulah," I told my belly. "Your mammy's name is Tallulah."

The Shepherd—I wish to God I knew his real name—he said none of us are to speak our real names ever again. The Shepherd picked me carefully, didn't he? Somehow, he had seen my self-doubt, nay, my self-hatred. And he had preyed on me. He had preyed on every one of us. Except Eternal Mist. She wasn't pregnant. Was she with him? Was she just pretending to be part of the Flock? I'd been such a stupid girl. I'm a girl no longer, and I will not act like one. Utopia does not exist. Or if it does—this is not it.

Back to my escape. What are my options? Find a way to run to the woods that back up to the property. We'd never ventured into them. The Shepherd said it's too dense. But maybe there's another reason. Maybe it's the way out. I don't know how deep the woods are, how long I'd have to travel. If I do this, I'll need enough food and water to last for days, if necessary. When they realize I'm gone, will it be the first place they check? And what about the others? How can I just leave them? I need to write down my escape plans so that if I'm successful, they can follow my lead. I need to find a way to get the plans to Red Rose and Morning Sun. Alana and . . . I realized I didn't even know Morning Sun or Eternal Mist's real names. I will never breathe word of my escape to Eternal Mist or leave her the escape plans. She is enemy number one.

The other possibility for escape is in the back of the van. The Shepherd does not always lock it. I could try and hide in the back, but if I was discovered, there would be no second chances, no explaining what I was doing. He was not the forgiving sort; he did not tolerate anyone going rogue. But maybe if I was discovered in the woods, I could say I got lost. I could tell them I was having contractions and needed to walk— and I didn't realize until it was too late that I had wandered into the woods. They probably would not believe me, but at least there would be a seed of doubt. I needed to write this down.

And there was a more dangerous part to my plan. I need to either drug Eternal Mist and the Staff or accidentally lock them in the storage pantry. The Shepherd keeps sleeping pills in the storage room. I have been so obedient that he trusts me. I have seen them. There is a trove of pill bottles in the pantry. And he's been bringing more and more food into the compound lately from the outside, as if he is preparing for the end of the world. And for me, this may very well be the end. The place that once seemed incredible to me now seems downright bizarre. This building is shaped like a womb. Everything in it looks like parts of the female body, even the fire pits and the bathing pool. Ovaries. Vaginas. Breasts. Wombs. Who would build something like this? I pray the bottle of sleeping pills are still stashed where I last saw them. As much as I want to implement this escape right now, I need to go slow to go fast. I need to take one day at a time and squirrel pills away.

It's definitely risky. I need Eternal Mist and the Staff to think I'm the one who is sleeping, and I need to make sure they don't bother me. I wonder if I should pretend there is something wrong with the baby. Would they take me to hospital? Doubtful. And if they truly thought something was wrong with my baby, would they kill me on the spot?

We are not allowed to lock our doors. Ironic, given that the Shepherd had no problem not only locking some of the women in, but also chaining them to their beds. *For their own good.* I could say I was deliriously tired, and I didn't even realize I had locked it. But that either meant climbing out the window—and I was only half-sure I could fit—or it would mean locking my door, making them think I am in there, then escaping through the woods. That was it. That was my plan. Wait for the Shepherd to go into town. Drug Eternal Mist and the Staff. Lock my door, as if I am inside. And escape through the back woods. I may not make it. But at least I will have tried. It is not a perfect plan, but at least I have a plan. Imagine that. Boring, ordinary Tallulah has a plan.

CHAPTER 27

*C*ORMAC HAD JUST FINISHED A BRIEFING WITH THE TEAMS SEARCHING for Dylan and Shauna. The cigarette butt found at the bog was indeed a Benson and Hedges 100s Luxury, the same brand Cahal Mackey had been smoking. The rain had made it impossible to source any DNA, and Cormac had already tried rattling Cahal by suggesting the cigarette butt found at the bog had been his brand. He'd stated that plenty of people smoked them, and he wasn't wrong. But it certainly made him think Neely was right all along. Cahal Mackey was masterminding all of this. Cormac was just about to check a message from Dimpna Wilde and return a call from the state pathologist, when a clerk hurried over to his office, a look of urgency on her face.

"There's a couple here who think their daughter is our Jane Doe."

"Is it Gary and Breanna Sheehan?"

"It is." *Finally.* The clerk took a deep breath. "I can't imagine what they're going through."

"Can you alert Garda Lennon that I'd like him in the interview room with me?"

"Of course."

"Then show them to the debriefing room—tea, biscuits, the works. And I'll need the file on Fiona Sheehan."

"Tea for you as well, Inspector?"

"Coffee would be a godsend."

"Straightaway." She turned and headed back to the reception

area. Cormac gathered his personal notes on the case and took a moment to be grateful for his support staff. He understood the clerk's sentiment—that she didn't wish tragedy on these parents, and of course neither did he—but as far as this investigation was concerned, the sooner they identified the woman found in the bog, the better. The state pathologist was still waiting for dental records, and they were also waiting on a court order to dig into Fiona Sheehan's medical records. None of her friends had heard from her, but they did finally have a partial name for her boyfriend—Tom. One of them thought he worked with windmills. Guards were currently making calls. Everything about this line of work was either painfully slow or wait, wait, wait. Torture. And as horrific as it was to think like this, he hoped their Jane Doe was Fiona Sheehan. If she was their victim, they could gain access to her flat and her medical records.

The Sheehans and Garda Lennon were already seated when he entered the room, the table set up with their tea and coffee and biscuits. Steam rose from the untouched tea mugs. They were an attractive pair, both slim and well-polished, but their faces were a portrait of desperation.

"Mr. and Mrs. Sheehan?"

They rose when he entered, and he gestured for them to sit back down. "Please. Gary and Breanna," Gary said as they sat.

"I'm Detective Inspector Cormac O'Brien." He gestured to Barry Lennon. "And you've met Garda Lennon." They all nodded.

"A detective inspector," Breanna said. "Good." Her voice wobbled. As Cormac took the seat in front of them and handed out his card, Breanna Sheehan glanced at the folder labeled BOG. A folder that contained photos they did not want to see. Breanna's hand flew to her mouth. Cormac covered the folder with his hand. It was best to ease in.

"I understand you've been on a cruise?" He tried to keep his voice friendly and light; things would get heavy soon enough.

"We were supposed to be gone a month," Gary said. "For our thirty-fifth anniversary." Breanna simply nodded, her jaw tight. Their eyes were both rimmed in red.

There was no use dancing around it. "I take it you have not been able to reach your daughter, Fiona?" He nearly choked on the words, for no matter how well one could empathize, the horror of this was beyond comprehension. He didn't know how people survived things like this; these kind of wounds never healed. They would have to learn to constantly weave around it, like a fairy tree growing in the middle of a roundabout.

They shook their heads, nodded, unable to speak.

Cormac slid a box of tissues toward them and gave it a beat. "When did you last speak with her?"

Gary squirmed, then cleared his throat and looked to his wife. "It's been at least nineteen days," Breanna said, in an anguished whisper. "Her phone has been going straight to voicemail." She let out a cry and slapped her hand over her mouth again.

Gary reached over and set his hand protectively on her arm. "She'd already taken her maternity leave from work, but when we called, none of them had heard from her either."

"And yet you remained on your cruise?" Cormac felt cruel asking them that question; if they were innocent, there was no doubt they were already punishing themselves for that, but the question had to be asked.

The couple exchanged a heartbreaking glance with each other. "We were not on the best terms with our daughter when we left," Gary said. "It's been six months since we've seen her in person."

Breanna's composure crumbled, and she began to sob. "She can be so stubborn. We just wanted what's best for her."

Cormac nodded, hoping to exude calmness, but his heart was dancing in his chest. He knew that Fiona Sheehan's car was parked on the street in front of her flat. No signs of trouble were found inside the car. It was locked up. They did not find any handbag, or personal items, and no sign that any violence had occurred inside the car. They'd even brought canine sniffer dogs, and they did not alert officers to a body. That meant the abduction had taken place there, or someone had picked her up, or she'd taken another mode of transportation somewhere. They were all threads he could pull on.

"Our neighbor said there was a ransom note in the postbox," Gary said.

"He's old," Breanna said. "Please tell us he's deranged."

"He's not deranged," Gary said.

"He could have memory issues. Or he's just being cruel."

Cormac sighed and opened the folder. The ransom note was encased in an evidence bag.

He slid it across the table. "By the time this note was delivered to us, we believe at least two weeks had passed."

They leaned in to read it. Breanna cried out, and Gary made a fist and put it to his mouth. "I told you we shouldn't have gone on the cruise," Breanna said. "We did this. We did this."

"Don't say that." Gary tried to touch her hand; she yanked it away. Gary looked at Cormac. "We had no idea anything like this was going to happen."

"I know this is tough," Cormac said. "But I need to ask."

"Anything," Gary said. "We just want to find our daughter."

"Unless she's already dead," Breanna said. "Unless *they're* already dead."

"We need to see the woman you found in the bog," Gary said, his voice breaking.

"We'll get to that," Cormac said. "I can understand you want that part over with, but I do need to take this step by step." Gary opened his arms, then folded them and waited. "You said you quarreled with your daughter," Cormac began. "What was it about?"

The Sheehans exchanged glances again. "She wouldn't tell us who the father of her baby was," Breanna said. "We didn't even know she was dating."

"We do not believe in sex before marriage," Gary said. "I know that might sound terribly old-fashioned. But Fiona was—is—our only daughter. And this wasn't what we wanted for her."

"We were going to support her and the baby," Breanna said. "We *are* going to support her and the baby. But the father has responsibilities. Financial responsibilities."

"It got heated quick. Fiona told us all we cared about was money."

"It's not true. We just wanted to meet him. And maybe—if we approved of the match—we'd suggest they could get married." She dropped her head. "We're devout Catholics, and Fiona was too. At one time, at least."

"She was very cagey after we started asking about the father," Gary said. "And very angry."

"Hormones," Breanna said. She wiped away tears. "Show us," she said. "Show us the woman in the bog."

"I understand you don't have keys to her flat," Cormac said, ignoring her request for the moment. They nodded. "We sent word that we did not want you to enter." They nodded again. "Did you comply?" Cormac knew what they'd done; he'd had guards watching her flat, but he wanted to see if they would answer truthfully. It was hideous, to suspect these parents and grandparents-to-be, but in murder cases, the culprit was often someone who was closest to the victim. And these two had remained on a cruise even after they had not heard from their pregnant daughter. He'd be a fool not to thoroughly check them out.

"We drove to her flat," Gary said. "It's a semi-detached. We helped her buy it."

"We didn't enter," Breanna said. "We just . . . stayed in the car— in case we saw anything."

Cormac nodded. They were telling the truth. They stayed there for twenty minutes, and Gary had gotten out of the car, but he only walked the footpath in front of her flat, end to end. Then he had knocked on the neighbor's door, but received no answer. Cormac knew the family who lived next to Fiona were out of town and had been for some months. Given that her flat was at the end of the street, there was nothing but fields on the other side. If she had been abducted from her flat and had screamed, no one but cows would have heard it. "Did you see anything amiss? Any signs of a break-in?"

"Her car," Gary said. "It wasn't on the street."

"It was," Cormac said, "but we discovered it was towed." Between the car and the ransom letter, it was apparent that whatever had happened to Fiona Sheehan had taken place at least a fortnight ago. Gary looked shocked, but clamped his lips shut. "It's been processed, and there are no signs of any foul play. You'll be free to pick the car up soon."

"We don't care about the car," Gary spit out. Breanna patted his arm.

Cormac slid a piece of paper and a biro over to the couple. "Please write down Fiona's phone number, her place of work, and any friends you can think of." Breanna began writing.

"Who do you think took her?" Gary asked. "Is it this cult leader from thirty years ago?" His voice rose. "Do you have him back in custody?" Devout or not, Gary had a look on his face that Cormac knew well. The look of a man willing to take things into his own hands if the investigation did not proceed to his satisfaction. And he wasn't alone. The harbor master had expressed grave concerns about the rumbling of men at the harbor and what they wanted to do to Cahal Mackey and Flynn Barry. Cormac had increased the number of guards patrolling the area. He was also working on a new work placement for the men, something else that was taking too much time.

"It's too early in the investigation to draw any conclusions," Cormac said. "Do you have a recent photo of Fiona?" If he could spare them the image of the woman in the bog, he would do it. Even if it was Fiona, there was a chance they wouldn't recognize her. Not the way they'd ever imagined her looking. Her face could not have been bloated from the degraded bog. It was nearly drained of water. He had a theory that someone tried to strangle her in a bathtub, but for some reason that didn't work, and that's why her throat was slit. She must have been left in the bathtub for days until the killer figured out he wanted to move the body to the bog. It was just a theory, but the state pathologist said it tracked. "Did Fiona have a tattoo?"

"No," Gary and Breanna said in unison.

This confirmed the state pathologist's finding that the tattoo was given postmortem. *Sick.* Guards were canvassing nearby tattoo parlors, but no hits so far. Donnecha Wilde had recently opened a tattoo shop. He wasn't even sure Dimpna was aware of that, as she hadn't mentioned it. Cormac planned on visiting that one personally and soon. They were looking for someone skilled in tattoos, although, to his eye, they looked crude. Given that Donnecha was new to the business and no doubt had to do his homework to set up shop, hopefully he could tell them who the local players were. And although Cormac had to keep all possibilities on the table, he did not see Donnecha Wilde as their killer. The young man was one of the laziest Cormac had ever met, but he did have somewhat of a charming personality.

"Just show us," Breanna said, as she zeroed in on the file. "Is there a photo in there?"

Cormac took a pause. "I do have photos," he said. "But sometimes it's a good idea for maybe a good friend of the family or—"

"I want to see," Breanna said. "Now."

Cormac nodded slowly. "I must warn you. Even if this is not your daughter, and by the grace of God, I hope it's not, the photo does not resemble the woman she was before." He paused as he watched them take this in. "You may not even recognize her, and we are waiting on dental records."

"We'll call her dentist," Gary said. "He's a friend."

"That would help tremendously," Cormac said. "We'd also like to talk to her doctors and learn any information you have on her birth plan."

"She kept all of that from us," Breanna said. "She did say one thing—I just remembered."

"Go on," Cormac said.

"She said the baby was going to be gorgeous. The most gorgeous creature anyone had ever seen."

Cormac nodded slowly. Did this suggest an extremely handsome baby daddy? "Do you know anyone in Fiona's life by the name of Tom?"

They both shook their heads. Gary leaned forward. "Who is he?"

"Maybe no one," Cormac said. "One of her friends thought her boyfriend was named Tom and he worked with windmills."

Gary frowned. "There are several wind farms nearby."

"We're checking them out," Cormac said. "I don't have to warn you not to start digging, now do I?"

"Not if you do your job," Gary said.

Breanna pointed to the folder. "I will recognize her," she insisted. "We will recognize her."

"Why don't you show me a photo first," Cormac said. He did not want this lovely couple to see the photos. He wanted to forbid them to see the photos. He wanted to pick up the now-cold cups of tea and spill both of them on the file so no one would ever have to look at them again.

Breanna reached into her handbag and brought out not just one, but a stack of photos. She slid them across the table. He gently flipped through them, images of a radiant young woman with raven hair. In the first photo, her baby bump was barely visible, but in the third, it was close to term. She had a beaming smile. He'd been wrong. The resemblance was still there. They no longer had a Jane Doe. They had a Fiona. Fiona Sheehan was their murder victim from the bog.

CHAPTER 28

MOTH MAN HAD BROUGHT IN AN INHALER, CRAYONS, AND A COLOR-
ing book. He dumped them in a pile with their other supplies.
Shauna wished he would let them out of this claustrophobic room.
Her fingers were raw from trying to pry the boards off the window.
She'd also been staring at the keypad by the door, but she was terrified to touch it. The window was a better bet. She needed tools.
What did the rest of the building look like? Not bothering to linger,
Moth Man exited quickly, slamming the door shut behind him.
Dylan immediately retrieved the inhaler and began to use it. Shauna
waited until Dylan's breathing had regulated before approaching
the lad with the coloring book and crayons. Now Shauna could
write. They could communicate. She picked up a red crayon and
watched him frown. She held up her index finger, then turned to a
page in the middle of the book. She wrote: S-H-A-U-N-A. She
pointed at herself. His lips moved, forming her name. She handed
him the crayon and slid the coloring book his way.

D-Y-L-A-N he wrote.

"Dylan," she pronounced. He nodded. "Hear? Him?" She
pointed to the door. "Bad man?" He tilted his head and stared at
the door. After a moment, he shook his head no. "Moth Man," she
said, picking up a gray crayon and drawing an ugly moth. When he
didn't react, she gave it eyes that crossed and a tongue sticking out.
Dylan finally laughed, and she was thrilled to see a smile finally
break out on his tear-stained face.

She gently took the coloring book back. *You hear what?*

This time he didn't hesitate; he grabbed the book and a blue crayon, then rested the coloring book on his knees, his tongue hanging out of the corner of his mouth as he wrote.

Drip. He drew a picture of water dripping and watched her face eagerly as she read. She nodded. "Good," she said. "More." He shook his head. "Birds?" He cocked his head, listened, then nodded. *Birds.* "Cars? People talk?"

He jabbed at the word *drip*, then at the word *birds*. They were somewhere remote, but they had running water.

"Okay," she said. "Water drip. Birds. Okay." She scooted away from him. "Color," she said. "Color." He needed to get his mind off their situation; he was only a kid. She rubbed her belly. Were his parents rich? Were their captors asking for money? There was no one to pay for her. Maybe the Griffins. Because of the baby. Either way, the guards had to be searching for them by now. But she didn't even know where they were. How would anyone find them? She had no idea how far they were from Dingle, from the bog. *Wait.*

She scooted back to the boy. "Man take you," she said. She took the coloring book and opened to the back page. "Car? Road? See? Hear?" He bit his lip. "Understand?" He shook his head. She gestured driving. She exaggerated looking around as she drove. "Where here? Where here?"

He wrote a single word: *boot.*

The bastard had thrown him in the boot of the car. The same as he'd done to her. She took another crayon. *How long drive?* He stuck the crayon on his chin and looked up. He frowned. *One hour?* she wrote. *More? Less?* He circled less. Shauna felt her heart beat faster. She'd been correct. Less than an hour's drive. They were still in the vicinity of home. A sliver of hope wormed its way into her.

Car stop. What happened? Carry you?

Dylan stood. He gestured. The boot opened. The man grabbed him, threw him over his shoulders. Walk. Grass. Wood. Hard floor. Just like her experience.

Dylan seemed to have a burst of energy. He took to the coloring book, drew grass, and then a straight black line. He drew a large building, somewhat oval-shaped. It looked like a giant UFO. He drew water around the building. He then mimicked being cold. That must have been when he entered. It was a cold building. How had he been able to see? She mimicked a blindfold and then pointed.

He nodded, then mimed a small opening in the blindfold. He'd been able to see, and they didn't know. He was a bit of a rebel, like her. The realization gave her another little shot of hope.

"More," she said. "Everything." She pointed to the coloring book. "Write." She'd never be able to read his little lips.

Enter. Dark. Cold. Walk walk walk. Bumpy.

She nodded. "What see?"

He shook his head. *Dark.*

"House?" she asked.

He frowned. Then shook his head. Then held his arms open. *Big.*

Maybe an old warehouse. Or an abandoned factory. But why the funny shape? It wasn't much to go on. But it was knowledge. And knowledge was power.

CHAPTER 29

*B*Y THE TIME CORMAC RETURNED TO HIS FLAT THAT EVENING, A FAMIL-
iar figure was standing by his front door. Just the sight of her lifted
his spirits. "Dimpna Wilde," he said, enjoying the feel of her name
in his mouth. "What a surprise." He was so used to seeing her in the
white lab coat that the sight of her in a soft dress nearly took his
breath away. Given all the darkness as of late, he took a selfish moment to drink her in.

She lifted an over-sized envelope. "I know you're busy, and this is
probably nothing—"

"Your voicemail," he said. "I'm sorry I got so busy—"

"I figured. But you really might want to know about this."

"Come in," he said.

"I don't want to disturb your evening."

"I insist. If you don't mind me eating a bit of dinner while we
chat, that is."

"I don't mind at all."

He opened the door and gestured for her to take the lead. He
then had to maneuver past her in order to turn on lights, straight-
ening as he went. As bachelors were concerned, he was tidy. But
these cases had been so consuming that his housekeeping had
lapsed. They passed through his small living room and into the eat-
in kitchen. He placed the envelope from Dimpna on the small dining table and pulled out a chair. Dimpna perched on the edge. He
opened his fridge. "Beer?"

"I have an early morning," Dimpna said.

He sighed. He did as well. "Tea it is." He put the kettle on, then realized the one thing he'd planned for his dinner might not be her favorite: liver and onions. He'd eat later, but decided one beer wasn't going to keep him from doing his best on the case, and he took one out.

He sat across from Dimpna and slid the envelope over to him. He was soon holding a photograph and two newspaper articles. "He was hunting," Cormac said, mostly to himself.

Dimpna swallowed hard. "But as you can see, I'm not even showing in that photo. In fact, I've had time to reflect, and I remember this day. I had just found out I was pregnant, and I swear, I hadn't even told me mother or father yet. Any guess how he knew?"

Cormac's stomach had twisted, and he felt a surge of anger toward the cult leader. The thought of him stalking Dimpna made him want to find him and settle this in the most unprofessional manner. "Tell me."

"He was hanging around the chemist's. I received this from Danny Maguire—Sheila's father, who used to be a chemist. It was Mr. Maguire I had to approach when I needed a pregnancy test."

Cormac put it together. "Cahal Mackey knew that women had to ask the chemist for a test. He was lurking to see who they were."

"Exactly."

"Women who fit his profile. Young, possibly pregnant, and vulnerable."

"That makes me sick."

Cormac nodded. "We're talking about a very sick individual." Cormac was glad he'd skipped dinner. The tea kettle shrieked.

"I'll get it," Dimpna said. She popped up to fix her tea, and he received a little jolt. He liked her about his place, making herself at home. He'd have to shove that thought far, far away. He could not afford any distractions, not if he wanted to find their missing persons alive. It was going on exactly forty-eight hours since they'd found Fiona Sheehan's body and learned of Dylan's disappearance. Slightly longer for Shauna Mills. His only hope that they were still alive was the baby. The kidnapper was waiting for the birth of the baby. In that sense, he was working against a biological clock. He could not let up for a second.

He continued to study the photograph. "Mr. Maguire has kept this all these years?"

"Apparently."

"And he just now decided he needed you to see this?"

Dimpna returned to the table with a mug of tea. "It seems so. Sheila's cousin is in town. Her name is Orla, and she looks to be about eight months pregnant. He's worried about her."

He should be worried. Every pregnant woman and her loved ones should be worried. "Why didn't he just call into the garda station?"

"He doesn't know you. He knows me." She shook her head. "He can barely speak, he's so ill. I don't think he has long to live."

Cormac sorted the newspaper articles. "Why do you think he saved these? The most recent one, okay—but why the one from thirty years ago?"

"I don't know. But the case did stir up everyone in town." If she searched through her father's boxes, it was possible he'd saved newspapers from back then as well. "There's more," she said.

"I'm listening."

"I saw him again recently."

"Yes," Cormac said. "I know. He gave you the photo—"

"Not Mr. Maguire," Dimpna said. "Cahal Mackey."

"What do you mean?" Cormac was on high alert. "Where did you see him? At the harbor?" Her brother lived seasonally on a sailboat in the harbor. Maybe she ran into him there.

"He came into my clinic."

Cormac knew for a fact the man did not have a pet. This also meant that the guards watching him had messed up big-time, including Garda Lennon. He was not looking forward to that conversation. "When did he come into the clinic?"

"Just the other day—before . . ." she swallowed. "Before you found that poor woman in the bog."

Fiona Sheehan. They would be announcing her identification tomorrow. "What did Cahal Mackey say he wanted?"

"He wanted to know if I could recommend a wolfhound breeder."

Impossible. He was in temporary housing for at least six months. A fucking wolfhound? "There had to be another motive—"

"That's what I was just about to say," Dimpna began. "Right before he walked in, a young couple came into my clinic for the first time as well. The woman I've just mentioned. Sheila Maguire's cousin, Orla." She took a sip of tea. "I think Cahal Mackey was following her."

Cormac slammed his beer bottle down. "Damn it." Maybe Neely was right. Maybe she was focused on the only person who mattered. He stood and began to pace his kitchen. "Neely was right. It's him. He's starting this all over again." On Cormac's watch. He'd never been violent with a criminal in his life, and he'd been around a lot of them. But this smug son of a bitch preying on pregnant women—stealing babies, murdering the mothers—that was the bottom rung of depravity. Evil. The man was evil. And now he was hanging around the woman he loved.

Yes, he loved her. He hadn't told her and he wasn't planning on telling her any time soon. But he loved Dimpna Wilde. And right now, imagining Cahal Mackey anywhere close to her, anywhere close to any woman, made him want to pick up one of the kitchen chairs and smash it against the counter. What was his move here? Did he let Cahal Mackey know he was onto him? "Did he threaten you or her?"

Dimpna shook her head. "Not at all." She pulled a card out of her pocket and slid it over to Cormac. NEW AWAKENINGS. "He gave both of us this card. Orla seemed to like him. She said she knew a wolfhound breeder, and he also overhead them saying they were looking for a flat."

"Where do they live now?"

"With Sheila." Dimpna was chewing her bottom lip again.

"Tell me," he said.

"It's my mother. Doing her thing again. She suggested I'd been around someone who was pregnant—obviously Orla, but possibly Shauna Mills; she said that the woman was in trouble." Dimpna paused. "And cold. They might be somewhere cold."

Cormac arched an eyebrow. Maeve Wilde was a character. A tarot card reader. Sometimes she was surprisingly on the mark. And she had a very unique personality. Dressed to the nines, even while living in a caravan in the field, like an aging actress who had put herself out to pasture, then forgot to die. She was direct—he liked that about her. But he wasn't going to count on a so-called psychic to help with this case, even if she was entertaining. "Do you have a way to get in touch with Orla?"

"Of course. Through Sheila. And they're also supposed to check back in with Niamh about a place to let."

"Will you please get her contact info for me?"

"Certainly."

"This case almost broke Neely. I'm starting to see why."

Dimpna rose and not only took her teacup to the sink; she washed and dried it and put it away. It was the most romantic thing anyone had ever done for him. "I'd better head home," Dimpna said. "Long day tomorrow."

For a second, he almost asked her to stay the night. Would she say yes? An attraction had been simmering between them since the first day he met her, standing in the courtyard of her clinic filled with animals, and even among that chaotic zoo, all he could see was her. That was nearly going on two years now. They were like shy children at a dance, afraid to cross the center line. But he didn't want their first time to be under such a cloud. They had just taken a step away from the table when it happened. The window above his kitchen sink exploded, and a red projectile sailed toward them along with shards of glass.

"Get down," Cormac yelled. Dimpna scrambled behind the kitchen table. A brick landed with a thud at his feet.

"Be careful," she called out.

Cormac crouched and hurried over to the closest living room window. Outside he could see a man, swaying and yelling at the top of his lungs. He was illuminated by outside security lights, and it took him only a few seconds to recognize him. Gary Sheehan. Fiona's father. He tried to make sense of it over the thudding of his heart. "Stay here," he called to Dimpna. "I know who this is."

* * *

Cormac flung open his door to find Gary Sheehan standing there, ready to lob a second brick.

"Hey," Cormac yelled. Unlike the put-together man who had sat in front of him at the station, this man was absolutely blotto. It was the first time anyone had confronted Cormac where he lived. And it had better be the last. "Gary Sheehan." He used his harshest voice. "You're not looking to get arrested on top of everything else, are ya?"

Gary stopped swaying and stared at Cormac. "Me wife has taken to her bed," Gary said. "Why did you let her see that photo? How could you?"

"Drop the brick," Cormac said. "Now."

Gary squeezed it for a moment, and a drop of blood appeared near his palm.

"I'll arrest you. I don't want to. But I will."

Gary opened his hand, and the brick dropped to the ground.

Cormac had made a practice of not engaging with drunks, especially ones who found out where he resided just so they could throw projectiles at his windows after dark, not to mention startling the gorgeous creature crouching beneath his table. But he had empathy for this father. He'd lost his daughter and grandchild in the most horrific way.

"How could you let me wife see that photo?" Gary crooned. "How could you?" Cormac had warned her—hell, he'd warned the pair of them, because he knew the lasting trauma it could cause—but they had insisted on seeing it. Saying "I told you so" to the man would only ratchet up the tension. He also didn't want to shame him on top of everything else. Gary took a step and then swayed, his feet as still as if they were entombed in cement and his eyes nearly black with fury. Cormac knew it wasn't really directed at him, but it certainly felt that way. "I'm going to kill him. I'm going to kill that cult man."

"You don't want to spend the rest of your life behind bars," Cormac said. "Fiona wouldn't want that either."

"I want them back," he moaned. "Me daughter and grandchild. Our first. Our first. I want them back now."

"I know," Cormac said. "I know you do." When he was sober and some time had passed, he would recommend grief counselors. He was also confident that the parish priest would reach out. "The entire town will want to rally around you and your wife. Let them. I can't imagine how you feel. But you need to remember that we're all on the same team. We need to focus on finding the monster who did this." And was still doing it.

"What are your leads?" Gary demanded, the words muddled, but his pain loud and clear. "Who the fuck did this to my daughter and her baby?" His face was red, spittle flew from his mouth.

"We're doing everything we can to find out." Cormac loathed himself for the vague and generic response; he wanted to summon Neely, wanted her to be here to promise Gary that they would catch Fiona's killer. But even as he thought all of that, he had to remind himself that they had yet to confirm that Gary and Breanna Sheehan were out of the country when Fiona's throat was slit. He didn't think it was them; he didn't want it to be them, but evil came in many forms. And good people did evil things. Anyone who thought otherwise was a fool. And given that their daughter had kept her pregnancy a secret, given that they hadn't seen her in nearly six months, hadn't spoken in nineteen days, and given that they purposefully left the country and had intended to miss their granddaughter's birth, he knew the relationship had been complicated and strained. Their regrets were fueling their anger. Which is why Sheehan stood in front of him now, drunk out of his mind and violent. Cormac could have him arrested, let him sleep it off in custody. Some days he hated his job, wanted nothing more than to play the squeeze-box and listen to old men at the bar wax on about ancient history. Walk the roads, stand at the edge of cliffs communing with the wild Atlantic Ocean, feel the spray of water on his face and see how close he could get to the edge without tumbling over. One short lifetime was what human beings were given, and even then, they still had to turn paradise into hell.

"Go home, Gary. Sleep it off. We'll discuss this case at a decent hour in the garda station. And if you ever come to my house again for any reason, whether or not you lob bricks at me windows, I'm not going to hesitate to slap cuffs on ya. Do I make myself clear?"

Gary's face radiated hatred, but he quickly crumpled and began to sob. "I was cross with her," he said. "The last time I saw her." His head dropped. "I was cross with her."

Cormac felt his heart squeeze. "We all get cross from time to time."

Gary shook his head violently, refusing the comfort. "I'd give anything to have me daughter back, Inspector. I would be a better father." Dimpna emerged from behind Cormac. "There are only two things keeping me going. Me wife—and finding the monster who did this to her so I can kill him meself." He pointed his finger at Cormac. "And I don't care what you do to me after that. I'll kill him with me bare hands. I'll do much worse than slitting his throat from behind."

"For heaven's sake," Dimpna said. "Bring him in for a cup of tea."

Gary shook his head. "I don't want tea. I want me daughter's butcher." He stuck his hand in the pocket of his trousers, then pulled out a piece of paper. He shoved it at Cormac. "Fiona's boyfriend," he said. "At the windmill farm. Tom Cunningham he's called. Tom Cunningham."

Cormac stared at the piece of paper. "How did you find this out?"

"Sheer will," Gary said. "Sheer fucking will." With that, he whirled around and staggered down the street. As he went, he made a sound halfway between a howl and a croon. It echoed throughout the darkness and gave Cormac goose bumps. He was failing. He was failing Fiona, he was failing Dylan, he was failing Shauna. He shared Gary's rage. If he thought it would bring them any closer to solving this case, he'd burst into Cahal Mackey's flat and drag him out of bed. He'd choke him until he was ready to confess. And he'd do it without a single regret.

"You'd better not be driving," Cormac yelled after Gary. Cormac lived in a walkable part of town, and he watched Gary to make sure he wasn't getting into the driver's seat of any vehicles. Up ahead, he watched Gary climb into the passenger side of a taxi. At least he wouldn't have to worry about him getting into an accident.

"Are you alright?" Dimpna asked quietly, slipping her hand into his and giving it a squeeze.

"No," he said. "I think it's going to be a long, long time before I'm anywhere near alright."

"Is there anything I can do?"

"Yes," he said. "Sometime soon I'm going to need your help."

"Anything," she said. "I'll do anything."

"Good," Cormac said. "Because I'm going to need to see a woman about a pig."

CHAPTER 30

AT THE WIND FARM, TWENTY-EIGHT GIANT WINDMILLS CHURNED LIKE synchronized swimmers. It was a brisk day, but the sun was finally making a cameo. Cormac and Neely stepped out of the squad car near the main office. Cormac took a moment to stare at the swirling propellers and gather his thoughts. There was something mesmerizing about them, bordering on hypnotic, especially when you factored in the rhythmic swooshing that he could feel in his bones. He wished he had time to get lost in them, see where his thoughts took him. He was a firm proponent of clean energy, harnessing the power of the wind for electricity, but in truth he knew very little about the business, and the questions they had for this one particular technician today would do nothing to broaden his knowledge.

The operations manager had showed them Tom Cunningham's photo, and soon they spotted him on the grounds with a clipboard. The pair of them headed over to him.

Tom was a short but muscular man in his thirties with a shaved head. One look at him and Cormac couldn't help but imagine him coming up from behind Fiona with a sharp knife. He knew nothing of the man at this point, yet seven times out of ten, the killer was someone close to the victim. *Intimate.* Let's face it, it had been an intimate murder. He couldn't begin to imagine the pathology of such a killer. It took Tom a moment to realize Cormac and Neely were standing less than a meter from him, staring at him.

His stance switched to a defensive mode: feet wide, chest out, and the hand with the clipboard dropped to his side. "You're not authorized to be here," he said. "Who are you?"

"I'm Detective Inspector Cormac O'Brien, and this is Detective Sergeant Neely." Cormac found himself yelling over the wind turbines; he'd been accused of expelling a lot of hot air in his day, but these contraptions had him beat.

Tom's expression immediately softened. "Fiona," he said. "You're here about Fiona."

"I'm surprised you're at work," Cormac said. "Given your double loss."

He stared at the ground for a moment before making eye contact. "Let's go into my office."

His office was in a trailer set back behind the main building. It was cluttered with papers. Nearby a radio murmured on low and an old coffee machine sputtered. Tom sat at a built-in table that must have doubled as his desk, for it was loaded with folders. He removed his hat and sat it on top of a nearby pile. "Tea? Coffee? Water?"

"No, thank you," Cormac said. He and Neely remained standing. The booth was too small for him to squeeze into, and he also wanted to keep Tom on his toes.

"Why are you working when your girlfriend and baby were just found murdered?" Neely asked.

"Staying home isn't going to bring her back." He rubbed his chin. "I'm in recovery," he said. "Clean and sober five years."

"Congrats," Neely said.

He waved it away. "If I'm left home on me own, there's no telling what I will do. I've even been sleeping here." He gestured to the back, where indeed there was a cot and mussed-up blankets. "Work is the only thing keeping me sane. And I use the word loosely."

"Which word?" Cormac couldn't help but ask. "*Work* or *sane?*"

"*Sane*, Inspector," Tom said, hostility creeping into his voice.

Has a temper. Now they were getting somewhere. Cormac pulled out his notepad. "When was the last time you saw Fiona Sheehan?"

"Last week. Thursday. Before we both left." He answered quickly and without hesitation. But no doubt he had been expecting this visit. He'd had time to prepare.

Cormac was on high alert. "Left?"

Tom nodded. "I've been gone all week doing an installation in Killarney. She was going to meet up with a group of friends. She was all excited."

Neely and Cormac exchanged a glance. "We're going to need someone who can confirm you were out of town all week, and I'm going to need the name of these friends Fiona was meeting up with," Cormac said.

"You can call me supervisor, and I can also provide hotel receipts, restaurants, gas stations, whatnot. But as far as Fiona's friends?" Tom shook his head. "I wish I could give them to you. It's just some group she hooked up with online."

"What kind of a group?" Neely said.

"Adoptees," Tom said.

Cormac tilted his head. "What?"

"Fiona was adopted," Tom said. "As a baby."

Cormac was trying to hide his emotions, but the information was presenting a challenge. Gary and Breanna had sat across from them at the garda station for nearly an hour, and they had never mentioned this. Perhaps Cormac shouldn't have let Gary off the hook the other night. "She was meeting with other folks who had been adopted?" Neely asked.

"Exactly," Tom said. "All I know is that they were all from Ireland—at least they'd been adopted in Ireland—and they had been chatting for nearly a year. This was their big get-together."

"Where was it supposed to take place?"

"Honestly, I have no idea. Had I known what was going to happen, I would have asked more questions." Tom ran his hand over his shaved head. "I would have been happy she was going because normally she hated me being out of town. But, given the circumstances, I offered to cancel me trip and take her to hospital. But she was adamant. We had a bit of a row." Guilt settled over his face.

"Did things get physical?" Cormac asked.

"What?" His mouth dropped open. "Of course not. I've never raised a hand to a woman in me life."

"What about a knife?" Cormac said.

Tom shot up from the bench. "My God. Are you serious?"

Cormac nodded. "As a heart attack."

Tom gulped. He strode over to a small filing cabinet, where more folders were piled on top. He dug through them until he found what he was looking for. He handed him a calling card. "That's me manager. I was in Killarney. I've been working overtime. For Fiona. For her baby. Ask him."

"Believe me. We will," Cormac said. "But if there's anything you need to tell us, now's the time."

"I wouldn't hurt anyone. Especially Fiona. I loved her."

"Do you know anything at all about the other members of this online group, or is there any place she may have written it down?" Neely asked.

"No, I swear to ye. I only knew she was involved in this online group and they were meeting up."

"Did she contact you at all when she was with them?" Neely asked.

"There was no point." He ran his hands over the top of his head. "I was so angry. I'd never known her to be so irresponsible."

Cormac didn't know what Tom was referring to, but he would circle back to it. He removed a swab kit from his pocket. "I'd like to collect your DNA," he said, holding it out. "I'm sure you want us to rule you out."

Tom stared at it.

"Unless you have something to hide," Neely said.

Tom shook his head and reached for it. He put it on his desk. "When should I drop it off?"

"No need," Cormac said. "Swab your cheeks now and put it back in the baggie, and Bob's your uncle." Tom looked as if he'd rather do anything else. "Something wrong?"

Tom looked as if he was going to be ill. After another few seconds, he opened the plastic bag, removed the swab, ran it along the insides of his mouth, and dropped it back in the bag. "Satisfied?"

Attitude. "For now," Neely said.

"You said this group had been meeting online for at least a

year?" Cormac asked. Cahal and Flynn had only been out a number of weeks. Was it possible one or both of them had organized some kind of group from within prison? Was it a coincidence that they had a missing baby (or babies) from twenty-nine years ago and a woman twenty-nine years of age looking for her birth parents? Shauna had been an orphan. Was this the connection between the two? Both in search of their past?

"Fiona had never expressed any interest in finding her birth parents until she found out she was going to have a baby. It was then she wanted to know her medical history." *That made sense. Shauna would want to know the same thing.* Tom sighed and poured himself a cup of coffee. "If only she'd learned it a lot earlier."

"Why the hell didn't you come into the station the minute you found out your fiancé and unborn baby had been murdered?" Cormac hadn't intended to raise his voice, but that was downright suspicious.

Tom tilted his head and glared. "I told you I was out of town on a job. It's long, intense work. I didn't watch the press conference. When I did find out there was a pregnant woman found in the bog"—he gulped—"I didn't want it to be her. So I did what addicts often do. I buried me head in the sand." He stared at them. "And you haven't officially announced that Fiona was the woman found in the bog. But now I know. And now I'm telling you everything I know."

"And we're going to need a full account of where you were every day and night that she was gone," Neely added. She was pissed too. Good.

"Not a problem," Tom said. "But you've got the short end of the stick."

"What's that?" Cormac asked.

"I was Fiona's boyfriend. But I wasn't the father of her baby."

This was indeed a surprise. "Do you know who the father was?" Cormac asked.

He shook his head. "She kept saying it didn't matter, it didn't matter. And then, of course, it really didn't matter."

Neely stepped forward. "What do you mean?"

"You don't know," he said. "She must not have told them."

"Them meaning her parents?" Neely asked.

"Exactly."

"What don't we know?" Cormac asked.

Tom set his coffee down and used his hands as he talked. "I wanted her to go straight to hospital, but she insisted that the doctor said it could wait a week—she said up to four weeks—which was her way of trying to make me feel better. But it wasn't right. How could she . . . I don't know how she could . . . I almost got the feeling that she didn't want this group to know what happened. As if she had disappointed *them* somehow. I don't think she was thinking clearly. Hormones, grief, what have you."

"I am not following this conversation," Cormac said.

"I second that," Neely said. "Spit it out."

"There were complications with her pregnancy," Tom said. "A few days before this big meet with the adoptees was planned, her baby died in utero."

Cormac and Neely leaned against the squad car, watching the windmills churn as fast as their thoughts.

"Do you think Shauna Mills was part of this meetup?" Cormac asked.

"Shauna was orphaned, but she was never adopted," Neely pointed out.

"Maybe he had the subject matter wrong. Maybe it was either adopted or orphaned adults searching for their birth parents."

"That would track," Neely said.

"And it started online," Cormac continued. "Dimpna said the paper Shauna dropped at the festival seemed to be some kind of email exchange. Maybe she'd been communicating with Fiona."

Neely sighed. "It's a stroke of bad luck that Dimpna can't find the email exchange."

"Cahal Mackey showed up at her clinic," Cormac said. "I can't help wondering if he took the email."

"How would he know about it?"

"He could have been following Shauna at the festival," Cormac said.

"I'm glad you're finally seeing the light," Neely said. "It all leads back to Cahal Mackey."

"We need info from Shauna and Fiona's laptops," Cormac said. "I'll see if I can apply some more pressure on the forensic team. I also want to find out what kind of computer access Cahal Mackey had in prison." Cormac consulted the Notes app on his phone. "We should talk to this woman Orla right away."

"He's recruiting," Neely said. "Just like he did twenty-nine years ago."

"We've nothing to charge him with yet," Cormac said. "And I have Garda Lennon tailing both him and Flynn Barry."

"I'm going to give him some backup," Neely said.

"That doubles the risk of him being made," Cormac said.

"That may be. However, leaving him alone doubles the danger he's in," Neely pointed out.

Cormac knew she was right, but he also knew what kind of shrewd monster they were dealing with. "Get a female guard. They can pose as a couple."

"His new bride is going to love that," Neely said. Garda Lennon was recently married. Blondies the pair of them, they looked like brother and sister. No one had said this to their faces, of course, but he could only imagine the sight of them when they had little towheads running around.

"He's a big boy; we'll let him sort that out." Cormac headed for the car, and Neely followed.

"We're going to need to talk to Fiona's doctors straightaway," Cormac said. "See if we can verify that she'd already lost her baby." Was that why she was killed? Because someone had only wanted her for her baby? Was that why she seemed paranoid about anyone in this group finding out the baby had died? Did she know they wanted her baby? Was this another case of giving a baby up for adoption? And if Tom wasn't the father, who was? "What if this group wasn't about folks who have been adopted? What if it was a group for women who were giving their babies up for adoption?"

"That would fit," Neely said. "That would fit."

"I'll have a few guards do some online searching, see if it uncovers any such group."

"What did you make of yer man?" Neely asked with a nod back toward Tom's trailer.

"You first," Cormac said.

"He was trying to keep it together, but I felt like it was taking considerable effort. If you ask me, I think he's the type of man who easily loses his temper."

Cormac nodded as he opened the car door. "Not to mention he didn't report his girlfriend missing, and he didn't come forward when the news about a dead pregnant woman hit the papers," Cormac said. "He's either one cold son of a bitch, or he's in on this up to his thick neck."

CHAPTER 31

"*I* NEED TO SEE SKY," SHAUNA DEMANDED. MOTH MAN LOOKED AT her and then the boy. "Need walk," she said. He shook his head. "Cruel," she said. "Need sky, need walk." Dylan had still not reported the sound of cars, or horns, or people. They had to be somewhere remote. It wasn't right to keep them locked in this strange, tiny room.

"No."

Even with his mask on, Shauna could read the cruel twist of his lips. "Doctor says walk. Help baby come." He visibly sighed, his shoulders slumping. She decided to try something.

"FiFoFum," she said. "Do you know her?"

He stopped moving and became deathly still. He did not respond. He knew her. It was plain as day. He knew FiFoFum. Or . . . he was FiFoFum.

Did he send that strange letter? Then again, if he was the danger, why would he warn them about the danger? Some kind of sick game? Was it to draw her into the open? Was it to draw her to the festival? But he didn't kidnap her from the festival. He went to the Griffins'. Before her. How did he know that's where she was going? How did he get into their house?

Did the Griffins know him?

Shauna suddenly lunged at him, grabbing at his ugly mask. "Who are you?" she yelled. "Who are you?" She managed to grab feathers, and then his hands were around her wrists, gripping them hard.

Suddenly, Dylan was punching his thighs. Moth Man kicked at him. Shauna screamed. It must have been loud, for Moth Man flinched and dropped her wrists. His mask was askew. Those cheekbones, those eyelashes. He was handsome. He was a stranger. He was a monster. He grabbed her hair and pulled her head back. Her hand flew to his hands, and she clawed at him. She could see Dylan screaming. Moth Man shoved her head forward, and she stumbled. She could feel his exit, the rush of air, the steel door slamming behind him.

Shauna sank to the floor and covered her face with her hands. She soon felt small hands on her head. Dylan had crawled over to her. She released her hands, and he put his head on her belly. She stroked his hair. "Alright," she said. "It's alright." But it wasn't. None of this was alright. And she had a sinking feeling she had just made everything worse. So much worse. She had simply reacted in the moment. She remembered a secondary schoolteacher writing that about her once. *Reactive.* At the time, she had no idea what it meant. But the teacher had been right. She was reactive. And now that trait might just have cost Shauna her life. But there was still a chance for the boy.

She spotted a cardboard box in the middle of the room. Moth Man—this was his name forever now—had dropped off enough food for a few days. Why? Was he was going to be gone for a few days? Sometimes he came into the room just to clean the buckets and wouldn't say a word to her or the boy, wouldn't even look at them. Shauna had been trying to count the days, but given that she couldn't see the sky, it wasn't easy. Three? Maybe four? They slept a lot, and she couldn't count sleeps. She'd taught Dylan a few signs—man, bad, room, eat, hungry, sleep, potty. She taught him how to spell his name—D-y-l-a-n. He cried every day, but at least now he was seeking comfort from her. Soothing him gave her a kind of confidence she had never experienced. She had never even had a pet. In those small moments when she told him over and over it was going to be alright, she almost convinced herself. But it wasn't going to be alright, was it? She had to do something.

Asking Moth Man for a walk wasn't part of a plan; she just really wanted to see the sky. She couldn't imagine dying in here, without ever glimpsing the world again. She wondered how many other people were involved in this, and she was obsessing on whether or not they expected her to have her baby here. Women died in childbirth, even under the best conditions. She needed to think. She had to get them out of here. Moth Man wasn't in charge. People who are in charge do not empty waste buckets. There was someone else. There had to be.

She needed to do something. *Take him down.* The thought kept looping through her mind. And even though Dylan was a child, there were still two of them and one of him. She'd never seen him with a weapon. But there was nothing she could use as a weapon either. The trick would be to get him to venture farther into the room while staying close to the door. Could they somehow shove him farther into the back while the pair of them ran out? She'd also been eyeing the disgusting potty bucket. They could wait until it was full and then dump it over him? And then run. And pray. There would be no second chances. It could mean their deaths.

Dylan was waving his arms, trying to get her attention.

"What?"

He gestured as if he was writing something down. She reached for the coloring book and crayon and took it to him. He scribbled a single word: *hammer.*

"Good lad," she said. "Brave." Somewhere out there, someone was wielding a hammer. Shauna spent the rest of the day trying to figure out how to get her hands on it.

Shauna woke up to Dylan's sticky fingers poking her. She'd barely opened her eyes when he shoved the coloring book at her. It took a moment before she could read the list of words in front of her: *clang, bang, saw, drill* . . .

She sat up. Gestured for a crayon. He scrambled away and soon returned with the box. She wrote: *here? close?* He nodded vigorously, then pointed to the far wall. Very close. First the hammer, now this. What were they doing? Was it their kidnappers or someone who could rescue them? She wrote another word: *voices?* He frowned as if listening, then shook his head. Maybe it was their abductors. Or maybe someone else was occupying the space. Would shouting for help be of any use?

Shauna got to her feet and began pacing the room. Was this her chance? Her only chance? Were there workers just beyond the steel door? Should she scream for help? Dylan joined her in the pacing; the pair of them crossed back and forth, keeping their blood flowing. Every time she came up with a plan, she was stopped by fear. Not for herself, but for her baby and Dylan. If she was alone, she would at least embark on a hunger strike. She could feign sickness. In fact, it wouldn't really even be faking it; she couldn't help but worry something was wrong with the baby; he had been so still lately. She didn't like the thought of him absorbing her terror.

Dylan wasn't thriving either. He was looking very pale. He'd been marking the number of puffs he had left on his inhaler in the coloring book. The walls here were concrete. Dylan had not once written down that he heard voices. If the pair of them yelled in unison, would it do any good? She was going to demand to speak with whomever was in charge—as soon as she figured out what she was going to say. She needed a plan, and she needed it yesterday.

She glanced at Dylan. He had something cupped in his hands. "What's that?" He looked up, startled. He clamped his hands together and shook his head. Now she really wanted to know what it was. "Show me." He stuck out his lower lip, bit it, and glanced at the door. "Did you find it in here?"

He shook his head and pointed. "Out there?"

He said something, but the only word she could lip-read was *man*. It was enough. "Moth Man?" He nodded, then set whatever it was on the floor as he mimed taking something out of his pocket, then switched positions and showed her how he bent down to scoop it up.

"Show me. *Please.*" He picked up the object, and brought it to her. It was a bracelet. Fancy looking. MÍORÚILT 1994 was written across the top. The flip side read LOVE FOREVER AND EVER AND EVER.

Someone loved Moth Man. Thought he was a miracle. *Gross.* Dylan held his dirty little hand out. He wanted it back. She shrugged and handed it to him. "Don't let him see," she said. He nodded and stuck it between his sock and his shoe. Shauna went back to thinking about the noise outside the room, wondering what it could mean.

* * *

She didn't have to wait long for an answer. The next morning, Moth Man opened the door and strode in. He was holding something in his hands. Were those collars? He approached Dylan first and knelt. When he stood up, Shauna could see that he'd placed the collar around Dylan's ankle. It was black with a green pulsing light. He then placed one on Shauna. Her ankles were swollen, and he paused to look and them, then looked at her.

"Need walk," she said, wishing she could spit on his face and actively fighting herself not to do it.

Moth Man turned to Dylan and began to talk. The lad's eyes grew wide. Shauna grabbed a coloring book and crayons and shoved them at the man. "Tell me."

Even behind the mask, she could see his eyes darken. After a moment of hesitation, he took the coloring book and plucked a black crayon from the box. He scribbled something and handed it back: *Ankle monitor. Electronic. Made from dog shock collars! I will show you the boundaries. If you go beyond them, you will get a shock. Let's demonstrate!*

Shauna stared down at the monitor, trying to take it all in. Dylan's bottom lip started to tremble. "Off," Shauna said. "Take them off."

He reached in his pocket and brought out what looked like a remote control. He pushed a button, and suddenly Shauna felt not only her ankle, but her entire body vibrate for a second. Dylan's mouth was open in a scream. Moth Man laughed. He scribbled once more on the pad: *That was NOTHING. Low voltage. If you go beyond the black boxes with green blinking lights, the shock will be TEN TIMES WORSE. Could trigger a heart attack!*

Dylan gulped. Shauna could still feel the tremors in her body. Moth Man walked out, leaving the door gaping open. Shauna stared in disbelief. Dylan rushed forward, but she held out her arm to stop him. This could be a trick. She would go first. She could see daylight streaming in from the next room, and her heart started to drum. They couldn't possibly be letting them go, could they? Before she could take a step, Dylan had snuck around her other side, and he dashed through the door. So much for listening to her. She wasn't his mother, but she felt protective of him. This was just more proof that she wasn't meant to raise a child. She couldn't even control a captive one. She hurried after him, suddenly not caring what the consequences might be. All that mattered was getting out of this cramped and stinky room.

She stepped out the door and was greeted by a small, curved hallway made of the same smooth concrete as her room. Windows, also shaped like ovals, treated her to a glimpse of the sky and, given that it was a bright day, she had to shield her eyes. For a moment, she was blinded; she had been too long in a dark room. She stood there, blinking away colored spots, both ecstatic that she could soon gaze upon the sky all she wanted and furious that her eyes refused to take it in. Once she could see again, she stared at the concrete floor. It swirled along like a river. She followed it into a giant oval room. More curved windows; outside, glimpses of green. *Trees.* Once Shauna's eyes adjusted, she drank it in.

She had never seen such a space. With its curves, it most definitely looked like a spaceship, stretched out and situated on the ground. All smooth concrete. Currently all the steel doors and windows were open, and all around there was nothing but open air. She ran toward the brightest opening and soon found herself standing just outside the building, staring at a lake. Beyond it, she could see nothing but grass and thick woods to the east. She turned back to the main room and saw the reason for all the construction noises. They had been setting up a new living space. There were two proper beds, a crib, a rocking chair, a small kitchen and bathroom, and an area with an examining table and medical instruments. There was a sofa and a television with a DVD player and discs piled next to it. Moth Man stood in a corner, watching them. Dylan was racing around the room. He felt excitement, but hers had faded, and dread was creeping in. Shauna looked down at her ankle monitor; it was still blinking green. She looked back up at the space. It was filled with everything. Everything they needed. Everything they needed to be captives forever.

CHAPTER 32

*D*IMPNA ENTERED HER CLINIC TO FIND SHE HAD SURPRISE VISITORS. Orla and Kevin were back, and this time, they were accompanied by an older woman. Standing by the woman's side was a gorgeous Irish wolfhound. Whereas it wasn't true that all owners looked like their pets, this woman and her dog had the same deep gray hair. The woman's hair was in a braid that fell down her back. She appeared to be in her late fifties.

"Look who's here," Niamh said, grinning at Dimpna and gesturing to the young couple. "They found a flat."

"Brilliant," Dimpna said. "How are you liking it?"

"It's lovely," Orla said. "And it's right in town. Close to the ice cream shop." She grinned and placed her hand on her belly. "This little one is mad for ice cream."

"I'm looking forward to the day when you can no longer blame your sweet tooth on our innocent baby," Kevin said with a wink.

Dimpna felt a great sense of relief that Orla was okay. She hoped she wouldn't upset her too much when she told her that a detective inspector wanted to speak with her. But even so, Orla would be smart to fear Cahal Mackey, and she needed to be warned that he might be stalking her.

"This is Cara Hayes," Orla said. "She's the wolfhound breeder I was telling you about."

"Hello," Dimpna said. "It's nice to meet you."

"You as well," Cara said. "It never hurts to get in good with the local veterinarians."

"A man was in here asking about reputable breeders," Orla told Cara. "I just knew he had to meet you." She glanced at Niamh. "I lost his calling card and was hoping you still had it?"

"He gave it to Doctor Wilde," Niamh said. Now everyone was looking at her.

Dimpna had thought she was going to have time to work up to this conversation. "I actually need to speak with you about that," she said. Normally, she would have this talk in private, but Cara should be warned as well, just in case Cahal Mackey came sniffing around the wolfhounds. "There's a detective inspector who wants to speak with you," Dimpna began, making eye contact with Orla.

Orla's eyes widened, and she placed her hand on her belly. "With me?"

Dimpna nodded. "The man you're referring to was not serious about adopting a wolfhound."

Orla frowned. "He seemed serious to me."

"I don't want to frighten you, but that man was Cahal Mackey."

Kevin put it together first. "The cult leader? The one who killed those pregnant women?"

"The one suspected of killing them," Dimpna said. She turned her gaze back to Orla. "And I believe he only came into the clinic because he was following you."

Orla gasped. "My God," Cara said. "That's terrifying." The wolfhound, sensing tension in the room, whined.

"I told her there was something off about that man," Kevin said. "My wife is way too trusting." He put his arm around her; she shook it off.

"There's no such thing as 'too trusting,'" Orla said. "I trust people until they give me a reason not to." She chewed on her lip.

"Have you seen him since that day?" Dimpna asked. She knew these were the questions Cormac would ask, but she had to know.

"No," Orla and Kevin said in unison.

"Let me write down the inspector's name and number, and if you don't mind, I'd like to get yours," Dimpna said.

"Sure," Kevin replied.

"I'll take care of that," Niamh said.

As usual, Dimpna was grateful for her staff. "Thank you." She turned back to Orla. "Please don't let this stress you out too much. Just be aware, and please don't go anywhere alone."

Orla chewed on her lip, but she nodded. Kevin put his arm around her again, and this time she let it stay. "Believe me," Kevin said, "I won't let her out of my sight."

Dimpna hesitated; she knew this next statement might be crossing a line. "Sheila told me you were thinking of leaving town. Going back to Waterford. I wouldn't blame you if that's what you decide."

Orla shook her head. "We just signed a lease."

"This is a small town," Dimpna said. "I bet we could help you break it."

Kevin looked at his wife anxiously. "What do you think?"

"No," Orla said. "We're set up with our doula and our new flat. I will not let some psychopath run me out of town."

Cara caught Dimpna's attention. "I know it's last minute, but could you possibly examine Wolfie?"

Dimpna turned to the schedule board. Her next appointment had yet to show. She glanced at the wolfhound. "Is there any particular health concern?"

Cara shook her head. "He's going to be in a competition, and I was supposed to get a physical."

"I suppose I can have a quick look." She glanced at Orla and Kevin. "I've texted the inspector that you're here. Do you mind waiting a minute in case he wants to pop over?"

"We're waiting for Cara anyway," Orla said. She lowered herself into a waiting-room chair. Kevin remained standing. He was protective; Dimpna was relieved to see that. She walked Cara and Wolfie back to Exam Room 1. As soon as they entered Cara spoke up. "I lied."

Dimpna was thrown off. "I'm sorry?"

Cara scratched the dog behind the ears. "Wolfie doesn't need a physical. There's something you need to know, and I didn't want to say it in front of them."

"What is it?"

"I didn't know who he was at first, but Cahal Mackey has already been in contact with me."

Dimpna was on high alert. "Recently?"

Cara nodded. "He asked if he could spend time with my dogs, volunteered to walk them. But, like Kevin said, he gave me the creeps. I told him I didn't allow anyone else to walk my dogs."

Dimpna's heart thudded. He was definitely stalking Orla and, it seemed, the people in her orbit. Cormac would need to know this. "I wish I'd spoken to you earlier," Dimpna said. "I'm so sorry."

Cara waved the apology away. "It was shortly after he left that I saw the newspaper article. I'm old enough to remember that cult, those poor women. I can't help but wonder if he wants to use my dogs to lure in more victims."

"Have you called the guards?"

Cara shook her head. "He didn't do anything wrong. I wouldn't know what to report, other than a creepy feeling."

"And you didn't mention anything to Orla and Kevin?"

"I didn't want to freak her out. She's already so vulnerable." She chewed on her lip. "He started asking me questions about Orla."

Dimpna felt the hairs on the back of her neck rise. "What sort of questions?"

"Had I met her, did she ever find a flat to let—those sorts of questions."

Dimpna curled her fists. "If the inspector doesn't arrive shortly, you need to call the Dingle Garda Station. Ask for Detective Inspector Cormac O'Brien. Tell him everything."

"Are you sure? He didn't really do anything wrong."

"If you don't, I will, and then he'll want to speak with you, so you should do it yourself."

"I suppose," she said. "Better safe than sorry."

"Definitely," Dimpna said. "Much better safe than sorry." They headed back to the reception area. Orla and Kevin stood.

"Have you heard from the inspector?" Orla asked. "I need to get some food in me or this baby is going to start kicking."

"He's going to be a footballer," Kevin laughed.

"You should go," Dimpna said. "Is it alright to give Inspector O'Brien your phone number?"

"Not a bother," Kevin replied.

Niamh held up a notebook. "I can take it down."

Dimpna looked to Cara, who made eye contact with Dimpna, then took out a calling card. "In case you need extras," she said. She was a good actress. It was best not to alarm Orla and Kevin. Or was that a mistake? Maybe they should be more frightened. Dimpna would let Cormac handle it. She took the card, then handed it to Niamh. The sooner Cormac spoke with them, the better. If she couldn't convince the couple to leave town, maybe he could.

CHAPTER 33

ALTHOUGH SHAUNA LOATHED TO ADMIT IT, THE NEW FREEDOM THEY'D been granted was making a big difference. Not only in their quality of life, but also their moods. Strangely, despite the shock collars around their ankles, the doors to the building were only open when Moth Man was physically present. Every time he left—which was at least once a day for hours at a time, sometimes longer (Shauna had been writing down every time he left and every time he returned)—he first would go into the closed-off wing of the building, and soon all of the steel doors would close and lock. He then used one key to let himself out of a door, and Dylan said he could hear the sounds of chains and a lock being engaged when he would leave. Then, when he returned, he'd open the single door, go to the closed-off wing, and minutes later, the steel doors would once again open onto the property, allowing them freedom once again. It was limited freedom, but it meant everything.

They were allowed to take the outdoor walkway to the edge of the pond. There were even fish in the pond, and it was a delight to watch them. Shauna loved watching the reflection of the sky in the water. And her onboard passenger loved it too. He was kicking again. Moth Man had written her a note that a doula would be visiting her soon to check on things and go over her birth plan. She was terrified and furious at the thought of giving birth here, but at least she wouldn't have to deliver the baby alone in some tiny, weird room. Dylan loved the television and DVD player. He watched the same movies over and over, and she was starting to wonder if she should set some sort of limit on his screen time. The very thought was startling. She wasn't his mammy, and he'd been kidnapped, so he might as well do whatever he wants. Even so, she did her best to pry him away. But lately not even the fish could lure him from the screen. Instead of enjoying the outdoors and the additional space, he was becoming withdrawn.

It was probably a trauma reaction, and again, maybe she should just let him be. She couldn't imagine what his parents were going through. Were they still looking for him? Was anyone looking for her? Was Liam still going out drinking with the lads? Were the Griffins looking at other babies to adopt? The thought of what was going to happen to her after the baby was born was starting to gnaw at her. What would they do with the baby? Sell him? Every time she went over it, her heartbeat ticked up and her breathing became difficult. She had to be careful. She was not going to let Moth Man have the baby. She'd kill him first.

The crib and the examining table were disturbing. It dawned on her that now was the only time she had any leverage. The baby and Dylan were the reason she was determined to fight. But it was hard to fight an invisible enemy. Who was he working with?

Right now, he could not hurt her or he risked hurting the baby. But despite knowing she wouldn't be a good mother, Shauna would never put her baby in jeopardy and would not use him as a pawn. But was there a way to make him think she would?

She tried to think of what this building had once been. It didn't look like anything she'd ever seen. Especially the security.

In addition to steel doors and blinking keypads inside the structure, the property had a high fence made of iron, with a matching heavy gate. Even if they could somehow get the doors open, withstand the shock, or find a way to get the ankle collars off, if they couldn't figure out how to open the gate, then the only way out was through the woods. There were times when a drone hovered over the property. She had a feeling Moth Man was operating it from his secret wing in the building, finding yet another way to let them know that eyes were on them at all times.

They had a full-sized fridge and a real restroom. There were a few baths in this strange building and one shower that barely spit out cold water. They could not take a bath with the ankle monitors attached, but they could stand partially in the pitiful shower with half of their body and even then, Shauna wrapped towels around the ankle collar as the Moth Man had explained. "Otherwise you might die," he said. "Electrocution." She was going to take his word for it. She didn't have to keep an eagle eye on Dylan when he washed up; he didn't seem to be a fan of it.

It was wild to Shauna that this place had electricity and plumbing. For heat, they had fireplaces. Moth Man usually tended to them, but he showed Shauna how to do it for when he was gone. She didn't mind; the wood was all loaded up in a hallway, and it felt good to keep busy. It also gave her a good excuse to roam. Near the pile of wood was yet another steel door. She assumed it was locked; she hadn't dared try it in case he could see it. For all she knew, he was watching them right now. Were there cameras installed in the building, in addition to the occasional drone? She hadn't spotted any, but she'd be surprised if they weren't secretly embedded somewhere. She had to proceed as if they were watching their every move. She had to figure out a plan.

He didn't seem to be a pedophile or rapist; at least she didn't think so. He'd been rough with them, but otherwise Moth Man hadn't touched her or Dylan in any kind of sexual way. Pondering it all made her realize something. She hadn't asked Dylan everything. "Dylan," she called. "Dylan." It took four tries before he finally looked away from the telly.

The look on his face was sour. "What?"

"Bad man took you . . . where?"

He frowned. "Here."

"No. Where were you when he took you?"

"The bog."

"What doing there?" she asked. At this, his eyes went wide; then his gaze flew to her belly. She frowned. "What?"

He shook his head.

"Tell me."

"Monster."

"Monster?" He was hiding something. "Tell me."

"Dead woman." He became animated. "Her face was all like this." Using his hands and facial expressions he showed her a bloated, dead face. "She was like you." He pointed to her belly.

"Pregnant?" Shauna said the word and signed it at the same time. She'd been doing this a lot; he was a quick study.

He nodded.

"You looking?" She imitated him looking at what must have been a horrific scene in front him. "Then? What?"

He reenacted the scene and began talking up a storm. She had to get out the notepad. It took a while, but she finally understood. A man in a flat cap had given them ten euros and dared them to go to the bog. There were two other boys. That was good news. That meant the guards knew everything she knew. But the dead pregnant woman was not good news. She was the "before" version of Shauna. They must have taken her—did they get her baby? Bellies could remain swollen for a while after birth. Were these baby collectors? Or had they killed her and the baby? Was the woman FiFoFum? Shauna felt a twist of sorrow, even though she had never met her. This was no longer some distant fear. They were going to kill her. Were they going to kill the boy too? Or were they . . . she hated to think about this, but she'd heard about people being sold. Used as sex slaves. They hadn't killed him yet, so they had something in mind for him. And here he was, happy-out with his videos. She didn't want him terrified, but shouldn't he know the kind of danger they were in?

Was it better to have an ignorant and happy Dylan, or an aware and terrified Dylan?

She decided it was better to have an ignorant and happy Dylan.

The thought of escape looped through her mind. The only leverage she had was right now. Her baby was still a part of her. She'd lost track of time in here, which meant she'd lost track of her due date, but it was soon. If they wanted her baby bad enough, they were going to have to let Dylan go. And if they agreed and took him away, she would need proof that he was alive and back with his parents. She would ask that they bring her a newspaper article about his return—a photo of them dropping him off at a garda station—something.

She was going to have to make them believe that she would hurt her baby—what a disgusting thought—if they didn't let Dylan go. She could threaten to kill herself. But how? Starve herself? Could they force-feed her? She'd seen a bottle of cleaning fluid in the corner of the warehouse. She hurried over. It was still there. An ordinary cleanser. She picked it up. The bottle was opaque. She could threaten to drink it. She could hold up the bottle when he was across the room—he wouldn't be able to reach her in time—

She could wash it out, put water in it instead. She'd have to wash it real good or she would end up poisoning herself. Just having a plan made her feel giddy. Dylan went back to his movies. She stared at the bottle of cleanser. But what if there were cameras? They would see that she'd replaced it with water, and it would all be for nothing. They might even punish her. Put her back in that tiny room, which would be like death. First things first. She was going to have to test whether or not he was watching them through cameras. She was going to have to find out if this strange circular building had eyes.

CHAPTER 34

WHEN DIMPNA FINISHED FOR THE DAY, SHE WAS SURPRISED TO COME
out and see Cormac standing in her waiting room. Just the sight of
him made her heart feel as if it was lifting out of her chest. But then
she saw how knackered he looked, and she just wanted to mother
him. When was the last time he'd slept? This case was haunting
him, and she could see it on his face.

He attempted a smile. "I don't suppose you're free to go on a
mission?"

"I am if it means helping to find our missing persons," Dimpna
said. Patrick had proved more than capable of handling the clinic
on his own. "What's the story?"

"I need to visit our sole cult survivor, Erin Tanner. And I'm
afraid you're not going to like the assignment."

"Tell me on the way," Dimpna said. She headed for the courtyard
with Cormac following. "What's this assignment I'm not going to
like?"

Once outside, he paused. "Have you heard of good cop, bad cop?"

"Of course."

"We're going to play good inspector, bad veterinarian," he said.

She laughed. "I'm intrigued."

"Last time I paid a visit to Ms. Tanner, she was very uncoopera-
tive. She's also an animal hoarder. Wait until you meet Wilbur."

"A pig, is it?"

Cormac shuddered. "The biggest yoke I've ever seen in me life."

Bad veterinarian. "You want me to threaten to report her for endangering her pets?"

Cormac nodded. "I want you to tell her you're bringing in the cavalry, and they're going to haul every last one of them out of there if she doesn't cooperate."

"You know I don't really have the authority to do that."

"I'm sure you have people you could call."

Dimpna sighed. He was right; she did not like the assignment. Especially if the animals weren't in any danger. "Even if she cooperates, if I go in there and I think any of her animals need care, I'm going to have to make those calls anyway."

"Don't tell her that until she spill the beans."

"Are you sure she has beans to spill?"

"She's a former member of the cult."

"I see." In that case, the woman was probably traumatized. She didn't want to threaten to take away her pets on top of it.

"Both Neely and I thought she was holding something back, if not downright lying."

"We could try being nice first," Dimpna said.

"I don't have time to be nice," Cormac said.

"I have to go back in," Dimpna said. "I need my medical bag."

"You're not going there to treat them," Cormac said. "You're going there to threaten her."

"I'm not trying to tell you how to do your job . . ."

Cormac arched an eyebrow. "However?"

"She joined a commune. That's how much she trusts the system. If we come in there threatening to take away her beloved pets— some might even think of them as their fur babies—we're going to be playing right into her narrative of distrust."

"What does that have to do with your medical bag?"

"Does she seem like the type of person whose animals get regular vet care?"

"No."

"There you have it. If I see any of her animals in distress, I can offer free vet care."

"It's not a bad idea. You can send the bills to the garda station. I'll see what we can do."

* * *

Dimpna and Cormac were headed out of the courtyard when a familiar couple was heading in. Orla and Kevin. Cormac noticed Orla's belly straightaway. "Is that the woman I've been trying to get ahold of?"

"She's the woman I told you about," Dimpna confirmed. "Sheila's cousin." She turned to the couple. Orla wore a serious expression. Dimpna felt a pinch of worry. "Is everything alright?"

"It will be," Orla said. She held out a flyer. "I hope you can attend."

Dimpna glanced at it:

COMMUNITY MEETING—TAKE OUR POWER BACK! DINGLE—FEMALES ONLY. EXPECTANT WOMEN WILL LEAD A DISCUSSION RELATED TO CURRENT EVENTS.

The date was set for tomorrow evening, and below that was an address. Dimpna recognized it; the space was in town, and on weekends, it was a dance hall.

In the middle of a flyer was a blown-up photo of Cahal Mackey. It looked as if it had been taken at the harbor. Next to it, in typed capital letters, a caption read:

IS THIS MAN FOLLOWING YOU?

Dimpna flinched as a feeling of dread sideswiped her. Should Orla be doing this? She glanced at Cormac. He caught her expression, and she handed him the flyer. Orla watched them intently, no doubt ready to go on the defensive.

"Orla doesn't want to feel like a victim," Kevin said, before Cormac could speak.

"How many of these have you passed out?" Dimpna could hear the alarm in Cormac's voice.

"At least a hundred so far," Orla said. "I think the event is going to be huge. I booked a dance hall, so there will be plenty of room. And if anyone wants to volunteer to bring a dish, that would be much appreciated."

"You should have discussed this with the guards first," Cormac said. "This is completely irresponsible and dangerous."

"Cormac," Dimpna said quietly. She was really torn. On the one hand, Cormac was right. On the other, she knew what it was like to feel vulnerable and terrified. Orla was taking her power back.

Orla scoffed. "*He's* the one who's dangerous. He followed me here, then pretended he wanted to adopt a wolfhound."

"Stirring up people in the town is not the answer. It's going to take precious resources away, and we have two missing persons and a murder to investigate."

Orla didn't back down. "I'm certainly not stopping your investigations. It's perfectly legal to gather and support each other."

"This photo is going to cause problems," Cormac said. "And advertising a gathering of all the pregnant women in the area in one place when there might be a killer actively hunting them? What were you thinking?"

Orla remained defiant.

"I was nervous about her showing his photo, as well, like," Kevin said. "Do you think there's a chance it might enrage him? Do you think he'd take revenge?"

"If she's already passed out the flyers, we should move on to whatever makes sense next," Dimpna said. "There's no use wasting time on what's done."

Cormac must have been thinking the same, for he was already on the phone. "Neely," he said. "We have a situation."

"No disrespect, Inspector, but you can't stop us," Orla said. "We are meeting. There's strength in numbers."

Kevin gave an apologetic shrug. "When she sets her mind to something, there's no talking her out of it." There was no doubt Orla was related to Sheila Maguire. Dimpna hadn't spoken to her since she'd blurted out the story about her father. She regretted it, of course. Sheila always did push her buttons.

"I need you and Garda Lennon at the station now," Cormac said to Neely. "I'm on my way." He took all the flyers out of Orla's hands.

"Give those back," she said.

"I'm trying to protect you and everyone else in town."

Orla shook her head. "I'll only print more, so you might as well give them back."

Dimpna touched Cormac on the arm. "She's already passed out hundreds," she said. "The horse is out of the barn."

Cormac gave the flyers back, but it was easy to see he was none too happy about it. "I'm going to post guards at the event," he told her. "I know you think you're helping, but you're not."

Orla threw her hands up. "I can't stand by and do nothing. If he was following me around town, who's to say he wasn't following others? I can find out for ye."

Cormac shook his head and turned to Dimpna. "I'm going to have to postpone our other visit."

Dimpna walked him to the car so that they would be out of earshot with the others. "What if I went alone?"

Cormac frowned. "To see Erin Tanner?"

"I have the time and my medical bag. If you give me her address, I can give it a go."

"I can't have you questioning her."

"Of course not. But I could introduce myself as the local veterinarian—pretend I'm giving a group discount or some such, see if I can get her to talk to me."

Cormac chuckled. "Group discount. Hoarders discount, you mean."

"It might just work. This way, when I return with you, I will already have built some trust."

Cormac appeared to be thinking about it. Dimpna knew he had too many things to do and he was just one man. "I don't want you there alone."

"I'll take Patrick with me."

"Alright. Don't raise her suspicions about the past."

"I'll only talk shop."

"Call me as soon as you're back." He glanced at Orla and Kevin. "They don't know what they're doing."

"For what it's worth, I empathize with Orla. Feeling helpless is debilitating."

Cormac nodded. "Believe me, I understand that. But let us not forget which road is paved with good intentions."

CHAPTER 35

SHAUNA STOOD IN THE MIDDLE OF THE OPEN SPACE. IT WAS TIME TO find out if there were hidden cameras, and she had a plan. Moth Man had returned, but he was in another wing of the property, behind a locked door. When he was giving them the tour, he made sure they knew that they could not access his wing. A stake was positioned in that hallway, with a green blinking light. Presumably, if he was watching them on some kind of security screen, the equipment was being kept in that wing. She swayed a bit, then, using the sofa for support, struggled to the ground as if something was wrong. Once she was flat on her back, she pretended to convulse. She lay there for what felt like a considerable amount of time, thrashing about. Dylan, glued to the telly, took ages to notice. But when he did, he freaked out.

He ran to her and started screaming. Shauna could tell by his red face, his round mouth, the spittle flying out. *Damn.* She hadn't counted on that reaction. She had been too rash. If anyone was nearby, no doubt he, she, or they heard Dylan's screams. Someone could come through the door at any moment. She sat up and tried to explain what she was doing in her best attempt at a whisper. It backfired. He couldn't understand her. Before she could write it down, the door burst open. There was no time to replace the cleaning fluid with water. She either had to drop the plan or fake it. "Stop," she said bringing the toxic bottle to her mouth. "Or I drink it." The man froze and held up his hands. "If I drink it, the baby dies." *Sorry, onboard passenger. I'm trying to save us.*

"You bitch." Shauna knew it wasn't "witch" from Dylan's reaction. His mouth was still hanging open. The man took another step, and she lifted the bottle closer.

"I'm not messing."

He shook his head. His lips moved. She nodded at Dylan, who cautiously approached the man, the notepad in his outstretched hand.

The man wrote furiously, then turned the pad around: *What do you want?* She nodded at Dylan, and he said something to the man. A second later, he threw the notebook, and Dylan picked it up and brought it to Shauna.

I want to talk to the woman.

The man read it, and she could see his eyes close behind his stupid mask. There *was* a woman. She knew it. She'd been giving this a lot of thought. Moth Man behaved like he had a boss. A boss desperate for a baby. She'd been pregnant long enough to clock the expressions on faces she'd seen out and about in the world before she was a kidnap victim. It wasn't the men who stared at her belly, some with envy, others with longing. It was women. Women who touched her without permission, women who gawped and grinned, women who longed. Some woman out there had seen Shauna and judged her. Thought Shauna would be a bad mother. Thought *she* deserved Shauna's baby.

Put down the bottle.

No. Talk to woman.

I'll make you.

She lifted the bottle. "I can drink faster than you can cross the room."

He began talking; she could only lip-read "stupid bitch." Dylan started to cry. But then the man whirled around and left. Shauna could feel the vibrations in her body from the door slamming shut. Dylan ran over to Shauna and tried to get the bottle away from her. "It's okay," she said. "I'm tricking them."

"Who is the woman?" Dylan asked.

"The boss," Shauna said. At least she hoped. Either the boss or, at the very least, someone who had considerable influence. "And I'm going to make her set you free." But nothing happened. Nobody else burst through the door. Shauna stood there for forty minutes. Either no one was watching or they were calling her bluff. And then something was slipped under the door. Dylan ran to see what it was. He soon held up a DVD. It had a label attached: PLAY ME.

Before Shauna could stop him, he ran to the DVD player and slipped in the disc. The telly came to life. A new video was playing. It looked homemade. The opening showed rolling fields with this sprawling oval building set in the middle, surrounded by the man-made lake. Women in long, plain dresses stood outside, holding baskets filled with veggies. A white horse galloped across the screen, a gorgeous creature lit by the sun. A title rose: WELCOME TO THE WOMB.

The Womb? Were they fucking serious? But now it made sense. The building was shaped like a womb. Every inch of it. Every single room another mini womb. Even the windows and doors. She could not comprehend it. Who had built this place? But more importantly . . . why? And despite the smiling women in the video, it didn't seem as if anyone else had lived here in a long time. The grass around the lake hadn't been tended in ages. The furniture looked brand-new and cheap, as if it had been purchased just for them and hastily set up. But whatever this was, it was much more elaborate than Shauna first thought.

Shauna turned to see that Dylan was staring at the screen; transfixed. Another caption appeared: WELCOME, DYLAN! Dylan's mouth dropped open, and he pointed to it as if Shauna wasn't already seeing it. WELCOME, SHAUNA . . . AND BABY . . . YOU HAVE BEEN CHOSEN! YOU ARE SO SPECIAL! THE GRAND RULER IS CALLING ON YOU . . .

"The Grand Ruler?" Shauna said. "Pure shite," she said to Dylan, waiting for him to agree. He didn't respond. Shauna lunged for the telly, looking for the remote. It wasn't on the coffee table or on the television stand. Now the screen showed a blurry image of two men, standing tall in the field with a young boy by their side. They each held a rifle. WHERE MEN PROTECT, read the caption. JOIN US. It was then that Shauna spotted the remote clutched against Dylan's chest. He didn't want her to have it.

"Give it," she said, holding her hand out and approaching.

He shook his head. "Watch." She was able to lip-read him now at least half of the time.

"It's a trick," she said. She whirled around, headed for the telly, and moved the stand until she could reach the plug. She yanked out the cord. She turned to see that Dylan was yelling at her. What was wrong with him? He raced over and reached for the cord. She blocked him. "Stop. Stop." His face was red; he pounded on her legs with his fists. "It's a trick," she said again. He whirled in the opposite direction, toward the door where the man always entered. It was opening, but slowly this time. Both Shauna and Dylan came to an abrupt standstill. There stood a thin woman in a long brown dress. She wore a mask too, but unlike Moth Man, this was a colorful butterfly. It was stunning, with glitter and so many vibrant colors. It covered nearly her entire face.

Her hair was long and black, but as she neared, Shauna could see it was a wig. She wore bright yellow lipstick that was garish under the warehouse lights. She smiled. Her fingernails were also long and yellow. The people in the video hadn't been wearing masks, but their faces were blurry.

The woman was holding something out to Dylan, and her lips moved. She was harder to lip-read than the man, maybe because Shauna needed time to get used to her. Dylan approached the woman and took the item out of her hands. It took Shauna a moment to realize what it was. An iPad. On the screen of the small contraption, the same damn video was playing. Dylan clutched it and hurried to his bed. The woman then pointed at Shauna and pointed to the small table. Shauna wanted to tell her to go to hell, but this was the moment she'd been waiting for. This was the woman behind the man.

CHAPTER 36

*F*ROM A TINY CRACK IN HER DOOR, ERIN TANNER STARED OUT AT DIMPNA and Patrick with one distrustful eye. "Go away," she said.

Dimpna wasn't going to be discouraged that easily. She smiled, despite the cold reception. "I'm Doctor Wilde with Wilde's Veterinarian Clinic, and this is my vet tech, Patrick. We're here as a preliminary courtesy to check on the welfare of your animals." Often women warmed to Patrick. He was young, tall, and handsome.

"How ya," Patrick said. He flashed a smile.

"You might be tiny, but you tell big lies," Erin said, addressing Dimpna. She slammed the door shut.

Dimpna stepped back and nudged Patrick forward. "Try again."

"She didn't even look my way," Patrick said. "My charm is lost on her."

"Try again."

He frowned, then cleared his throat. "Ms. Tanner," he called out. "It's free. No cost to you."

The door swung open again. "I know the definition of free," she said. "No need to be patronizing." She looked like a wild mountain woman, her long gray hair in gnarls past her shoulders. "It's the guards, is it? Threatening to take them away. This house belongs to my creatures as much as it does to me, and I'll defend them and me property with my last breath."

"We're here voluntarily based on anonymous concerns," Patrick said. "But we don't wish for anyone to remove your animals, and if

you allow us to come in, we can vouch that they're living in safe
conditions and that we've attended to all of their health needs."

"Why would you do that?" Erin Tanner's voice was filled with distrust. She sounded as if the Devil himself had come to her door.

Just then, something grunted from behind them, and Dimpna
whirled around to see a giant pig standing before them. A Large
White. "You must be Wilbur," she said. "How old is he?"

"His name isn't Wilbur," Erin said.

"What is his name?" Patrick asked. "He's a big boy."

Erin finally looked at Patrick. "I could say the same thing
about you."

Dimpna didn't have to be watching Patrick to know he'd just
turned about three shades of red.

"May I?" Dimpna asked, turning toward the pig.

"Billy don't like strangers," Erin said. "And neither do I."

"I'll have to introduce myself then," Dimpna said. She knelt before the pig and removed an apple from her pocket. "Heya, Billy.
Look what I have here." He toddled up the stairs, and within seconds, his wet, hairy tongue had inhaled it, leaving her palm a slob-
bery mess. "He's limping," she said. "Have you checked his hooves
lately?"

"I'm no pig doctor," Erin said. "But he's been doing that for a
few weeks now."

"Patrick," Dimpna said, handing him the small bag of apples
she'd brought for this occasion. "Can you keep feeding him?"

As Patrick plied him with more apples, Dimpna quickly checked
Billy's back hooves. He snorted his disapproval but didn't dare turn
away from the apples. Sure enough, his back left hoof had some
swelling just above it. "Looks like a wee infection," she said. "I have
a salve and antibiotics that will clear it right up."

"He'll be fine," Erin said, but her voice betrayed her worry.

"He'll be fine once we clear it up," Dimpna said. "But if you let
this go, the infection will spread."

"Your father was the tall vet, was he not?" Erin asked.

"Eamon Wilde," Dimpna said. "Yes, he was. He's still with us, but
he's retired now."

Erin stared at Dimpna as she rummaged in the bag for the salve
and antibiotics. "I bet he wanted a son."

Patrick looked startled, but Dimpna just laughed. "It's quite possible," she said. "Luckily, I've given him a grandson."

Dimpna finished applying the salve, then held it and the bottle of pills out to Erin. She narrowed her eyes, then finally took the offerings and opened her door. Dimpna spotted six cats on the sofa in the dim room behind her. Cormac must have been in hell. She wished she could have been here for that.

Dimpna wondered how many more animals were inside. "May we come in?"

"Don't touch a thing," Erin replied, but she stood to the side to allow them entrance.

Dimpna thanked her, and they stepped in. "I'm going to need more light," she said.

Erin huffed, and then, to Dimpna's surprise, soon three old gas lanterns were flickering.

"How many cats do you have?"

"Fifteen," Erin answered without hesitation.

"And when is the last time they had veterinarian care?" Dimpna asked.

"The twelfth of never," Erin answered. "And low and behold, they're all still alive."

"That may be," Dimpna said. "But that doesn't mean some aren't suffering, like your Large White out there." Dimpna nodded at Patrick, who took out a notebook and approached the cats on the sofa.

"Life is suffering," Erin said. "The more you suffer, the more you'll be welcomed into Grand Ruler's everlasting paradise."

Grand Ruler. Was that the lingo of the cult? If so, she was still tied to it. Now that Dimpna's eyes had adjusted to the lanterns, she could see that the place had an old granny feel about it. Cat hair, dust, and a slight smell of mold. She had a feeling Erin Tanner had never seen a doctor in her life either. She casually tried to look and see if there were any framed photos about, anything to show a personal relationship with another human being, but so far there were none in sight.

"Might we have a cup of tea?" Dimpna asked.

Erin grunted, then nodded and headed out of the sitting room.

"They're all matted," Patrick said, his hands lifting a giant clump on the cat before him. The cat yowled and backed away with a hiss. Erin charged back into the room.

"Get out!" she said. "Get out!"

"Ms. Tanner, he's not hurting them," Dimpna said. "But this matting is. They all need to be shaved down, and if they're not used to humans touching them, they'll need to be tranquilized while they're tended to." And that was without checking anything else about their health. This was way more than she'd bargained for.

"They're grand!" she said. Given that Erin's hair was nearly as matted, the state of the cats was no surprise.

"They are not grand," Dimpna said, keeping her voice level. "I'll need to do a few at a time, which would mean picking them up in crates and taking them back to the clinic. While there, we'll also make sure there aren't any other underlining health issues."

"No." Erin violently shook her head.

"That's your decision," Dimpna said, waving Patrick to move back. "But that detective inspector wants to use them against you. He sent me here to check on their conditions. And when animal welfare checks in with me, I will have no choice but to tell them that these animals have not been properly looked after."

"The Devil at my doorstep," Erin said. "I knew this was going to happen. I told him. I *told* him." Her eyes widened as if she'd just thought of something. She turned away. "That's why," she said. "That's why."

"Why what?" Dimpna asked.

"Seven Star," Erin said. She looked to the ceiling as if gazing into the heavens. "Is this your doing? Is it?"

"Who is Seven Star?" Patrick asked.

"The original sinner," Erin said, as she began to pace. "Our downfall."

Dimpna was at a loss. Erin Tanner's level of agitation was frightening. She certainly hadn't come here to cause damage. "Ms. Tanner, although we are here about the animals, I did want to say that I think what you did all those years ago—coming forward as a witness against the Shepherd—was very brave."

Erin Tanner let out a sound that was more of a snort than a laugh. "How little you know," she said, as a smile spread across her face. "How little you know."

"I'd like to know more about Seven Star," Dimpna said.

"Her powers have risen," Erin said. "She wants revenge."

Dimpna had no idea if Erin's words were the ramblings of a woman suffering from a mental decline—understandable, given how terribly isolated and alone she'd been for nearly twenty-nine years—or if her cryptic words were part of a larger manipulation. She knew they were here on behalf of Cormac, and she knew exactly who Cormac was investigating. *How little you know* . . . What did she mean by that?

"Seven Star and her damn journal," Erin said. "Blasphemy."

"Can I fix you a cup of tea?" Patrick asked. "Or maybe call for a takeaway? My treat."

Erin narrowed her eyes. "I thought she was dead. I really thought she was dead."

Patrick wandered to a nearby table. He made eye contact with Dimpna, gave a slight nod, then moved back to the sofa. "There are seven cats here," he said. "Where are the rest?"

"They like to hide," Erin said. "They don't trust you."

"I don't blame them," Patrick said. "Trust needs to be earned."

Dimpna casually made her way over to the table where Patrick had stood. She looked down to see a white chemist bag. Sitting on top of the bag was an inhaler. Next to the inhaler was a calling card, but Dimpna needed to get closer to read it. She dropped down and pretended to tie her shoe. On the way up, she rose slowly, enough to be on eye level with the calling card. A familiar name stared out at her: CARA HAYES. The wolfhound breeder. Dimpna wished she could take a photo, but Erin was now eyeing her from across the room. She backed away. "What will it be, Ms. Tanner? Will you let us look after your cats in addition to your Large White?"

"I'll think about it," she said.

"While you're thinking, don't forget you could lose them all if you don't." Dimpna headed for the door, with Patrick close behind her. Once they exited, Erin made sure to slam the door behind them. Billy grunted and followed them to their vehicle, as if he too wanted to make sure they left. As soon as they were inside Dimpna's VW bus, Patrick turned to her.

"The inhaler," he said. "Do you think it's hers?" A reporter had broken the story that Dylan Walsh's inhaler was found near his bicycle.

"I don't see her as the type to buy anything to help with her health," Dimpna said. "And what about the calling card next to it?"

"Cara Hayes?" Patrick asked.

"Yes. She's been in the clinic several times, and on the most recent visit, she claimed Cahal Mackey was nosing about her wolfhounds."

What on earth was Erin doing with the wolfhound breeder's calling card? Could Cara have a closer relationship to the Shepherd than anyone realized? Cult leaders rarely got their hands dirty. They were evil puppeteers manipulating others instead. How did Orla get to know Cara? Perhaps it hadn't been accidental after all. The thought of Cara secretly working with the Shepherd to manipulate Orla made her sick to her stomach. Was this what her mother meant when she'd said, "How does this involve you?"

Dimpna had enough to worry about. Her father. Her son. Her practice. Her lovely creatures. Sheila Maguire. Her growing desire for Cormac. And now these kidnappings and murders. It was bringing up too much for her. She was going to have to go on a long hike with her four-pack and soon. If she didn't, the world was going to swallow her whole and spit out her bones.

Cara Hayes. How did she know Erin Tanner, and what the hell were they up to?

CHAPTER 37

*C*ORMAC STOOD INSIDE FIONA SHEEHAN'S FLAT, HOPING IT WOULD talk to him. He needed to get to know her as a person, not a victim. Through her identification and death certificate, they had finally spoken with her doctors, and it was confirmed that her baby would have been a stillbirth and that she had decided to delay the procedure to abort the fetus. Cormac couldn't imagine how agonizing it would have been be in that situation, but what he couldn't wrap his head around was the fact that she wanted to postpone it.

Cormac had guards going through every adoption site online, any kind of support group, anything. But, so far, they hadn't been able to find any specific mention of a group meeting in Dingle. Perhaps this was a very small group, and the only way he was ever going to know was if someone else in the group came forward. The tech team would go over her laptop, but they'd had Shauna's laptop for some time now, and they still hadn't found any threads. He was praying Dimpna would find that printout of the email exchange Shauna had dropped at the festival. What were the odds that it had gone missing? Had someone stolen it from her clinic? Was it the true reason Cahal Mackey had recently wandered in? Or was someone acting on his behalf?

Cormac wasn't expecting to find any kind of direct answer in Fiona's flat, and the forensic team had already combed through it. Her laptop had been bagged and was on its way to the technical team. Fiona's flat was slightly messy, but not to an embarrassing degree—no dirty dishes lying around or anything of that sort, but it had a lived-in feel. A complete luggage set was lined up in her cupboard, her car was once again parked in front of her flat, and there were no records of any kind of travel thus far. This added to the likelihood that, regardless of whom she was meeting with, they were staying local.

He stood in front of her refrigerator, which was littered with photographs, a few takeaway menus from nearby restaurants, and a calling card. She was a beautiful, smiling young woman. Dark curly hair, blue eyes, and a peachy complexion. His heart squeezed. She'd had her entire life ahead of her. From all accounts, she was always a bit of a spitfire, a rebel, and an adventurous girl. She was on maternity leave from her job as a publican at a bar on Strand Street. She'd been off for the past few months. The current staff did not report any kind of trouble—no stalkers, no worries that she voiced, no threats. They were all shocked to learn that the baby was going to be a stillborn. Fiona wasn't the type to easily spill her secrets.

Fiona's mobile had not been located in or around the bog, but they had requested records; unlike for Shauna, they had least had her mobile number. He prayed the records would come in sooner rather than later. Then again, if she had been part of some kind of adoptee ring, that suggested meticulous planning, and Cormac very much doubted that whoever was in charge would have communicated with her through her mobile phone. Had she been given a burner? Where had she been killed? What vehicle had been hidden in the woods, and where was the wheelbarrow or cart that had most likely transported her body to the bog? Somewhere out there was the hard evidence he needed.

They had narrowed down Fiona's close circle of friends, and guards were in the process of interviewing them. He prayed she'd confided in at least one of them about this online group of adoptees. He still didn't know where poor Dylan Walsh fit into the picture, unless they were dealing with a random kidnapping—but no, the lads had been *sent* to the bog to find Fiona. These cases—or this case, as he was framing it: one big messy ball of twine—was absolutely maddening.

Cormac took one of Fiona's photos off the fridge; she stood out-side with Tom Cunningham, the pair of them with their arms around each other and grinning. Her hair was blowing back in the wind, and she had her hand resting on a small baby bump. Who had taken the photo? Cormac wanted it for their investigative wall at the station—the largest wall they'd ever constructed. It covered all three cases—Fiona Sheehan, Shauna Mills, and Dylan Walsh. They were connected. He needed photos of all of them "before." He wanted his men and women to see the living people they were fighting for. "I'm sorry," he said to the rest of her smiling faces on the fridge. "I'd be a fool to make promises, but I will tell ya that I'm not resting until your coward of a killer is brought to justice."

He had nearly turned to leave when he caught sight of a calling card on the fridge. He plucked it off and looked at it: CARA HAYES, WOLFHOUND BREEDER. *Interesting.* He had just heard from Dimpna, and she had found the same calling card in Erin Tanner's cottage. This was a breakthrough. Somehow, this woman was involved. He'd already interviewed Cara, and she'd informed him that she thought Cahal Mackey was once again stalking young pregnant women; at the very least, he was stalking Orla. She seemed forth-coming, but what was her card doing in Erin Tanner's cottage and on Fiona Sheehan's fridge? He didn't know what, but this was something. And something was so much better than nothing. He had picked up his mobile to call Neely when it rang in his hand, startling him. It was the Office of State Pathology. He answered straightaway.

"Detective Inspector?"

"Speaking."

"Marjorie here from OSP. We just compared that DNA sample you dropped off to the unborn baby. It's a match."

"Are you sure?"

"Yes. Tom Cunningham was the baby's father."

"You have a lead?" Neely asked straightaway. Cormac met Neely outside the station just as she had arrived. The skies were gray and spitting.

"Two things. The state pathologist just phoned. Looks like baby daddy is a liar."

"Tom Cunningham?"

Cormac nodded. "The DNA sample proved he was the baby's father."

"Hmm," Neely said. "It's possible that Fiona lied. To him."

"Possible . . . but why? There's a photo of them on the fridge. All lovey-dovey. Why wouldn't she want him to know?"

"Worth a follow-up," Neely said. "What's the second thing?"

He handed her Cara Hayes's calling card, encased inside an evidence bag.

Neely raised an eyebrow. "A wolfhound?" She let out a wry laugh. "I can see that alright. It's about time you got over your fear of four-legged creatures."

"Allergies," Cormac said. "And hilarious."

Neely's smile soon disappeared as she studied the card. "What's the story?"

Without discussing it, they began to head inside the station. They had a debrief meeting that was starting soon. "She happened into Dimpna's clinic the other day with the young pregnant woman I've mentioned," Cormac said. "Orla. She told Dimpna she was worried Cahal was stalking Orla."

Neely returned the evidence bag to Cormac. "I remember."

"Dimpna paid a visit to Erin the other day offering free veterinarian care." He stopped as he realized that he had yet to fill Neely in on that development. There hadn't been time.

"She did what?" Disapproval was stamped on Neely's face.

They reached the Incident Room, and Cormac set the evidence bag on the front table. This discussion with Neely was an opportunity to practice laying out the case. The chief inspector and chief superintendent were now involved—from a distance, but that would change if they didn't start making headway. "We needed a way in with her. The stick hasn't worked so far, so Dimpna volunteered a carrot."

Neely sat on the edge of table. "If this case weren't so important, I'd be giving you a lecture right now."

That was exactly what he was trying to avoid. "Don't you want to know where I'm going with this?"

Neely pursed her lips. "I don't know. Do I?"

Cormac picked up the evidence bag. "She found Cara's calling card—one just like this—in Erin's sitting room."

Neely paused to think about this. "And?"

"And?" He waved the evidence bag. "I just happened to find the same card on Fiona Sheehan's refrigerator?"

"Interesting." Neely crossed her arms. "Have you set up an interview with this wolfhound breeder?"

"Not since this discovery. Our initial interview was brief; she was pointing the finger at Cahal Mackey."

"Then she's on our side."

"She's now linked to one of our victims. You need to take your blinders off."

Neely's face turned red. He could almost hear her counting to ten in her head. "Maybe she's playing amateur sleuth, and she knows as well as I do that the Shepherd is up to his old tricks."

"Whatever it is she's doing, I intend to find out." Cormac's instincts told him to hurry. Shauna was most likely days from giving birth. Dylan's parents had not received a single request for a ransom. He had to remind himself that slow was fast. He needed to be meticulous in his approach. If Cara Hayes was somehow involved and he came at her too hard, he might lose his advantage. "I'm thinking of having her tailed for a while. Before she knows we're on to her."

"What does Dimpna know about the woman?"

"She said that, until the other day, she'd never even heard of her, but it doesn't end there. Before she met her, Cahal Mackey pretended to be in the market for a wolfhound. Asked Dimpna if she knew any breeders."

"It's all a bit strange, but what are you thinking?"

"I'm thinking it's a dog whistle. And somehow Cara is connected to Erin and Fiona, and Cahal, and most recently, she's been hovering around Orla Quinn." He shook his head. "No matter what else takes place, I will not let anything happen to another young pregnant woman."

Neely hopped off the table. "Orla Quinn is the same young woman who's organizing the rally and has blasted a photo of Cahal Mackey on her flyer?"

"'Tis."

"She's putting a target on her back."

"I'm aware."

"Have you ordered a background check on Cara Hayes?"

Cormac nodded. "I have guards working on it now. But what I really want to do is to get Erin and Cara at the station for questioning at the same time."

"Erin Tanner? The woman never leaves her house."

"She still has to obey the law, doesn't she?"

"She may have a true disability. I don't see you getting what you want by ignoring that reality."

Cormac turned to the evidence wall and wandered over to the section on the cult. "How many women were in the cult?"

"Five, as far as we know . . . but most of them are presumed dead." She paused. "Are you thinking . . . do you think Cara might be another cult survivor?"

"She's the right age." Fifty-something. "What other possible connection would she have with Erin Tanner?" *And Cahal Mackey . . .*

"Maybe Erin was looking to add to her ark," Neely said.

"She seems more of a cat person to me," Cormac said.

"We need to nail Cahal and Flynn on charges—*any* charges," Neely insisted. "We need them behind bars while we untangle whatever mess this is."

Cormac glanced back at Neely. "It sounds like you're thinking of crossing some lines." Cormac waited for her to deny this, but Neely simply stared back. "I know they're scum. And they should have paid for their sins. But we have no evidence they're involved in the recent murder or kidnappings. I'm trying to follow up on Cara Hayes as well as this adoptee group. I think they're key to unlocking this entire thing."

Guards began to filter into the room for the debriefing. Soon the media would descend. Neely joined Cormac at the wall. "Unless boyfriend Tom was lying," Neely said in a quiet voice. "He's the only one suggesting there was some kind of online group."

"Did Tom give you any reason to believe he's lying?" Cormac asked.

"You mean besides pretending the baby wasn't his?"

"Isn't it possible that's what Fiona told him?" Their background check had not yielded anything disturbing, and he had given his DNA to compare to the fetus. "I think he was being truthful. We'll have to see his reaction when we give him the news."

Neely nodded. "Let's hope this meeting is quick," she said. "We've got Michael and James coming into the station today with their parents."

Cormac had been eager to speak with the lads. "I hope they'll let us speak to them alone. They aren't going to be as forthcoming if their parents are listening in."

Neely sighed. "I've heard the parents don't want them talking at all. No one wants to put a target on their child's back."

"But the kidnapper has already seen them—and none of this would be happening if they hadn't abandoned Dylan at the bog." It wasn't their fault. But he couldn't help thinking they could have done more to try and save him. That Dylan had also been the victim of bullying.

The room was now full. Neely took a seat in the front. Cormac took a deep breath and turned to face the men and women on his team. It was show time, and on his end, there was no big song and dance to deliver. Unless one of the other teams had something new to share, this episode was going to be a rerun. Someone at the back of the room was waving his arms. Garda Lennon. He jerked his head for Cormac to meet him in the hall. This must be something big. He'd never delay a briefing otherwise. Please, God, let it be something big. Cormac hurried into the hall. Lennon had moved far enough away from the door that they couldn't be overheard.

"What's the story?"

"A double hit," Lennon said. "The tire marks in the woods by the bog. We were notified that they most likely belonged to a Ford Ranger Raptor."

"And you've already done a search on locals who own Ford Ranger Raptors?"

"You bet your arse." Lennon was radiating excitement. "There's one name that stands out above the rest."

"Who is it?"

"Liam McCarthy," Lennon said. "Liam McCarthy owns a blue Ford Ranger Raptor."

CHAPTER 38

*C*ORMAC AND LENNON STOOD IN FRONT OF LIAM'S TOWN HOUSE. Neely was conducting the briefing on her own, and Cormac prayed that, at the next one, they'd have big news to break. But there was no Ford Ranger parked anywhere on the street. Liam was also registered as driving a yellow Fiat, and that was nowhere in sight either.

"We also found out Liam manages rental properties," Lennon said. "Maybe the truck is parked there?"

"How many properties?"

"Three."

"Let's start with the closest one."

The first property was a semi-attached town house much like the one Liam and Shauna lived in. It took several tries, but eventually a woman opened the door. She appeared to be in her fifties, but was well-preserved. Blond hair without a streak of gray, slim, and apparently about to go somewhere, for she was wearing a long robe. She waited with the door only half-open. Cormac felt as if he knew her, but he couldn't place her. He flashed his badge and introduced himself and Garda Lennon. "And you are?"

She crossed her arms. "What can I do for you, Inspector?"

"I assume you're renting this flat?"

"Is that against the law?"

"Do you know a Liam McCarthy?"

She squinted. "He's the property manager."

"Have you ever seen him drive a Ford Ranger?"

"I wouldn't know one truck from the other."

"But you have seen him drive a truck?"

She shrugged. "I'll have to ask my son. He would know for sure. He's not home at the moment."

Cormac was still trying to place her. "Have we met?"

"Are you playing some sort of game?" She put her hands on her hips. "Is this about his missing girlfriend?"

"Had you ever met her?"

"She was with him when I first moved in. But she stood by the car. A yellow Fiat. We never spoke."

"What is your name?"

She simply stared at him. "I can find out quite easily," he said. "Is there a reason you don't want to give it?"

From behind her, a phone began to ring. "That's probably my son now," she said.

"Fantastic," Cormac said. "Please ask him about the Ford Ranger. We'll wait."

Fifteen minutes later, they pulled up to derelict cottage. A FOR RENT sign was posted in the yard. The tenant's son had viewed this property before renting the town house for his mother. He said there had been a truck parked in back, but he didn't know the make because it had been covered with a tarp.

"This property isn't on the list of rentals," Lennon said.

"Maybe Liam removed the listing," Cormac said. "Maybe there's a reason." He reached into the glove compartment and took out two pairs of gloves. He handed one to Lennon. "Just in case," he said. The house sat back in a field. Leaning up against the side was a wheelbarrow. Cormac put on his gloves, then tipped it back. There was very much nothing to see, and that's what caught his eye. It looked as if it had been scrubbed. Whereas most of it was covered in rust, there was a portion inside where it had been scraped down to the original paint. On full alert, they headed for the back of the property. There they found a pickup truck hidden beneath a tarp. Cormac lifted the tarp from the back. "It's a Ford

Ranger Raptor," he said. He continued to lift the tarp. The back of the truck bed had also been scoured clean. He walked around every inch of it. Water pooled on the edges, which was not unusual, given the recent rain. "Call this in," Cormac said. "We need to process it; maybe he didn't wipe it all away." They could always hope.

"What's that?" Lennon was shining a torch at the far side of the truck. Cormac edged in and squinted until he saw it. A splotch of red.

"Blood," he said. "That, my friend, is blood."

CHAPTER 39

"I'M SO HAPPY TO SEE ALL OF YOU HERE TODAY," ORLA SAID. SHE stood in front of the large crowd of mostly women, many of them pregnant, gathered in front of her. "Today is the day we stop being afraid. Today is the day we let everyone know that we will not hide in our homes until this monster is caught. Today is the day that we show everyone. We. Are. Not. Weak."

Given that Sheila was sitting up front, Dimpna stood in the back of the cramped room. It was standing room only. She'd learned too late that the flyer Cormac had taken had the wrong date. Orla had tried to explain it was simply a printing error, but as Dimpna watched her fiery speech, she was starting to think that Orla had intentionally fed the guards the wrong date. Her rebellion was very much a Maguire family trait. Dimpna was in support of women gathering, women feeling their strength, women banding together in times of crisis. But these weren't normal times, and Dimpna couldn't help but worry.

Women had come from all over Ireland, and she knew this because many of them had their counties proudly displayed on their signs. Orla had done an extensive outreach. Dimpna was so lost in her speech, she didn't realize that Sheila had left her front-row seat until she was standing right next to her.

"Can you believe it?" Sheila said. "This is amazing." She had either let their past argument go, or she was up to something.

"The guards should have been aware," Dimpna said. "But yes.

It's good to see so many women banding together." Later they planned on marching. There were so many things they hadn't considered. Traffic, civil order, safety. On the other hand, she couldn't imagine the nightmare Cormac would be wrapped up in if they tried to arrest women—many among them pregnant—on the streets of Dingle. What a pickle.

Men had turned out too, including Sheila's father. He was seated in the back, an oxygen machine at his side. Sheila noticed Dimpna taking this in. "Orla is family," Sheila said. "He insisted on coming." She paused. "I hope the mere sight of him doesn't creep you out."

Zinger. "It's in the past," Dimpna said. But she knew how much the past could cling to a person, influence them. She didn't have to like Danny Maguire, but as a human being, she still could still feel for a dying man. "I'm glad he was able to come." Family was family. Family stuck together.

"We're going to gather outside in just a moment," Orla said. "We did not get city permission to take over the streets, but I feel if we take over the square near the Fungie the Dolphin statue, we can march in a circle. It's the heart of Dingle; we'll capture the attention of tourists and journalists."

At least she had enough sense not to disrupt traffic.

"We're going to demand that Cahal Mackey and Flynn Barry either be arrested or removed from this town," Orla said. "We're not the ones who should hide; they are the ones who should hide."

The room erupted in applause and cheers. Dimpna felt a prickle of fear travel up her spine. She flashed back to a moment in time when she'd accepted a ride home from one of Sheila's boyfriends. She'd been cramped in the back seat, only to find out the seat belts were missing and this particular boyfriend had a lead foot. He sped down curving roads in the rain, nearly colliding head-on with multiple cars. Dimpna had felt so helpless and close to death. For some reason, as she listened to the growing rage in the room—justified or not—she had the same helpless feeling of an impending crash.

Liam McCarthy was sweating. His leg bounced up and down, and he continuously glanced at the clock in the interrogation room. Things had moved quickly since they had discovered the truck. The owner of the rental property had died this past year, and the house had been vacant since then. Liam was insisting he hadn't touched that truck in ages.

"Anyone could have taken it," he said. "Anyone."

"Someone just happened upon it and decided to hot-wire it?" Cormac asked.

Liam squirmed. "I didn't say that."

"Well, you'd better say something. Because if you don't talk before that blood comes back, and it turns out to be Fiona Sheehan's, you're going away for a very long time."

"I don't know Fiona Sheehan," he said. "I'd never met her in my life."

"And yet your girlfriend was in communication with her."

Liam frowned. "What are you on about?" His surprise seemed genuine. But sociopaths were often excellent liars.

"Shauna and Fiona exchanged emails a month before Shauna's abduction, and most likely days before Fiona's murder," Cormac said. They had no actual proof that Fiona was writing the emails, but he suspected that was the case, and Cormac wanted Liam on edge.

"That online group?" Liam said. "Fiona was part of that?" He seemed to be concentrating on something. "This has to be someone I know," he said. "Or someone who knows me."

"I'm going to ask you again: Do you honestly think someone hot-wired your truck? Is that what you're asking me to believe?"

"I left the keys hanging in the house," Liam said. "Were there any signs of a break-in?"

They had found a busted window in the back that had been boarded up. Cormac kept this to himself. "Why would you keep the keys to your truck in an abandoned house? And, on that subject, why would you hide your truck there as well?"

"It's a 2000 Ford," Liam said. "It's falling apart." He threw his arms up. "Hell, I wouldn't have cared if it was stolen." He leaned in. "I swear. I haven't driven it in a year."

"Why didn't you sell it?"

He shrugged. "I wouldn't get enough for it. I thought I'd use it to haul wood."

"Haul wood."

"Yes, Inspector. Haul wood."

"When is the last time you set foot on that property?"

Liam sighed. "I hung out there when I first found out Shauna was pregnant. It did me head in, to be honest. I needed a place to think." He shrugged again. "I mean, the house was just sitting there. The previous owner had no family left. It's probably going to sit there for ages." He sighed. "He could have left it to me."

Cormac leaned across the table. "Tell us where Shauna and Dylan are being held. I'll make sure the DPP knows you cooperated."

"DPP?"

"Director of Public Prosecution."

"Jesus. I didn't do anything. You've got it all wrong."

"Then who did? Because whoever it is this person is framing you."

"That's what I've been saying all along!"

"Who's the last person that rented that house?" Cormac just couldn't see Liam McCarthy for this. It was too planned out. What killer would leave the wheelbarrow leaning up against the house and the truck that he transported the body in in the backyard? And how did this killer manage to scrub everything down to the paint and yet miss a glaring splotch of blood?

"No one's rented it since the old man died," Liam said.

"Who knows about it?"

"What do you mean?"

"Did you ever have the lads over to the house? Do a bit of drinking? Play a bit of cards?"

He squirmed. "Once or twice."

"I'm going to need the names of everyone you ever had over to the place."

Liam gulped. "There's something else."

"Yes?"

"I let it out once in a while."

"Pardon?"

"It's a perfectly good house! Just sitting there. I thought it wouldn't hurt to rent it out. Earn a bit of cash on the side. "Nothing permanent, mind you. But sometimes men need a bit of space. Entertain a friend or play cards, like you said."

"And how many people have you rented it to?"

"I'd have to check. Maybe six or seven."

"Six or seven. In the last month? How many in the last month?"

"Only two."

"And they are?"

"I want to speak with a solicitor."

"Your pregnant girlfriend is missing. Along with a lad ten years of age. You're sitting here in a heap of trouble. And if you're telling the truth—"

"I am—"

"Then give me the names. Don't you realize one of them could be the man who took Shauna? Who killed another young pregnant woman and dumped her in a bog? And then just because he could, snatched a lad ten years of age from the same bog after sending him there?" Cormac hadn't realized he was yelling until he saw Liam McCarthy flinch.

"Will you protect me?" Liam said.

"Protect you?"

"If I give you the name, I don't want him coming after me, like."

"Who is it?"

"He paid in cash. A lot of cash."

"Who the fuck is it?"

"You have to know this was before they found that body. This was before Shauna went missing. It was two men. I didn't know if they were a couple, but I'm not some nosy homophobic bastard. And it's not like there was a lease. Don't you get it? I didn't even know their names. It was a cash deal. Told them if they were still there in thirty days, I'd throw them out. I still wouldn't know one of their names, except I saw him in the news." Liam gulped. "I should have told you, alright? But I was scared. That woman was already dead, and Shauna was already gone." He leaned in. "I knew you'd blame me. I was well and truly in a bind. Hell, even I'd think I was guilty." He shook his head. "Plus, if I said anything and they were involved in Shauna's kidnapping? Who knows what they would do. I was trying to follow them. Figure out a plan. Don't you see? Don't you see how I had to keep me gob shut?"

Cormac didn't want the sob story. There were days when he sorely regretted that he wasn't allowed to beat subjects to a pulp. And he had a feeling this one wasn't guilty; he just wasn't smart. "Is there a bathtub in the house?"

Liam frowned. "Yes." He gulped. "Why?"

"It's now a crime scene," he said. "No one is going to be allowed in until we're finished." It was Fiona's last resting place, a bathtub in an illegal rental.

Liam's knee started to bounce. "Do you believe me? Do you?"

Cormac leaned back and crossed his arms. "I'm not going to ask you again."

"Flynn Barry, alright?" He gulped. "I rented the house to some dude and Flynn Barry."

CHAPTER 40

*C*ORMAC CLOSED THE DOOR TO THE INTERROGATION ROOM, LEAVING a sobbing Tom Cunningham to collect himself. Tom's reaction to the news that he was the father of Fiona's baby had been instant grief, the type you cannot fake; if it wasn't real, Cormac would retire on the spot and live out his days in Ibiza, Spain. That didn't mean he wasn't a killer. According to him, Fiona had insisted the baby wasn't his. She'd also kept the name of the father from her parents. Why wouldn't she want them to know? Did she truly think someone else was the father? Or did she not want Tom to have a claim over the baby? Had Tom been violent? There had to be a reason she lied to him. He could have killed her out of rage; he wouldn't be the first jealous lover to do such a thing. Maybe his grief now was over the fact that he had murdered her for an infidelity that never occurred. When asked why he thought Fiona would lie, he insisted her behavior had become secretive soon after meeting with this online group of adoptees. The tech team had still not found any leads on this supposed group. There was another rub. Tom's alibi checked out. He was out of town installing windmills the entire week Fiona was murdered. He could have paid someone to do the evil deed, but there was no evidence to support that as of yet. But things had progressed on another issue—the original crime scene.

Cormac had been to the abandoned house, and the entire upstairs bathroom smelled of bleach. Technicians were trying to find any scrap of evidence they could, but Cormac had no doubt that bathtub had been the last place Fiona had been alive. Her body had decomposed too much to tell if there had been a struggle or if Fiona had trusted her killers and willingly followed them into the house, perhaps lured in by the prospect of a secret meeting with fellow orphans looking for their birth parents.

"There was a phone call for you, Inspector." Cormac had just stepped out of the interrogation room when the female clerk blocked his path. "I think you'll want to call him back straightaway." She paused. "If you can."

"It will have to wait." He was on his way to haul Flynn Barry's arse into the station.

The clerk nodded slowly, but she remained in his path, her face radiating panic.

"Who was it?" Cormac asked. He needed her to spit it out.

"Flynn Barry," she said.

"You're joking me."

She frowned. "No, sir. He said it was urgent."

"What else did he say?"

"He said, 'They're after him.'"

"I'll call him back," Neely said, coming up from behind them.

"No," Cormac said. "You haven't heard the latest."

Neely stopped. "Go on, so."

"Thank you," Cormac said to the clerk. "I'll take care of it." She still didn't leave. "What's the story?"

She looked nervous, as if she was afraid to tell him. "When I told Mr. Barry you were in a meeting and couldn't be interrupted—I'm quoting here, Inspector—he said, 'I had something to confess. This is going to fucking cost him.'"

"I see," Cormac said. *Something to confess . . .* It was as if the man knew he'd just hauled Liam McCarthy into the station, and maybe he did. Or maybe he'd been watching the property and knew the guards were all over it. The clerk was still hanging around. "Something else?"

She nodded. "There are a lot of women gathered in Dingle—some kind of a protest."

Orla Quinn. He tried to remember the date on the flyer; it was supposed to be days from now. "Are they taking over the streets?"

She shook her head. "They're gathered in the square near Strand Street."

He sighed. "Do we have enough guards on it?"

"As many as we could spare."

The clerk finally made her escape, and Cormac turned to Neely. "Whatever you're about to tell me, it's going to have to wait," she said. "Michael and James are in the meeting room with their parents." The lads who left Dylan at the bog. He did need to speak with them. He felt a sense of urgency, as if everything was happening at once. "Send Garda Lennon to pick up Flynn Barry straightaway," he said to Neely. "And then join me in the meeting."

Michael and James were seated next to each other with their parents bookending them. Cormac arrived with biscuits and Coke. The parents might kill him because of the sugar load, but the lads would love him; after all, they were willing to go all the way to the bog for ten euros, just to buy sweets. Let them have all they want; he needed them to help him find Dylan—needed to know anything, anything at all about the man in the flat cap. Neely was already seated, and she gave him a nod confirming that Lennon was on his way to find Flynn Barry. Given that she had a maternal way about her, Cormac thought she might put the lads at ease, not to mention the parents.

It began pleasantly enough. The lads tore into the biscuits and the Cokes, and Cormac did his best to try to convince the parents to wait out in the hall. They refused, so there was nothing to do but proceed as if they weren't in the room.

"I'd like to know everything the man in the flat cap said or did," Cormac began. "And did you bring the ten euros?"

Michael's father slid a plastic baggie across the table with a crumpled ten-euro note inside. There was probably nothing they could glean from it, but Cormac was grasping at straws. He pulled out two ten-euro notes and handed one to each of the lads, which garnered him big smiles. He felt sick to his stomach, imagining what Dylan was going through at the moment. "Let's start with everything you remember," Cormac said. "You were at the art fair, and it was getting late, is that right?"

The lads nodded their heads.

"Michael was supposed to be headed home," his mother said.

"As was James," the other mother said.

Cormac made eye contact with the parents. "I know this is difficult, and there's no judgment here. But if you're going to remain in the room, I need you to keep silent." Despite Cormac first being treated to a look only an Irish mammy could give, the parents nodded.

Michael was the first to talk. "We were on our bicycles in front of the ice cream shop," he said. "The man in the flat cap came up to us. He said, 'Hey, lads. Lads on the bicycles.'" He glanced at the recorder in the middle of the table, and then at James.

"That's right," James said. "That's exactly what he said."

"Go on, so," Cormac said.

"He was holding out ten euros," Michael continued.

"We thought he was going to give it to the beggar woman, like," James said.

Cormac raised an eyebrow. "Beggar woman?" They nodded. This was the first he'd heard of a beggar. She could be an eyewitness. His mind flashed to the woman who had come into his station claiming to have known Shauna. Was this the same woman? Was she involved somehow? Was that why she wouldn't give her name? He'd have to mention this to the guards going through the CCTV footage, as well as canvass the shopkeepers again. They would likely remember her. And if she was the same woman who had come into the station, Cormac could get a sketch artist on it. "What all can you tell me about this beggar woman?"

"She smelled," Michael said, wrinkling his nose.

James bobbed his head in agreement. "She wanted to snatch the tenner, but he told her to go away."

"He wanted to give *us* the tenner." Even after all that had taken place, Michael sounded excited.

Michael's father turned his gaze on his son. "I never knew me son was so stupid," he said. Michael's face turned red, and he stared at the table. This was exactly the scenario Cormac had been trying to avoid, and now he was wrestling with his own temper as well. He wanted to yank the father up by his shirt collar and shove him out the door.

"Please," Cormac said. Beneath the table, he clenched his fists.

Not only were they the exact type of comments that were going to make the lads clam up, they were also most likely the kinds of comments that had created little hellions in the first place. He was going to put an end to it right now. "I can get a solicitor to sit in with us—I'll even let you choose him, free of charge. However, if any of you say one more word while I'm having a chat with these lads, you will be removed. By force, if necessary." The lads' jaws dropped open, and although they didn't dare look at their parents, Cormac could see the amazement on their faces. Cormac had had a lifetime dealing with bullies, one of the fallouts of being a short man. A Napolean complex, he'd heard more than once. A tall man could get angry, and no one batted an eye. When a short man got angry, it was a complex. Dimpna Wilde not only had the same issue to contend with, she faced extra discrimination for being a woman. But he digressed. He stared at Michael's father until the man gave a curt nod.

"When you got near the man, did you get a good look at his face?" Cormac asked, turning back to Michael and James.

"I reckon," Michael said. "He looked kind of old."

Cormac wondered what old was to these lads. "Old like me?" he asked. Barely over forty. No doubt ancient to these lads.

Michael shook his head. "Definitely not as old as you."

"Would you say he was in his twenties?" They looked at each other.

"Ryan's age," Michael's mother said. Then, stricken, she looked at Cormac. "Sorry. He's me brother. In his twenties."

"You're alright," Cormac said. "Was he Ryan's age?" he asked the lads.

They nodded.

Not Cahal. Not Flynn. Did that mean they weren't involved? Or, as several people had mentioned, was Cahal manipulating someone else into doing his dirty work? It wasn't necessarily the man in the flat cap who abducted the boy or killed Fiona. A man in his twenties would be easy to manipulate, especially if he needed money. And it wasn't that difficult of a task, was it? Give a couple of lads ten euros, and dare them to go to the bog . . .

But wouldn't that person have come forward when he heard

what had happened? If he was only peripherally involved and had any conscience at all?

"Was he a beggar?" Cormac asked. "Did he smell?"

Michael wrinkled his nose. "No. Just the woman."

"He was giving us money, not asking for money," James said. "That's no beggar."

The kid had a point there. Then again, he could have been paid double or even triple by the perpetrator to approach the lads. "Did he seem drunk?" Michael shook his head, then shrugged. *Fantastic.* "What color were his eyes?"

Another shrug from Michael, then he looked at James.

"I was only looking at the money," James said.

"Dark," Michael said. "Maybe they were brown. Or blue."

And this was why children made terrible eyewitnesses. "Was there anything funny about his face? Big nose? Could you see any hair? Lips, teeth, did he have any tattoos?" He was firing questions too fast. He wanted to pick them up and literally shake the answers out of their heads. He wanted to get a hypnotist, but he had a feeling that would be a battle royal with the folks. Cormac gently slid photos of Cahal Mackey and Flynn Barry across the table. The boys stared at them. "Have you seen either of these men?"

"Yes," Michael said.

"Yes," James agreed.

Cormac was stunned. "Is he the man in the flat cap?" If so, these lads were terrible judges of age.

"No," Michael said.

"Definitely not him," James said.

Neely frowned. "Then where did you see him?"

"On the telly," Michael said.

"And the paper," James added.

Cormac exhaled. *Kids.*

"Is there anything else you can think of from that night that it would be good for us to know?" Cormac asked.

The lads sat in silence. Finally, Michael raised his head. "I think the man dropped something," he said. "And Dylan picked it up."

Cormac straightened his spine. "What did he drop?"

"Some metal yoke," Michael said. "He said we could only see it if we didn't go to the bog."

Dylan didn't want to go. Cormac's heart nearly broke into pieces. Was this why Dylan was taken? Did the man in the flat cap somehow know Dylan had nicked something from him?

"Detective Inspector?" The same young clerk who had intercepted him in the hallway poked her head in the room. "May I please speak with you for a moment?" This had to be something major. "Excuse me for a moment, lads." He stood and hurried into the hall where the clerk was waiting nervously.

"Yes?" Cormac said.

"There's been an incident at the harbor."

She gulped. "What kind of an incident?"

"A savage riot. There are at least a hundred men fighting." She gulped. "And Cahal Mackey and Flynn Barry are at the center of it."

CHAPTER 41

*D*IMPNA HAD BEEN STANDING IN THE SQUARE WITH THE PROTESTORS, listening to Orla continue her speech when she saw the commotion out of her periphery. A male voice rose above Orla's, and the distinct verbiage and pattern of someone preaching rang out. She caught something about "the end days," and "Satan himself." The preaching man drew closer. No sunglasses, no hat, but Dimpna knew exactly who it was. Cahal Mackey. The group of women clocked him at about the same time, and for a moment, everything fell silent as he strode toward them. He began to run.

And then she saw that Mackey was being followed. She recognized Gary Sheehan in the lead. Fiona's father. The one who had thrown a brick through Cormac's window. He was holding a baseball bat. And so were the twenty or so men behind him, all brandishing some sort of weapon.

"Oh my God. Sheila!" Dimpna yelled. "Move out, move out—back to the meeting room." Dimpna began touching and talking to as many women as she could. Some stood frozen; whether it was fear or fascination, the result was the same. "Move!" Dimpna yelled. "Move!" The group of vigilante men had now surrounded Cahal Mackey, and the women began to scream. Sheila came to life and began following Dimpna's lead, urging the women to drop their signs and run. They were finally moving, en masse. Dimpna feared a stampede. She'd never been in the middle of such a dangerous situation, and it had come on without warning.

"My father," Sheila yelled, as she passed Dimpna. "I can't find my father."

"Let's get these women safe. We'll find him," Dimpna said. No matter her feelings for Danny Maguire, she did not want to see him crushed. The group of men seemed to double in size. Pure chaos. "Stop," Dimpna screamed. "Stop!" She saw several guards, young, fresh-faced lads, running toward the scene, terror stamped on their faces. They were hardly equipped to handle a riot, and from the looks on their faces, they knew it. A woman screamed, and Dimpna whirled around to see a pregnant woman on the ground. Before Dimpna could reach her, other pregnant women were already helping her to her feet. As the group of men moved toward where the woman once stood, like a giant floating amoeba, the air vibrated with screams. As Dimpna grabbed the arm of the woman closest to her and began pulling her away, she couldn't help but think how thin the thread of civility stretched, and how easily it could snap.

Multiple squad cars headed for the harbor, lights and sirens blaring. Cormac and Neely were in the lead, and they were being brought up to speed by a guard in the back seat. "Cahal Mackey was walking the harbor, preaching that they were all sinners and the Grand Ruler was coming for them soon."

"Flynn Barry's call," Cormac said. "Maybe if I had been available, none of his would have happened."

"Don't be a fool," Neely said. "If he was trying to save anyone, it was only himself."

"He said he had something to confess."

"That man wouldn't confess to the mirror."

Cormac glanced at the garda in the back. "And then?"

"Then there was a group of men carrying baseball bats and whatnot following him."

Cormac groaned. A riot. Just what they fucking needed. He was balls to the wall, finally seeing tiny cracks in the case, hoping to make a giant breakthrough, and now this.

Ireland had a Public Order Unit, but they were deployed for big events and mostly worked out of Dublin. Every guard on duty was headed to the scene, with all the riot gear they possessed. His head was going to roll for this one, but right now, all he cared about was putting a stop to the bleeding. Literally.

"People are scared," Neely said. "With Cahal and Flynn working at the harbor, this was inevitable."

He could hear a bit of resentment. It was true she had repeatedly said they needed to find a way to lock up Cahal and Flynn. "We didn't have cause," Cormac said. "I would do the same again." It would do no good to state that he'd repeatedly warned them. He should have found a way to force the issue. He felt defensive, but now was not the time to win arguments. They were finally pulling up to the harbor. Cormac screeched to a stop, not caring where he was parked, and they scrambled out of the car. The crowd was massive and the sound deafening. As instructed, guards with riot gear assembled into a straight line and began leading a formation toward the center of the crowd. A loud boom rocked the street. Cormac turned to see a car erupt in flames.

Neely had gotten ahold of a bullhorn and demanded folks put down their weapons. Cormac joined the formation just behind the guards with riot shields; he could hear rocks bouncing off them as they moved forward.

Soon shouts of "The guards are here" rang out and rippled through the crowd. As they pressed forward, men dropped off, throwing bottles, spitting, or pumping fists as they left, any last bit of rebelling they thought they could get away with. As they advanced forward, the crowed thinned. All dashed off, apart from a pile of men in the center. Cormac heard the unmistakable sounds of fists on flesh. They had someone in the center of all that rage. On his command, guards charged the group, dragging the men away one by one. By the time they had six in handcuffs, there was only a single man left. He was bloodied and on the ground in a fetal position. Even then, Cormac recognized Cahal Mackey.

"Ring the paramedics," Cormac shouted, and a guard replied that he had done so. Cormac knelt by Cahal. His eyes were swollen shut, his lips were three times their normal size, and blood oozed from his mouth. Cormac couldn't help but wonder about Flynn. Were his phone calls a warning about this? Was this the "something" that was going to cost Cormac?

The paramedics arrived, and Cormac stepped out of the way.

Cahal Mackey suddenly opened one eye; the other was swollen shut.

"He did this," he said. His voice was gravelly and barely audible. "He's still in control."

"Who?" Cormac asked. "Flynn?"

A paramedic gently shoved him aside. Cahal turned his one good eye away from him. "The Shepherd," he muttered. "The Shepherd."

"Over here!" The scream came from the other direction. Cormac turned to see that a flurry of activity had erupted down the docks. Cormac was on his feet and running toward the area before his thoughts had even caught up. He had to push through yet another group of men huddled around something.

"Out of the way, inspector coming through." As the men parted, Cormac spotted blood on the wood planks of the boardwalk. Next to it, a blue baby blanket. His heart leapt into his throat. But as they parted, it wasn't a pregnant woman on the ground, but another man soaked in blood. His eyes were closed. Strewn all around him was baby paraphernalia. A blue blanket, a pacifier, a teddy, a piece of white typewriter paper with some kind of email exchange between someone named FiFoFum and DeafGirlsRule. Shauna and Fiona. The exchange Dimpna Wilde picked up from the festival. Whoever took it had been in her clinic. Two words appeared on the planks ahead of him, written in blood: BABY KILLER. His throat had been slit. *Flynn Barry.* Cormac stood over him, staring. The Shepherd had survived the attack, but the Staff was dead.

CHAPTER 42

ELCOME

The woman had slid the first message across the small table. It was written in green crayon. She smiled behind her colorful butter-fly mask. Shauna did not return the smile. She picked up a black crayon and scribbled.

Why mask? Why butterfly?

Butterflies are free!

Ironic, because Shauna and Dylan were not.

Let us go.

Another sickening smile from the woman, as she patiently waited for the notepad to slide back her way. This time she used a purple crayon, as if she was mimicking the myriad of colors in her mask.

After my baby is born.

Tears welled in Shauna's eyes as she read it, and she was furious at herself for them. She wanted to lunge across the table, rip the mask off, and gouge the woman's eyes out. *My baby*, Shauna thought. *My baby.* It was the first time she had ever had that thought, and there was a strange power behind it. She had to make it through this. She had to get away from this place and this woman and that man. She had to do it for her baby. *Her baby.* He wasn't even born, and Shauna knew she loved him more than she had ever loved any-thing or anyone in her life. Shauna stuck to the black crayon. Everything in her world was going to be dark until they were free. They slid the notebook back and forth.

You're not keeping my baby.
You ALREADY decided.
KIDNAPPERS won't raise my baby.
Join us!!

There was something about the woman's handwriting that felt familiar—the capital letters, the big loops, what was it? Shauna's brain felt stuck between gears; there was too much happening at once. *Join them.* They were crazy. There was no explanation other than they were out of their minds. The strange building. The butterfly masks. The homemade videos. The friendly smiles, as if they weren't being held here against their will. Except Shauna wasn't sure if that was true for Dylan anymore. Ironically, they had drawn him to them like a moth to a light. Who were these people? Shauna had heard of secret societies—cults—but she'd never paid any attention to the stories. Half the time, she felt as if she lived on an island, wanting nothing more than to be surrounded by deaf people so that the hearing didn't outnumber them. But this was a whole new level of ostracizing, and she refused to be manipulated. Had they targeted her because she was deaf? Did they think she was too stupid and naïve to fight back? If so, they had another think coming. Join us. Who the hell did this woman think she was?

NEVER EVER EVER
We are different. Special. Like you. Like the lad.

Shauna didn't need to write anything more. She crossed her arms. "No," she said. "Evil."

Dylan doesn't think so.

Shauna didn't want to, but she couldn't help but turn and look for Dylan. He was playing chess with Moth Man. He was laughing. She curled her fists at her side. Whatever plan she came up with, she was going to have to implement it without Dylan's help. "I need a doctor," she said. "Hospital."

Doula. You will meet her soon. It's almost time.

Shauna wondered what would happen if she lunged across the table and drove the black crayon into the woman's eye. She'd been in fights when she was younger. She could be a scrapper. The baby weighed her down, but not as much as the fear of hurting him. But after the baby was born? She wouldn't hesitate to hurt this woman.

Maybe everyone was right about her. Because she knew one thing for a fact. She wouldn't just be capable of hurting her; she would enjoy it. Shauna picked up a red crayon.

DYLAN'S PARENTS ARE WORRIED SICK. THEY ARE LOOKING FOR YOU.
They won't find us.

Shauna was used to reading people's expressions, but the mask was making it impossible. However, her posture showed a woman who was secure in her statement, not someone looking over her shoulder. Then again, the mask could be giving her a false sense of confidence. Beards often hid men's expressions. Sunglasses could also provide a type of privacy. Even caps pulled low could offer protection. All methods to help human beings hide something. Was that why they were wearing them? Shauna hated that she was now genuinely curious about this woman and what had brought her to do something so evil. That, and it had been too long since she'd spoken with another adult. Whereas Shauna had no connection with Moth Man, maybe Butterfly Woman was someone she could glean just a little bit of information from. Information was power. Shauna continued the conversation.

Why masks?
Change. Transformation. JOIN US AND I WILL TAKE IT OFF!
I am your prisoner. Can only join if I am free.
STAY AND RAISE YOUR BABY YOURSELF. WE WILL HELP.

Bullshit. More game-playing. Shauna was angry now, and anger was not good for her onboard passenger. He didn't deserve it. *NO DOCTOR? NO DEAL.*

"Good news. We have a doula. Do you know what that means?" The woman spoke instead of writing. Shauna glared. She only understood one word: *doula.*

She was tired of hearing about this doula. *WHEN?*

Shauna wanted to continue to argue, but it was pointless. She needed help; the baby was coming soon. The thought of giving birth alone was terrifying.

A FEW DAYS . . . Are you excited?

"You must think I'm stupid. Let me go. Let Dylan go."

NOT STUPID. YOU ARE SPECIAL.

"Because I'm deaf?" The woman was patronizing her now.

BECAUSE OF YOUR MOTHER.

The sentence stopped Shauna cold. She stared at the woman. The woman sported a smile now, at least from what Shauna could tell. Part of her mouth was hidden behind the mask. "Doula now. I haven't felt the baby kick in a while. I need to know if he or she is okay."

"She?" Butterfly Woman leaned forward. *You said you are having a boy.*

How did she know? It was none of this woman's business. Shauna did not reply. Butterfly Woman continued to write. *A boy. My baby boy.*

Shauna crossed her arms, shoved the paper and crayons away. She was done talking.

You don't want to know about your mother? Not even her name?

Shauna simply stared. The woman held up her index finger, then leaned down beside the table. Shauna had failed to notice that the woman had come in with a satchel. When the woman straightened up, she was holding an old book. She set it on the table, then reached into the satchel again and brought out a stack of papers. She opened the older book to show Shauna that someone had been writing in it. A journal. Then she closed it and tapped the stack of papers. *I give you a copy of journal. It belonged to your mother.*

Shauna pointed at the original. "That one."

Butterfly Woman shook her head. "Mine." She lifted it and held it to her chest, then nudged the copies forward. "Yours."

Shauna wasn't going to fall for it. She had to force herself to focus on what mattered. *Why take Dylan? TELL ME.*

Butterfly Woman hesitated. *I need him.*

Shauna read it and frowned.

The woman kept writing. *He's mine.*

Crazy. A madwoman. "He's not yours."

Dylan's parents abused him. He's safe now.

Shauna slid her chair back and stood. She pointed at the woman. "Liar. You're a liar. You're a kidnapper."

The woman's mouth twitched. She removed yet another item

from the satchel. She held it up. It was a photo of a pregnant woman with long dark hair. Next, Butterfly Woman held up a newspaper article: DEAD PREGNANT WOMAN FOUND IN BOG. This had to be the one Dylan mentioned. Shauna slapped her hand over her mouth, then scrambled to her feet and began to back away. Butterfly Woman stood as well, but grabbed the notebook and a crayon on her way up. She wrote furiously on the notebook:

WE DIDN'T DO THIS. We are saving you from the monster who did.

"Liar!"

I know this killer. He's targeting our group.

"What fucking group?"

The woman grabbed the old book from the table. The journal. She went back to the notebook and wrote once more: *Your mother started a revolution.*

Shauna stopped moving. Butterfly Woman nodded vigorously and wrote again:

Read it.

Butterfly Woman once more shoved the copy of the journal across the table. Shauna shook her head, but she couldn't tear her gaze away from it. The woman had written another message, this one three times bigger than the others. It was also underlined and topped off with three explanation marks:

IF WE LET YOU GO, HE WILL KILL YOU!!!

"Who? Moth Man?"

Butterfly Woman seemed startled by the suggestion. She shook her head. *He's my son. Good man.*

"Why? Why me?"

You are special. And he wants to kill you. You carry MY baby. We save your life.

"Why would he kill me?" It didn't make any sense.

You are evidence.

"Stop riddles! Stop!" Shauna could feel her throat burn. "Evidence of what?"

"The truth!" This statement Shauna could lip-read. The woman must have seen Shauna hesitate. She wrote one last message, her hands flying across the page:

The Shepherd killed Fiona. He is a monster.
Evidence of what?
Your father. You are the Shepherd's daughter.

The Shepherd's daughter. What did that even mean? Who was he? Shauna stared at the photocopied journal. She'd placed it by her bed. Should she read it? Was it really written by her birth mother? Was the woman in the bog really FiFoFum? And was FiFoFum the woman named Fiona? And was Fiona the dead pregnant woman in the bog? Was Butterfly Woman telling the truth? Were they protecting her? Protecting her from her own father?

Shauna had no idea whether or not what the Butterfly Woman said about Dylan's parents was true. What if he *had* been abused? Learning that might go a long way to figuring out if anything else she had said was true.

She was going to have to talk to Dylan, but he was becoming more and more withdrawn from her, and more and more attached to their kidnappers. She needed him to trust her again. And then she needed another plan. Maybe it was time to let them believe that she was starting to like and trust them. She wanted to think that Dylan was pretending too, but she feared he was not. He was curled up on his bed. She scooted over to him. She had to call out his name three times before he looked up from his iPad. She hoped whoever raised her onboard passenger would limit his screen time. It wasn't healthy. It turned them into zombies. "Dylan," she said louder, giving him a little pinch.

He shrieked. She could not hear it, but he jumped, and she saw how wide his mouth opened.

"Sorry," she said. "Let's play a game."

"No." He rolled over, turning his back to her.

"I'm your friend," she said. "I'm trying to help you." He turned his back to her and buried his face in the iPad. Shauna snatched it from behind. Dylan whirled around, his eyes crazed, his mouth open in that familiar scream. "Just take a break," Shauna said, panic rising in her at his extreme reaction. She didn't realize until she felt a shadow fall over her that Moth Man had entered. Dylan looked at him, and now the lad's eyes shone with excitement. Before Shauna knew what was happening, Dylan had scrambled off the bed and was holding hands with Moth Man. They waked toward the door. Panic seized her. She screamed. They did not turn around. She ran toward them screaming. Moth Man whirled around and dropped Dylan's hand. Dylan looked terrified, but not of the man—*of her.* She was watching him change before her very eyes, get sucked into this evil couple. Moth Man grabbed her arms and twisted them behind her back.

"Dylan," she yelled. "Run!" Moth Man couldn't chase them both. But Dylan stood still. Moth Man marched her to the door where they used to live. The tiny room with no windows, the room with no sky.

"No," she said. "Baby not happy."

He kept moving toward the door. Did he understand her?

"Dylan," she screamed. "Run! Run!" Would he listen? Would he run? Would he find a way out?

Moth Man opened the door and shoved her into the tiny room. Then he turned on a bright light before exiting and treated her to a strange smile as he shut the door. She had been prepared to fling herself at the door when the photos on the walls stopped her. They were of the dead pregnant woman from the bog. Not a newspaper article of an eerie but empty bog, like Butterfly Woman had showed her, but genuine photographs. Of the dead woman. There were shots from multiple angles. The poor woman's bloated corpse, a jagged red slash across her neck, her belly straining beneath a short white robe. *Robe.* She whirled around to see if it was still there. It was. A short white robe just like the one on the corpse. "No," she screamed. "No!" She ran to the door and pounded on it. Was Butterfly Woman still here?

She could not look at those photos. She could also not look away.

These photos weren't a warning. They were a promise.

Butterfly Woman had not seemed as threatening. Was it an act? She said Moth Man was her son. Wait a minute. Dylan's bracelet. MÍORÚILT—1994. LOVE FOREVER AND EVER AND EVER. It was to Moth Man from his mother. She said they were protecting Shauna. From the Shepherd. Who she said was Shauna's father. And her mother the writer of that journal. The journal that was now out there while she was in here. Which statements were lies and which were the truth? What if Butterfly Woman didn't know her son was evil? What if she truly thought they were doing the right thing? What if Moth Man was fooling her too?

Shauna slowly got to her feet. Maybe Butterfly Woman had no idea her son was a killer. Who else would take these photos? Display them. And if that were true, if she did not know her own son was evil, then Shauna had something. Something she could use to create a divide between them. She needed Butterfly Woman to see this room. She needed to convince her that her son was a monster. And then maybe, just maybe, she would let them go. If she was smart, Butterfly Woman would come with them. But they needed to leave soon. Before it was too late. Before it was all too late.

CHAPTER 43

ORMAC HAD TO STEP AWAY FROM FLYNN BARRY'S BODY. ON THE SURface, this murder seemed straightforward. A group of vigilante men started a riot, attempted to murder Cahal Mackey, and succeeded in murdering Flynn Barry. But now, looking at the man's slit throat, Cormac wondered if something else was at play. It occurred to him that the riot and the men beating up Cahal Mackey could have been a cover for a lone killer. Had this person instigated these men so that attention would be drawn away from the harbor, away from a now-defenseless Flynn Barry? By a person with a history of slashing throats? What if the same person who had murdered Fiona Sheehan—and Alana Graves and who knows how many others—was the person who slashed Flynn's throat while the crowd was distracted by the riots?

But why target the number two? Was it possible that Flynn Barry had been telling the truth? Had he something to confess? Something that cost him his life?

"Here," Neely said from behind him. He turned around. She was holding a bottle of water.

"Thanks." He took it and took a drink, although it was only to make her happy. It was a reminder though that he'd barely eaten, slept, or drunk anything other than coffee in days.

"What if he knew who took Dylan and Shauna? What if he knew who killed Fiona?" Cormac couldn't help but torture himself.

Neely shook her head. "He was trying to mess with your head.

Full stop." And yet here Flynn Barry lay. Neely knew he was still obsessing on his failures. "You know better. Pull yourself together."

Ironic coming from her. But she was right. Her words were like a blast of cold water in his face. "Is the team ready?"

She nodded. "Coroner, technical team, photographer." She glanced toward Strand Street, which was still blocked off. "We have a lot of our men on riot duty," she said.

It was a bit late for that. "We need to question Cahal Mackey," Cormac said. As soon as the hospital would allow it. "He said something odd when he saw me."

"I'm listening."

"He seemed to be referring to the Shepherd as someone else."

"What do you mean?"

"He said, 'He's still in control,' and when I asked, 'Who?' he said, 'The Shepherd.'"

Neely frowned. "He was just beaten to a pulp. Or he's a split personality, for all I know."

"Do you see now that, whatever is happening, this isn't all about them?" Cormac didn't want to alienate Neely—he needed her, he respected the hell out of her—but he also needed to know if she was ready to take her blinders off.

She chewed on her lip. "They're involved," she said. "But there has to be someone else as well."

"More puppets," he said. "More believers." Believers so brainwashed they would kill for another man. Human beings. They never failed to disappoint him.

"Inspector."

Cormac turned to see Garda Lennon holding up an evidence bag. Inside was a gold cross that had fallen near Flynn Barry's body.

"What is it?" Cormac bridged the gap between the two and took the evidence bag.

"Look at the name engraved on the back."

Cormac turned it over and stared. SHAUNA MILLS. The gold cross belonged to Shauna Mills.

Neely and Cormac waited outside Erin's house for Cara Hayes to show up. Given Erin's severe isolation, he'd given up on the idea of

YOU HAVE GONE TOO FAR   281

forcing her to come into the station. He needed her to be cooperative. He needed answers. The pig was sunning himself on a patch of dirt nearby. They had told Erin they wanted him in an enclosure for their visit. He hoped the fact that she'd done no such thing was not a harbinger for the rest of the interview. On the positive side, Cara Hayes pulled up bang on time. The pig lifted his head and grunted, then set it back down with a snort.

"He's growing on me," Neely said.

"More bacon for me," Cormac replied. Neely gave him a look, and he laughed. "I'm only messing."

Cara smiled as she emerged from her truck, but from the tight pull of her thin lips, Cormac registered it as fake. She was in her fifties, like Erin, and wore no makeup. Her hair was black freely mixed with gray and pulled back in a severe bun. As she approached, her eyes flicked around the property, and she wiped her forehead with the back of her hand. The pig suddenly squealed, then got to his feet and toddled over to her, faster than he looked capable of moving.

"He knows her," Neely said, reading Cormac's mind. "She's been here before."

"He's fond of you," Cormac called out.

Cara flushed. "Is he?" She smacked her lips and shrugged. "Maybe he smells my wolfhounds."

"Are you saying you've never been here before?" Neely asked. "Never met that pig? Is that what you're telling us?"

"Why would you think I have?" Cara asked. Another deflection. *Interesting.* What was the connection between Erin and Cara?

Cormac had taken prescription allergy meds before this visit, and they were making him loopy. That and no sleep, topped off with insane amounts of caffeine, had him on edge.

Neely was studying him. "Shall I ask Erin to join us out here?" she asked.

Cormac glanced at the skies, which looked as if they were about to split open and bucket down on them. "Inside is fine," he said.

Neely nodded, then proceeded to the front door and banged on it.

"Why am I here, Detective?" Cara asked. "I don't know this woman."

"Why do you assume we're here to see a woman?" Cormac had only given her an address, nothing else. She had just given herself away. Cara's face reddened. "I'm going to give you one chance to stop lying," he said. "If I were you I'd take it."

"Excuse me?" Her face tightened.

"We know you've been here. We know you know the pig. We know you know Erin. Any stories you make up are going to make you look guilty."

Anger radiated from her. "Guilty of what?" Cormac could imagine her surrounded by a pack of wolfhounds.

The front door swung open, and a voice from within called out. "Come in."

Neely entered, followed by Cara and then Cormac. He kept the door open and stood near it.

"Why is she here?" Erin whined. Not "Who is she?" but "Why is she here?" More confirmation that they had a past.

Ironically, it was the first question for which Cormac really wanted an answer. Unlike Cahal and Flynn, who were used to keeping their mouths shut—permanently now, in the case of Flynn—Cormac was hoping that, if these women refused to say anything, they could turn them against each other and at least squeeze something out of one of them. It was pathetic that this was where he was at in this investigation. Regardless, one had to play the cards one was dealt.

"I'm not feeling well," Erin said, clutching her stomach. "I need to lie down."

"The sooner you tell us how you know each other, the sooner we will all be out of here," Cormac lied.

Erin suddenly hurtled herself toward Cara, much like her pig. "Is it true?" she asked. "Is he dead?"

Cara shook her head, and Cormac couldn't help but think she was warning Erin. "I don't know what you're on about."

Flynn Barry. This was a pot Cormac could stir. He turned to Erin. "The Staff, isn't that what you called him?" She pursed her lips, then looked away. He turned to Cara. "Are you telling me you didn't hear about the riot near the harbor?"

"I've been busy, Inspector. Was there a riot at the harbor?" But she was starting to sweat.

"He's dead," Erin said. "He can't do any damage." A smile came across her face, and it changed her completely. Cormac shivered. She was off today; was it a medication issue, or was she regressing into her cultish state? She clapped her hands together. "It's as if Seven Star has risen from the dead." She winked at Cara. Cara glared.

"Seven Star," Cormac said. "She was one of you?"

"If there's nothing else, I'm leaving," Cara said. "This poor woman is obviously mentally ill."

Erin turned to Cara. "If hers has come back, what about yours? Are you going to search?"

Cara's face paled. "Shut. Up."

"Her what?" Cormac said. Neither woman even glanced his way. He was starting to feel as if he was invisible, but at least they were talking.

Cara moved to the door. "I'm leaving."

"Whatever you two are involved in, it's getting serious," Cormac said. "You need our help."

"The butterfly has emerged from its cocoon," Erin suddenly said. Her eyes danced with excitement. "The wings are flapping. One down and four left."

"One down?" Cormac said. "The Staff?" Who were the four that were left?

Erin simply blinked, then tilted her head and twirled a strand of hair.

"Seven Star," Neely said. "What was her name before her transformation?"

Transformation? Neely apparently knew some of the cult lingo. He should have taken a deeper dive.

"You seriously cannot be listening to this woman," Cara said. "She's obviously not well."

"We do not speak their former names," Erin said.

"And yet you are using yours," Cormac pointed out. Erin narrowed her eyes and glared at him.

Neely turned to Cara. "You're here because we found your business card on her table."

Cara stood by the door and shrugged. "She's obviously an animal hoarder. I don't know where she got my card, but there's no way I'd let her adopt one of me wolfhounds."

"Butterflies are free," Erin sang. "Butterflies are free." Erin began to laugh. "I never thought she had it in her."

Butterflies. Her. Erin Tanner knew a hell of a lot more than she had ever let on. But she also seemed mentally unwell. If it was an act, it was a good one. He had to hit the right notes with her or she would clam up. "What else do you know about butterflies?" Cormac tried to keep his voice casual.

"They're free," Erin said. "That's what I know about butterflies."

They're free.

"What about butterfly tattoos?" Cormac asked. "Or masks?"

Erin's face went blank, and she zoned out. He glanced at Cara. "What do you know about butterflies?"

"That a single flap of their wings can cause a tornado halfway around the world?" Cara asked.

Neely snorted. "We're more interested in tattoos and masks."

"Can't help you there," Cara said. "You should check with a tattoo shop."

Cormac's gaze fell on the fireplace mantel. There was now a black-and-white framed photo sitting atop it. He could see a group of women standing together, all in long dresses. Twentysomethings, and it appeared as if they were all in various stages of pregnancy. Neely had noticed it too, and while Erin's back was to her, she snapped a photo with her mobile phone.

Good woman. Neely and Cormac exchanged glances; then they both looked from the photo to Cara. He and Neely had the same thought at the same time. It had been said that Erin was the only female survivor of the cult. But looking at Cara now as she locked eyes with Erin, the answer about how these two women were connected was obvious. Cara Hayes was another cult survivor. He grabbed the photo off the mantel and approached Cara. He pointed to the one he pegged as Cara in the photo.

"You're telling me this photo isn't of you?" Cormac asked. Cara didn't reply. "I did you a courtesy of meeting here," he said. "And since you've chosen to lie, I'm hauling you into the station next."

"I've done nothing wrong," she said.

"Your lies are hindering my investigation. You can pretend you didn't hear about the riot—"

"I *didn't*—"

"But I know you've heard about the dead pregnant woman in the bog—"

"Fiona," Erin said. "Red Rose, Red Rose." Erin clucked her tongue.

"Shut up," Cara snapped.

Neely stepped forward. "Red Rose was one of the cult members. Was Fiona her baby?"

"Seriously?" Cara was red in the face. "If our babies were stolen from us, how are we to know? I could be standing in a crowded room with my child, and I don't even know if I'd recognize her."

Her. Now they were getting somewhere. Cara was beginning to crack. "Online testing," Cormac said. "If the now-grown babies wanted to find their birth mothers, there are ways." *Some kind of online group . . . adoptees.* "Oh my God," Cormac said. What if the grown children who had been snatched from the women of the cult had started looking for their birth mothers? He hadn't meant to speak out loud, but it was too late to take it back. Every head snapped in his direction. He stared at Cara. "You swear no one from any kind of online adoption group has been in touch with you?"

Cara bowed her head and shook it slowly. Cormac looked to Erin. "They're free," he said. "You mean the children of the Flock, don't you?"

Erin blinked, but a smile broke out on her face. "They're free," she repeated.

"Has anyone contacted you in any way?" Neely asked Cara. "Anyone claiming to be your child?"

"I wish I could help you," Cara said. Her mouth was quivering.

"I'm taking you both to the station," Cormac said. "And I'm going to find reasons to keep you there until you tell me something useful."

Erin shrieked and huddled in the farthest doorway. Cara sighed, then snatched the photo out of Cormac's hands. She brought it close to him and pointed to a young woman. Even in black and white, Cormac could tell her hair was a light shade. She was radiant. "Golden One," she said. "I never knew her given name. She said she never wanted to utter it again."

"What about her?" Cormac asked.

"She was the first to give birth. The first one to be chained and have her baby ripped out of her arms." Erin squealed, and Cara shushed her with a look. "It was a boy. According to the Shepherd, he was born frail. He immediately took him to hospital. That was his version."

"And Golden One?" Cormac asked. "What was her version?"

"That he was kidnapping the child."

"You should have listened to her."

Cara's anger returned. Her nostrils flared. "We all made mistakes. But if you think you can punish me more than I've already punished meself, you're going to be sorely disappointed."

"I see," Cormac said. "What happened to Golden One after he took her child?"

"She vanished. The very next day. The Shepherd swore to us that he dropped her off in town." She shook her head. "But none of us believed that."

"You don't think it's possible?" Neely asked.

"She would have gone straight to the police. She would have moved heaven and earth to find her boy." Cara's gaze returned to the photo. She pointed to another. This one had soft brown curls and looked as if she was the youngest. "Morning Sun," she said. "You found her at the base of the mountains."

Neely came to attention. "Alana Graves?"

"Yes," Cara said. "Alana." Her voice trembled. "We failed her. We should have listened to Golden. And when Golden disappeared, we should have listened to Seven." Cara looked wistful. "Seven was the second of us to realize we'd been duped. And the bravest. She managed to escape before it all imploded."

"Excuse me?" Cormac said. He and Neely came to attention.

"She drugged me!" Erin blurted out. "Betrayed me. She was the Devil's child."

Cara pinched the bridge of her nose, then focused on Cormac. "On this matter, Erin speaks the truth. Seven Star drugged Eternal Mist and the Staff while the Shepherd was away. I saw her do it. And even though I didn't help, I didn't stop her either."

"She was still with child when she escaped?" Cormac asked.

Cara nodded. "I don't know what ever happened to Seven or her baby. I don't know if they're alive or dead. I do know they weren't anywhere near the property. The Shepherd and the Staff searched everywhere. And it wasn't long after that that they were arrested."

"The anonymous letter," Neely said. "The anonymous caller."
Seven Star.

Cormac grabbed the photo and once again presented it to Cara. "Show me."

"Seven Star," Cara said, pointing to the woman in the middle of the photo. Her voice caught. She was a strikingly beautiful woman, even in black and white. Tall, with chiseled cheekbones and intense eyes. "Her name was Tallulah." Cara gently touched the photo. "For thirty years, I've imagined what became of her. Imagined her getting to spend the rest of her life with her child. Somewhere far, far away. I hope they're happy. I hope she's a grandmother now."

"Devil!" Erin said. "Devil child."

"Tallulah," Neely said. "What was her surname?"

Cara shook her head. "I couldn't tell you."

"He's going to find out about this," Erin crooned from the corner. "Why are you doing this?"

Cormac whirled on her. "If by 'he' you mean the Shepherd, he's lying in hospital and may not even make it. I've got guards stationed at his room. He can't hurt you. You have to help us find Dylan and Shauna."

"He's fooling you," Erin said. "He's still fooling you."

Cormac sighed and focused again on Cara.

"Eternal Mist." Cara pointed at Erin Tanner's photo.

"Eternal Mist," Erin Tanner repeated. "I am Eternal Mist."

"And you?" Neely said. "What was your name?"

"You already know," Cara said.

"Red Rose?" Neely ventured.

Cara nodded. "I gave birth chained up. They tried to put me out. But I was still half there. I never even got to hold her."

Cormac bowed his head. He couldn't imagine the horror. Not only of that moment, but every moment since for the past thirty years. Why were they so reluctant to talk? "The compound," Cormac asked. "Did we find the right one?"

Cara bit her lip. "I told you. That's all the help I can give you." But there had been a slight shake of her head. A negation. They hadn't found the compound.

Erin walked up to Cormac, snatched the photo from Cormac's hand, and walked out of the room with it. "One down and four left," she said again as she disappeared.

Cormac faced Cara. "What is she talking about?"

"*Who* is she talking about?" Neely chimed in. Cara remained silent. "Tell me you know *something* that can help us find Dylan and Shauna." Neely was practically begging.

"I wish I could," Cara said. "I couldn't even find the compound if I wanted to."

Cormac stepped forward. "It *is* safe."

Cara shook her head violently. "It's not."

"We thought Erin was the only survivor," Neely said. "How did we not know about you?"

"I'd had enough drama for a lifetime. I wanted to leave the past where it belonged."

"Why did the Shepherd come to see you?" Cormac asked.

"He didn't," Cara said. She shivered. "But if you let it be known I've spoken with you, he will. He will." She stared at him. "Don't you see? *One* down? Flynn? Four left? Four people who could expose the truth. I'm one of the four left, Erin is one of the four. Cahal Mackey. I swear I don't know who the last one is. But if I had to guess? Seven Star."

Cormac felt he was being conned. But what if he wasn't? Is that what Erin meant? "Don't lie to me. You told me the Shepherd visited you. You told Dimpna Wilde. You pretended he was asking after a wolfhound."

"Oh," Cara said. "Right." She suddenly looked nervous.

"Why didn't you come to us?" Neely asked. "Why didn't you tell us who you were then?"

"There are things you don't understand," Cara said. "I won't risk any more lives."

"We can help," Cormac said. "We're your lifeline. *Take it.*"

Cara walked into the adjacent dining room. The table was piled with papers. She returned with an envelope and a biro. She began to sketch. When she handed it back to Cormac, he found himself looking at the strangest building he had ever seen. It almost looked like a giant UFO, surrounded on all sides by smaller ones, circled by a lake. "I can't tell you how to get there. I know it's under an hour's drive. Dense woods border the property to the east. It's surrounded by a man-made lake and enclosed by an iron gate. Before you reach the iron gate, there is a long drive. I never heard any neighbors. It's less than an hour's drive from here. I swear that's all I know. I *swear*." She ran for the door, and before either Cormac or Neely could stop her, she was gone.

"Have you ever seen anything like this?" Cormac asked, staring at the sketch.

"No," Neely said. "But a building in Ireland that looks like *that*? Someone has to have seen it."

She was right. "We'll start online," Cormac said. "Let's get back to the station. We also need to see if we can find out more about Seven Star."

Neely glanced toward the back of the house. "We're leaving," she called out. There was no answer. They had just opened the door to exit when they were startled by a loud thump. Neely and Cormac stopped in their tracks. And then, they ran toward the dining room. The sound had come from that direction, but farther away. A doorway in the back of the dining room exited into a hall. They dashed through it. To the left was a closed door.

"Erin?" Cormac called out as they approached the door. "Are you alright?" There was no answer. Cormac took out his gun. Neely followed suit. They approached the doorway on either side. "Erin," he said. "Say something." They listened. Silence.

On three, Cormac mouthed to Neely. *One, two*—on the count of three, he shouldered the door. It cracked around the knob, allowing him to reach in. A key rested below the knob. He turned it, then tried the knob, and the door swung open. The sight before them was heartbreaking.

Erin Tanner hung from a rope tied to a heavy chandelier. Above the waist, she was struggling, her hands clutching at the rope.

"Jesus," Cormac said. "We're coming." Below her, a chair had been kicked to its side. Neely cried out, and they rushed for the chair at the same time. Cormac was the first to get it upright. He leapt on top of it and struggled to undo the heavy rope around her neck. It was tight, but he was able to loosen it a smidge. He grabbed her around the waist and lifted her, hoping to ease the pressure even more. "Call 999," Cormac yelled.

"I already have," Neely said.

"Find a knife." Cormac held the woman by the waist, trying to loosen the tension around her neck. Her nails dug into his arms, scratching, scratching. She pummeled him with her fists. She was having an internal struggle as she battled the will to live and the will to die.

"Your animals," Cormac said. "They need you." The scratching stopped. Cormac could feel her laboring to breathe.

"I'm coming," Neely yelled. "I have a knife."

"We won't take your lovely pets away. I promise you. Are you listening to me? I *promise*. We'll help get them well. You're alright, luv. You're going to be alright." Cormac was straining under the weight. Despite her being a petite woman, it was not easy holding her up from this position. "Do it for all your animals, will ya? Live for them. They need you, Ms. Tanner. They need you."

CHAPTER 44

*E*RIN TANNER WAS IN HOSPITAL, AND SHE WAS GOING TO SURVIVE. Cormac did not like that she was at the same hospital as Cahal Mackey, but at least they were on different floors, and if he could help it, neither would ever know the other's exact location. The only reason Erin was giving so far for her attempted suicide was ramblings about Cara saying too much. "He'll get us," she said. "He'll get us." Cormac didn't know why her solution to that was to beat him to the very thing she was afraid of, but the woman was not mentally stable. She had to be sedated when she realized she'd been taken out of her home. He'd put a call in with Dimpna, and she was going to make sure Erin's animals were taken care of for the time being.

Cormac had been replaying his conversations with the women over and over again, especially the part where Cara Hayes said she wouldn't know her own child if she was standing before her. First, he wasn't sure he believed that, but second, he couldn't help thinking about Fiona. If she had been a member of a group trying to find their biological parents, had she found out who her mother was? And if so, could he somehow get access to those records?

There were two DNA samples the state pathologist did have handy. Fiona Sheehan and Alana Graves. He slipped outside and put in a call to the state pathologist. Could she compare the two DNA samples? See if they were related? Normally, such tests could take weeks, but she said she would try to rush it. Headquarters had already made it clear to all involved that this case was the highest priority. After the call, he pocketed his mobile phone and headed back inside.

A guard was stationed at the door to Cahal Mackey's room. The sketch drawn by Cara was now in the hands of a small team of guards, and they were scouring the internet, property records, and social media for anything resembling the strange building. He did not want any public announcements; if this was the location where their victims were being held, he could not afford any public inter-ference. Cormac and Garda Lennon were informed that Cahal was awake, but he was on heavy painkillers. Cormac still wanted to speak with him, but mainly he just wanted to get it over with. It seemed the entire town had come out to beat up the former cult leaders, and how could he arrest the entire town? Even the har-bor's CCTV footage had mysteriously disappeared. But if those men did know where Dylan and Shauna were being kept, Cahal was the only one left who could tell them, and Cormac wanted to make damn sure he got a statement before it was too late. Given what had happened to Flynn Barry, Cahal Mackey would be defensive, terri-fied, and inclined to flee.

They were shown into his room right away. Cahal was lying in the bed, and given that his left eye was swollen shut, it was his right that took them in. He briefly shut it when he recognized Cormac and shook his head.

"If you're here to protect me, you're too late," he said. His head was tilted to the side, and his words were slurred. From the looks of him, he was on strong painkillers.

"I never wanted that to happen to you or Flynn," Cormac said. That was only partly true. He'd keep the bad part to himself.

"Flynn," Cahal said. "Poor bastard."

"I received a message from him hours before he died," Cormac said. "He said he had something to confess."

"Did he now?" Cahal started to chuckle, which turned into a hacking cough that made him wince. "Wonder if he grew a pair."

"Any idea what he wanted to tell me?"

"That's probably what got him killed." Cahal's head tilted to the side.

He was definitely out of it. If Cormac played his cards right, he might be able to get something out of him. He decided to play it as if he knew what the hell they were talking about. "It was bound to get him killed, don't ya think?"

Cahal nodded. "I'm surprised he kept his mouth shut this long. But what's he going to do to him now?"

"What's who going to do to him now?"

Cahal studied Cormac for a moment, then wagged his index finger. "You know who."

"Right, right," Cormac said. "It's obvious, isn't it?"

Cahal shrugged. "I never did find out how much he was paid."

This was definitely the drugs talking. But was it truthful? Cormac edged in. "What do you think he got paid?"

"Had to be enough to take care of his family."

Cormac nodded. "Gotta take care of the family."

Cahal shrugged. "He was going to be arrested anyway. Eventually. He was born to be a criminal."

What in the hell was he talking about? "You're the only one who can speak his truth now," Cormac said.

Cahal turned his face to the wall. "I won't betray the Shepherd."

What the hell? Was he once again talking about himself in the third person? "What are you saying?" Cormac asked. Cahal kept his face to the wall. "You won't betray yourself? Is that it?" A nurse entered the room to check his IV. Cahal continued to mumble. "What is he saying?" Cormac asked.

She shrugged. "He's on heavy painkillers."

"Does it make you hallucinate? Forget your own identity?"

She did not look worried. "Patients will say anything. Have you ever seen those viral videos where dental patients still under medication say the craziest things?"

"No. I can't say that I have."

"They're all on YouTube. Hilarious. One guy thought he was a carrot." She laughed for a moment, then stopped as if she had just remembered who Cahal Mackey was.

"Have you heard him say anything strange?" Cormac asked.

She shook her head. "No, but the drugs would have kicked in only recently."

"Has he had any visitors?"

"For this one?" She shook her head. "No. But Trisha Barry was in, hoping to find her brother alive. She'd heard about the riot and that one of them was rushed to hospital. Unfortunately, I had to give her the news."

"Trisha Barry?" Neely had mentioned her. "That's his sister?"

"Yes. I went to primary school with her, only she was a year older and Flynn a year younger. They lived in a shack. But you should see her now. She's in a fancy house. Done well for herself, despite her brother."

He was going to have to speak with the sister. "I'm sorry you had to break the news to her," Cormac said.

"She wanted me to know he had nothing to do with that cult. But I know better."

"She said that? That he wasn't part of the cult?"

The nurse nodded. "She said, 'Hasn't he paid enough? He wasn't even one of them.'"

It was similar enough to what Cahal had said when Cormac first walked in. Cahal slowly turned his head and grinned at Cormac. It gave him the creeps. Cormac focused on the nurse. "I take it you've seen this fancy house of hers?"

"I might have passed it once or twice."

"I'm going to need that address."

"Not a bother. I'll write down it down for ya."

"Trisha Barry wasn't able to tell us anything back then," Neely said. "She went to university in the States." Cormac and Neely stood outside the hospital. Neely had flowers for Erin, and Cormac was on his way to see Trisha Barry, but first he was getting the scoop from Neely. "When we finally got ahold of her, she became a pain in my arse."

"How so?"

"She was adamant that her brother would never join a cult. Rang me up to tell me that nearly every day. She admitted he had a criminal bent, but she just couldn't swallow the rest. Even *after* she visited him in prison and he told her he'd been the number two, she still wouldn't believe it."

"Maybe she has something to say now," Cormac said, jingling his car keys. "Maybe she knows what he was going to confess."

"From your mouth to God's ears," Neely said.

"Anything on the UFO building yet?"

"It's a womb," Neely said. "It's shaped like a womb."

"Ahhh," Cormac said. "That's what it is." He shivered. "How can that place be hidden?"

"It has to be in a remote location—Cara mentioned woods and an hour away—I've got six men on it."

"Keep me posted," Cormac said. "And wish me luck with the sister."

"Good luck," Neely said. "You're going to need it."

CHAPTER 45

TRISHA BARRY'S HOUSE WAS INDEED WHAT ONE MIGHT CALL "FANCY."
A decent-sized limestone house set back on a bit of property. The
door and windows were all painted a cheerful blue. There were at
least four cars in the drive; it looked as if she had company. He was
glad she still had friends and support, despite the life her brother
had lived. He wondered if she lived in this big house all alone. Cormac rang the bell, and minutes later a petite woman in her fifties
with cropped brown hair answered the door. Her hair was mussed
up, and her eyes swollen, no doubt from mourning her brother.

Cormac gave a polite nod. "I'm Detective Inspector Cormac
O'Brien. We spoke on the phone."

She nodded. "The other one didn't want to show her face, is
that it?"

Cormac bristled at the tone, but didn't replicate it. "And by 'the
other one' you mean . . . ?"

"Detective Sergeant Neely."

"She's very busy at the moment, but she sends her regards."

Trish snorted and crossed her arms. "I told her at the time that
my brother was not part of that commune. I tried to give her
proof." She looked at Cormac as if waiting for a response. "I told
her over and over and over. She wouldn't listen. And now he's
dead!"

"I was told he admitted he was part of the cult," Cormac said
calmly. "And that he never wavered on that."

"Because they would have killed him," she moaned. "Maybe even me."

"May I come in, Ms. Barry?" Cormac asked. "I just need a few minutes of your time."

She glanced into the room behind her. "I have visitors."

"I'm afraid this can't wait," Cormac said. "I need to discuss a message your brother left me shortly before he died."

"Died?" Anger coursed through her. "He was murdered, Inspector. He didn't just lie down and die."

"I'm deeply sorry for your loss," he said. "I meant no disrespect."

"And Cahal Mackey nearly beaten to death. You're the ones in charge, are ye? How could you let that happen? How could ye?" Tears ran down her face, and she wiped them away with the back of her hand.

"I won't offer any excuses for what happened to those men," Cormac said. "And you're right; I'm the one in charge, and I take full responsibility. I'm also actively trying to find the killer of a pregnant woman and locate two missing persons—another pregnant woman and a lad ten years of age."

"Then why are you wasting time standing here looking at me?"

"Because your brother told me he had something he wanted to confess, only I never got to hear what it was."

"If you think I have any idea what you're on about, let me assure you, I don't."

"Fifteen minutes," Cormac said. "That's all I need. And whether you believe it or not, we're also trying to find your brother's killer. Questioning those closest to him is our first step. If you want us to find who did this and bring him to justice, you'll let me in."

Trisha sniffed then stood aside. "We can go to the kitchen," she said. "Where it's quiet." They passed through the sitting room, where about half a dozen people were gathered. He could feel eyes on his back all the way to the kitchen. The space felt like a spot of sunshine. It was modern and bright, with a marble island. Trisha pointed to white leather stools along the island, and Cormac sat.

"I'll put on the kettle."

"Appreciate it," Cormac said. "But that won't be necessary."

She opened a bottle of red wine on the counter and poured herself a large glass. "You don't mind, do ye?"

"Not a bother," Cormac said.

"I don't know how I can help you, Detective, but ask your questions."

Cormac glanced at his notepad. "Did you have much contact with your brother after his release?"

"I told him he could stay here. But apparently he had a flat associated with this work program at the harbor." Tears came to her eyes again. "That put a target on his back."

Being associated with a cult that murdered pregnant women and sold their babies put a target on his back . . . Cormac wanted to say it, but he didn't want her on defense. "Your brother said he'd changed in prison," he said instead. "And shortly before he was killed—"

"Murdered—"

She wasn't wrong. He was murdered. In fact, he was butchered. "Shortly before he was *murdered,* he left me a message. He said he had something to confess."

"You mentioned that already."

"I'd like you to give that some thought. Do you have any idea what it might have been?"

"I have an idea." She stuck her bottom lip out. "But you aren't going to believe me."

"Try me." Cormac felt his hopes rise, but just as quickly, the defiant look on her face shot them back down.

"He was going to tell you the truth. That he was never a member of that cult."

Cormac was tired of her already. "Why would he confess to being a member if he wasn't?"

She sighed. "Because he would have gone to prison anyway. For crimes he did commit. And at least this way . . ." She stopped and bit her lip.

"Go on."

"He was paid off, alright? He agreed to take the fall because . . ." She choked up. "Because he wanted me and my kids to have a home." She gestured around. "This home."

"I see."

"You don't believe me?"

"I didn't say that."

"I've been a hairdresser me entire life. You think I could afford this house on that kind of a salary?"

"I don't know."

"He gave me cash. Loads of cash."

"Doesn't that suggest he was in this cult?"

"It suggests he was paid off."

"By whom?"

"I told the other detective all of this a long time ago. I was willing to give up the house to clear his name. He was furious when he found that out."

He was going to have to try this again. "If your brother wasn't the Staff," he nearly cringed saying the nickname, "then who was? Who paid him off?"

"Cahal Mackey," she said without hesitation.

Cormac sighed. "The Shepherd."

She laughed, then shook her head. "Cahal Mackey was the number two. Cahal Mackey was the Staff." Cormac stopped writing and looked at her. If—and it was a mind-bending if—if she was telling the truth, that would explain the things Cahal Mackey had said to him from his hospital bed, and it would also explain Erin Tanner telling them they weren't even close to the truth. Was it possible? Was it possible that neither Cahal nor Flynn were the Shepherd? Trisha leaned in so close he could smell the wine on her breath. "I swear on Flynn's grave. That is, as soon as he has one." She was trying to hold back, but the tears were coming. She backed away.

Cormac sketched the strange building on his notepad and turned it to face her. "Does this mean anything to you?" If Flynn Barry wasn't the Staff, chances are he had never been to the property. But if he was, there was a chance his sister would recognize it.

She stared at his drawing, then shook her head.

Cormac put his notebook down and stared at the wine, wishing he could swill down the rest of it. One thing was for sure. As soon as this case was solved, he was going to get drunk. Off his head, mind-numbingly, happily drunk. He decided to ask her one more time. "If Cahal Mackey was number two, then who was number one?"

"Flynn wouldn't tell me," she said. "He said if I knew, I'd be in danger. The only thing I know is that it sure as hell wasn't Cahal Mackey." She looked Cormac dead in the eyes. "And whoever the Shepherd is, he's been running free for the past thirty years." Her words echoed in his poor head. "And do you really think," she continued, "that a man like that is going to let you catch him now?"

CHAPTER 46

SHAUNA HAD BEEN LOCKED IN THE TINY ROOM FOR A DAY, A NIGHT, and another day now. They had all the power. No matter what she tried to do, they had the upper hand. If they succeeded in taking her baby, she had already decided that she would want to die. She had started to read the journal. It read like a horror story. It had to be made up. Butterfly Woman was trying to mess with her head, right? Why didn't she let her have the original? Had she changed it? She could only read a little at a time. Every word was forming an image of her mother. Shauna felt drawn to her at times and repelled by her when she read other passages. It was a game. It had to be. She wanted to get her hands on the original. Shauna had a feeling it was down the corridor where Moth Man stayed. The only space in this strange building where they were not allowed to go. Where they would be delivered a shock that could kill them.

Dylan was getting further and further away from her. She suspected that, while she was in here, Moth Man had been spending more time with him, pretending to be his friend, something that infuriated Shauna. She was losing him. And maybe she couldn't blame him. If he wasn't ever going home, why wouldn't he want to get close to his kidnappers? Especially if they were doting on him, making him feel special. They had probably thought they could do the same with her.

Shauna stared at the concrete walls. In a burst of fury, she had ripped down all the horrific photos of the poor dead woman and shoved them under her cot. She slid them out again and retrieved one. That one she slid down her pants and prayed that, when he came for them—which he would the minute Butterfly Woman was due to arrive—he wouldn't realize that one was missing. She stared at the now empty walls and wondered, Would there come a day when there would be another pregnant woman in here staring at a wall with photos of dead Shauna?

The door opened, and Moth Man stepped in. He immediately clocked the photos under the cot and took them. He left the room with them, closing the door behind him. A few minutes later, he returned, and at first, she was terrified that he was going to demand the remaining picture. Instead, he held out a sheet of paper: DOULA COMING. CLEAN YOURSELF. AND DON'T EVEN TRY ANYTHING. SHE WORKS FOR US.

He left her alone again, and as she cleaned herself with the wet wipes, she tried to think about this visit with the doula. Even if this woman did work for them, was there any way of reaching her? Should she show her the photo? But hours went by, and the door remained closed. At some point, Shauna dozed off. When she awoke, she thought she was dreaming. There was a woman in the room with her. She too wore a butterfly mask, but unlike the previous woman's festive one, this mask was more like Moth Man's— black and orange that blended in with brown hair streaked with gray. She wore an old-fashioned dress; it went all the way to her ankles and was drab and brown. Shauna detected a strange scent in the air, like that of a wet dog. The woman carried a medical satchel. It dawned on Shauna, along with a sense of panic: This was the doula. If she didn't manage to escape, this was the face she would see hovering over her when her baby was being born. Were they also the hands that would take her baby away forever?

The woman turned the lights up. Shauna had preferred the dark, had wanted to sink into the abyss. But a funny thing happened when the doula illuminated the room and could now see Shauna clearly. Her mouth dropped open, and she froze. Even behind the mask, Shauna could feel her intense gaze and knew that something had just happened. Shauna scrambled to her feet. "Help me," she said. "They kidnapped me. They kidnapped Dylan."

The woman came close then, too close too fast, and her mouth was moving at a speed that was too fast for Shauna to comprehend. Panic bubbled up in her as she stared at the dark hairs above the woman's lips. Before Shauna could utter a single word, the door opened again—perhaps the doula had been too loud—and Moth Man stepped in. The doula immediately stopped talking, her lips stilled. It was as if Shauna had just watched a human being turn into a waxy doll. As Moth Man stood and watched, the doula removed a blood-pressure cuff from her bag, along with a thermometer and a stethoscope. She approached Shauna with the cuff. Her back was to Moth Man. Her lips moved one more time, slowly, and in an exaggerated manner. And this is what Shauna thought she said: *Trust me.*

The woman hurried out of the room. When she returned, she was holding another notebook. Moth Man stepped forward; then the woman spoke to him. Whatever she said seemed to calm him down. The woman took the notepad from him and wrote on it: *Use this to write down your contractions daily.* Shauna took it, then opened it:

I'm sorry. I can't help you.
I have to protect my daughter.
—Morning Sun

Morning Sun. From the journal. The doula had been one of the women. She'd known her mother. That is, if there was any truth to the journal. Shauna still hadn't finished it. Was the doula just messing with Shauna? Shauna stood still as she was checked out. Blood pressure, temperature, heart rate for both her and the baby.

The woman looked around then, as if looking for something. Moth Man must have said something, for she turned to him, and they spoke to each other. He had not left Shauna with anything to write with or on. Soon they both left the room, but before shutting the door, the doula turned to her once more. This time she put her index finger up to her lips: *Shhh.*

What. The. Fuck. The doula obviously worked for these people, so what game was she playing? If she didn't leave and go straight to the guards, then Shauna could not trust her. Period. If she had known the doula was finally coming, she would have thought of another way to make herself look ill, see if they would be so panicked they'd take her to a doctor. Then again, they'd probably just let them both die.

Shauna wondered if they were ever going to let her out of here. She felt a slight cramping. What if something was wrong with the baby? Is that why the doula had looked around and then left so quickly? Shauna wished now that she'd kept the photos of the dead pregnant woman on the wall. How would the doula have reacted when she saw the photos?

You eejit. The woman had been wearing a mask, just like them. She *was* one of them. She could not be trusted. Shauna paced the tiny room until her cramps subsided. By then, she was exhausted. She lay down on the hard cot, and even though she didn't think it was possible, she fell asleep. She had no idea how long she was asleep, but she awoke, disoriented and groggy, to find Moth Man standing over her. He was grinning. Then he whirled around and once more left the room, the door shutting behind him. It took her a minute to realize what he'd done. The photos were back on the wall. Crumpled, but menacing. Her bloated face. That bright red slash across her neck. Reduced to a creature lying in a degraded bog with a stomach just like Shauna's. But this time there was something else. A message. Spray-painted in red across the wall were two words: YOU'RE NEXT.

Stomach heaving, Shauna sat on the bed and picked up the journal. She turned to the first page: THE WOMB—1994. And she began to read.

CHAPTER 47

SHEILA MAGUIRE HAD CANCELED ALL HER TOURS FOR THE DAY. IT didn't feel right, entertaining tourists with all the trauma happening in the area. And then there was her father. She hadn't seen him since the riot. By the time she went into his room, she noticed his closet door was open and a good portion of his clothing was gone. Just as she'd been about to call the guards, he called. He told her he wasn't coming back. He said he knew his time was coming and he didn't want to die in the house. He didn't want Sheila to have to see that. He told her he would send word through a friend when he was gone and his body would be sent to the funeral home he'd chosen. Sheila had tried and tried to talk him out of it. He severed the call. She didn't even recognize the number, but when she called back, it had been disconnected. She called her mother, who was now living in Cork.

"That sounds like something he would do, doesn't it?" Patty Maguire said. "He always did dance to his own drumbeat." She didn't sound sorry that he was dying, but Sheila could hardly expect that. He'd hurt her deeply. Betrayed her. Had a second family.

Orla. Did Orla know he was gone? Sheila called her, but her phone went to voicemail as well.

Dimpna. She ached to talk to her. Even after she'd said what she'd said about her father. Dimpna could be spiteful, but Sheila could hardly blame her. Sheila could call the guards, but her father was probably within his legal rights to disappear. What was he thinking? Slinking off to die? It wasn't right. She had to find him. What "friend" could he possibly be staying with? He'd lost so many friends his age. He'd hardly be staying with Orla and Kevin, would he? She kept returning to his room. This was the only place he'd been for the last few weeks. If there was any clue to where he was now, it would be in here. Resentment filled her as she headed for his closet. This wasn't how she had planned on spending her day, and her only hope now was that she'd figure out where he was sooner rather than later.

Cormac stood in front of Maeve Wilde's caravan clutching his sketch of the womb building, praying that, if anyone saw him standing outside her door, they would think he was there on official police business. Technically he was, but consulting a psychic would not just get him laughed out of the station; he was convinced it might even get him booted out of Dingle altogether. But he was desperate enough to try anything. Their victims had been gone way too long. According to Jane and David Griffin, Shauna was only a matter of days from her due date, and he feared what would happen to her once the baby was born. Dylan's parents were desperate for news, as was the entire town, as was he himself. The lack of progress was maddening, and he couldn't stop playing out the fantasy in which they found where they had taken them, burst in to save them, and arrested the kidnappers.

With all this weighing him down, what harm would it be to see if Maeve Wilde had any insight? He was just about to knock on the caravan door when it swung open.

"Hello, Inspector." Maeve was dressed up as usual; today it was a light blue pantsuit with a white ruffled top. Her hair was feathered, her makeup was on, and she wore white high heels. She was so different than Dimpna, yet equally fascinating.

"Hello, Maeve. I'm sorry I didn't call ahead of time."

"It just so happens I'm free," she said. "It's like I knew you were coming." She fixed him with a penetrating gaze, and he had to laugh. She had a way of disarming him. He followed her into the caravan.

"I've been dreaming about the lad and the young woman who've been taken," Maeve said. She pointed at the built-in dining table. "Have a seat. I'm going to choose a tarot deck."

The place looked exactly like it had the last time he'd wandered in. Neat as a pin. Violets on the windowsill. He sat in the booth as she put the kettle on, then proceeded to the press, where she took her time choosing a deck. She brought a placemat over to the table, a fancy cloth designed for her cards, and set the deck on top of it. It was housed in a little velvet bag. She then set about making them tea. When it was ready, she brought it over with a tin of biscuits and took the seat across from him.

"They're still alive," she said. "But they're running out of time."

He hoped to God she was right about the former and wrong about the latter. But anyone could have told him he was running out of time; he could feel it in his bones.

"Dylan's mother has been to see me," she said softly. "But I couldn't read her."

Cormac sat up straight. This was news. "When did she pay you a visit?" he asked. "And why couldn't you read her?"

"She was here three days ago. Her energy was too chaotic. She's out of her mind with grief. It's understandable, of course, but it gets in the way of a reading."

"Did you tell her you thought he was still alive?" He prayed she did not. The one thing he always made sure of in an investigation like this was to be transparent with a victim's family. It was the reason he'd been so startled when Neely promised during the press conference that they would get the killer. Because there was always a chance they would not.

Maeve was watching him. She removed the deck of cards and began to shuffle them. "No, Inspector. You'll be happy to hear I said nothing to her at all."

He let out his breath. "Listen," he said. "I don't know whether I believe in this stuff or not. But we have two missing persons and an unsolved murder. I guess I'm just curious what you'll get. And if it helps, I do have some items."

She nodded. "Set them on the table."

He set down the sketch of the womb building, then pulled out a photograph of Shauna, then one of Dylan, Fiona, and finally the black-and-white photograph of the women from the village. Maeve Wilde raised an eyebrow. "You came prepared." She picked up the sketch of the womb building first. "Is this where they're being kept?"

"It's a lead," Cormac said. "But as of yet we do not have a location."

"Remote," she said tapping it. "Someone knows. Someone nearby."

Cormac sighed. Unless it was the violets on the windowsill, that wasn't terribly helpful. She picked up the black-and-white photo of the women and stared at it for a moment. "There's a lot of energy here," she said. "A lot of trauma." She set the items to the side and formed a Celtic cross with the tarot cards on the table.

"The young woman who's been taken," she said after a minute. "I'll be frank. I know that she's deaf. But I see her using a variety of ways to communicate."

"I wouldn't be surprised. She learned Irish Sign Language later in life, so she's been lip-reading and speaking, and writing with most folks." He had learned recently that sign language wasn't universal; each country had their own. He'd found that fascinating. He just assumed they all used the same signs. That was the problem with investigating. One might make assumptions that were unhelpful, steer an investigator in the wrong direction.

"That explains all these modes of communication around her," Maeve said. "I think they're being kept together."

"Dylan and Shauna?"

Maeve nodded and tilted her head. "But I see it splitting. Maybe they were together at one point, but now they've separated them."

"They?"

She nodded slowly. "There's more than one. There may even be three or four."

Fantastic. Was it some kind of kidnapping ring? Cormac was waiting to see if she would pick up on anything that wasn't in the press. He'd heard back from the tech team regarding Shauna's laptop.

Shauna had erased her history and not just like a casual user would, but the tech team said it was a solid wipe. Either Shauna had more computer experience than they realized or someone had given her clear instructions on how to permanently get rid of her history. They were still digging, but he'd found no information on whom she had been chatting with or what had been said. It was possible she used a special platform to communicate, or her phone—one of those apps that are supposed to be untraceable. The last tower where her phone had pinged wasn't far from the Griffins'. After that, the phone went dead. Her kidnappers had no doubt either destroyed or disabled the phone. He couldn't see Cahal or Flynn keeping up to date with technology from prison.

"I'm primarily interested in any kind of location you can pick up on," Cormac said.

"I feel cold. I've been feeling cold ever since they went missing."

"How cold?" If they had been locked in some kind of freezer, they were probably dead.

"Damp. Not freezing. But in need of a jumper or an extra blanket. I see mattresses on the floor." She stopped and tilted her head again. "Wings," she said. "But don't worry. I don't think they're angels. Wings. A bird? Something flying?"

He'd made a mistake—this wasn't going to be helpful. He felt like an idiot. She didn't have any kind of magical powers. But he was already here, so he might as well let her finish. "Colorful wings," she said.

Butterfly. Was that what she was picking up on? Because that information had not been in the press. He was back to paying close attention.

"I have read about Fiona," Maeve said. "I feel there is a connection been herself and Shauna."

"It's possible they were both involved in some kind of online group." He wasn't going to say adoptees.

"That would fit," Maeve said. "I don't see it as a close connection, but there's definitely some kind of bond."

"That's good," he said. "Anything else?"

"My guides are telling me you're headed in the wrong direction. Everyone is headed in the wrong direction."

He had to swallow his frustration. Couldn't she just tell him the right direction? "There's something you're missing. I'm sorry, I don't know what it is, but someone on your team has his or her mind made up—only it's steering you wrong."

Neely. And her obsession that this was Cahal Mackey, still manipulating the murders from behind the scenes. Was she wrong?

Cormac's mobile rang. He let it go to voicemail, but he stood. "I've taken too much of your time already," he said.

Maeve walked him to the door. "Someone's hiding in the shadows," she said. "It's like a masquerade ball. No one is who they seem." Cormac nodded. He thought of his suspects. Gary and Breanna Sheehan. Jane and David Griffin. Liam McCarthy. Tom Cunningham. Cahal Mackey. Cara Hayes. Erin Tanner. Previously Flynn Barry, but there was no way to follow up with him. Any of them could be lying. Hiding something. But he was starting to think he was never going to find out. He had his hand on the door latch when Maeve stopped him.

"Have you ever considered getting a tattoo?" she asked.

Tattoo. None of their searches at tattoo parlors had yielded anything. He whirled around and stared at her. "What do you mean?"

"Don't get me wrong; you're a very handsome man. But maybe you'd like to get . . . I don't know . . . the Scales of Justice or some such?" She snapped her finger. "A squeeze-box," she said. "You could get a squeeze-box. I've seen you play. With Dimpna. You're both quite good. You're both quite good *together.*"

"Tell me what else you're getting about tattoos?"

"Getting?" she said. "This isn't a psychic thing. It's a mother thing."

"I don't understand."

"One moment." She hurried to the small fridge in her kitchenette and returned with a flyer. Ink-ling. "My son, Donnecha, is opening a tattoo parlor. He had personal instruction from a top tattoo artist and everything." Cormac stared at her. "I'm sorry," she said. "I suppose I'm quite out of line. It's just—he's not even open, and someone has stolen some of his paints and needles."

He'd forgotten all about Donnecha. Things had been too crazy. *Someone had stolen all of his paints and needles.* Cormac could hardly contain himself. "Maeve Wilde," he said. "You've done it. I should have come to see you ages ago."

Maeve grinned. "Thank you, Inspector. It's a gift."

CHAPTER 48

*D*IMPNA WAS ALMOST FINISHED FOR THE DAY WHEN NIAMH POKED HER head into Exam Room 1. Dimpna knew from the expression on her face that something was up. Dimpna raised an eyebrow.

"Dylan's mam is here," Niamh said. Ava Walsh. "With Dylan's dog."

"Emergency?"

Niamh shook her head. "She said something about his tummy being off."

Dimpna's heart squeezed. "Send her back." Normally, they did not take walk-ins unless it was an emergency, but being a mother of a missing child was emergency enough for Dimpna.

"I'll send her back and put the tea on," Niamh said.

"You don't have to stay," Dimpna said. "I know your shift is over."

"We're both staying." This came from Patrick, who was also due to go home.

"You two are the best," Dimpna said. They both grinned.

"We know," Niamh said. Patrick winked.

Ava Walsh was quickly ushered back. She was a thin woman with pale blond hair. Her face, which was probably normally pretty, showed the signs of strain. Her lips were cracked, and her eyes were rimmed in red. Tucked under her arm was a Jack Russell terrier. Ava's eyes were swollen, and just looking at her made Dimpna tear up. She turned her back and bit her lip; she wanted to be strong for her. "Hello, Ava," she said. "Please come in." The dog squirmed in her arms and wagged his tail. "Who do we have here?" she asked.

"Patches," Ava said in a gravelly voice. "Dylan named him."

"Hello, Patches," Dimpna said, reaching over and giving him a scratch behind his ears. "How are you, luv?"

"He's an absolute wreck," Ava said. "He doesn't understand why Dylan isn't home. He goes into his room and just whimpers. Is that normal?"

"Why don't you put him on the exam table, and you can have a seat right there," Dimpna said, gesturing to a chair in the corner. "Niamh has the kettle on; we'll have a cup of tea to you right quick."

Ava's shoulders slumped in a relief as she set the dog on the table, then sunk into the chair. Dimpna petted the dog and went through the motions of checking his vitals. "Is he eating normally?"

"I suppose."

"Are his bathroom routines normal?"

Ava chewed on her lip and nodded. "He's sad," she said. "He's so sad."

Dimpna wanted to tell her that her son was going to be home soon. That he hadn't been harmed. That whoever did this would be punished. She would give anything to make it so.

"Has your mother said anything?" Ava asked casually. "Is she getting any ideas?"

That's why she was here. Her husband most likely did not approve of Maeve Wilde's tarot card readings or psychic abilities, but here was a desperate mother trying anything she could. "She doesn't know where he is," Dimpna said. *I'm so cold, why is it so cold?* Dimpna would not fill this woman's head with any of her mother's utterings; even if her mother was somehow getting impressions from their missing persons; none of it was helpful. "I'm sorry," Dimpna said. "I wish there was something I could do."

"I know," Ava said. "Everyone in town has rallied around us and searched, and brought us food." From the looks of Ava, she wasn't eating any of the offerings. Dimpna couldn't blame her. If it was Ben—especially at that age—Dimpna would have been out of her mind. "I can't tell you how much we appreciate it." The tears came then, and soon the woman was hunched over, sobbing. Dimpna set the pup down and gave him a chew stick while she knelt in front of

Ava. She rubbed her back until Niamh came in with the tea; then they found a small table to set up in front of her where they placed the tea and biscuits. Patrick brought in chairs, and soon they were all sitting in a semicircle around the grief-stricken mother.

"The last time I talked to him, I was harping on him about his shoes," Ava said. "I don't care about his shoes. I don't care about his shoes." She looked at them as if pleading with them to do something.

"All mammies fuss over their children like that," Dimpna said. "Try not to be so hard on yourself."

Ava shook her head. "He's a young lad; he should be playing, should be getting dirty. Why did I give him a hard time about his shoes?" She wiped her tears and shook her head. "What if that's his last memory of me? I'll never forgive meself. Never."

Dimpna took her hand, and Niamh took the other. "My mam says they're together," Dimpna blurted out. "And they're still alive."

Ava's head popped up, desperation and hope radiated from her in equal measure. "But you just said she didn't know anything."

"She doesn't know *where* they are," Dimpna said softly. "And I figured that's what you need to know."

Ava leaned in, desperation clinging to her. "She thinks he's with the missing deaf girl?"

"That's what she thinks."

Ava nodded and began rocking. "I hope she's kind. I hope she's kind. But she can't talk to him. She can't talk to him."

"I bet they've found ways to communicate," Dimpna said. "Take it from me—there are many, many ways to communicate."

Ava nodded again, but suddenly she was anxious to go. She stood. "I'm sure I'll see you at the vigil?"

They were all meeting at the harbor tonight, to carry candles, condemn the violence that had taken place at the harbor, wanting to get the focus back on finding Shauna and Dylan.

"Of course," Dimpna said.

"We'll all be there," Niamh added.

Ava glanced at the dog. "I think he should stay with you for a while," she said, her voice cracking once again. "I can't watch him. I can't watch him go into Dylan's room and cry."

That's the other reason she was here. Dimpna totally understood. They didn't have the bandwidth or the time to take care of an active pup. "I'd be happy to mind him," Dimpna said. "As long as you need."

"Maybe you can keep him until Dylan is back," Ava said. "He'll be so happy when he's back."

They all walked Ava outside. They were standing in the court-yard, finishing their goodbyes, when Cormac O'Brien emerged from Maeve Wilde's caravan. He didn't clock them until he was halfway across the field, and when he did, Dimpna could see a pan-icked expression come over his face. Ava pointed at him. "That's the Detective Inspector," she said. "Was he visiting your mother?"

Dimpna, who was also processing this revelation, wanted to say something that would help Cormac save face, but she couldn't think of a single plausible explanation. "I don't know," she ended up saying. "They're still doing house-to-house inquiries; perhaps he simply wanted to know if she's seen or heard anything."

"I wonder if she told him what you told me," Ava said. "That they're together and still alive."

Dimpna felt a wave of terror come over her. What had she done? Cormac was going to be furious.

"Mrs. Walsh," Cormac said as he drew closer. "Are you looking for me?"

"No," she said. "But I am surprised to see you here." The look on her face said it all: *Why aren't you out looking for my son?* "I didn't re-alize the guards consulted psychics."

Dimpna felt a little defensive. One minute, Ava had been beg-ging to know what Maeve Wilde saw in her cards, and now she was admonishing Cormac for doing the same thing. On the other hand, Dimpna was surprised by it as well. Neither Cormac nor her mam had mentioned this little visit. What *had* her mother told him? And why didn't he tell her he planned on speaking with her mother? Not that he owed her anything, but she felt strangely left out. Then again, this was not about them. This was about two miss-ing persons and an unsolved murder.

"Now that you're here, can we go over a few more questions?" Cormac said.

"If it will help," Ava replied. "Doctor Wilde told me that Maeve thinks my baby is still alive. And that he's being held with that poor deaf girl. Is that what she told you?"

Cormac's gaze slid to Dimpna, and the look on his face cemented her shame. *Sorry*, she mouthed. He looked away from her and focused on Ava. "Would you like to go somewhere private?"

Ava shook her head. "No. I have nothing to hide."

"I'm working on a theory that this wasn't an impulsive snatch. That maybe whoever took Dylan and Shauna had been watching them for a while." Ava's lip quivered, but she held it together. "Did you notice anyone you hadn't seen before—maybe someone you suddenly saw in your vicinity more than once? Or did Dylan mention anyone new hanging around?"

"I don't have an answer at this moment, but I'll have a think on it."

"You heard about the violence at the harbor?"

"Of course." She set her mouth in a thin line. "We didn't ask for that. We didn't tell anyone to do that."

"Of course not. Where were you and your husband during the riot?" Cormac knew exactly where her husband was. He'd been in with the crowd. Several witnesses had mentioned that, and CCTV backed it up. Cormac needed to find out if Ava would answer his questions truthfully.

"With me," she said. "We were at home all night."

Cormac sighed. If she was willing to lie about this, what else was she lying about? "I'd like to speak with your husband about that," he said. "But right now, I need to speak with Dimpna."

Dimpna stood in front of him with the look of someone about to be scolded. "Your mother said that Donnecha had some supplies stolen from his tattoo parlor."

Dimpna tilted her head. "I hadn't heard," she said. "But surely that's the least of your worries at the moment?"

"Can you take me there?" he said. "Now?"

"Can you tell me what this is all about?"

"I'm not accusing Donnecha of anything, and what I'm about to tell you isn't public information."

"I'll guard it with me life."

"Fiona Sheehan was given two tattoos postmortem."

"That's strange. And awful." She frowned. "How can Donnecha help?"

"We've tried every tattoo parlor we could find, and no one has had any equipment stolen or aroused any other suspicions. I didn't think to include Donnecha's parlor in my search."

"That's because he's not officially open yet, waiting for a few permits. The pre-opening work he's been doing is free—for practice." She stopped talking, and a strange look came over her face. "He did say that he had a tattoo artist who had come to town to train him."

Cormac straightened up. He didn't dare hope too much, but he could feel his blood pressure tic up. "What's his name?"

"I don't know," Dimpna said.

Cormac nodded. "Well, let's hope to God Donnecha does."

CHAPTER 49

SHAUNA NOW HAD AN EXTENSIVE ACCOUNTING OF THE TIMES MOTH Man came and went. The least amount of time he'd ever been gone was two hours. He'd also been leaving more and more lately, and he seemed nervous. "He's excited about the baby," the doula told Shauna. "And I'll be moving in soon, so that you'll never have to worry about giving birth alone."

"He's a killer," Shauna said. Morning Sun shook her head.

Shauna grabbed the notebook. *I can prove it. Will you help me?*

Morning Sun slowly shook her head. From under her pillow, Shauna grabbed the photograph of Fiona—her bloated face, her slit throat—and forced Morning Sun to look at it. "He did this," she said. "He's going to kill me too."

Shauna was now convinced the journal was the real deal. She wanted to get her hands on the original. The same book her own mother had held, the book where she'd written down all of her secrets. Shauna knew from the journal that there used to be prescription medication in the storeroom. She needed to give birth *without* the doula. Weeks ago, that would have terrified her, and it still did, but she knew her baby's only chance to get away was if she and Dylan were alone. She then showed Morning Sun the section of the journal that mentioned the medication her mother had given Eternal Mist and the Staff. "Storeroom," Shauna said. "Can you get it? Still there?"

Morning Sun continuously shook her head. She grabbed the

notebook: *I'm going to be a grandmother too. My first. I can't help you. I'm sorry.*

She was just as bad as Moth Man and Butterfly Woman. Worse. She cringed, realizing that Golden One had felt the same about her mother. They'd all been victims. And in the end, they had all tried to save only themselves. Maybe Shauna would do the same. The same for Dylan, the same for her baby.

There was one saving grace. Dylan was starting to come around. Yesterday, after the doula left, she saw the woman talking to him. Afterward, Dylan seemed troubled. He was pacing instead of lost in his iPad. Shauna went straight to him. "What's wrong?" Dylan turned and grabbed his iPad then opened it to notes.

She's mental, he typed.

"What did she say?"

He looked at Shauna. *I miss my mam and da.* For the first time in ages, he began crying again. She sat on the edge of his bed and invited him over. He sat next to her and placed his head on her shoulder. She stroked his hair. After a few moments, he grabbed his iPad. *Butterfly woman said you're my lad. You're my lad.* He shook his head. *I am not her lad! I want to go home,* he wrote. *I want to go home.*

This was it. This was the moment she'd been waiting for. *I have a plan,* she wrote. *To get us all home.*

He nodded, then jumped to his feet. He grabbed the notebook they used to use to communicate. Shauna had missed her chats with him. He was back now. He was back.

I'm sorry. I trick you.

"What?" She didn't need to write; he understood her voice, and some of her signs.

I explore. I make them trust me.

Shauna's heart swelled. She grabbed the notebook. *Like a spy?*

Dylan's head bobbed up and down. *Like a spy.*

What did you find?

Moth man's room. Computer.

"You went into his room?" She pointed at the ankle bracelet.

He nodded, then pointed at the ankle bracelet and shook his

head. Then he mimed Moth Man using the remote. Then held up a finger. "One time."

"Computer? In room?"

Dylan nodded. *Open and close doors.*

The building doors?

He nodded again, then turned to another page in the notebook. There he had written down a series of words and numbers. Butterfly. Moth Man. Spaceship . . . The page was filled with words.

"What?"

Password. If I can get in again, I can try these.

Her heart squeezed. The chances were nil. Not only would he get shocked, there was little chance he'd be able to guess a password.

But he was thinking of a plan, and that's exactly what they needed. Shauna had been trying to formulate her own plan. And there was one thing she would definitely need from Dylan. Help giving birth. There was no other choice. For any plan to work, she was going to need his help. She took the journal. She would need to draw pictures. Pictures would help. Dylan was about to get homeschooled.

She'd been reading Dylan the journal. At first, he refused to believe it. But he had more freedom inside the Womb than she did, and he had found chains in some of the smaller rooms. He had yet to be able to access the storeroom; it too was protected by the black box with the green blinking light. In case they could ever figure out their way around that, Shauna opened to the page in the journal where Seven Star listed the medication she'd used to drug Eternal Mist and the Staff. She made Dylan read it over and over.

Shauna had also been thinking about Liam. She hadn't been fair to him. He would have been willing to raise their baby, but she didn't give him a choice. Shauna now knew how it felt for all her choices to be taken away. And if she lived, she swore she would never do that to another human being, ever. And there was something else. She couldn't give her baby to the Griffins. He was hers. They'd already been through so much together. If she could survive this horrible place, she could do anything. She could be a mother. She thought of the homeless woman who always greeted her. *You would be a good mother.* Maybe she was right. Maybe she should have paid more attention to that sign.

Wait. The image of the sign rose in front of her again. The handwriting. The handwriting was the same as Butterfly Woman's. The homeless woman on the wall was Butterfly Woman. Was that possible? She'd been watching her. Following her. Trapping her. Who was she? How did she know Shauna?

The doula—Shauna had stopped thinking of her as Morning Sun; she was no longer anyone she could consider an ally—returned that day, and she brought baby clothes. All blue. All boy related. "I don't know for sure I'm having a boy," Shauna said.

The doula whipped her head around, alarm stamped on her face. She mimed writing. She wanted the notepad. Shauna found it and handed it to the woman. She wasted no time in scribbling. *Do not ever say that again. You are having a boy!!!*

She stared at Shauna as if waiting for a response. She smiled, even though she felt sick to her stomach. *Sorry, baby. I sounded just like her. If you are a girl, I will love you just as much. You can be anyone you want to be. Girl, boy, non-binary. You are my child.*

Shauna didn't mean for tears to come to her eyes. The woman cocked her head and then placed that gloved finger on her face, wiping off the tears. Then she grabbed the notepad again.

Going home to get my things! Moving in! Hang tight for a few hours.

She wagged her finger at Shauna as if warning her not to be naughty while she was gone. And as she left, with a skip in her step, Shauna knew it without a doubt. This woman wasn't well. And if Shauna didn't have this baby before she got back, they were all in a world of trouble. She had one thing going for her. The contractions weren't a lie. They'd been coming on steady now. And it would be up to Dylan to help her. It was time for another lesson.

Shauna had never taught anyone a single thing in her entire life. The most surprising bit was that she liked it. It made her feel as if she was doing something important. It gave her confidence. The baby kicked something fierce as she went through her diagrams with Dylan; it was as if he knew preparations were being made for his arrival. Strangely, teaching Dylan about the childbirth process wasn't as embarrassing as she thought it would be. And even more strange, when she was the one explaining it, she wasn't afraid. Even when his mouth dropped open and his eyes widened and he told her for the umpteenth time it wasn't that way with baby lambs, and he would know because he helped birth a lot of them with both a tall animal doctor and a really, really short one—

The lad could talk. But they were communicating well now through a combination of gestures, signs, lip-reading, pictures, and writing. Dylan and her baby were her only goals. *Save them.* She was starting to figure out a plan for them—and she knew her survival was not part of this plan. That would be up to God. Her job was to save *them*. She never knew there was such power inside her.

The mother lambs thrashed and moaned. Are you going to thrash and moan?

Yes. Probably even louder. But don't let it scare you. I can't hear me anyway.

It was true, but it struck Dylan's funny bone. He started laughing. He curled up, and his little body was shaking. It made Shauna laugh too. It made her laugh until Dylan suddenly stopped, then sat up straight, his eyes wide and his face still. *Fuck.* Shauna hadn't even felt him behind her. The next thing she knew, Moth Man's face was right beside her as he knelt down. His *face.* He wasn't wearing his mask. She could barely see him out of her peripheral vision, but he was talking to Dylan. Dylan was shaking his head no. The next thing she knew, Moth Man had grabbed one of her diagrams and ripped it up. Then she felt his hands on her breasts, and he started bouncing them up and down as he talked to Dylan. He squeezed them. He laughed. He wanted Dylan to laugh. Shauna felt hot shame rip through her body. She felt like a thing. That's exactly how Moth Man saw her. A thing to use. A thing to torture. And after the baby was born? A thing to kill. He pinched her nipple hard, and she cried out. He laughed again. He would enjoy it. He would enjoy watching her die. Dylan ran for his bed as Shauna bit her lip. It was everything she could do not to drive her elbow into Moth Man's black heart.

He dropped his hands and stood. Shauna recovered enough to whirl around. Was he going after Dylan? But no, Butterfly Woman had come into the room. Had she seen what her pervert of a son had done? Maybe it was time to show her Fiona's photo.

"Take off your mask," Shauna said to the woman. The woman shook her head. Why? If her son was showing his face, why wouldn't she? "You're the woman who sat on the wall. Told me I would be a 'good mother.' Liar." Butterfly Woman's mouth dropped open. Shauna was right. The woman spoke to her perverted, evil son, and his face immediately flushed red. He huffed off in the direction of the sealed-off wing.

"I'll show you," Shauna said. She marched to her original room, the tiny prison. She stopped long enough to see that Butterfly Woman was following. Ever since Moth Man had put those horrific photos back on the wall, she had left them there. She would show her who her son was. Butterfly Woman was following, but so was Dylan. Shauna reached for him. "Just her," she said. "It's okay." Dylan chewed his lip and glared at Butterfly Woman. The woman went to touch him with a gloved hand. He whirled around and ran. "He's not yours," Shauna said. "He'll never be yours."

The woman's mouth twisted in a snarl. Shauna continued to the room. When they reached it, she gestured to all the violent photos. "See? This is your son. He murdered her." Shauna waited for Butterfly Woman to break down. "Monster," she said. "Monster." But the woman's cruel mouth wasn't open in shock. It was smiling. *She knew.* She knew exactly who her son was and what he had done. Maybe they had done it together. There was no one to save them. It was going to be up to her. Shauna was standing closer to the door than the woman. Did Butterfly Woman know the key to enter on the pad? If Shauna locked her in, would she be able to get out? Sometimes Moth Man exited through this wing and didn't come back. Did the steel doors automatically lock when closed? There was no keypad on the outside of the room, so they had to. This could be the smartest thing she'd ever done, or the dumbest. Shauna darted for the door, and once outside, she slammed it shut.

Her last image was Butterfly Woman flying toward the door, trying to stop her.

Shauna leaned against the wall, trying to catch her breath. She wouldn't be able to run. Her contractions were irregular but getting stronger. Sometimes women had fake contractions; she remembered this from her lessons. Were hers fake? They felt fucking real. What was she going to do now? Was Moth Man here?

And then, as if she'd called out for the Devil, there he was. From the look on his face, he could hear his mother screaming and pounding on the door. Dylan was back too, and Shauna had never seen such terror on his little face. She'd blown it. She'd made the wrong decision. Moth Man whirled around, and Shauna knew he was going to unlock the door. Shauna reached for Dylan's hand, and together they hurried back to their beds. Shauna didn't know what was going to happen now, but she knew she wasn't going to like it. They'd just better not punish Dylan. If they did, she was going to kill them. She didn't know how. Or where. Or when. But she would find them one day, and she would kill them.

It was at least a half an hour that Shauna lay in her bed, terrified about what punishment they would soon deliver. And then there she was. Butterfly Woman stood over her, holding the photocopied journal. She placed it right by Shauna, who was curled up on the bed. It was only a few pages. The last few pages. Butterfly Woman had written in red: READ TO THE END!!!

Lessons from *Outside* the Womb—1994

When rescued, circus elephants that had been on a short chain most of their lives were finally set free, they still believed they were chained and never ventured farther than the confining distance they'd been conditioned to go. *Psychological chains*. Those woods had been behind us the entire time, and I had imagined they were dense and impenetrable. Because that's what we were told. But it was shockingly easy to get through them. I had finally managed to get enough sleeping pills crushed up and put in the Staff's whiskey and Erin's tea. The Shepherd had been gone for two days. I waited until an hour after they had gone to bed and grabbed the makeshift bag made out of one of my dresses and filled with as many supplies as I could think of. I truly thought I'd be in those woods for ages. How wrong I was! And how free it felt. I'll never forget it. The air was so fresh I kept swallowing it. *Free. Free, free, free.*

And before I knew it, I was on the other side of them, and there, just ahead—a road! I began walking along it, hoping a car would take pity on me and give me a ride. But I was also terrified that the Shepherd would be in the next car. My heart tripped in my chest. I wanted to head straight to Dingle, or a hospital, or a garda station. But in my mind, I was still chained. And even though I no longer trusted the Shepherd, and had never trusted the Staff, I also didn't trust anyone in the outside world. I was terrified that they would find me and bring me back and chain me up. I had one goal. And that was to safely have my baby and put him or her somewhere safe. This was what I thought. Only I had no idea what—make that who—was out there. Waiting. Very patiently. For me.

There were only two more entries left in the journal, and, skimming through it, Shauna could see that the handwriting in the very last entry was completely different than all the rest, and it was today's date. That's what Butterfly Woman had been doing since she was let out of the tiny room. She'd written an addition to the journal. Shauna felt a strange foreboding come over her. There was something else on one of the last pages. Dark smears. *Blood?* Why would there be blood? She kept reading. She read it all. The horror. The horrible, horrible ending. Butterfly Woman wanted her to know it all. Now Shauna knew she had to get her hands on the original journal. It had to be in this building. In the closed-off wing. And if they could get it and somehow figure out the password to open the steel doors, then maybe, just maybe, Shauna's plan would stand a chance.

CHAPTER 50

"*H*E WENT OUT," BEN SAID. "SHEILA MAGUIRE CALLED HIM IN A panic." Dimpna and Cormac had just entered Ink-ling, looking for Donnecha. Ben was alone in the shop, filming. He turned the camera on them until a look from his mammy forced him to put the camera down and pay attention.

"Sheila?" Dimpna asked. "Why?"

"I don't know," Ben said. "She said something about her father."

Dimpna glanced at Cormac. "We'll head over," he said. He stuck his hand in the pocket of his blazer to fish out the keys, and the sketch of the compound tumbled out. Ben automatically knelt to pick it up off the floor.

"I'll take that," Cormac said quickly.

Ben shrugged and handed it to him. "The spaceship house," Ben said. "Isn't it wild?"

"The spaceship house?" Cormac asked. He felt as if all the oxygen had left his lungs. "You know this house?"

Ben nodded. "Some fellow YouTubers walked through it and filmed it," Ben said. "It's wild."

"When? When did they walk through it?"

Ben frowned. "Like six months ago." He gestured to the laptop on the counter. "I can show you the video."

"Do you know exactly where it's located?" *Please, God, please.*

Ben shook his head. "Nah. YouTubers never give up their secret locations. Original content is king."

"I need you to contact them. I need you to call them right now. Do you understand?"

"And say what?"

"Tell them a detective inspector needs that address right now, and it is a matter of life and death." *Three lives.*

Ben's eyes widened. He nodded. Dimpna was grateful he didn't ask any more questions and got on the phone straightaway. Dimpna's phone pinged. *Donnecha.* "My brother is texting," she said. The text was a photo of a white robe edged in emerald green. *Odd.* Dimpna typed first.

where are you?

danny maguire's closet. i don't think sheila knows.

Cormac looked over her shoulder. "May I see that?" Dimpna handed him the phone.

"What am I looking at?" he asked.

"Danny Maguire's closet. And the same robe that's in the photo."

"Danny Maguire," he said. "Sheila's father."

"The local chemist," Dimpna said. "I didn't tell you this, but he gave me a really hard time when I had to ask him for a pregnancy test years ago." She took a deep breath. "He called me a sinner. He called me a whore." She'd finally said it aloud. The part of the story she'd never told anyone. It was ironic, given how many times she'd replayed it in her head. *Hundreds.*

"He would have known all the young girls who were pregnant in the area," Cormac said.

"He told me Cahal Mackey had been lingering in the shop."

"Tell me more about Danny Maguire." Cormac sounded intense. What was happening?

"Like what?"

"Anything."

She told him about Danny watching her in the dark. How he gave her the creeps. Cormac nodded, encouraging her to continue. "Right after I left for Dingle, he moved out. Had an affair. Had a second family. At least that's the story."

"A second family," he said slowly. "Did he by any chance suddenly come into money?"

"How did you know that?" Cormac didn't answer. "He lost it just as quickly. Gambled it away."

"My God," Cormac said.

"What's happening here?" Dimpna asked.

"Cahal Mackey told me he wasn't the Shepherd. And he wasn't the only one. Erin Tanner and Flynn Barry's sister said it as well."

"If he wasn't . . ." *Danny Maguire.* "Oh my God." She could see it. It was both shocking and somehow . . . *it fit.* Did Sheila know? Did she suspect? Was she helping him get away?

"Where is Danny Maguire now?"

"That's the thing," Dimpna said. "Sheila hasn't seen him since the riot at the harbor."

Cormac turned to Ben. "Donnecha mentioned being trained by a visiting tattoo artist."

"Kevin Quinn," Ben said straightaway.

"What?" Dimpna said. "Are you sure?"

Cormac turned to Dimpna. "You sound surprised."

Dimpna nodded. "He told me he was a consultant. I just assumed it was something in the business arena."

"What else do you know about Kevin Quinn?" Cormac asked Dimpna. He felt he was nearing the end of a puzzle, but a few pieces needed to be switched. But there was a timer counting down, with only seconds left to figure it out. One wrong move and the entire picture would vanish forever.

"They were looking for somewhere to let," Dimpna said. "Orla didn't want to live with his mother—I guess she's a bit of an odd bird, not to mention was smoking in the house—and the place where they originally let had a horrible smell."

A horrible smell . . . The house Liam McCarthy had rented out to Flynn Barry and *some dude. Kevin Quinn.* "Do you have any idea where this place was? The one with the smell?"

Dimpna hesitated. "I do. It's a property Liam McCarthy manages. Kevin and Orla rented the flat, and then when they complained of the smell, they moved in with Kevin's mother, who was letting a town house—also managed by Liam McCarthy."

He knew her. The tenant whose door he'd knocked on. Kevin Quinn's mother. "Do you know her name?"

Dimpna shook her head. "All I can tell you is Orla said she was strange. Smoked in front of her. Kept strange scrapbooks. Treats her son like the moon and the stars."

"Do you have any idea what brand of cigarettes the mother-in-law smokes?" Cormac asked.

"No," Dimpna said.

"I can add something," Ben said. "He wasn't who Donnecha imagined. And he fired him straightaway."

"Why?" Cormac was growing more panicked by the second. He wasn't trying to alarm Ben, but he literally wanted to shake answers out of him.

"He said ink and his syringe gun, or whatever you call that yoke, went missing. Only meself, Donnecha, and Kevin were in the shop. And he knows I didn't nick them."

"Let's put Kevin Quinn aside for a moment. What do we know about Orla?"

Dimpna raised an eyebrow. "Sheila's cousin." There was a trace of doubt in her voice.

"You don't sound confident."

"I felt as if whenever Sheila talked about Orla, she was hiding something."

"What do you think she was hiding?"

"I don't think Orla's her cousin. I think Orla is her half-sister. I think Orla is also Danny's daughter."

"The 'secret family' he supposedly had," Cormac said.

Dimpna nodded.

"And now Danny Maguire is in the wind?"

"That's what Sheila said," Dimpna said.

"Could she be covering for him?"

"I'd like to say no," Dimpna said. "But with Sheila Maguire? Anything is possible."

CHAPTER 51

Outside the Womb—2005

My darling girl. I need to write this down because if there's one thing I've learned, tomorrow is never promised. I must leave you for now. I promise you, it is not forever, and I'm not leaving you because I do not want you. I've never wanted anything more. And I would do it all over again for you. To hold you in my arms. To see your tiny hand wrap around my finger. So tiny, and you already have such a strong grasp. I'll never forget the sweet, sweet weight of you in my arms. How overcome with joy I am when I gaze at those beautiful eyes. I love you more than life itself. You are the sun, and the stars, and the moon. And now I know what she lost. Why she's so angry. She has already found me and made that clear. She threatened me. I think she might have gone mad. It's partially my fault, and I vow to make amends. I will even help her find her son.

Therefore, I am temporarily hiding you with people I know will take good care of you, because she is very dangerous. She is after me, and therefore she is after you. I will not let her have you. I named you Shauna. It means a "gracious gift," a "gift from God." And that is exactly what you are. But your caretakers must know, I am a little worried. You do not babble as much as I thought babies were supposed to, and the other day, the loudest noise went off—firecrackers, no doubt young lads acting the maggot—but you didn't startle or seem to notice it at all. I am leaving a note for your caretakers so that they can take you to a doctor straightaway. The Staff has been arrested, so you are safe from him. Strangely, he was arrested with another man I'd only seen once or twice at the compound when they needed manual labor. They were "discovered" at some burned-down property. It seems as if the Shepherd orchestrated all of it. But I know who was really behind their arrest. I know who wrote letters and made phone calls alerting the guards.

Golden One.

It is a miracle. She is alive after all. How I cried when I saw her again. It was as if she had risen from the dead. The Shepherd must have had a soft spot for her. Or she clawed her way out of his grasp; how she managed to survive, I do not know. And now it seems the Shepherd is caving to her demands. She was perhaps the most clever of us all. And she has gone mad with grief. I fear it is directed at me. And now that I have you, I can understand how that has happened, and deep down, I know that I owe her my life. And yours.

The Shepherd is back in town, trying to slip back into his old life. I want to tell the guards how wrong they have things, but I don't think I'd be believed. The only "proof" is you. Your DNA proving that he is your father. But I don't expose him or even dare to ask for money. He's already given it to Golden One, and the men taking the fall. The Staff. And the laborer. Why not me? Where is my share? I am going to confront her. I am going to make her split it with me—whatever she has been given. I suffered too. And I have you. I must be able to take care of you. Golden One will see the light. I will make her see the light.

CHAPTER 52

"Why?" Cormac asked as he and Barb stood near his car. They were in front of the garda station, waiting for the address of the spaceship house. Dimpna had gone to speak with Sheila. Time was of the essence, and they needed to divide and conquer. "Why would Orla and Kevin target Shauna Mills and Dylan?" Cormac needed Neely's help with the last of their puzzle pieces. They needed to get this right.

"Could Orla be faking her pregnancy?" Barb asked. "Maybe they're after Shauna's baby."

"And Dylan?"

"I don't know." Barb put her hands over her mouth and shook her head. Were they forcing things to fit? Cormac's mobile phone rang, interrupting the moment.

"Inspector O'Brien."

"Hello, Inspector. This is Margaret." The state pathologist.

"Hello, Margaret. Do you have news for me?"

"Indeed. Your hunch paid off. Fiona Sheehan is a genetic match to Alana Graves. I'm within a ninety-nine-percent certainty that she was the biological mother."

Mother, daughter, and baby. Three generations of women murdered young. Cormac didn't always know what he believed in, but no one had to convince him that life wasn't fair. "Thank you."

"I suppose it's good to fit the puzzle pieces together, but I wish I'd been calling with better news."

"Me too," he said. They hung up, and he filled Neely in on the conversation.

"The children had been seeking their parents," Neely said. "I wonder if any of them actually made contact?"

"I feel they must have. I think it's what set all of this in motion."

Cormac jingled his keys. "Let's pay Orla and Kevin Quinn a visit, shall we?"

Neely raised an eyebrow. "Now?"

"Yes. Now." Cormac couldn't sit still. He had to keep moving. "If the address of the compound comes in, we'll go immediately, along with every other garda we can spare." They just had to be stealthy. If anyone from the compound heard them coming, they could find themselves in a hostage situation. They could lose the upper hand.

"How do we find out without alerting Orla and Kevin?" Neely asked. "If they're in on this—"

"You're going to do something a bit sketchy," he said. "You're going to touch her stomach."

Barb took this in and nodded. "What's our excuse for going over there? How can we do it without alarming them?"

"We have a legitimate reason. To interrogate Kevin about the tattoo."

"Let's go talk to Kevin's mother. She's the closest to us. After that riot, where else would Orla go?"

Cormac nodded. "Let's go."

Neely held up keys. "I'll drive."

Minutes later, they pulled up to the familiar-looking town house. They hurried out of the car. Halfway up the walk to her front door, it came to him. "The homeless woman," he said, "who came into the station to report Orla missing."

"The one who wouldn't give her name," Neely said. "What about her?"

He pointed to the town house. "It was her. I knew she looked familiar, but I couldn't place her."

"You're saying it was Kevin's mom?"

"The one who wouldn't give her name," Cormac said, with a nod, "who pointed fingers at the Griffins." Now that he had the image of her in his mind, he had no doubt the homeless woman and the woman who answered the door to this town house were one and the same. How did she fit into this mess, and what in the hell was she up to?

"Kevin and his mother went out," Orla said, shortly after inviting them in. She made a face at the mention of his mother. "They should be back in a few hours."

"We'll come back then," Cormac asked. He was lying. They were going to wait here until they had the address of the compound. But he did not want Orla on alert.

Orla placed her hand on her belly. "Can I ask why you want to speak with him?"

"Tattoos," Cormac said. "We had some questions about tattoos."

Orla swallowed. "What kind of questions?"

She seemed on edge. Was she in on this? Or had she started to suspect her husband was in on this?

"Questions relating to Fiona Sheehan," Cormac said. He needed to see how she would react.

Orla's mouth dropped open. "The woman you found in the bog?" If she was an actress, she was a good one.

"She had a tattoo," Neely said. "It looks recent. We're hoping Kevin might be able to tell us something about it."

"I hope he can," Orla said. She didn't make a move to pick up her phone. Cormac wanted to know if she was so alarmed that she planned on contacting him.

Barb smiled. "Is the baby kicking yet?"

"Is she ever," Orla said. "Want to feel?"

"If you don't mind."

"Not at all."

Barb placed her hand on Orla's belly. Orla moved it around. "There."

"I felt it," Barb said with a slight nod to Cormac. "I felt it."

"How is it going with the mother-in-law?" Cormac asked.

Orla rolled her eyes. "I'm trying to be happy for Kevin," Orla said. "Happy that he's finally connecting with her. But she doesn't make it easy."

"Finally connecting with her?" Cormac asked.

Orla nodded. "Kevin was adopted," Orla said. "Just like me. Goldie is his biological mother." She laughed. "Funny being so intense and having a name like Goldie."

"Intense, is she?" Cormac asked, as his heart began to trip.

"Is she ever," Orla said. "The way she looks at him. Clings to him. They spend loads of alone time together. Making up for lost time, I suppose. I swear, some days I think she's so possessive of him that she'd love nothing more than to get rid of me." Orla shivered. "Lucky for me, I'm giving her a grandchild."

"I heard your mother-in-law is a smoker," Cormac said.

Orla made a face. "Disgusting habit. And she was smoking in the house! With her door shut and apparently blowing it out the window, but I was furious."

Cormac nodded. "What brand does she smoke?"

Orla frowned. "Does it make a difference?"

"It might."

"Benson and Hedges Luxury 100s," Orla said wrinkling her nose. "As if there's anything luxurious about carcinogens."

Back in the car, they sat in silence for a moment. "I owe you an apology," Neely said. "You were right. I was blinded by the past." She shook her head. "And I had the past wrong." Cormac had broken the news that he believed Danny Maguire was the Shepherd. He knew it was difficult news for her to process.

"You might have had the wrong fella, but you were still right that the Shepherd was the one who set this entire horror story into motion. He ripped that woman's baby out of her arms."

Cormac's phone rang, startling them. "Let's hope this is an address," he said.

Neely clasped her hands. "From your mouth to God's ears," she said. "From your mouth to God's ears."

Sheila and Donnecha were standing in front of her house when Dimpna pulled up. From the looks on their faces, they were arguing.

"Fantastic," Sheila said when Dimpna got out of the car. "Did you tell her your crazy theory too, like?" She threw Dimpna a desperate glance. "He's gone round the bend. He thinks me father is the Shepherd."

"I know a way to settle this," Dimpna said.

Sheila stared at Dimpna for a moment. "Oh my God. You as well?"

"Last time I visited, you said you thought your father took your car."

"So? What does that have to do with anything?"

"Do you have GPS memory?"

Sheila narrowed he eyes. "Why?"

"Maybe that's where we find him. Wherever he went before." Dimpna doubted he would have realized the car was tracking him. What if he went to the compound?

"He's not the Shepherd," Sheila said. "And he probably just went to the shops. But you're right. It's worth a try." Sheila reached into her pocket and brought out a key fob. She pressed it, and they heard the car beep. Sheila headed for it.

"We're coming with you," Dimpna said. She would find out the address and text Cormac on the sly. "You drive. But we have to stop at the clinic."

"What for?"

"I'm babysitting a dog, and he can't be left alone." Dylan's dog. He wasn't an official tracking canine, but maybe he would know the lad's scent. And if Dylan was there, he would be comforted by the sight of his dog. "Please," Dimpna said. "It'll only take two shakes of a tail."

They'd been driving for fifteen minutes. The last destination on the navigation system was about an hour away. It fit with what Dimpna had heard of the spaceship house. "This is ridiculous," Sheila said. "This far out? Where the hell did he go?"

"We'll find out," Dimpna said.

"I don't know," Sheila said. "He doesn't have my car now. How would he even get there?"

Someone picked him up. Or even an Uber. Or he was on the run. All Dimpna knew was that they might very well be on the way to where

Dylan and Shauna were being held. She texted Cormac, hiding her phone under her purse. Sheila still picked up on it.

"What are you doing?"

"Answering a text from Niamh. I had appointments."

Sheila swerved, and Dimpna was thrown against the passenger door.

"You'd better not be lying to me."

"Sheila!" Donnecha said. "Calm down." Never, ever tell a woman to calm down, Dimpna tried to tell him through telepathy. Sheila sped up, glaring at Donnecha through the rearview mirror. "Jaysus," Donnecha continued. "Can you drop me home?"

Sheila seemed to be considering it. Donnecha had no idea they were perhaps on their way to finding Shauna and Dylan. *Please, God.*

"I'll take you home," Sheila said. "As soon as I find a place to turn around."

"No," Dimpna said. "Keep going."

"What is with you?" Sheila demanded.

Dimpna took a deep breath. "I think your father was the Shepherd. I think we're going to their compound. And I think that's where we'll find Shauna and Dylan."

"My God," Donnecha said. "I changed me mind. I'm staying with ye."

Sheila nearly swerved again, and Dimpna had to lunge to straighten the wheel. "Focus," she said, "or you'll get us all killed."

"You're wrong," Sheila said. "You're wrong." She pounded the steering wheel. "You think he slit that poor woman's throat? He can barely walk."

Maybe that was all a lie. "I don't think that," Dimpna said. She didn't know what to think, but she had to placate Sheila. "I think there's someone else. I think they're trying to set your father up to take the blame." *He deserved it.* Dimpna left that part out. This would take Sheila a lifetime to process.

"You're wrong," Sheila said again. "You're wrong." But she kept driving.

Dylan's dog whined in Dimpna's lap and stuck his face against the window. Dimpna texted Cormac again.

In Sheila's car
Following GPS of last location
When D.M. took car

"What's the address?" Dimpna demanded. "I have to call the guards."

"This is crazy," Sheila said. "This is crazy."

"Please," Dimpna said. "This isn't about you. Or your father. This is about a missing boy and a pregnant woman. You have to do the right thing. You have to."

Sheila touched a button on the screen. An address came up. Dimpna texted it straightaway. "Thank you," she said.

"I want an apology," Sheila said. "When I prove you wrong."

"I swear to ya," Dimpna said, "I'll apologize. If you'd like, I'll tattoo it on me arse."

"I'd like," Sheila said.

"I'm not doing that," Donnecha said. "Hard no. I'm drawing a line."

"Not a bother," Sheila said. "I'll do it meself."

CHAPTER 53

Last Journal Entry—The Womb 2024

Seven Star Seven Star, how I wonder where you are...I know exactly where she is. Your evil mother. I know where her bones lie. She thought she was so clever, didn't you, darling Tallulah? The look on her face when she escaped and came to see my mother, only to find me! And even though she thought she had brought her baby somewhere safe, I found you, Shauna. I found all the children. I was surprised you realized who I was. You're right. I am the woman on the wall. I'd been watching you. I was nice to you. I told you you would be a good mother. It was one of the biggest lies I've ever told. Any mother who would give up her baby is evil. You had a miracle inside you, and you were going to give him away. A boy. MY BOY.

Do you want to know what happened to your mother? She became a falling star. After all she'd done to me, she tried to get the money that I got out of the Shepherd. It was money to find my son. She had some nerve. I brought her back here

and chained her to the very bed where I
BEGGED her to help me. I BEGGED you, Seven.
And what did you do? You slapped me. You are
WORSE than the Shepherd. You allowed that man
to lie with you. To impregnate you. As if that
made you special. As if he wasn't going to rip her
from your arms like he did mine. The Staff may
have been less powerful, but his sperm gave me a
son. The Shepherd sold my son, Kevin; he sold his
daughter with Cara—Orla; and he sold Alana's
baby—Fiona, only she ended up with her throat
slit, just like her mammy. He didn't want Seven's
baby; he didn't want YOU, Shauna. What did
anyone want with a disabled girl? Kevin is
perfect except for one thing. He's all grown now.
He married Orla—and before you go thinking
anything disgusting—they're no relation
whatsoever. She is, however, your half-sister. Sorry,
this isn't going to be one big happy reunion.
Fiona was convinced it would be. Stupid girl. By
the way, you met Cara. Your doula. And she isn't
Morning Sun. She lied. She's Red Rose.

Your mother's betrayal could not go
unpunished. There is no forgiveness in me. And
now you will die, just like your mother. After MY
baby boy is born, I will slit your throat and
watch you bleed out, and then I will throw you
into the lake. And then I will have every age I
missed out on. Newborn, young lad, grown son.
Only then will my shattered heart be healed. It is
my destiny. Can you believe I ended up back at
the Womb? I've made it mine. My son has
improved the security. I will create what the
Shepherd failed to create. Utopia. This place will
experience a new birth—a transformation. I am a
butterfly, and this is now my cocoon.

And even better, I am going to be a grandma!

Kevin and Orla are the only children of the Flock that mean anything. Fiona was such a disappointment. My son befriended her, swapped out her birth control for candy—yours too, as you somehow guessed. Luckily, you didn't blame the tenant that came and went; you blamed Liam. Perfect. Fiona almost ruined it by telling the father of her baby all about us. Thankfully, we convinced her to lie to him. By then, she knew enough about us to be afraid. But then she killed her baby boy with her evil heart. She didn't take care of herself. She tried to lie; oh how she lied! She said it wasn't her fault her baby died. But I knew better. It was the sin in her blood, and savage daughters MUST pay for their mothers' sins. My beautiful boy helped take Fiona's body to the bog. Your time is coming, Shauna. This is no longer just a journal. It's a scrapbook. Taped to the very last page of the original is the knife I killed your savage mother with. Soaked in her blood. Soon to be soaked in yours. How does it feel, knowing it's here somewhere, but you can never get your hands on it? Don't worry. You'll get it soon. I only wish your mother were alive to see me slit your throat. May you rest in eternal torment, Seven Star. You weren't so shiny after all.

Love and kisses,
Butterflies are free!
Golden One

CHAPTER 54

SHAUNA AND DYLAN STOOD IN FRONT OF THE BLACK BOX NEAR THE storeroom. *Circus elephants.* Moth Man had just left. They had at least two hours. Ever since reading the rest of the journal, she'd been thinking about those circus elephants. Every time they'd experienced a shock, Moth Man had been standing there with the control. He'd let Dylan into his room once, and Dylan had not experienced a shock. And he still locked all the steel doors whenever he left. Shauna stood near the black box. According to Moth Man, one step beyond it and they would receive a shock. It might be fatal. It could kill her baby. But maybe . . . maybe they'd been duped. Maybe they'd been like those rescued circus elephants.

Shauna took a deep breath and then stepped beyond the box. Dylan grabbed onto her, his mouth open in a scream. He stumbled past the box as she kept moving forward. They both stopped. *Nothing.*

"What?" Dylan said, staring at his ankle. "What?"

"Circus elephants," Shauna said. *Fucking circus elephants.* "Hurry," she said. "Show me his room."

Dylan took the lead, and they headed down a small hall to a room on the right. Inside was a bed and, across from it, a table with two large monitors. She headed for it. Cameras showed all the rooms in the Womb. Dylan rushed to her side and grabbed the mouse. He brought up a screen. It was for an electronic locking system. *The doors.* He held up a finger, then ran out of the room.

Shauna crossed the hall to another room. *Butterfly Woman.* This room was smaller, with only a bed. Was the journal in here? Was the knife that killed her mother *really* taped to the last page? If it was, and she could get it, and they could somehow figure out how to open the doors, they could run to the woods. But there wasn't much time—and she wasn't even talking about the two-hour window in which Moth Man could suddenly return. Her contractions were getting stronger and closer. The baby was coming soon. Her fears flooded her once more. All the things that could go wrong. All the things that had gone wrong for other women. Losing their babies. Losing their lives. Why wouldn't it happen to her too?

She felt vibrations through her feet and turned to see Dylan barreling toward her holding his notebook. He sat down and began to type usernames and passwords. It was never going to work. He tried three and stopped. The screen was blinking: ONE MORE ATTEMPT AND THIS SYSTEM WILL LOCK.

"Wait," she said. Passwords were personal. What was personal to these people? *When Moth Man met Dylan, he'd dropped something. Something personal.* "Bracelet."

Dylan reached into his shoe and brought it out. He looked at her and nodded. Then flipped between the front of the bracelet with *Miracle* written in Irish, along with 1994, and the back, which read LOVE FOREVER AND EVER AND EVER. Which was the username and which was the password? They had one more try. Shauna grabbed the notebook. *Passwords use numbers often. Right?*

Dylan gulped and nodded.

"Wait," she said. "Need journal first." She'd told him about the knife. She'd taught him how to help her give birth. And, finally, he knew her plan. What there was of it. And the minute they opened those doors—if they could open them—they would be racing against two clocks. The baby's arrival and Moth Man's return. "Look for journal," she said. "Gather supplies." The supplies were part of her plan too. Dylan nodded, his expression matching the panic she felt. Their adrenaline was pumping. This was their one chance. There would be no turning back. A contraction hit her, and she doubled over. This was the worst she'd felt so far.

Dylan began tearing around the room, looking under pillows,

under the mattress, under the bed. He then crossed into Butterfly Woman's room. She stumbled toward her room for the supplies, trying to remember her breathing.

She grabbed the towels and sheets she had gathered, every little thing the doula had left in her room for the birthing day, which wasn't much. Wet wipes. Sterilizing wipes. She was coming out of the room, holding as much as she could in her hand, when Dylan appeared, a book in his hand, triumph on his face. The journal. "Last page," she said.

He opened it. And there it was. A knife. Blood. Taped to the last page. The knife that slit her mother's throat. "Kettle," she said. "Hot water, clean knife." If nothing else, they could use it to cut the umbilical cord.

Dylan nodded as he grabbed the knife, his hands shaking. She touched his face. "Sweet, brave lad."

It was time to try the password. She set the bundle by the door that opened onto the lake and ran back to Moth Man's room. Her fingers trembled as they hovered over the keyboard. The password made some sense, but Loveforeverandever was a very strange user-name. Moth Man wasn't the boss. Butterfly Woman—Golden One—was the boss. She thought back to her first meeting with Butterfly Woman. She'd written "Butterflies are free." It had also been on the letter that Shauna had thought was from Fiona. But Fiona was already dead, lying in the bog. The letter had been a trick. She'd lured Shauna out into the open. *Butterflies are free.* She wrote it as the username, without any spaces, and then put in the password before she could change her mind: MÍORÚILT1994. Her heart tripped as she pushed ENTER. At first, nothing happened. And then the screen filled with light as the doors to the Womb began to open. This was it. Their one chance. But just as her joy was peaking, the screen shifted, and an image of the front gate appeared. It was opening. He was back. Somehow, he was back. Maybe the ankle bracelets had set off some kind of alarm. "Dylan!" She screamed as she ran from the room. "Now. Run! Run!" She grabbed the bundle she'd dropped in front of her door, the key to her plan. Dylan appeared by her side, hysterical and crying, holding the knife, dripping with water.

"Run," she said. "Run." He needed to save himself. She needed him to think of himself.

Together, they hurried for the exit. The iron doors were open, and beyond the doorway, a car idled. What was he waiting for? "Run," she said when they reached the end of the pier. "Woods. She touched his shoulder. "Run fast," she said. "Don't stop. Just run."

They ran. Dylan was ahead, although he kept turning to see that she was still behind him. Her contractions continued, slowing her down. When Dylan reached the edge of the woods, she was only halfway through the field. This baby was coming. She couldn't stop it. A strange feeling of peace came over her. There was no time to torture herself; it would soon be over. One way or another. "Run," she said to Dylan. "Drop blanket." She would need that; it might bide him time. He ran, but he took the blanket with him. Maybe he hadn't understood her. The woods were in sight. She was hit by a contraction so hard it stopped her in her tracks. She couldn't keep going. It was now. It was happening now. Babies, she realized, came whenever the fuck *they* wanted to come. Her baby was stubborn, just like her. Her baby was just like her.

The woods were dense. Dylan wanted to find a spot to lay down the blankets. But when he looked back, he could no longer see Shauna. It was getting hard to breathe. He'd forgotten his inhaler again. It felt like he ran a long time before he finally saw her. She was on all fours in the field. She was making awful sounds. And then he heard what she could not. The sound of a car door slamming. The bad people were back. They would see Shauna, and they would go to her. They would be focused on the baby. He had time to get away. But she needed the blankets. And she was afraid. And there was going to be a helpless baby. Why was he the one making the decision? Wasn't he a coward? He thought back to the baby lambs and that little veterinarian. "Where there's life, there's hope," he could hear her saying. "Where there's life, there's hope." She said childbirth was natural. There was nothing to be afraid of. But he knew that part was a lie. Shauna needed help. But then maybe both of them would die. He made his decision. He picked a direction. *No turning back*. He took a deep breath and, giving it all he had, he ran.

Dylan was trying to follow everything Shauna and her pictures had said to do, but Shauna was thrashing and moaning, sounds he'd never heard before in his life. He wished she would stop; it seemed it hurt worse than the mother lambs, and one of their babies had died. Would this one live? He wondered if it was a sin to see her without any of her clothes on down below. But he knew the baby had to come out there; Shauna's pictures had made that very clear. He was glad he wasn't a girl. He barely had time to see the man who emerged from the black car. It wasn't Moth Man or Butterfly Woman. From this distance, he looked old. Dylan didn't know whether or not to yell for help. The man got out of the car, but then he didn't move. Dylan had just enough time to see that the man had slumped to the ground when Shauna grabbed his hand and let out a scream. Whoever that man was, Dylan couldn't help him. He let Shauna hurt his hand. "You can do this," he said, even though he knew she wasn't watching his lips. "We can do this."

CHAPTER 55

*T*HE LANDSCAPE WAS BECOMING MORE REMOTE, THE ROADS CURVIER, the woods closing in. Dylan's dog began to whine and twirl in Dimpna's lap. They were only five minutes from the address on the navigator. Ahead, the road forked. Sheila's directions said to go right. But Dylan's dog was suddenly alert, and he lunged toward the left, emitting a high-pitched whine.

"Left," Dimpna shouted at the last minute. "Left."

Sheila looked panicked as she jerked the wheel to the left, sending them all shifting sideways. Sheila stepped on the gas; she was going too fast, and suddenly there was something in the middle of the road in front of them.

"Stop!" Dimpna shouted again as the dog began to bark. Sheila saw the small figure in the road; there was blood—he was covered in blood. She slammed on the breaks. The dog scratched furiously at the window. "It's Dylan Walsh," Dimpna said. "Call 999."

Shauna was staring at the sky, hoping to see a message in the clouds. She was silently cheering Dylan on. She could barely move, drenched in sweat, with the knife resting on her belly. Clutched in her arms was the little bundle. She had just given birth to the placenta. It was over. It was all over. She closed her eyes for just a second and opened them to find a pair of masks huddling over her. Butterfly Woman reached for her bundle. Just as those gloved hands touched the blanket, Shauna lunged with the knife. The blankets that Shauna had wrapped to look like her baby fell open, bloody and empty. She stabbed Butterfly Woman first, aiming for her heart, but at the last minute, the knife sunk into Butterfly Woman's hand instead. *Golden One.*

Golden One pulled back, mouth open in a roar, as Shauna yanked out the knife. Golden One reared back, and then Moth Man was suddenly on top of Shauna, his large hands wrapped around her neck. He started to squeeze. But she'd been holding the knife on her stomach, blade facing up, and when he shifted to put his weight on top of her, it sunk into his stomach, and he released his hands. Golden One was coming at her again, and Shauna knew she had run out of miracles. But then suddenly Golden One toppled over. Standing behind her was an old man. He hauled Moth Man off her. He was now on his back, blood covering his chest and abdomen, mouth and eyes open—and still. He was dead. Moth Man was dead. Terrified, Shauna stared up at the man. And she knew. Before he spoke a word, she knew who he was. The Shepherd. Her father.

Just as Dimpna reached the terrified and bloody lad, she heard a sound rise from the bundle in his hands. The unmistakable cry of a newborn.

"Help her," Dylan said. Dimpna reached for the baby. Dylan shook his head. "Shauna," he said. "Help Shauna."

A horn sounded from behind. Dimpna whirled around to see a familiar red Toyota. *Cormac.* "They're the police," Dimpna said. "Trust them."

"Help her," he said. By now, Sheila and Donnecha were out of the car and by her side.

"Which way?"

Dylan pointed to the woods. "Hurry," he said. "They came back."

CHAPTER 56

ALTHOUGH THIS WASN'T THE FIRST TIME SHAUNA HAD BEEN IN HOS-pital, she had never had this many people gathered around her. And flowers, there were flowers everywhere. Her baby girl was asleep in her arms. Dylan was here with his parents, and Shauna wondered if they would ever stop smiling. Cameras were hovering in the hall, but Shauna didn't like them. She had been terrified to face Jane and David Griffin and Liam, but before she could apologize or explain, they had all three embraced her. And somehow, the Griffins knew. They gave her a card. It read: *Congratulations on your Baby Girl*. Liam's face radiated love. Shauna would never forget the look on his face when he held his tiny daughter in his arms. They couldn't stop smiling, but she couldn't stop crying.

Butterfly Woman was dead. The Shepherd had stabbed her. Danny Maguire. Her father. But Moth Man hadn't been dead after all. Kevin Quinn. He had survived the attack. He was in hospital now, just like her, but as soon as he was well, he would be going to jail along with Danny Maguire. The Shepherd. Her father. He had been a monster, but in the end, he had saved her life. Kevin's wife Orla was Shauna's half-sister. Shauna's baby was going to have family. A cousin. And a mother and father. And love. So much love.

The lake was being dredged for her mother's body. Seven Star. Tallulah Mills. But Shauna knew it was only her bones they would find. Her soul was free and had been looking out for her. Her angel. *Love*. Pure love. Speaking of love, a familiar chubby face came into view. Shauna held her free arm out, and Dylan nestled into it. He stared at her baby with wonder. "My hero," she said.

Dylan beamed. He lifted his head and enunciated clearly. "What's her name?"

"Sky," she said. "Her name is Sky."

CHAPTER 57

*T*AKING DOWN THE CASES LAID OUT ON THE BULLETIN BOARD IN THE Incident Room gave Cormac the same bittersweet feeling as taking down Christmas. There was relief, but a strange hole snuggled up beside it. He and Neely stood for a moment, looking at all the faces that had consumed them for the past few weeks.

"Danny Maguire, the Shepherd," Neely said, shaking her head. "I would have never guessed in a million years."

"We finally got him," Cormac said. Although most of the evil deeds in the present day had been done by others, Danny Maguire had been the one to kill Flynn Barry. Apparently, when Cormac didn't answer Flynn's call, word had reached Danny Maguire that Flynn was going to talk. He was going to finger him. Danny, a man barely able to walk and talk, had summoned the last of his energy to start a riot during Orla's gathering so he could slit Flynn's throat and keep his mouth shut forever.

"He's dying," Neely said. "But that's not enough for me. I want him to suffer more."

Cormac stared at the women who had been part of the Flock. He began matching them up with their grown children. First, their abductors. Moira and her son, Kevin. Kevin had told them that he had been contacted by Danny Maguire, the Shepherd. Danny hadn't told him who he was at first, only that he had located his birth mother. Did he want to meet her? Kevin had grown up with a somewhat decent family in Waterford. They weren't perfect; after all, they hadn't asked any questions when approached by Cahal Mackey with a newborn for "adoption." The adoption fee was fishy—all cash, and no records. The same went for Fiona's parents. Desperation. Secrets. Kevin's adoptive parents were told Cahal was the birth father, which was true, but that his wife had died in childbirth and he couldn't raise the lad on his own. At the time, Danny Maguire's wife had been a nurse and had been involved with adoptions through a hospital program. She didn't know she was being manipulated, but Danny had access to a list of people who were desperate to become parents.

Once Kevin reunited with his mother, she began implementing her revenge plan. Cara Hayes was in the area and desperate to know her daughter. She'd threatened to expose Moira if Moira didn't help find her. And so they found her too. Orla. Given that the Shepherd was Orla's father, there was no blood relation between Kevin and Orla; and Moira, seeing them together, played matchmaker. And then Cara Hayes was indebted to Moira. Cahal Mackey and Flynn Barry were being released from prison. And even though Moira had her grown son, she was still missing her newborn and her young lad. She began hatching her plan. Find the others. Danny knew exactly where the other two had gone. He had never lost sight of any of them: Fiona and Shauna were in County Kerry. Danny only knew that Moira wanted to find them all. He had no idea that she had, in essence, become what he no longer was. A Grand Ruler. The Decider. And she had an army of people who were desperate to keep their pasts hidden and do her bidding. But Moira and Kevin were the ones who'd slit Fiona's throat. It was Danny Maguire's preferred way of killing; she was trying to frame him. He'd slit Alana's throat and taken her baby. Fiona. And then she met the same cruel fate, but this time at the hands of Moira and Kevin. Mother and son, once victims, turned into monsters themselves.

One by one, they took the photos down. "Are you going to rest easier now?" Cormac asked.

"I don't know," Barbara said. "Are you?"

"Shauna and Dylan are safe. That's success."

"It is."

"You're part of this. Your drive helped propel me."

"I know what you're doing."

Cormac raised an eyebrow. "What am I doing?"

"Trying to woo me. But I'm still retiring."

"You'll be sorely missed."

"Don't worry. I'll still be hanging around."

"I'm sorry that we butted heads."

"Don't be. I had blinders on. And I'm ever so grateful you're one stubborn arsehole of an inspector."

The rain was hitting his roof so violently that Cormac wasn't sure if he had a knock at the door or if Mother Nature was playing tricks on him. He opened it to find Dr. Dimpna Wilde standing on his stoop, drenched and shivering. He pulled her in, and the door slammed shut behind her. For a moment, they just stared at each other as the wind howled and the gorgeous creature dripped rainwater onto his floor. Her hands went to the buttons on her blouse and one-by-one she began to undo them. "I'll get a towel," he said, his voice husky and foreign to his ears.

"Don't bother," she said, as ripped the rest of her top, removing it and throwing it to the floor.

"Do you need some help?"

"I thought you'd never ask," Dimpna said.

He reached around and unhooked her bra. It joined her blouse on the floor. Her breasts, slick with rain, were works of art, her nipples rock hard from the cold. His eyes traveled to her denims, clinging to her legs. She stepped into him, and he wrapped his arms around her waist. Their lips met as her wet hands wrapped around the back of his neck. Without breaking the kiss that sent desire surging through every cell of his body, he gently backed her into the nearest wall. A photo fell to the floor with a clunk. Thunder rumbled, the wind howled, and lightning cracked, momentarily spotlighting the pair. She broke off their kiss, shimmied out of her denims, then her knickers. He wasted no time removing his clothes, and they sank to the floor.

"Are you sure about this?" he whispered as she climbed on top of him.

"No," she said, bringing her soft lips to his ear, tracing his neck with her tongue, making him shiver. "Are you?" She pulled back and rested her palms on his chest, her eyes staring into his, making him feel more alive than he'd ever been.

"No," he said, as she positioned herself to rock his world. "I've never been more unsure of anything in me entire life."